SUDDENLY, TH
PRESENCE OF A

It was very near and he cursed himself for having missed it till now. Soon a hand snaked out of the gutter to snare his ankle. Before he could react, he was toppling to the pavement. Rolling as soon as he hit the ground, he caught a glimpse of a manhole cover blowing into the air. A shadow followed the disk, erupting like a demon from the nether hells. The dark figure landed lightly on the street and snaked by, turning in a rustle of black fabric and the glint of polished steel.

As he faced his opponent, Theodore realized he had been hit because there was blood on the other's blade. The wound felt small, a tiny cut just above the left hip. He hoped his body was not lying to him, concealing the awful truth of a mortal wound. He had no more time to wonder. The other was moving and Theodore must defend himself. . . .

FASA

RELENTLESS ACTION FROM BATTLETECH®

BATTLETECH®

HEIR TO THE DRAGON

Robert N. Charrette

A ROC BOOK

ROC
Published by the Penguin Group
Penguin Books USA Inc., 375 Hudson Street,
New York, New York 10014, U.S.A.
Penguin Books Ltd, 27 Wrights Lane,
London W8 5TZ, England
Penguin Books Australia Ltd, Ringwood,
Victoria, Australia
Penguin Books Canada Ltd, 10 Alcorn Avenue,
Toronto, Ontario, Canada M4V 3B2
Penguin Books (N.Z.) Ltd, 182-190 Wairau Road,
Auckland 10, New Zealand

Penguin Books Ltd, Registered Offices:
Harmondsworth, Middlesex, England

Published by Roc, an imprint of Dutton Signet, a division of Penguin Books USA Inc.
Previously appeared in a FASA edition.

First Roc Printing, September, 1996
10 9 8 7 6 5 4 3 2 1

Copyright © FASA Corporation, 1989
All rights reserved

Series Editor: Donna Ippolito
Cover art by Bruce Jensen

ROC   REGISTERED TRADEMARK — MARCA REGISTRADA

BATTLETECH, FASA, and the distinctive BATTLETECH and FASA logos are trademarks of
the FASA Corporation, 1100 W. Cermak, Suite B305, Chicago, Il 60608.

Printed in the United States of America

This one's just for you, ERJ

The author wishes to thank all of those who helped in their varying ways and degrees, especially Donna Ippolito, Jim Musser, Boy F. Petersen, Julie Guthrie, Eric Johnson, and Anthony Pryor.

Prologue

Unity Palace, Imperial City, Luthien
Pesht Military District, Draconis Combine
3 February 3004

Subhash Indrahar seemed a solidification of the night as he stepped between his minions and into the bedchamber. His black ISF duty uniform was immaculate from the high collar to the soft, split-toed boots. Unlike the men who preceded him, he had made no sound while crossing the nightingale flooring of the porch between the room and the private gardens.

The Assistant Director of the ISF swept the room with his eyes, swiftly filing away a mental picture for later reference. His own Internal Security Force men took up strategic positions, discreetly covering all exits. None of the five showed any reaction to the blood-spattered corpse sprawled on the sleeping mats at the center of the chamber. Four of the other five men in the room were Otomo, the vaunted bodyguards of the Coordinator. They shifted nervously, showing the proper amount of fear and respect at Subhash's entrance. The fifth man was Takashi Kurita, his long-time friend.

Takashi stood still, his back to Subhash. The younger man was looking down at the body lying at his feet, the corpse of Hohiro Kurita, Takashi's father and Coordinator of the Draconis Combine. With the murder of Hohiro, Takashi succeeded him as the head of House Kurita and ruler of the star-spanning Draconis Combine.

Indrahar found Takashi's lack of emotion mildly disturbing. Briefly, he wondered how much more the Otomo must fear this calm acceptance of death. The bodyguards, having failed in their duty to protect their master, waited anxiously for Takashi's reaction. They had been entrusted with protecting the life of the Coordinator. Indrahar's arrival was a reminder that they would have to answer for their failure when the ISF questioning began. No one kept secrets from the watchdogs of Kurita society, save by taking those secrets to the grave. Some of the bodyguards were doubtless contemplating suicide to expiate their shame, assuming they were not executed for the failure.

Silently, Takashi knelt by the body, heedless of the pool of congealing blood that began to soak sluggishly into the knees of his tan military fatigues. He reached out his right hand to lay gentle fingers on the cheek of the face ravaged by the sword stroke that had split Hohiro's skull. Takashi remained so for several minutes, ignoring Indrahar, who stepped closer.

"The circumstances surrounding my death will not matter to me, for I will be on my way to heaven," Takashi said softly. Subhash recognized the words as Hohiro's own, spoken by the arrogant lord just two years ago. "Is it so, Father?"

Subhash remembered something further the late Coordinator had said. "It is only those I leave behind who will discuss the matter." Subhash knew that discussion of this night's "matter" would soon begin, for the murder of the Coordinator would shake the Combine.

Abruptly, Takashi seemed aware of Subhash's presence. The ISF man bowed and said, "The Otomo have captured the assassin near the tea house, Takashi-*sama*."

Takashi grunted acknowledgement. Starting to rise, he slipped on the fouled mats. As he reached out his left hand to steady himself, it fell into a puddle of blood, splashing his sleeve and sliming his hand. Takashi stood without further incident, oblivious to the bloody picture he presented.

Subhash fell in behind his friend and they headed for the garden. Throughout the room, Otomo and ISF men bowed to the new Coordinator.

The two friends entered the garden, stepping out into the starlight and shattered peace. Around them, the palace churned with reaction to news of the night's disaster. Hand-held lanterns bobbed among the cryptomeria trees as servants and minor officials scurried about asking each other for information concerning the disturbance. More Otomo and ISF agents stood scattered among the bushes and rocks, silent and still as the stone and bronze statues that graced the gardens.

Before the two men were halfway to the teahouse, the slap of bare feet on the wood of the garden's drum bridge caught Subhash's attention. He turned to speak to Takashi, but found him already looking in that direction. Coming toward them was Takashi's wife, Jasmine. She wore a hastily wrapped evening kimono and her long black hair was still tangled from sleep.

"Husband!" she cried, relief flooding her voice as she recognized Takashi's familiar, stocky silhouette. She slowed her run to a more sedate walk. "I awoke to find you gone and heard the guards running. I feared something had happened."

"Something *has* happened," Takashi stated in a quiet voice. As he turned to face her, the lights from the house caught the dark stains on his uniform and hands. Jasmine halted. Her fist rose, covering her mouth and masking all of her face save the horrified eyes. Comprehending her reaction, Takashi said quickly, "I am uninjured, but Hohiro is dead."

Subhash watched Jasmine's face as relief at her husband's safety struggled with grief at the passing of his father. The ISF man noted that she came no closer to her husband, her fastidiousness seeming stronger than her need to confirm Takashi's words with more than her eyes. She was a delicate flower to be wed to a samurai like Takashi, a man who would soon take the reins of controlling the destiny of billions of loyal citizens.

A slight movement in the crowd caught Subhash's attention. Forcing his way between the legs of an ISF man, a small figure burst through the assembled servants and courtiers. Subhash memorized the agent's face. He was lax to let a child past his guard, even if that child was Takashi's son and a member of the ruling Kurita clan. The agent did stop the taller figure toiling in the wake of the scrambling boy. The boy's pursuer was the portly old monk Zeshin, an initiate of the Order of the Five Pillars and the man charged with watching over the nights of Takashi's child. Subhash observed the chagrin on the monk's face as his struggles with the guard drew the attention of the exalted personages in the center of the garden. Subhash could see that the monk expected punishment for the failure to control his charge.

Jasmine stooped and held out her arms to her son as he ran across the garden. She gathered him close and hushed his excited questions with shushes and soft promises of explanations to come in the morning. She rose, lifting the gangly weight of the six-year-old with a mother's quiet strength. Their way was blocked by a stocky shadow that raised a bloody hand to seize the boy's arm.

The boy looked down at the hand gripping his left arm and saw the blood that slicked it. His head jerked up to find the owner of the hand was his own father. Subhash could see the child's eyes go wide, not with fear but with anticipation.

"Has there been a war?" the boy asked, voice full of excitement. "Have you been killing Fedrats, Father?"

"Hush, child," Jasmine admonished. "Children should not be out this late at night."

The boy frowned at his mother, making clear his opinion that mothers always spoiled the fun. Before he could reply, Jasmine continued, "You are going back to bed. Tomorrow. . . ."

"No!" Takashi's forceful interruption startled Jasmine. "You have shielded the boy long enough, woman. I have humored you until now, but tonight that must end. Let him see the world as it is."

Takashi pulled the boy from his wife's arms and into his own. The boy went gladly, ignoring his mother's protests.

"My son," Takashi said, "this blood you see on my hands is not that of the enemies of our clan. It is not that of a Fedrat, not that of House Davion. Nor does it belong to any weak-spirited popinjay of House Steiner, nor of any other House who shares the Inner Sphere with us. This is the blood of our clan and our House, the blood of the Dragon."

"Do not do this," Jasmine protested, light glinting from the tears in her eyes. "He is too young."

She started to take the boy back, but Subhash reached out to grasp her arms. She turned to him. "You are his friend. Tell him. The boy is too young to be frightened by the death that surrounds us."

"Takashi-*sama* does what he must, Lady Jasmine."

Facing such adamant will, she slumped in surrender. Takashi turned away as Subhash gave Jasmine over to the care of her maids hovering at the edge of the crowd, fearful of intruding until summoned. Now they came forward to escort her back to her own chamber.

With Jasmine cared for, Subhash again became a shadow at Takashi's back. Still holding his son, the new Coordinator strode into Hohiro's bedchamber. Subhash stepped up in time to see the boy's eyes go wide at the carnage in the room.

"Grandfather?" asked a young and tentative voice.

"Yes," Takashi answered, leaving no room for pity in that single word. "That was your grandfather. He was also the Coordinator of the Draconis Combine. That is your future if you are not strong.

"I am Coordinator now, and you are my heir. We are Clan Kurita. We must have the strength to rule, the strength to avoid such an end. We must always do what is necessary for the survival of our House and of the domain that we rule. It is a trust we must never betray. Not for any man or woman, nor for any personal feelings or weakness of spirit. If we are weak, this is the fate that awaits—ignominious death. *Wakarimasu-ka?*"

The boy said nothing. Wide blue eyes still riveted to the corpse of his grandfather, he swallowed, then nodded.

"Good," Takashi said as he turned to leave the room. "We must see to his assassin."

"I want to kill him," the boy declared in a small voice full of determination. His earlier excitement had turned to grim seriousness.

"You cannot," Takashi told him, but seemed pleased at his son's response. "I know that clan honor calls out to you. I know this because it calls to me as well. Let this be your first lesson as you now step from your mother's shadow. Personal violence is not the way of the Coordinator. Our destiny requires us to work through others. This assassin must meet justice, not vengeance. It is best for the Combine. *Wakarimasu-ka?*"

This time the boy shook his head, a confused look on his face.

"In time you shall, my son," Takashi assured him.

The trio stepped back into the chill night air. Despite the dark, Takashi missed no step in the short walk to the group assembled around the teahouse.

In the center of that gathering was an Otomo *Tai-i* who

stood behind the huddled figure of a man. As Takashi came to a halt, the *Tai-i* reached down and grabbed a handful of the man's hair. He yanked the assassin's head back, letting light fall on the blood-streaked face. One eye was swollen shut and already purpling from the blows he had received.

"Talon Sergeant Ingmar Sterenson," the *Tai-i* announced.

Subhash could see that the man was nearly dead from the battering his captors had given him, but a defiant light still shone in his open eye. That eye fixed on Takashi. Subhash felt the man focus on the Kuritan lord, narrowing his world to include only himself and the Coordinator.

The assassin started to speak. The *Tai-i* raised his hand to cuff the man to silence, but froze into immobility at a small shake of Takashi's head.

"Tonight a lie comes to an end," Sterenson croaked. "For years, I served you as a trusted and valued aide. I espoused the cause of House Kurita. Tonight, no more."

Sterenson could speak no more for the coughing that racked his whole body, but when he finally found his voice, it was stronger, tinged with the conviction of the true fanatic. "Tonight I have struck a blow for freedom in killing the tyrant. Independence for the people of Rasalhague!" he shouted. "Death to the oppressors!"

The *Tai-i* slammed his fist into the side of Sterenson's head, and the bound man crumpled to the ground. He twisted and moaned as Otomo kicked and spat upon him.

"Enough!" Takashi barked.

The Otomo ceased instantly. Sterenson twisted around and raised his head to stare Takashi in the eyes. Subhash felt the passage of understanding between the two, each acknowledging and accepting his part in the night's drama.

"Shoot him," Takashi said, his voice flat and dead.

The *Tai-i*, eager to win the regard of the new Coordinator, drew his pistol and fired. The gunshot rang from the garden walls.

In the dying echoes, Subhash whispered to Takashi, "My superior, the Director of the Internal Security Force, would have wanted to question him, Takashi-*sama*."

Takashi looked his old friend full in the face. "Do you question my judgment?"

Subhash searched Takashi's blue eyes, testing the strength of the Kurita lord's *ki* shell. Impressed, he replied, "It is not my place, *Tono*."

"A man must know his place," Takashi observed as he looked away. "I will see the Director at dawn, with questions of my own. A traitor should not have been allowed to reach such a trusted position. This is not the Free Worlds League."

Takashi turned back to meet Subhash's eyes.

"*Kendo* at noon, Subhash-*kun*? We will have much to discuss."

Subhash bowed, acknowledging and accepting the appointment.

He straightened to watch his childhood friend, now the Coordinator, walk at a calm, steady pace toward his own bedchamber. Takashi held his son secure in his arms. In the darkness, the pale oval of the boy's face shone over his father's shoulder. Even in the poor light, Subhash could see that confusion and fear had taken over from the boy's initial reaction. Subhash offered the child a smile of reassurance and reached out with his *ki* to calm the child from his own well of tranquility and strength.

I will guard your future, young Kurita.

The boy managed a half-smile and Subhash sensed his relief.

BOOK 1

Bravery

=== 1 ===

Streets of Kuroda, Kagoshima
Pesht District, Draconis Combine
17 May 3018

Breath came hard through the suit filters and sweat ran into his eyes. Rising nausea forced Theodore Kurita to take a risk. He pulled out the heat vents on his suit, cracked the seal on the faceplate, and slid the visor up over his forehead. The open vents would increase his heat signature to any observer with infrared capability. Without the light-amplification circuits and the bi-level circlevision device that made up the faceplate, he was almost blind in the oily darkness of night in Kuroda. More visible and blind he might be, but at least he could breathe again. As he struggled to keep his gulping breaths quiet, the rush of oxygen cleared his brain and fought back the nausea that had threatened to overwhelm him.

The ISF sneaksuit he wore was not designed for the sustained exertion of his run across the warehouse district. The infrared signature-suppression fabrics and noise-deadening air filters had been overworked, becoming dangerous as they overheated his body and limited his air. Theodore's instructors had often warned him that it was hazardous to try a long-distance run while wearing such a suit. Only a fool or a desperate man would make such an attempt, they said. Theodore did not consider himself a fool, and he hoped his pursuers would not consider him desperate enough to try it. In fact, he was counting on it.

His plan seemed to be working. He had neither seen nor heard any sign of them for half an hour. That meant nothing, of course. They wore sneaksuits like his, standard-issue for the Combine's Elite Strike Teams and the storm troops of the Internal Security Force. That meant that whoever was behind this attack had powerful forces at his disposal, men expert in "black" operations. Such men would be relentless. And very dangerous.

Such considerations made his decision to run justifiable.

The need to open the suit had strong justification as well, but it annoyed him all the same. He needed to stop the fire in his muscles, needed the air. So Theodore took another risk on top of the risky run, and stopped before being sure he was in the clear. He expected better of himself. He wanted to cover three kilometers before resting, but his body betrayed him. Too much easy living at the academy, he concluded.

As his breathing steadied, he considered how differently the night had begun. He was not expecting any trouble on the eve of his graduation from Wisdom of the Dragon School. Four long years of advanced strategy and combat training were over. He had thought that a tryst with his current paramour, Kathleen Palmer, would be an ideal tension-reliever before the ceremonies tomorrow. Kathleen had been a breath of fresh air when they first met four months ago while Theodore was on holiday from the school. She had seemed so far from the taint of political intrigue, uninterested in talk of war and warriors. She had been truly an anodyne after his years of study and training. In her arms, he could forget his obligations and duty.

One way or another, that was over now. Theodore had seen the assassin's image reflected in her eyes as the black-clad figure approached. That warning allowed him the fraction of a second he needed to avoid the knife-hand the man aimed at his neck. His sudden reaction had thrown the assailant off balance. While Kathleen fled screaming from the room, Theodore counterattacked and struck the man down with a well-placed kick. She had been aware of the intruder's presence, but she had not warned her lover. That was something Theodore could not, would not, forget.

He had wanted to follow and force an answer from her, but decided that questioning Kathleen would have to wait. Instead, he had stripped the man of his sneaksuit. Assuming that the failed assassin had back-up, Theodore knew that his sneaksuit would be far more useful than his own fancy dress clothes, strewn about the room with abandon. He had taken the man's gear as well, not having armed himself before a peaceful lark in the old town. Except for the traditional *katana*, a blackened steel blade with black braiding and non-reflective fittings, the man carried no lethal weapons.

Presumably, his master wanted Theodore alive, perhaps to be used as a bargaining chip. If they wanted him alive, Theodore reasoned, they would be holding back, careful of harming him seriously. He had no such qualms regarding their health. His first priority was to escape and survive. He had no desire to be anyone's prisoner.

Once outfitted, Theodore had exited the building, rappelling down the side with the man's utility line. Thus had he avoided the doors, which must surely be under close watch. His short cut had allowed him to elude the mesh of their net. When he hit the ground, only one black-clad figure opposed him. He took the man down without needing the sword, and started directly back toward the academy. Then he noticed three more assassins on his trail.

Fearing that they would catch him, or worse, call in reinforcements to intercept him, he cut away and headed for the Desolation. There, amid the ruined buildings and rubble of that long-abandoned quarter of Kuroda, he hoped to throw them off his trail. The academy often conducted city-fighting exercises in the Desolation. To improve his scores, Theodore had memorized maps of the region and made a regular effort to keep up on the changes the exercises wrought in the cityscape. He hoped that such knowledge would give him the advantage he needed to elude the pursuit.

As soon as he had lost sight of them, he began to run. Now he stood here, less than a kilometer from the academy. His panting had almost stopped, but his breathing was still ragged. Concentrating on his *hara,* he willed himself to center. Slowly his breathing became regular. He accepted the fatigue in his limbs and banished it. Calmness suffused him, and in that calmness, he found another presence.

He snapped his head up, eyes working to pierce the darkness. There, standing still on the roof of the gutted shell across the road, was a silent, black-clad figure, starlight glinting from the circlevision visor. The figure bowed to him. Theodore snapped his own visor down, only to find that the slim figure had vanished.

One has found me.

No, he admonished himself. I have seen one. *I might hope only one is there, but I cannot assume so. Never underestimate an enemy.*

He checked the street and found it deserted. Deserted of people, that was. The derelicts and criminals who occasionally hid among the ruins had gone to roost. Only the night vermin prowled on their own life-and-death hunts. Theodore decided that the small scurryings were a good sign, for it meant that no human presence disturbed their ground-level hunts. Perhaps there was only the one. That thought set him to scanning the roof again, but he found no sign of his pursuer. While checking the ground level, he had left himself open to a long-range attack from above.

No attack had come. He did not know why, but he did know that he was lucky. He presumed that the other was on his way to street level. By heading up, Theodore hoped to confound that maneuver and recover the moments he had lost.

Peeling back the leather palms of his gloves, he uncovered the microhooks set there. A swift crouch and spring started his climb up the side of the building that sheltered him. Fingers and toes sought the minute purchase offered by the crumbling mortar between bricks. Where there were no useful cracks, the microhooks penetrated and took hold of the porous surface of the brick, the barbs offering a secure grip. A flexed palm released tension from the hooks and they slid free, allowing him to reach for a new, higher grip.

All the way up the wall, Theodore berated himself for his foolish lapse. In his mind, he heard the voices of his teachers. Two were most insistent. Brian Comerford, his Special Operations tutor, had nothing good to say about his delays or his physical stamina. Tetsuhara-*sensei* nagged him to reach for and trust his center, promising him all the strength he needed if his *hara* control were strong. While listening to those inner voices, he climbed the fifteen-meter wall in less than half a minute.

On the roof, Theodore checked his surroundings again, but found no sign of the other. He set out across the roofs at a pace that would not overtax the sneaksuit. Eventually, the deteriorating quality of the buildings he crossed forced him to abandon his aerial path and return to the ground. His speed increased when he was no longer concerned that a misstep might send him plummeting through a rotted roof.

Theodore knew that he was not alone, but none of his tricks succeeded in forcing the other to show himself. Discarding the attempt to confront this lone hunter, he resumed the effort to lose his dogged pursuer.

Suddenly, Theodore sensed the other's presence very near and cursed himself for having missed its brief absence. *Another mistake,* chided the ghostly voice of Comerford-*sensei.* *This time a costly one,* Theodore agreed.

A hand snaked out of the gutter to snare his ankle. Before he could react, he was toppling to the pavement. He tucked to minimize the shock and realized that the hand was gone. *That's bad,* he told himself, feeling the agreement from Comerford-*sensei*'s spirit.

Rolling as soon as he hit, he caught a glimpse of a manhole cover blowing into the air, impelled by a near-silent huff of compressed gas. A shadow followed the disk, erupting like a demon from the nether hells. The dark figure landed lightly on the street and ran toward him.

Theodore regained his feet and cleared his sword in time to parry a passing cut as the other snaked by, turning in a rustle of black fabric and the glint of polished steel.

The two stood frozen for a moment, the other in *muniken,* Theodore in *tensetsu.* He recognized the other's command of the ancient Yagyu sword technique and shifted to *katsuninken.* The other hesitated a moment, then started a shift to *kojo* that was never completed. At that instant, the manhole cover returned to the street with a ringing clatter, startling Theodore. The other, clearly expecting the clamor, converted the shift of stance into a lightning attack. Theodore's counter was too slow. The other flashed past.

As he turned to face his opponent, Theodore knew he had been hit because there was blood on his opponent's blade. The sword was so sharp that he had not felt its touch. He felt for the pain as he readied himself. The wound felt small, a tiny cut just above the left hip. He hoped his body was not lying to him, concealing the awful truth of a mortal wound. He had no more time to wonder. The other was moving and Theodore must defend himself.

The next exchange was no passing attack. Each black-clad

figure stood its ground, trading attack for counter. Unexpectedly, in the middle of Theodore's attack pattern, the other crumpled to the ground. Theodore's stroke whistled through the air above the falling body, pulling him off balance when it did not meet the expected resistance.

Theodore recovered, returning to a cautious guard-posture as he looked down at the unmoving figure. He was puzzled. He had not thought that he had pierced the other's guard.

There was no time to consider. In the distance, he heard the soft slap of running feet. Whether it was his pursuers or local inhabitants drawn by the clamor of the manhole cover, he did not know. Either was more trouble than he wanted. Turning, he ran down a narrow alley, risking a look back just before he rounded the corner. Three black-clad figures pounded down the street toward the alley, but of his recent opponent, there was no sign.

Knowing that the shadows offered no protection from the light-amplification equipment of his pursuers, Theodore ran on.

2

By the time Theodore recognized from the echoes that he had entered a dead end, his pursuers had rounded the corner and entered the alley. There was no time to climb away from them unless he could delay them somehow. Reaching for his pouch of flash grenades, he found it gone, cut away in the sword fight. He steeled himself to turn and fight for his life as a stirring in the gloom told him the situation had just gotten more complicated.

From the darkness at the alley's end stepped another black-clad figure. The hood of this one's sneaksuit was pulled down around his neck and his faceplate swung from a loop on his belt. Apparently, he disdained the advantage of night vision to face his cornered quarry. His face was hard, its flesh glistening with a light sheen of sweat. The red-headed man held a *katana* in his right hand. With his left, he reached into a pocket set into the sleeve of his sword arm and laughed confidently.

Theodore skidded to a halt, his own hand snaking behind his back. *Arrogance has no place in a warrior's heart,* reminded Tetsuhara-*sensei*'s voice. *Quite right,* Theodore agreed. *And this man shall pay for his arrogance.*

He drew a packet from his pocket and squeezed it hard before flinging it at the new opponent. Simultaneously, he dove to his right, using the momentum of his throw to pull himself into a roll.

The sudden move saved him from the redhead's missile, which whizzed past Theodore to strike with a meaty thunk at one of the other pursuers. Hearing a clatter of debris and a whuffing sigh, he reckoned that one of the three behind him was out of the fight.

Theodore's own missile disintegrated in flight as the chemicals released by his squeeze ate through the thin walls of the bag and released the contents. A fine mist wreathed the head of the bare-faced man. He collapsed in a fit of coughing, temporarily incapacitated.

Coming out of his roll, Theodore was beset by the remaining two. They circled him, maneuvering as a team. Every time Theodore tried to draw his sword, one or the other would press an attack, forcing Theodore to abandon his attempt and concentrate on blocking or avoiding their blows.

They were cautious, having seen how well Theodore fared against their comrades. They took their time, contriving to set him up for a decisive attack that would not expose either of them to a crippling counterattack.

Watch the pattern, Comerford-*sensei*'s ghostly voice advised.

Control the ma-ai, Tetsuhara-*sensei*'s spectral tones demanded. *A true warrior is always in control of the distance of engagement.*

"*Hai!*" Theodore shouted as he caught the pattern and acted. He spun on his heel and launched a flying kick at the shorter of his two attackers. Thinking himself safely out of range, the man failed to counter completely and tumbled backward into the grime-smeared bricks of the alley wall.

Theodore's rebound dropped him to the ground, where he lay loose-limbed and sprawling. The tall one dove on him to take advantage of his disorientation from the bad fall, only to find Theodore's helplessness was a sham. Rolling away from the attack, Theodore let the man slam into the refuse-strewn ground. His own kick at the man's head was weak, but did serve to further daze his opponent.

Heedless of proper form, Theodore scrambled on top of the man. The man struggled to avoid his grip as Theodore slipped a choke-hold around the assassin's windpipe. Not trusting his strength at this point, Theodore went for a steady choke rather than trying to snap the man's neck. His opponent's struggles were slowing when a hand gripped Theodore's shoulder.

"Enough."

Theodore spun, awkwardly because he was straddling a body. The backfist he threw in turning was caught effortlessly by the new arrival and held in a grip of titanium. His knee, directed at the newcomer's groin as Theodore tried to straighten up, was adroitly deflected by the man's hip. The man effortlessly redirected Theodore's energy, crashing him onto his back.

"Enough, I said."

Wind gone, Theodore lay weak and vulnerable. He squinted his eyes down to a slit in an effort to steady the doubled images he perceived. Even with his blurred vision, he recognized the smiling face of Subhash Indrahar, the man his father had elevated to Director of the Internal Security Forces.

Such a highly placed traitor, Theodore lamented. *My mentor, a man I had thought a friend. You always took my side against Father. Now your true colors show. Now, it seems, my life is forfeit to misplaced trust.*

"Do not think me a traitor, my young friend. As ever, I stand behind you as heir to the throne of the Draconis Combine. And do not think too unkindly of poor Kathleen. She only followed my orders. These men you have faced are a final exam of sorts, a test of your mettle," Subhash said, sweeping his arm to indicate the six men gathered around them, including the teary-eyed redhead and the one wearing Theodore's own discarded finery. "You have passed quite well."

"You had me in fear for my life."

"Of course. Only at the edge of death does a man truly live, and show whether he is truly a man." Subhash extended a hand to help Theodore to his feet. "You have shown that you are a man. Rough around the edges, perhaps, but refinement will come with time.

"I have known you since childhood, and I believe that I know the sort of man you are. You see the Combine as I do, the strongest hope of unification for the Inner Sphere. You believe, as I do, that the Combine must come before all, that is must be preserved to perform its destiny of reunification.

"Now I ask you to join with these men in a society dedicated to that end. I ask you to join the Sons of the Dragon."

Subhash waited for Theodore's reply. Though his mentor smiled benevolently, Theodore sensed the taut expectancy. Around him, the other men began to shift nervously.

He was at once touched and alarmed by Subhash's offer. The ISF Director was a man he had idolized for many years. His belief in Theodore's potential was something the young heir wanted to reward after his long and difficult childhood and adolescence. Yet this secret society of Indrahar's whispered of intrigues and dark alleys, things alien to the samurai Theodore believed himself to be.

The offer lay before him. If he refused now, it would never come again. Something in Subhash's voice and the tense stance of the men around him spoke eloquently of a unique opportunity. If he did not join, they would go their own ways and he would hear no more of it. Until he crossed them in some way. Subhash had become one of the most respected, and feared, ISF Directors in centuries. He was a good man to have as an ally and a bad one to have as an enemy.

Theodore smiled and executed a sharp bow. "I am honored."

Subhash clapped him on the shoulder. "I am pleased."

The tension in the alley evaporated. In the joking and verbal replay of the combats that followed, Theodore ventured, "Subhash-*sama,* wouldn't you say that seven opponents were too many for one not well-versed in this type of nighttime activity?"

"You handed all six agents quite well, Theodore-*sama,*" Subhash replied with a pleased grin. "And I was no opponent at all."

Theodore was taken aback by the ISF Director's response, but said nothing. He looked carefully at the men around them, noting their height and build, the way they moved. Thinking back over his night's adventure, he was certain that he had encountered each only once. Moreover, none of the group fit the physical type of the swordsman who had wounded him. There was more going on than he understood. The words of old Zeshin, his childhood companion, came to him: *A wise man listens when he has no words to speak.*

Given what had happened this night, Theodore decided that was very good advice

3

"**D**o you think he'll come?"

Of the five men and two women in the back room of Snorri's Tavern, the speaker was clearly the most nervous. Having drawn stares from the others with his question, he began to fidget with the gold braid decorating the shoulders of his tunic. His restless fingers had already unraveled one of the tassels and added to the frayed look of the ancient uniform jacket.

The bearded man sitting at the head of the table knew, as did all present, that the fat man in the outlawed uniform of the Rasalhague Prince's Guard was not entitled to wear it. His fellow conspirators tolerated his affectation because of the wealth he brought to the enterprise. The bearded man suppressed a sigh. Leading this odd assembly of personalities was a trial, made no easier by the wretched places where they often met. Slums were hardly in keeping with his dignity or that of their cause.

"Of course he will come," the leader assured the agitated man. "This matter touches too closely his own interests."

"He could betray us," warned one of the women. She was grim-faced and apparently calm, but her voice held just a hint of fear.

"He won't," the leader said, stroking his salt-and-pepper beard in a casual gesture of confidence meant to bolster his fellows. "His position with the Dragon is shaky enough. He has let his ambitions show too clearly of late, and his enemies in the court on Luthien are almost in position to deny his petition for elevation to the status of Archduke over the five worlds he controls. Add to that the fact that the Coordinator sent no Kurita troops to help him defend against the recent raids by House Steiner, and you will find a man who believes he has no future with the Dragon."

"He might see betraying us as a way to regain favor," countered a tall man, pacing back and forth like a caged animal. His carriage showed him to be a military officer, but his drab, worn clothes were those of a mercantile messenger. A DCMS-issue laser pistol, its grip stained from years of use, rode in his low-slung messenger's holster.

"Such a betrayal might, indeed, gain him influence at Court, but there will be no treachery." The bearded man smiled with satisfaction. "As I said, our friend's ambitions have been all too obvious of late. More to us here in the District than to Luthien. I have accumulated certain evidence and prepared it for release to certain individuals. In doing so, I have guaranteed that if he betrays us, he will fall with us. He won't risk that."

"Hassid Ricol is a daring fellow," the military man warned.

Several in the circle drew in sharp breaths at the mention of their expected visitor's name. "No names," one hissed.

The military man harrumphed in contempt of the others' timidity. "Jessup has assured us that the lostech artifact he brought will mask our talk from any ISF listening devices."

"I said *should*, not *will*," Jessup shouted heatedly. "You endanger us all with your loose talk."

The military man started across toward Jessup, but the bearded man blocked his path, catching the other man's arm.

"At ease, Colonel. He's just upset at your breach of the agreed-upon protocols."

Jessup had scrambled back, knocking over his chair when the Colonel started forward. Now, from the safety of his position behind two other conspirators, he taunted the other man. "And rightly upset, you loose-mouthed warhorse! If you can't be trusted to control your tongue in a relatively safe place, how can we trust you when out of our sight?"

The Colonel bristled at the slight to his honor. Despite the drag of the bearded man's grip, his hand closed around the butt of his pistol. "Why, you little . . ."

"Such a cozy circle of friends. Reminds me of the court on Luthien."

The squabbling group of schemers froze in place. Heads turned toward the man who spoke from the doorway.

Tall and well-built, he was a sharp contrast to the mousy fellow at his side. The man's athletic build was cunningly accentuated by a finely tailored suit of deep burgundy cloth, trimmed in gold at cuff, collar, and lapel. A scarlet sash hung to his left hip, where a *katana* in *tachi*-style mount rode in a vermillion scabbard. A velvet half-cape, of a red so deep that it appeared black in the low light of the room, hung suspended from his right shoulder in the style of high courts throughout the Inner Sphere. Coolly surveying the assembled conspirators, Duke Hassid Ricol casually removed his fine oxhide gloves.

The bearded man was quick to recover. He waved away Ricol's guide, ignoring the man's apologies for failing to warn the group of their guest's arrival. Also ignoring the still angry Colonel at his side, he stepped forward, smiling.

"You are most kind to join us, Your Grace."

"I have not joined you yet, Jarl . . ."

"You know us, friend, and we know you," the bearded man cut in before Ricol could speak his name. The naming of ranks was dangerous enough. Though he had confidence in Jessup's device, he was not the sort of man to take chances. "Show us the courtesy of using no names save those we give you here."

Ricol inclined his head to show he understood and gave a small smile. Something in that smile struck the bearded man as a trifle condescending, but he dismissed his unease.

"I am Diamond," he announced, and then proceeded to introduce the rest of his group. Each conspirator went by the name of a gemstone. He concluded by giving Ricol a codename. "And you, my friend, shall be known as Ruby. Together we are the jewels of the princely crown of Rasalhague.

"Sit here," said Diamond, indicating a seat next to a compdeck. "Let us show you an outline of our plan."

Powering up the console as Ricol sat down, Diamond then slipped an iridescent disk into the slot and settled himself next to the Duke. The rest of the conspirators watched anxiously as Ricol began the long process of reviewing the data.

At one point, he paused and looked up. "There are some areas that seem ill-defined."

"Make your inquiries of the computer, friend Ruby," Diamond directed. "All the information you desire is included in the databank—but without the risk of being overheard."

Turning back to the screen, Ricol did not bother to conceal his annoyance. Diamond ordered refreshments to occupy the others while they waited on the Duke. Finally, Ricol sat back, massaging a stiffened neck.

"Will you join us?" blurted the man in the outlawed military uniform.

Ricol looked him in the eye, and the man's stare faltered. "I'll take it under advisement."

"That is not a commitment," Diamond observed.

"You are not yet successful," Ricol countered.

"Uncommitted men are dangerous," the Colonel observed, his voice hard with implied threat. "Dangerous men have accidents."

"People who react when there is no threat are nervous. Nervous men have accidents, too," Ricol replied, but his tone was nonchalant. Focusing on the Colonel, he added, "Stay out of my way and I will stay out of yours. Make my life difficult and I will take yours."

The Colonel stiffened. His eyes narrowed at the threat, but he said no more. The bearded man hoped that it was the beginning of caution in the Colonel's headlong attitude. He pulled his thoughts back to their guest as Ricol addressed his next words to the group as a whole.

"Your plans do not conflict with mine. For the moment, I suggest that we all pursue our own interests. Perhaps we can help each other when circumstances arise later. Say, when such actions are mutually beneficial."

"I'm sure we will find many such mutually beneficial circumstances in the future," Diamond assured him.

Ricol smiled as he stood. "Your scheme is intriguing. We can talk again after you have carried through on your next steps."

Diamond admired Ricol's composure as the Duke turned his back on the conspirators and left without a further word. As soon as the Duke was out the door, his former guide stuck his head through the doorway. Diamond nodded to him, indicating that the man should follow Ricol as planned.

In hushed whispers, the group assessed the result of the meeting. Diamond watched the silent Colonel, observing the roiling emotions the military man so injudiciously allowed to show on his face. He was not surprised when the Colonel silenced the conversation by slapping his hand hard against the table.

"Kill him," the Colonel said simply, brown eyes locked with Diamond's own cool blue.

"No," the leader responded. His voice held conviction and the authority of a man who had spent years as a planetary ruler.

The Colonel was not subdued; he had stood up to planetary rulers before. "He will betray us."

"Again, no. We've persuaded him. He will come to us when the time is right."

Diamond had no trouble seeing that the Colonel was not convinced, but the man's shrug showed that he was willing to wait. The others were relieved when the man retreated from the room and expressed confidence in their leader's assessment of the situation. Then they, too, dispersed.

The bearded man was equally relieved. With Ricol, he had secured the last of his preliminary supporters. One final piece to set in place, then he could order the start of action.

His goal was in sight. While the others dreamed of freedom and national sovereignty, he looked further. They would never understand his vision, he knew, but that was unimportant. They only needed to play their parts, unwittingly setting him on the path to rulership. He looked forward to the power he would wield. There was so much good he would do, so many wrongs he would right. His name would be remembered forever.

4

Constance Kurita stifled a yawn. She automatically arrested the hand that rose to rub her sleep-filled eyes, then remembered she wore no cosmetics to smudge. She allowed herself the luxury of freeing the hard particles that clung to her eyelashes. Then she gave all her facial muscles a hard rub. She was never at her best in the predawn hours, and years of meditation vigils had done little to change that.

The urgent summons brought by her maid had left no time to apply her usual court make-up. She had chosen her simplest garb, an amber-colored Pillarine robe, and bound her lustrous black hair at the nape of her neck after only the most cursory brushing. *Shudocho* Oda would not look kindly on a tardy novice, even if she was a member of the ruling Kurita clan. Within the Order of the Five Pillars, Oda was her superior. As long as she was an active member of the Order, Constance was obligated to respond when he called. He never abused the privilege and was most circumspect about her social position, so far above his own.

The message had mentioned that she was to meet with Florimel Kurita, her great aunt and Keeper of the House Honor. Constance believed she knew the true author of the summons.

The Keeper was the custodian of the Combine's religious, ideological, and social codes. In her charge was the Dictum

Honorium, a detailed and complex set of conventions and axioms originally compiled in 2334 by Omi Kurita, daughter of Shiro, first Coordinator of the Draconis Combine. Much like the samurai "house codes" of ancient Japan, the Dictum set forth guidelines for the proper conduct and concerns of a subject of the Kurita clan. Centuries had enlarged that document with the wisdom, and sometimes the follies, of succeeding Coordinators and Keepers. As custodian of the document and the ultimate authority over its contents, the Keeper of the House Honor was a powerful figure in Kurita society and a significant check on the office of the Coordinator. As part of that check, the Keeper ruled the pervasive Order of the Five Pillars, known colloquially as O5P.

Constance herself had joined the Order after secondary school when her sex barred her from further formal education. She knew that O5P was in part a teaching order. Those who teach, she had reasoned, must hold the knowledge that is taught. Her action had galvanized her father, Marcus Kurita, to action. He had arranged for her to be tutored in law by one of the finest lawyers in the Combine, in the hope that she would renounce the Order to follow the lure of knowledge he dangled before her. She had accepted the tutor, but remained with the Order, dreaming of rising to the honored rank of *jukurensha*. Vowing that his daughter would not be sent to wander as a penniless teacher in the Combine's outback, Marcus then used his influence as Warlord of the Rasalhague District to persuade the masters of O5P to keep her on Luthien, where he might see her during his sojourns in the capital.

Constance had accepted with delight, for she had not relished giving up the pleasures of court life. She also realized that she would better tread the path of an Adept if nearer to the center of power and wisdom.

Constance's musings were cut off as the door slid open to reveal *Shudocho* Devlin Oda, back-lit by the lamps in the corridor. Oda slid the door closed and walked silently across the mats to the east wall to bow before the small shrine, lit softly by light from the *shoji* walls of the corridor. The shrine was in the ancient *Ryuboshinto* tradition, consisting of an intricately carved gilded box in decorative and figurative motifs. The box stood on a pedestal of ivory carved in the serpentine shape of the Kurita dragon. Surrounding it were five candle stands, each of a different material: gold, ivory, steel, teak, and jade. Each material symbolized one of the five Pillars that supported Kurita society.

The *shudocho* reached out to each of the stands in turn, lighting a red wax candle there. The last one he lit was the Pillar of Ivory, which Constance took as a sign. Ivory symbolized religion and philosophy, the realm of O5P itself.

Oda knelt across from Constance. Though bursting with curiosity, she said nothing, for the *shudocho* gave no sign that speech was allowed. When Constance flicked her eyes in the direction of the low dais that formed the northern end of the room, she found Florimel seated there. At some point, the old Keeper had silently taken her place.

The Keeper was dressed in a floral-printed formal kimono whose colors hinted properly of the spring. Her posture was straight, causing only the absolute minimum of folds in her garb. She was seated on a stool, a concession to her seventy-six standard years. Florimel's cerulean eyes gazed from a porcelain face, composed and painted with formal court make-up despite the hour. The effect denied her years, making her look thirty years younger. Those eyes seemed kindly now, but Constance knew they were capable of sudden shifts. She had seen them flash hard and unforgivingly toward enemies of the realm.

"*Shoshinsha* Constance," Florimel began. "The dawn will bring a new day, graduation day for the current class of the Wisdom of the Dragon School. This night there is another graduation, one not marked with the pomp and ceremony of a military academy. This graduation will be one of simplicity, pure in its essence and harmonious with the Way. So it must always be for the Order of the Five Pillars.

"We only recognize what is."

Florimel stopped speaking. The silence grew so long that, had the old woman on the dais been anyone other than her great-aunt, Constance would have assumed she had fallen asleep.

"This night we recognize that you, Constance Kurita, are no longer a student. Accept our congratulations, *Jukurensha* Constance. You shall greet the sun as an Adept of the Order of the Five Pillars."

Constance found herself unable to think clearly. Here, unlooked for, was the goal she had sought for years. She had not thought herself ready. There was so much more to learn.

"Well, child, have you nothing to say?" Florimel asked with a smile in her eyes as well as on her lips.

"I am surprised," Constance said haltingly. "I had not thought to achieve this goal so soon."

A little of the joy left Florimel's smile. "Your journey is far from over, daughter of my heart. You have *achieved* nothing, save another step. An Adept is not perfect. Perfection is a journey, not a goal. Honor is found in that journey. To have achieved the goal, or more accurately, to believe that one has achieved the goal, is failure.

"My confidence in you is great. There will be no failure."

"I am honored by your confidence, *Jokan* Florimel," Constance replied.

Oda's laugh shattered the tranquil formality.

"You are to be honored by more than that, Constance-*sama*," Oda assured her in a dry voice.

Constance looked up sharply at the *shudocho,* but his expression was closed, his intent shuttered from her view. She turned to her great aunt.

Florimel gave her a comforting look before turning her gaze toward Oda. "Oda-*kun,* you are less distant from the confusions of youth than am I. If I can show tolerance, so can you. Mind your manners."

"Very well, *Jokan,*" Oda acquiesced with a bow. When he straightened, he faced Constance. His voice was harsh with a leashed emotion that Constance could not identify. "It is true that you shall greet the dawn as a *jukurensha,* but by the sun's setting, you shall no longer be one."

"What!" Constance's eyes went wide with shock.

"Regrettably, it is necessary that you leave my Order."

When no further words were forthcoming from the *shudocho* and a search of his stony face yielded nothing, Constance turned to her great-aunt. Her dismay dissolved as she caught a gleam of mischief in the old woman's eyes.

"He is quite correct, Constance," Florimel said, her voice stern. "You must leave the Order if you are to take the next step on your journey.

"This day, before Devlin Oda, Lord of the Pillars, I declare you my successor as Keeper of the House Honor."

"What!" Constance gasped, feeling foolish for repeating herself. Her wits had deserted her. The sharp reactions of what her father liked to call her "lawyer's mind" had vanished. Embarrassed, Constance reached deep within for the calm she had been taught to cultivate. After a shamefully long time, she stammered, "How can I accept? I am unworthy. I am not prepared."

"Of course you are not prepared," Florimel said, her voice softer. "That is why I make this declaration now. I'm not getting any younger, you know.

"To everyone outside this room, you will become one of my aides, little more than a servant. They will not know you are my successor, Oda-*sensei* and I will help you prepare to take my place. It will not be easy, but much of the work has already been done in your Pillarine training. You have learned our philosophy and goals, and partaken of our mental and physical disciplines. Now we shall focus that training and expand that learning."

Seeing that Constance was still distressed by the sudden changes in her life, Florimel added, "It is proper that you should feel unworthy. Had you felt deserving of the position, you *would* be unworthy, totally unsuitable.

"Make an old woman happy, Constance. Say you will take my place."

Constance searched Florimel's eyes, reaching to feel the old woman's heart as the Pillarines had taught her. She found the strength she knew to be there, strength that proved Florimel's plea of old age a sham. Florimel asked from strength, not weakness. Her desire that Constance succeed was a fierce flame that cindered Constance's objections.

"*Jokan* Florimel would not make a mistake in this matter, *Jukurensha* Constance," Oda declared, trying to push Constance toward the decision she had already made.

"*Jokan* Florimel, I bow to your wisdom," Constance said with a smile, and Florimel's answering smile sealed the pact.

Oda harrumphed his approval of a recalcitrant girl's reluctant acceptance of duty.

"Now then, Constance, I have another bit of business tonight," Florimel announced. "Come kneel beside me here. It is time for you to begin learning more about our affairs."

As Constance took her new place at Florimel's side, Oda opened the door to admit five persons. Four wore the rust-colored robes of Pillarine monks, their shoulders broadened by the stiff, yoke-like collars of off-white armorplast. Each of the four wore a sash and collar tie of a different color: green, brown, gold, and ivory. Four of the five pillars, Constance noted. Each monk's sash was tied in the simple knot that indicated a high-ranking Adept. All wore the hoods, complete with one-way visors, that hid their faces as thoroughly as their robes hid their body contours.

The fifth figure was bare-headed and wore a black ISF sneaksuit. Constance was amazed at the beauty of the woman's delicate features. She needed no cosmetics to enhance the even, golden glow of her skin or her dark-lashed, slanting eyes. The combination of asian features and skin tone over the her strong caucasian bone structure was exquisite. Her shining raven hair was curled close to her skull like a helmet, the ends stirring only slightly as she strode into the square formed by the monks.

All five bowed to the shrine, then to Florimel, and finally to Oda. Without a word, the woman advanced to Oda and knelt before him. He placed a Pillarine collar over her shoulders. As she rose, she tugged the attached hood up and slid the visor down over her features. As the dark-haired woman returned to the other monks, Constance saw the steel grey sash and observed the practiced ease with which she tied it into an Adept's knot.

All five bowed again to Florimel. The woman advanced and knelt before the dais. Head bowed, she offered up a dark leather pouch with a cut strap.

"Here is his pouch," she announced. "I have failed."

Florimel signaled Constance to take the pouch from the woman's hands. "You have brought what you were sent after. Why do you speak of failure?"

"I cut him. His blood is on my sword." Hands now freed from their burden, she placed her palms on the floor and deepened her bow. "Please accept my request for dismissal from the Order."

"How did this happen?" Oda asked from the back of the room.

"He was too strong for my technique," the woman answered, without moving.

From the corner of her eye, Constance saw Florimel smile.

"You bring good news, *Jukurensha,*" Florimel declared, rejecting the request for dismissal by her use of the woman's rank within the Order.

The woman straightened, confusion and surprise evident in her posture. Reflecting on her own confused night, Constance sympathized with her.

"It is important to know that the heir is strong. It is even more important that I know you have not fallen into the trap of believing yourself perfect and invulnerable. No one is ever invulnerable. You have pleased me, *Jukurensha*.

"I have more work for you." Florimel beckoned the monk wearing the colors of the Pillar of Gold. "*Jukurensha* Sharilar, help her to prepare. She is going to have a busy day."

Florimel signaled the end of the audience with a curt nod. As the others left the room, she turned to Constance. "You, too, have a busy day ahead. Many busy days. Let us greet the dawn together. We have much to discuss."

Constance smiled in anticipation.

5

"Theodore Kurita."

Theodore stiffened as his name was called. *He was first!*
The warmth of the morning sunlight that drenched the courtyard was swallowed up in the heated rush of victory. Until
this moment, he had not known. Now that he did, he could
have shouted his victory among the stars. But of course he
did not. He bowed stiffly toward the dais and the assembled
dignitaries before rising from where he knelt among the
graduating class. He strode to the aisle in the center of the
rows of kneeling officers, turned sharply, and headed for
the dais.

Theodore was acutely aware of all eyes on him as he
walked the length of the academy courtyard. Theodore imagined that he could feel the heavy gaze of his father boring
down from the elevated gallery surrounding the courtyard.
As much as Theodore wanted to meet his father's eyes, he
refused to break the discipline of the occasion.

Take a good look, Father, he said silently. *I have beaten
your mark here. Now you must surely see that I have proven
myself worthy.*

As Theodore neared the dais, he focused on the frowning
face of *Tai-sho* Zangi, commandant of the Wisdom of the
Dragon School. *Smile, Old Leather Face,* he thought. *I am
your best.*

The *Tai-sho* continued to frown as Theodore mounted the dais and knelt before him. As Theodore executed the formal bow, the *Tai-sho* spoke in a voice so soft that even the officers kneeling three paces behind could not hear him.

"You have not done your best here."

"But I am first," Theodore replied.

"You are arrogant," Zangi retorted. "You still have much wisdom to learn."

"Not from you."

"As you say."

Zangi held his right arm out to his side. An aide approached and handed him a sheathed *katana*. The *Tai-sho* held the weapon out crosswise to Theodore and spoke in a voice that carried through the courtyard.

"This is the fighting sword of a Kurita samurai. Elsewhere you learned the arts of a MechWarrior and the science of a tactician. Here you honed those skills and learned the art of strategy. Will you accept this sword to use in the service of the Draconis Combine?"

"*Hai!*" Theodore answered. Taking the sword from Zangi's hand, he slid it through his sash and completed his formal acceptance with a bow. Only the mat saw his smile of jubilation.

Zangi held out his arm again. This time the aide handed him a *wakizashi*.

"This is the honor sword of a samurai of the Draconis Combine. Elsewhere you learned the code of *bushido*. Here you learned to live *bushido*. Will you accept this sword, joining your honor to that of House Kurita?"

"*Hai!*" Theodore repeated. His motions were fluid as he placed the second sword in his sash.

Even as Theodore bowed, Zangi reached to the black lacquered tray at his left and removed the top sheet from a stack of brilliant white rice paper. With brisk motions, he folded it closed and sketched on the outside the characters for *sho-sa*. Careful of the wet ink, he held out the packet to Theodore.

"These are the commands of the Dragon. By accepting the swords, and with them your duty, you have accepted these orders."

As custom demanded and heedless of the still-damp ink, Theodore tucked the orders unread into his tunic. The orders were also a promotion, the prize for the first in the class. Even his father had not managed this coup.

Theodore bowed to the *Tai-sho* and stood, carefully steadying the swords as they tugged at his sash. He walked backward to the edge of the dais and bowed again before turning and descending the five steps. In response to the cheers of the crowd, his reserve cracked and he smiled broadly for all to see. As Theodore strode down the aisle, discipline vanished completely and he searched the gallery with his eyes. He sought his father among the ranking guests, but did not find him.

Theodore's first thought was that his father had been somehow delayed. Perhaps there had been a minor mechanical difficulty with the DropShip, the planetary spaceship that an interstellar JumpShip used to convey passengers to and from the jump point at the edge of a star system. Or perhaps there had been some delay in aerospace traffic. Theodore knew better, though. The Coordinator's space transports were maintained to the highest standards, and no air traffic controller would dare interfere with Takashi's chosen time or path of arrival. His father had been here, but had not chosen to witness his son receiving the swords and the coveted first ranking, with its attendant promotion.

Your father only wishes to see you succeed, old Zeshin's voice told him again, as it had for years.

Liar, Theodore thought. *I have succeeded and he refuses to see it. Was I a fool to believe that this success would change the way he treats me?*

Confucius speaks highly of the duty that a son owes to a father, but duty is a curious river. It flows uphill as well as down, Tetsuhara-*sensei*'s voice counseled obliquely.

So why can't he see that?

This time, the voices offered no answer.

Barely noting his surroundings, Theodore entered the honor court. He walked carefully along the stones of the path and took the central place of honor among the carefully tended trees and precisely raked patches of gravel. Lost in his thoughts, he experienced the continued calling of names and shouted cheers as a meaningless susurrus of sound. Those sounds were absent for some time before he noticed.

While he had been contemplating his situation, the honor court had filled with the other graduates, each taking his place according to class ranking. All kneeled in silence, meditating on their new lives in service to the Dragon. Custom demanded that they remain so until the first in the class released them. Without opening his eyes, Theodore finally remembered where he was, and spoke the phrase they awaited, "We begin."

Around him, more cheer broke out. The normally restrained Kuritans cut loose with yelps of joy as they flung their gray academy caps into the air. Some left the court, searching for family members to share their happiness. Most simply jostled and pummeled each other in a tumult of rejoicing and congratulations.

"*O-medeto,*" said a soft voice beside him.

Theodore opened his eyes to look at the speaker. The late afternoon sun, peeking over the garden wall, haloed her black hair and threw her lovely features into shadow. It was a face he knew well from these years at the academy and one he had preferred to see on his staff rather than the opposition's. What was new was the open smile on her face.

"So, Tomoe Sakade, you are friendly now," he said. "What brings a sudden thaw to such ice?"

"We are no longer rivals, *Sho-sa,*" she replied. "Now we can be friends. There is a celebration at the House of Tawamure."

"I'm not interested in a rowdy party."

"Neither am I," she said with a devilish grin.

He was intrigued by her statement, but before he could investigate the possible meanings, a man in a *Chu-sa*'s uniform thrust himself to Theodore's attention.

"*Sho-sa* Kurita, the Coordinator requests your presence in the Agate Pavilion."

Theodore was almost surprised to find his father wearing his formal ceremonial garb; Takashi Kurita had not participated in the ceremony. The black cutaway tailcoat revealed a gray satin waistcoat stretching over the expanse of his belly. The gray pinstriped pants fell without a crease to touch the white spats that covered the mirror-polished black shoes. His short black hair, with its white temples and forelock streak, matched the outfit and lent him the air of a distinguished diplomat of ancient Terra. Theodore had always found the diplomatic garb as anachronistic as the traditional Japanese garb affected throughout the Combine.

As Theodore entered, Takashi turned and dismissed his

aides. He studied his son from head to toe with his ice-blue gaze. *"O-medeto, Sho-sa."*

"Domo arigato, Otosan," Theodore responded automatically. Though he heard the sharpness in Takashi's tone, he could not help but ask, "Are you pleased?"

"Do you expect me to be?" Takashi retorted, all trace of politeness gone. "The ISF has informed me that you have not worked to the best of your ability. I have received reports of shirking, liaisons in the town, and missed assignments. Disgraceful."

"Yet I am first in my class," Theodore said, lifting his head in pride.

Takashi's eyes narrowed. After a moment, he turned toward the window that overlooked the multi-roofed buildings of the academy and stood there for a long moment. Takashi's voice was gruff when he spoke.

"I see that *Tai-sho* Zangi has accorded that honor to you. You should thank him before he leaves for Brihuega and his new command there."

Theodore was surprised and shocked. "That is ridiculous. He would not request an assignment to such an outpost world. Training warriors is his life."

"He did." Takashi waved a hand toward the desk where lay a pile of papers topped by a DCMS request for transfer form. "He found it preferable to the alternative."

Theodore realized suddenly that something was wrong, but he didn't know what. Zangi had been judged guilty of some crime and offered the usual "alternative." The injustice rankled him. "*Tai-sho* Zangi is an honorable man."

Takashi spun around and crossed his arms over his chest. His face was granite. "He has disobeyed me by showing favoritism to my son. I have been lenient in permitting him this recourse."

"He does not deserve this treatment. He showed me no favoritism."

Takashi dismissed his son's defense of Zangi with a slashing motion of his hand.

"Do not demean yourself with lies to defend the false honor he has accorded you. It is unbecoming to a Kurita." Takashi's voice softened. "You shall retain the rank. The people must see my son as an outstanding MechWarrior."

"That is all you care about, isn't it? Appearances!" Theodore spat out the words in disgust.

Takashi turned a cold, hard stare on him.

"We are Kurita. Across the stars, what we appear to be, we *are*. Appearances are all-important. That is something you seem unwilling or unable to learn." After a pause, Takashi added quietly, "Your mother is disappointed, too."

Theodore clenched his jaw to keep from flinging a sarcastic retort at his father. He hated it when Takashi brought Jasmine into arguments to cover his own feelings. In as calm a voice as he could muster, he said, "If you have no further need of me today?"

Takashi looked at his son with calculating eyes, sifting and weighing the effects of the day's confrontation.

"You may go."

Theodore turned and walked slowly from the chamber, controlling the desire to rush out, to be free of his father's suffocating presence. He walked through the building, ignoring the greetings and congratulations of all he passed. On the steps outside the Agate Pavilion, however, he was confronted by someone he could not ignore. Subhash Indrahar clapped him on the shoulder.

"*O-medeto, Sho-sa,*" the man said with a smile full of approval.

Theodore looked at the ISF Director with no thanks in his eyes. "The ISF has informed me," he quoted in a voice filled with the pain of his father's continued rejection. He shook off Subhash's hand, overwhelmed by the need to escape. He ran down the steps.

Shoving his way through the celebrating crowd, Theodore could hear Indrahar calling his name.

6

They found Theodore sitting on a bench in a quiet garden. At his feet lay a crumpled sheet of white rice paper, tightly covered with calligraphic characters.

Even in his despair, Constance thought him romantically handsome. The slightly tousled dark hair and the rumpled uniform added just the right touch of pathos to his tall, lanky frame. Lover and child at once. What woman could resist? *If only he were not my cousin*, she mused.

Great-Aunt Florimel had noted Theodore's abrupt departure from the Agate Pavilion and sent aides to follow him and report where he stopped. When that message came, she had ordered Constance to print a hardcopy of a certain computer file, all the while criticizing Takashi's treatment of his son. From her earliest childhood, Constance remembered Florimel's loving concern for Theodore. Florimel believed that it was her karma to assist and guide him toward his destiny, for he had been born on her estate at the outskirts of the Imperial City. Constance had been born there, too, and that seemed to link her somehow to Theodore as much as their shared childhood at the court on Luthien.

Constance had been there when Theodore was born. She had been only seven years old at the time and remembered little of the event that had so racked Jasmine with agony. At the time, Constance had not understood the whisperings that Jasmine could bear no more children.

That had made her only child all the more precious to Jasmine, and she had protected and pampered him beyond the time proper for a Kuritan boy-child. His mother had not always been able to shield Theodore from his father, however. Constance remembered too many occasions when she had held her sobbing young cousin in her arms while he choked out a story of Takashi's coldness or unthinking cruelty.

Now Theodore was here alone on a day when he should be rejoicing with his family, with his friends. Once more his father had rejected him. Constance thought it intolerable, but she had no power to change it. Even Florimel could do little. She never confronted Takashi about his treatment of Theodore, but protested it in her own way. Through subtle manipulation of his environment and well-timed encouragements, she worked to sustain Theodore's spirit.

Constance knew from the printout she carried that Florimel had a good one today. She sneaked a glance at her great-aunt. Florimel's concern for Theodore showed clearly, but beneath that concern was strength and confidence. Constance was relieved, her own confidence bolstered. Great-Aunt Florimel would save this day.

Theodore stood as the two women entered the garden and pretended surprise at finding him there. Florimel dismissed his attempts at formal courtesy, reminding him that they were all family. Then Theodore helped her to a seat on the granite bench he had just vacated. Heedless of the damp ground, Constance settled at Florimel's knee in a rustle of fine *dai-gumo* silk. After a pause, Theodore joined her, seating himself cross-legged directly in front of his great-aunt.

Florimel's manner suggested that nothing existed outside the garden where they sat. Caught in her spell, the two younger Kuritas found themselves immersed in the moment. The smell of the shower-soaked earth. A *tatsugonchu* flitting and hovering over a puddle. The cool air in the shade.

Florimel herself broke the enchantment, nudging the crumpled rice paper with her toe. "There is a problem with your orders," she said.

Theodore looked down at the ground as though ashamed.

"It is unworthy, but I am unhappy with the BattleMech that Father has assigned for me."

"And what is it?" Florimel asked, though Constance was

quite sure she already knew. Theodore's quick glance at his cousin showed that he thought the same.

"A DRG-1N *Dragon*."

"A noble choice and most symbolic. The Dragon is the symbol of our House and of the whole Combine."

"And Father is very keen on symbols," Theodore said, shifting uncomfortably where he sat. "A *Dragon* is at the bottom of the heavy class of BattleMechs. I have little doubt that it was the least he felt he could give me and still maintain appearances. He probably wished he could have given me a light 'Mech, perhaps a *Locust*. After all, I am such a plague to him. Never good enough."

Florimel quietly cut off Theodore's increasingly bitter speech. "You don't have to fight in it."

Thrown off stride, Theodore paused with his mouth open.

"Of course I do," he said, recovering a little.

"Nonsense! A Kurita samurai has the privilege of fighting in any BattleMech he owns."

"But I don't . . ." Theodore began, puzzled.

"It seems that this is registered on the rolls of the Draconis Combine Mustered Soldiery in your name." Florimel held out the hardcopy that Constance had printed for her. Attached to the cover was a pocket containing an iridescent data disk on which was emblazoned in black the alphanumeric code "ON1-K".

"This is the technical manual for an *Orion* 'Mech," Theodore said in surprise.

"I know what it is," Florimel conceded indulgently. "I had hoped to present it to you on a more auspicious occasion, such as your twenty-fifth birthday."

She started to say more, but refrained when it was obvious Theodore had no attention for anything beyond what he held in his hands. While he paged through the manual, she exchanged amused glances with Constance.

"This was General Kerensky's 'Mech!" Theodore blurted, eyes wide.

"An amazing discovery, wasn't it?" Florimel inquired nonchalantly. "It was found on an asteroid during the course of a minor investigation I ran several years ago in the New Samarkand system."

"You found a Star League depot and kept it secret?" Theodore's voice was full of disbelief.

"Really more of a Star League junkyard. Nothing was

functional. The 'Mechs and other equipment we found there were most likely cast off by General Kerensky and his loyal troops, jettisoned before they exited the Inner Sphere for parts unknown and left us to the Succession Wars. Likely they only had space for a limited amount of materiel.

"The *Orion* was practically a shell, all its important parts removed or ruined. I could not offer such an empty gift, however. The 'Mech has been refitted by the finest technicians in the Combine and with the best equipment, including some brought from the Free Worlds League factory that is the last one in the Sphere producing *Orion*s."

"This is too great a gift," Theodore said, holding the manual out to Florimel. "I cannot accept it."

Florimel ignored his outstretched hand. "In my eyes, you have earned it."

Theodore dropped his arm. Constance could see through his show of humility that he was pleased with Florimel's gift and even more pleased to have her acknowledge his achievements.

"You show greater concern for the heir than the Dragon himself," Theodore said, accepting the gift. His tone revealed a trace of bitterness.

A slight frown crossed Florimel's face. "Try to understand him, Theodore. He has great concerns."

"Too great to be concerned about his son."

"Not too concerned to give you a good assignment," Constance interjected.

Florimel glanced at her sharply, and Constance realized that she had revealed knowledge of Theodore's orders, which he had not yet given to them.

Theodore showed no sign of having noticed. "Perhaps," he admitted grudgingly. "A command lance of my own choosing is an honor, and a posting to the Steiner border is certainly better than the tour of the Periphery border that I expected. Surely, with a battalion to command, I can win some honor for the Dragon against our hereditary foes in the Lyran Commonwealth."

"And you will be near your fiancee," Constance added.

"*Soka,*" Theodore snorted. "That must be the old man's reason. He is so concerned that there be heirs. He must feel that if I am near the woman, I cannot but act as a rutting stallion." Theodore shook his head sadly. "As if he could take care of any heirs I produced. He cannot even handle his own."

"His concern for heirs is valid," Florimel stated firmly.

"Well, he needn't be so concerned," Theodore said, a wide grin beginning to show on his face. "I probably have many already. And I'm sure the ISF will keep him informed."

"It is their duty," Florimel reminded.

Theodore was silent for a moment, then he nodded. Whether in recognition or resignation, Constance could not tell. "*Wakarimas*. As it is my duty to carry on the seed of the Dragon."

Theodore rose, loose-limbed and relaxed.

"I have recently had what I believe is an offer in that department, so perhaps I'll do something about it." Consulting the timepiece in his ring, he added impishly, "And it seems I'm late."

When Theodore had excused himself and left the garden, Constance stood and helped Florimel to her feet.

"His spirits are lifted and he seems once more in control of himself," she offered.

Florimel nodded. "As much as one in his position can be."

7

Lotus Theatre, Munich, Radstadt
Rasalhague Military District, Draconis Combine
29 July 3019

The bearded man known as Diamond frowned, waiting for the last arrival. Opal was late, and the fat merchant was usually early. That might mean trouble if Opal had run afoul of the ISF. Diamond considered dispersing the gathered conspirators; the abandoned theatre might be a good place to hold a clandestine meeting, but they could not defend it if the ISF came calling.

The banging of an open door caught by the wind announced Opal's arrival. He forced the battered door closed, shutting out the dismal, wet gloom. His feet made a squishing sound as he hustled through the lobby and seating area to join the others in the orchestra pit. Murmuring his apologies, the latecomer shook oily water from the slick surface of his foul-weather coat.

At least the fool didn't wear that damning uniform this time, Diamond thought. The group humored the eccentricity when meeting on the merchant's home world, but here, in the shadow of the Black Tower, it was too dangerous. It was one thing to hold the meeting under the tyrant's noses, and quite another to flaunt it. If the authorities spotted such a blatant tie to the Free Rasalhague Underground, no amount of explanation would suffice. The merchant and anyone found with him would be tossed summarily into the Tower to join others who dared openly oppose the Combine government. Anyone who entered that grim, windowless concrete monstrosity never saw the light of day again, not even that of the dismal, cloud-shrouded local star.

" 'Bout time you got here, Armandu," snarled a man in a military issue jumpsuit whose identifying rank and unit insignia had been carefully removed. The lack of markings did not disguise the fact that the hostile speaker came by his outfit legitimately.

"Must I remind you about names again, Colonel?" the bearded man snapped. Over the past year, the Colonel had become increasingly intolerant of the need for secrecy. It was just one more sign that he considered himself vital to the cabal and that he expected much power in the new order.

"No need to get testy, oh most noble leader," the Colonel replied sarcastically. "The ISF goons would never think of listening for treason within earshot of the hell they built for political prisoners."

"We must always be cautious," Diamond said.

The Colonel shrugged his indifference and went back to scanning the summary brief that Diamond had provided earlier. Diamond decided not to press the issue.

"Now that we are gathered . . ."

"Where is Ricol, uh, I mean Ruby," the soggy newcomer nervously interrupted.

Diamond scowled. *If it were not for the fool's money . . . .*

"As I told the others before you arrived, Opal, Ruby has business elsewhere."

"Damned convenient," the Colonel growled.

"Ruby has provided valuable assistance to us in certain ventures," Diamond said, more to remind and reassure the others than to placate the Colonel. The hard-faced military man and the aloof Duke Hassid Ricol had been at odds from the first.

"Ruby's presence is unnecessary," Diamond declared. "So let us not descend to squabbling so early. I have good news."

Expectant faces turned toward him.

"Last week, final negotiations were completed for the marriage of Theodore Kurita and Anastasi Sjovold. The wedding is to take place in Palace Hall in the city of Reykjavik, former capital of the Principality of Rasalhague."

Murmurs of jubilation and congratulations burst from the conspirators. They all knew the difficulty the negotiator had faced in gaining this concession. The agreement to hold the marriage in the Rasalhague District, rather than at the traditional site of Imperial City on Luthien, was crucial to their scheme. It meant that the highest nobles of the court would be traveling into the District, and if all went according to plan, many would never leave. Takashi Kurita had agreed to enter their trap.

"Takashi," Diamond said. By uttering the name of the man they most despised, he seized his fellow conspirators' attention. "Takashi Kurita has agreed to the request of his cousin, our benevolent Warlord Marcus Kurita, to conduct an inspection of the District's military forces. The tour will take place immediately after the wedding and is to be conducted by the notable *Tai-sho* Vladimir 'Ivan' Sorenson, may ravens feast on the traitor's eyes.

"By activating a sleeper agent in Sorenson's entourage, we can kill two Snakes with one blow. Our cause has been handed a most pleasing gift."

"But when is this to happen?" someone asked insistently.

"Soon. Now that arrangements have been completed satisfactorily, the Coordinator wishes no delays." Diamond paused to pick up a datapad. "We shall have to step up our timetable."

An uncomfortable silence followed Diamond's announcement, and the conspirators looked nervously at one another. Opal broke the silence.

"How soon?"

"In two months," Diamond said softly.

Agitated voices expressed alarm, just as he had expected. Unlike him, most of the group would not be able to return to their homeworlds to oversee final preparations and still get to the Rasalhague system in the time remaining. Individual components of their plan might be jeopardized by the need for haste. But, he believed, not dashed to ruin. The main portion of the plan remained sound.

Out of the chaos came a voice, that of the fat plotter Opal. "I will provide funds for everyone to send priority messages through the ComStar communications system. We cannot allow the delays of interstellar travel to halt our divinely ordained mission."

Diamond was surprised at the conviction in Opal's voice. Now that action was near, the man seemed possessed of an unexpected inner fire. Even as he began to wonder how to put this new fervor to use, the Colonel interrupted his thoughts.

"What about the Heir Designate?" the man demanded. "Has there been time to ascertain the pup's stand?"

"Not as well as I would like," Diamond admitted. He knew he had to distract their attention from the problems and refocus it on the possibilities of success. This was no time for defeatism. "But all the signs are positive. He has met Anastasi and raises no objections to the match. He even pays her formal court on his furloughs to Rasalhague. Most interesting is that he seems to be finding a favorable reaction among the general public. The people seem to take his estrangement from his father as a sign that he will be favorable to them."

"The people are fools who don't understand what happens around them," sneered the Colonel, who obviously considered himself no fool.

"Regardless, my friend," Diamond said quietly, not wanting to lose the thread he was weaving. "Theodore's estrangement is something *we,* ourselves, should find encouraging. The latest news may not be favorable for the people, but it certainly augurs well for us.

"Our agents report that he has had another major argument with his father, this time over military matters along our border with the Lyran Commonwealth. Theodore believes that he discerns a weakness in House Steiner's troop distributions, one that could provide the opportunity to take the Tamar system and break the stalemate in that sector. The Coordinator explicitly forbids his son to take action and refuses to authorize any major incursions. I think it likely that Takashi remembers his own father's failed attempts to take that system. They were very costly to the Dragon. Our Coordinator shows little faith in his son's abilities, and seems skeptical that Theodore could better the efforts of the redoubtable Hohiro.

"That leaves us with one very frustrated fellow. Our Theodore may be an astute military man, but he is a child when it comes to politics. I feel sure that he will welcome the removal of obstructions to his ambitions and will reward those who aid him. He will believe that our actions and support free him to pursue his military ambitions."

"We do not need another Kurita tyrant," the Colonel ground out.

"No, we do not," Diamond agreed. "We will not accept such a tyrant, but Theodore need not know that. When our position has been solidified and he has given Anastasi a child to inherit the throne, we will have no further need of him. Isolated from the court on Luthien, as he has been, he will have no friends to warn him and no allies to defend him. In his isolation, he will be vulnerable. Should it come to pass that he is branded a patricide, who would object when loyal citizens rise up and dispose of him?"

8

Ochre light from Rasalhague's midday sun flooded the great bay of the DropShip *Mukade,* overwhelming the glow of the light strips on the wall of the bay. The trip in from the station at the nadir jump point had taken three-and-a-half days, even at the 1.5 G acceleration Theodore Kurita had ordered from the *Mukade's* captain. The crew and his own MechWarriors had griped about the extra half-gee, but Theodore ignored them. Anxious to be down, he had made the descent from orbit seated inside his BattleMech and had freed it from its travel moorings as soon as the DropShip touched down.

Now he sat in its cockpit, waiting for the bay doors to open wide enough to clear the machine's bulk. Around him the ship's crew were busy helping the MechWarriors power up their machines and ready them for debarkation. The rest of the lance would not be off the *Mukade* for many minutes yet.

The orange light of Rasalhague's distant sun reflected in sparkles from the lubricant-shiny metal of the ramp extenders, but automatic compensators kept the glare from Theodore's eyes as he pushed down on the throttle pedal, starting the 'Mech lumbering down the metal runway. BattleMech footsteps rang in dull thunder as the seventy-five-ton mass of armor and armament strode forth from the DropShip.

Tai-i Tomoe Sakade stood on the ferrocrete near the 'Mech hangar, waving. She had left their assignment on New Caledonia weeks ago and traveled to Rasalhague. Once onplanet, she had begun liaison work with the Twenty-second Rasalhague Regulars on Heiligendreuz, the lance's next duty stop in Theodore's shuffle through the Draconis Combine Mustered Soldiery. Theodore keyed up the magnification as he slid the focus point of his head-up display onto her face. The image enlarged until it filled his screen, and her smile filled his heart. Theodore raised one of the *Orion*'s tubular arms and swung the medium-class laser back and forth to return her wave.

As his olive-drab *Orion* began its trek across the landing field, Tomoe disappeared into the hangar building. Rather than switching to IR or light-amplification circuits to follow her progress in the darkness of the structure's cavernous interior, he elected to do something more useful. He began running his checklist of monitor circuits to verify that the machine had survived its transport across the gulf of space. All circuits read green on his status board. Good. No lengthy maintenance would be necessary, and he could shut down the machine as soon as it was safely parked.

The heat indicator showed a level slightly higher than the maintenance manuals predicted for the 'Mech's current activity level, but Theodore wasn't worried. The discrepancy was due to the dark olive paint worn by the *Orion*. The paint had a lower albedo than the manuals recommended, but Theodore was happy to live with the increased solar heat absorption. He had spent weeks of patient research discovering the color scheme carried when the machine had served General Kerensky. Once the colors were authenticated, he had painted the 'Mech himself. Only the insignia were different. Instead of Star League markings, the *Orion* now carried the serpentine dragon of House Kurita. Within the gaping jaws of the dragon, clear upon the red field of the disk, was a silver star, the cadency mark of the Heir-Designate. He was very proud of the 'Mech and had named it the "Revenant."

The "Revenant" entered the shadows of the hangar and headed for a gantry. With the delicate touch of an expert, Theodore maneuvered the blocky, humanoid 'Mech into the waiting cradles. As soon as the 'Mech was locked in, he cracked the access hatch at the back of the machine's "head" and squeezed his lanky body down the narrow, low corridor that led to the opening. Once outside, he kept his crouch until he was sure he would not clip his head on the rearward-projecting, rectangular horn that held much of the *Orion*'s comm gear.

As soon as he had cleared the horn's shadow, Tomoe was in his arms. Their lips met, and her deft hands twitched open the closures of his cooling vest so she could slide her arms around him. When they stopped to catch their breaths, Tomoe smiled radiantly. "Hardly the behavior of a man who is to be married to someone else in three days."

"Maybe so," Theodore said, returning her smile. "If I loved her. The marriage is only political."

"I thought you hated politics."

"I do. This is necessary, as you well know. The Combine must have continuity in the line of the ruler, and my father arranged this marriage to ensure that I will have a sound claim to Rasalhague. My bride-to-be is the daughter of the District Governor, and her family has strong ties with both the Sorensons and McAllisters, two ancient and honorable families in this region. The marriage will serve to bind this oft-rebellious district closer to the heartland of the Combine.

"It is my duty and I will do it."

"Quite a speech," Tomoe said with a frown. "And quite political. You must be coming to like politics after all."

"You know that's not the case," Theodore insisted. "It is *giri*. I am a samurai and must do my duty."

"Yes, you are a samurai," she said, caressing his cheek. "Always *giri* rather than *ninja*. Always duty before human feelings."

Tomoe stared deeply into his eyes. He wondered if she was searching for a denial of her statement. If so, she would not find it. At last, she sighed and lowered her head to rest it against his chest.

"I had hoped you would return early from the drill and give us some time together before the wedding," she said, voice muffled in the folds of his vest.

"And I have done so." Theodore rested his chin against the soft pillow of her glossy black hair.

"I know. I shall treasure that for the rest of my days."

The sorrow in her words was painful to him. "It doesn't have to be this way."

"Oh, but it does, my brave samurai," she sniffed. "We have been through it all too many times. I will not be your concubine. Once you are married, we will be lovers no more."

"That's not what I want," he insisted, holding her away from him and tilting her face to his.

"It's not what I want, either, but it is the way it must be."

He started to object, but she held her fingers to his mouth. "Don't spoil the little time we have left."

She took his hand and led him to the gantry elevator. They said nothing during the ride down and the subsequent walk to the barracks. As soon as they had closed the door of Theodore's room behind them, she slid his vest over his shoulders. Before it hit the floor, she had started in on the closures of his tunic. For an hour, they had no more need of words.

She lay with her head on his shoulder and ran her hand down the length of his body, back and forth, pausing occasionally before sliding past the bony curve of his left hip. Theodore relaxed, enjoying her gentle touch. He wanted to convince himself that it would go on forever.

"Your father has been delayed," she said without preamble.

"An attack?"

"Nothing so dramatic," she said with a shake of her head. "Court business. His JumpShip is due in-system tonight, and *Tai-sho* Sorenson's DropShip awaits him at the zenith station. They will have to make the trip from the jump point under high-gee to arrive in time."

"Rest assured that they will. Father must be here to bless the union; anything else would undermine what he hopes to gain." Theodore shook his head ruefully. He had received no more than the barest acknowledgment of the wedding date from his father, and now the Coordinator would be pushing men and machines in order to be present. "What about Mother? The *Mukade* received no communiques through the ComStar network while we were enroute."

"Your mother and the rest of the court is already inbound from the jump point. They delayed departure from Luthien somewhat when it looked as though Takashi might be able to accompany them, but they finally had to leave without him. You know Takashi won't risk her on a jump to a nonstandard point or allow her to travel at more than one gee. That puts quite a constraint on travel time. Her DropShip has been inbound for over four days. Morning update put ar

rival in"—she pulled his hand over to check his ringwatch—
"one hour."

"I should be there to meet her," Theodore said, rising
from the sleeping mat.

They showered together, using much of the hour. He was
half-dressed before noticing that she was only watching him.

"You're not dressing."

"I'm not going with you," Tomoe said simply.

"Why not? You're my Command Lance second. As my
executive officer, you are entitled to be present at formal
gatherings."

"A position, it is well known, that I earned on my back."

Theodore walked across the room to the comm unit,
which Tomoe had warned him contained a listening device.
Slipping a prepared disk into the slot, he pressed down on
the receiver three times, activating a recorded conversation
that would drown out anything they said. He turned to
Tomoe.

"That's not true. We may be sleeping together, but you
have earned your position in my lance fairly. Your record at
Wisdom of the Dragon speaks for itself. The simple fact that
you, a woman, could graduate from the academy shouts of
your ability."

"Tell it to the troops, especially Tourneville," she responded bitterly. "Most believe that you carried me through
the academy as well."

"Tourneville is my father's creature," he said, as though
that explained everything about the man. "He is a bad echo
of the Coordinator's short-sightedness. My father should be
glad I have a regular, careful lover who is loyal to the
Dragon. Here, in the heart of restless Rasalhague, I could be
running around making bastards and creating future pretend-
ers to the throne."

"This is not a joke. Tourneville is dangerous. It's bad
enough that you insist we live with his bugs and his peeping,
but his talk when you are not around is insufferable. Why
did you choose him for your command lance? With the se-
lection privilege as first graduate of Wisdom, you could
have chosen another fine MechWarrior like Sandersen. One
who would be as loyal to *you* as Tourneville is to Takashi."

"Tourneville is a spy I know, and he is not very good at
his job. That is exactly why I chose him. Had I chosen
someone loyal to me, I would never know who of those

around me worked for my father. This way I have some control over what the Coordinator hears about my actions. After all, we always know where Tourneville's bugs are." He reached out to caress her hair. "It's not important what they think. I want you with me."

Tomoe shook her head. "I am enough of a scandal. It wouldn't be wise to flaunt me before your mother and the courtiers."

"To the seven hells with them," Theodore said.

"Cursing won't change it," she insisted. "I'm only thinking of your political welfare."

"To the hells with politics, too."

"Get used to it, lover," she snapped, stepping away from him. "Politics will be your bedfellow for the rest of your life. Politics is your duty."

Theodore scowled at her. He hated it when she wouldn't listen to him. "If you won't go under your own power, I'll carry you. Naked, if I must," he said, making a grab for her.

Tomoe slipped to one side. He felt the firm, smooth curve of her breast just before she seized his arm and twisted. He landed in a heap on top of the rumpled blankets.

"Go on with you," she said, turning her back on him. "Do your duty."

"Damn!"

Theodore stood and smoothed out his rumpled uniform. Grabbing up his combat vest, he started for the door. As he opened it, he thought she said something. "What was that?"

"I said," she repeated in a very small voice, "spare me a little more time before I lose you."

"All that I can."

He closed the door so that he would not hear her cry.

Teary-eyed and naked, Tomoe turned to the computer and called up the duty files. When the commander was off partying, the executive officer had to run things. She scanned the lists and began to enter commands.

"Damn duty," she snarled at the empty room.

9

Senior Tech Beorn Karlborgen looked down at the small green tablet lying in the palm of his hand. He stretched his thumb over it and rolled it around. It was smooth, hard, and cool. And deadly.

Three days ago, CommTech Fletner had passed him a personal communique. Fletner's face showed what he thought was the proper amount of sympathy. The message stated that Beorn's brother Alfred had died in the crash of a commercial air flight into the capital. Fletner had been impressed with Beorn's fortitude upon receiving the message.

As for Beorn, he had never had a brother named Alfred.

The message was from the Rasalhague underground. He was to proceed with Plan A, as in Alfred. He was to implement that plan on this incoming flight.

For weeks, he had been making subtle alterations to the control systems of *Tai-sho* Sorenson's DropShip. He had smuggled on all the components of the bomb and installed them under cover of normal maintenance work. No one had suspected or questioned him. Why would they? Had he not served loyally as Sorenson's chief technician for two years? Had he not uncovered three bombs planted in various vehicles that the *Tai-sho* was to have used? The *Tai-sho* had complete confidence in him. Indeed, Beorn was a man considered above reproach.

He was a sleeper agent. A time bomb.

Three days ago, the message had come to activate him. The shift of plans meant that Takashi Kurita would die before the wedding. The ceremony scheduled for tomorrow would certainly be postponed, but the leadership of the underground must be confident enough that it could still take place after the official mourning period. At least, they were confident enough to take a chance, and use this rare, and perhaps unique, opportunity to dispose of the tyrant.

With Takashi dead, Theodore would be under more pressure than ever to produce a legitimate heir. A marriage arranged by his father could hardly be ignored, especially when that marriage would calm a potentially rebellious portion of the realm.

Beorn looked at the junction box on the wall in front of him. From here, he could activate the assassination devices. Concealed among a myriad of ordinary instructions were the override programs. Once activated, there would be no escape for Takashi. The bomb would detonate at fifty meters above Rasalhague mean sea level, almost exactly ten meters above the runway of the Reykjavik Starport. The explosion would gut the *Leopard* Class DropShip. Its flaming mass would continue on the course he had locked into the autopilot and then plow straight into the Kurita military sector of the starport. There would be no survivors.

Innocents would die, both aboard the DropShip and at the port, but that could not be helped. This was war. A dirty and undesirable one, but war nonetheless.

A klaxon sounded through the ship. First warning to take stations before final approach. The stress aboard would be nothing like the three-G press they had endured under the Coordinator's orders, but the captain would want everyone safely strapped in anyway, taking no chances while the Kurita tyrant was aboard.

Beorn looked again at the tablet in his hand. Closing his eyes, he popped it into his mouth and swallowed it. There was no turning back now.

He slid out the wire support frame, unlocked the box, and lowered the lid onto the frame. Carefully, he tapped the activation codes onto the membrane keyboard in the box lid. Three green lights flashed within the box. Satisfied, he closed the lid and reinserted his maintenance key into the lock. From his tool box, he took a hydrospanner, and with a sharp rap from the tool, snapped the key off in the lock.

Those on board were doomed, but they would never know it until the pilot tried to adjust the ship's approach vector. By then, it would be far too late. The ship and its passengers would be irrevocably headed for impact with the Kurita military sector of the starport.

Beorn squeezed his eyes together, suddenly drowsy. They had said it would be fast. Legs numb, he slid to the floor. *Goodbye, Hilda. I wish there had been more time for us.*

Beorn Karlborgen closed his eyes and slept.

Theodore frowned at Tourneville's fussing.

"Shouldn't you have had the unit flash on your cap changed, *Sho-sa?*" the man chided. "We are no longer with the An Ting Legion. After the wedding, the lance moves on to the Twenty-second Regulars. I realize that you will not join us on Heiligendreuz for several weeks, but you *are* our commander, and it's only proper that you wear current insignia on your uniform. If you had gotten a manservant, as I suggested, all these little details would have been cared for."

"I don't need that kind of help, Tourneville. For today, the cap will do as it is," Theodore said, hiding his irritation with a smile. *And you don't need a helper in your spying,* he added silently, accepting the proffered cap and settling it on his head.

Ignoring his companion's frown, Theodore shrugged into a nonregulation battle vest. The dark-brown, padded garment almost covered the red diagonal stripe on his dark gray jersey. Theodore knew that Tourneville was as bothered by the scruffiness of the vest as by the fact that it covered the identifying stripe that was the most prominent feature of a Kurita MechWarrior's noncombat uniform. For a spy, Tourneville had a most curious desire to see things identified for what they were.

As soon as they were ready, Theodore led the way from the barracks to the motor pool. After a short delay in which Tourneville dealt with a runner from the comm center, they mounted an open-topped groundcar and sped away with a soft electric whine.

"What was that all about?" Theodore asked as they had cleared the gate.

"Nothing important, *Sho-sa*. Some minor official has been

trying all morning to speak to you. I told the comm center to hold all messages. Warlord Marcus Kurita's summons has higher priority than some local's desire to have his picture taken with the Heir-Designate."

"Is that all he wanted?"

"Who knows?" Tourneville shrugged. "These provincials have no sense of importance. Warlord Kurita's desire to see you at the port control has priority."

Tourneville had shown rare initiative in determining the relative importance of messages to Theodore. Though undecided whether he was more annoyed at Tourneville's temerity or by the man's fawning reverence for cousin Marcus, Theodore merely replied, "Mustn't disappoint the Warlord."

10

"That is the first approach warning, Coordinator," Ivan Sorenson announced. "Time to prepare for the descent to the port."

"Very well, *Tai-sho*," Takashi Kurita said as he stood. "I have found our little talk about the Rasalhague situation quite interesting. Your perspective on my cousin Marcus's performance as Warlord is most enlightening."

As the two men left the tiny captain's lounge and entered the bridge of the DropShip, a pasty-faced crewman burst through the hatch.

"Body ... dead ... purple splotches," the man stammered.

Sorenson was on him in an instant, his two-meter height looming over the crewman.

"Stop babbling, crewman!" he growled. "I want a clear report."

The man made a visible effort to control himself. "Senior Tech Karlborgen. I found him in Engineering. He's dead, sir. It's awful. He's all covered in purple spots."

Sorenson wasted no time. As he turned to exit the bridge, he shouted, "Pull us back to a holding orbit, *Dai-i* N'kuma. I don't want us down till we find out what happened."

As he pounded the length of the ship, Sorenson considered the possibilities. He knew of no disease that would cause purple spots, making it likely that Beorn Karlborgen was the victim of foul play, be it some hideous poison or a tailored bioweapon. Whatever the cause, there was a murderer aboard. That meant trouble—and trouble was the last thing he wanted with the Coordinator of the Draconis Combine on board his DropShip. He had considered it a bit of good fortune when Marcus Kurita had suggested that the *Tai-sho* personally meet the Coordinator at the jump point. Now that fortunate assignment was on the verge of becoming a curse. *My honor becomes nil,* he told himself, *if anything threatens the Coordinator while he is in my care.*

Sorenson reviewed his enemies, searching for a possible author for the day's trouble. When he could think of no one who had the opportunity, he started on possible enemies of the Coordinator. His thoughts shuddered to a halt when he confronted the backs of the crewmembers gathered around the body.

Sorenson shouldered his way through and looked at the body. The calm, composed face of the corpse struck him at once. Not murder, then. *What have you done, Beorn?*

Sorenson bent to examine the body. After a quick search, he was even more sure that the Senior Tech had killed himself.

"The ship controls are frozen," said someone at his shoulder.

Sorenson started at the voice, which was as cool and detached as though coming from beyond the grave. He turned, half-expecting to confront Beorn's ghost, and found himself looking at Takashi Kurita. The Coordinator had followed him.

"It seems that your Senior Tech wished to be an assassin and had not the courage to face the death he would give us."

Recovering his composure, Sorenson asked, "What do you mean?"

"The *Dai-i* says that the command of the ship is locked into autopilot. We are committed to a course that will crash us into the control center of the military portion of the spaceport at Reykjavik."

Takashi's words sparked a panic in the crew around them. Men and women scrambled in all directions, shouting and fighting among themselves. Several headed straight for an escape pod. The leader of that trio slapped the access control, screaming for the door to hurry up. All three wailed their dismay when the pod launched without ever opening its door.

"Very thorough," Takashi commented. "All outbound communications are blocked, replaced by computer simulations of routine messages. The control center is unaware of our plight."

"He was a superior Tech," Sorenson agreed, infected by the calm of the Coordinator. "Does the *Dai-i* think the override could be broken?"

"Not in time."

"Then we are trapped."

"Unless you can grow wings or walk on air like the fabled *tenshin*."

Sorenson started to shake his head. The Coordinator's comment sparked a desperate plan.

"There may be a chance," he said. "Come, *Tono*."

Sorenson led the Coordinator to the BattleMech bay.

The Coordinator must have divined Sorenson's plan as soon as they reached their destination.

"The 'Mechs are not equipped for orbital drop."

"No, *Tono*. We have the shells and maneuver units on board, but there is no time to rig them up. My *Grasshopper* has jump jets, though, and we have already entered atmosphere. If we can get a 'Mech outside the ship, it may be possible to ride it down. It won't be a pleasant trip and the landing will be rough, but it's a chance."

"The Dragon approves audacity, *Tai-sho*."

Sorenson suspected that Takashi was a superior 'Mech pilot. Hoping that the Coordinator would understand, he said, "There's no time to clear the safety locks and to wipe the neurocircuits clean for you, so I'll have to pilot it."

The Coordinator nodded.

They rode the lift to cockpit level in silence, rising high above the deck where crewmembers scurried in panic.

"Better let me in first, *Tono*. I'll never get my bulk past you otherwise."

Sorenson squeezed through the narrow entry hatch. As he passed, he tugged the lever that unfolded the jumpseat and locked it in place. Most 'Mechs had such accommodations for passengers, but they were cramped, uncomfortable. The rider was locked in, able to see nothing more than brief glimpses of the controls and screens, unable to affect his fate. Briefly, Sorenson wondered how Takashi would take such helplessness. He himself would have been frantic.

As he settled into the command couch and keyed in his computer identification code, he heard the Coordinator strapping in. Sorenson slapped on the biomonitor patches and jammed the plugs into their neurohelmet sockets before rocking the massive helmet free of its cradle. He settled the helmet over his head, feeling the weight pressing down onto his unprotected shoulders. *Damn! That will bruise,* he thought, but there was no time to don the cooling vest whose padded shoulders normally protected a MechWarrior from the oppressive mass of the neurohelmet.

The lack of the cooling vest was a problem. No MechWarrior ever wanted to operate his machine without one. As heat built up in the cockpit, a man could be cooked. He and the Coordinator would have to take their chances.

"All belted in, Coordinator?"

"Hai," came the answer, still cool and sounding far more ready than Sorenson felt. "The reactor is cold."

The Coordinator hit upon another flaw in Sorenson's plan. It normally took several minutes to safely bring a Battle-Mech's fusion reactor to operating temperatures. Minutes they didn't have. Starting the 'Mech cold was another risk that only a desperate man would take.

"We're going to have to chance a cold start, *Tono.* I'm trying to set up a power feed through the DropShip's monitor cables."

Sorenson completed the circuit just as an explosion rocked the ship. *Damn, Beorn. Nothing left to chance. You set explosives as well.*

The BattleMech jerked as power flooded into it. Limbs spasmed as random surges activated the myomer pseudomuscles that moved the massive alloy bones of the machine's skeleton. In the midst of the jerky dance, Sorenson sent the signal to open the bay doors.

There was no response.

He tapped the unlock code again. And again. The titanium alloy doors remained immobile, as unmoved by his repeated signals as by his curses. The damned traitor had been too thorough.

There was only one chance left.

Sorenson triggered the 'Mech's head-mounted missile launcher.

Crashing detonations filled the bay as its door shattered under the explosive power of the warheads. Strips of steel ripped free of the ship, scattering free into the sky like chaff. The *Grasshopper* was knocked free of its mooring as a tremendous blast spun the ship. A tumbling whirl of clouds was the last thing Sorenson saw as the BattleMech toppled backward, jarring its pilot, and sending him straight into darkness.

"Good to see you again, Duke Ricol," Theodore said, straightening from his bow and extending his hand to the man.

"The pleasure is mine, Highness." Ricol's tone was as suave as his dress. His natty red garb was a distinct contrast to the drab gray and brown that dominated Theodore's uniform. "What brings you out so early in the morning, after so long a night of celebration?"

"A message from my cousin Marcus," Theodore answered, wondering if Ricol really knew how he had spent his night. "He asked me to come to the control center."

"I would have expected him to be here to meet you," Ricol said. "His lack of grace in not meeting *me* is understandable. I am but the lord of a minor house, expected to wait on the whims of the mighty."

Theodore gave Ricol a sidelong glance. He couldn't be sure just what part of the man's comment was sarcasm and to what part he was supposed to respond. Theodore elected to deal only with the factual statements.

"Then you were to meet him, too."

"So his message implied, Highness."

"Curious."

"Yes, isn't it?"

The two men lapsed into thoughtful silence. Theodore looked out of the command center at the dawn rising over the starport. Condensate clouds rose from vents on the roofs of buildings across the field, as heated exhaust met the chill atmosphere. Workers moved about their business, taking care to spend most of their transit time in the light of the rising sun, avoiding the frost-cloaked shadows. Less lucky were a company of *Tai-sho* Sorenson's Eight Rasalhague Regulars. The MechWarriors' physical fitness instructor led them on a prescribed course that took no account of personal comforts as they jogged off to begin an early morning run.

All was ordinary, another typical day. Order was serenity, something Theodore wished he had more of after the bustle of the previous day's hectic wedding preparations and the uneasy night with Tomoe.

"Ah," Ricol said, drawing his attention. The Duke pointed at a speck in the distance. "A DropShip is approaching. I believe that your father will be making planetfall soon."

11

***Draconis Military Starport, Reykjavik, Rasalhague
Rasalhague Military District, Draconis Combine
22 September 3019***

A commotion in the outer reception room drew the attention of those awaiting the incoming flight. Through the transparent barrier wall, Theodore could see Tourneville arguing with a new arrival. The newcomer still wore an aviation helmet concealing all his features except for the salt-and-pepper beard that bobbed up and down as he spoke and gesticulated at the main reception area.

Theodore recognized the beard as belonging to Ottar Sjovold, Governor of Rasalhague District and his future father-in-law. Excusing himself from Duke Ricol, Theodore headed for the other chamber. As he penetrated the white-noise curtain masking the observation area, his ears filled with Sjovold's urgent demands to see him.

"What is the problem, Jarl Sjovold?" Theodore inquired.

Slipping past Tourneville's outthrust arm, Sjovold hurried toward Theodore and grabbed him by the arm. "Hurry, your Highness. Your man wouldn't let me through and there is little time. We must get you out of here."

"What are you talking about, Governor?"

Sjovold swept his eyes across the chamber before stammering nervously, "Ah . . . an accident. Yes. There's been an accident! You must come with me."

"Have you notified the authorities?" Theodore asked, suspicious of the sudden shift from assurance to distress.

"No. No time," Sjovold babbled as he continued to tug the resisting Theodore toward the exit. "It's ... it's your mother."

Concern swept away Theodore's wariness. "She's been injured?"

"No," the Governor answered. "At least, nothing serious. But she wants to see you immediately. We must hurry!"

The Governor urged Theodore into a waiting VTOL craft. Theodore dropped onto the perforated metal bench seat in time to see Duke Ricol and Tourneville climbing in after them. Sjovold seemed as surprised as he was. Ricol made a remark, but his words were lost in the scream from the turbines as the craft rose from the pavement.

Theodore was forced into his seat as the craft lifted rapidly. The thunder of the rotors changed pitch when the wing tilted, bringing the whirling blades down into position for effective forward flight. The pilot had begun a sharp bank over the outskirts of the spaceport when the VTOL bucked as a shock wave hit it. The sound of thunder followed.

As the craft banked in the other direction, Ricol tugged Theodore's sleeve and pointed out through the still-open hatchway. Framed in that patch of sky was a scene of horror. The incoming DropShip was trailing smoke and flames. Explosions erupted along its length, scattering smoking debris and burning fragments. As they watched, a BattleMech toppled out through a great rent in the heavy metal bay doors on the ship's side. It fell in a loose-jointed tumble to crash and shatter on the ferrocrete. A huge fireball erupted from the descending spaceship's nose and enveloped the fuselage. Out of the flames shot another 'Mech. One arm flopped loosely, trailing fire as the 'Mech traveled in a low arc away from the the burning ship. The DropShip's nose lifted slightly, as though the pilot had somehow regained control of his plummeting craft. The illusion was shattered as the ship plunged into the control center and erupted in flames.

The men in the VTOL shielded their eyes from the fireball's intense flare. Dark, deadly smoke billowed up in death's umbrella over the site. Theodore was appalled. No one could survive that crash.

His father had been aboard that DropShip.

Governor Sjovold struggled across the compartment and slid the hatch closed. The noise level dropped instantly as the sealed cabin's sound buffers muffled the engine sounds. Sjovold dropped into the seat next to Theodore.

"You could have died in the crash, your Highness."

With a start, Theodore realized that Sjovold was right. If he had remained in the control center, now an inferno, he would have died at the same time as his father.

"I risked my own life," Sjovold continued, "to get you out of there. I tried to get a message through to you all morning and arrived at your barracks to find you had left for the port."

Theodore held up a hand to stop Sjovold. "*Chu-i* Tourneville, perhaps you had better go up to the cockpit and use the radio to ensure that the emergency facilities are mobilized. Get the fire under control before it jeopardizes the rest of the compound."

Tourneville looked on the verge of refusing the suggestion, clearly wanting to remain. Theodore raised his chin slightly in a way he had seen his father do many times when wishing to reinforce his orders. Chastened, the *Chu-i* gave a sketchy bow and vanished up the companionway to the cockpit.

Theodore turned to face the puzzled Governor. "Tourneville screened my calls this morning," he explained.

Sjovold nodded his understanding, and a slight smile crept onto his face. "I see you begin to understand what has happened. You will appreciate that I have your best interests in mind."

"I appreciate that you saved the life of the man who is to marry your daughter. A man who would become . . . no, *has* become Coordinator. I do not think that you have only *my* interests in mind."

Sjovold rocked back into his seat and stroked his beard, a sudden, new respect coming into his eyes. "I would be a fool and a liar if I denied that. Our paths take us in the same direction, and we can be of great help to each other.

"For years, I have studied your career. The more I came to know of you, the more I was impressed. I have worked to see you replace your father. My people and I have worked alongside the Warlord, planning to rid ourselves of the tyrant, a man who has oppressed you as much as he has this District. Though we worked with Marcus, assuring him that we would support him as Coordinator, we worked for you. Marcus has betrayed us all by trying to kill you today, too.

As soon as I learned of his message to you, I tried to stop you."

"You did not try to stop *me,* Jarl," Ricol drawled.

Sjovold, his concentration on Theodore broken, looked blankly at the Duke.

There was something between the two men that Theodore did not understand. It was unimportant compared to what the Governor had said. "You say that you were involved with my cousin Marcus in a plot to kill my father."

"It was necessary. But Marcus double-crossed us. He wishes to be Coordinator. It was always my intention to see you on the Coordinator's throne. We did this for you."

"And now you expect me to work with you."

"You will be Coordinator. We will all benefit. As your Warlord here, I can assure you of a peaceful, loyal district."

Theodore stood and paced across the compartment. Sjovold's ambitions had been revealed, naked and ugly. He was now double-crossing Marcus even as he said the Warlord had double-crossed him. His back to the Governor, Theodore said, "You have an interesting opinion of the Kurita clan, Governor Sjovold. In general, and of me, specifically. If you know me so well, you should realize that I will not be a party to regicide."

A sudden, meaty smack and yelp caused him to turn. Ricol and Sjovold were wrestling, rolling back and forth across the deck.

Theodore stared at the struggling men, disturbed that he had felt no warning, no sense of danger to himself. His early training with Tetsuhara-*sensei* and later sessions with Director Indrahar had taught him to trust that sense. He did not believe it would betray him here. This was between the two of them. He held himself aloof from the struggling men on the floor of the compartment.

The combatants bashed up against the aft bulkhead, Sjovold on top. The Governor's hands were locked around the Duke's throat. Ricol's arm snaked out to one side, slamming a fist into Sjovold's left elbow. Having weakened the grip, Ricol broke it completely in a convulsive heave. He drove a stiffened arm forward, catching Sjovold's chin with his palm. The Governor's head snapped back with a brittle crack and he collapsed onto the Duke. Ricol untangled himself and slowly rose from the motionless body of his opponent. Stepping back, the Duke clearing Theodore's line of sight and pointed to a slim blade lying next to the Governor's outstretched hand. "He meant that for you, your Highness."

"And you threw yourself in his way to save me," Theodore stated flatly.

"As you say," Ricol said, inclining his head, "Coordinator."

Theodore was taken aback at being addressed by his father's title. It did not sound right. He wondered about Ricol's motives, about the fight he had witnessed. "Did you wish to cover your own connections to him, or did you act only out of loyalty to the Dragon?"

"Coordinator, I shall face any allegations of disloyalty in the circle of honor," Ricol replied, nonplussed by Theodore's bluntness.

"And triumph, no doubt. I have heard of your skill with blades. Of all kinds."

Ricol's face betrayed nothing.

Theodore shrugged. "Tell the pilot to take us to the Hotel Kiruna. My mother must be informed of today's events."

Ricol bowed, as befitted a loyal servant of the Dragon.

12

Sorenson had no idea how long he had been unconscious, but he knew it must have been only briefly. When he came to, the *Startreader* was still plummeting toward the surface of Rasalhague.

Ignoring the warning buzzes and flashing system failure lights, he forced the *Grasshopper* from its bed of smashed machinery. The BattleMech wobbled as it reached its feet, sending a feedback of dizzying vertigo through the neurocircuits to increase the ache that filled his skull. The 'Mech staggered forward toward the rent his missiles had torn in the bay door. He reached out with the machine's arms and grasped the ragged edges. Metal tore like paper as he applied the herculean strength of the seventy-ton machine's myomer muscles.

A high-pitched whine warned him of an actuator failure. He stabbed a hand forward even as his eyes registered the lights signaling a myomer failure, but was too late. Before he could hit the cut-off, the *Grasshopper*'s left arm twitched, then went rigid as the motivating myomers, already stressed by the cold start, locked in spasm. Sorenson snapped the switch, cutting the power and unlocking the tension on the main myomer bundles. The smoking arm flopped uselessly to the side of the 'Mech, but the irregular motion of the failing arm twisted the 'Mech off-balance. Before the dazed

Sorenson could compensate, the 'Mech crashed into the edge of the bay door, its upper torso jutting through the opening. The screaming wind of the DropShip's passage smashed the *Grasshopper* firmly against the frame of the ship, doubling it over like a ragdoll.

Cursing the useless arm, Sorenson used the machine's remaining limb to lever the 'Mech into a more favorable position for firing the jump jets. As he did so, his sensors registered a tremendous explosion near the bow of the *Startreader*. Fearing that he would not clear the wreckage of the dying DropShip, he speared the red jump button.

Fire from the captive sun at the heart of the BattleMech's fusion engine vaporized a minute quantity of the mercury reaction mass, transforming it instantly to plasma. Flame and superheated air rushed out the exhaust ports in the *Grasshopper*'s back and legs, thrusting the 'Mech through the growing fireball enveloping the *Startreader* and away from the doomed vessel.

Heat deluged the cockpit, and the *Grasshopper*'s computer voice warned of imminent shutdown because of it. Sorenson, barely conscious, cut in the override, stilling the voice. Stubbornly, he worked the controls, trying to bring the wobbling 'Mech under control. As it spun, his cockpit screen gave him alternating views of ground and sky.

"At least we're not heading straight down," he croaked, his throat gone dry from fear and heat.

There was no answer from the jump seat.

Sorenson had no time to wonder if his passenger was still alive. The ground was coming up too fast. There was not enough time to gain control of the wounded 'Mech's flight. In a desperate attempt to minimize crash damage to the cockpit, he forced the machine around until its head was pointed away from its direction of travel. The legs and torso could absorb far more damage than the relatively fragile head structures of the BattleMech.

When the altimeter LED readout clicked to thirty meters, he opened the jets all the way, burning all his reaction mass in a single burst. The flight system monitor board flashed red. He had only begun to hope that they had burned long enough when the 'Mech smashed into the ground.

Thrown violently against his restraining straps, Sorenson felt his skin slice open along their edges. Red failure lights filled his board, then blinked out as cockpit power failed. He was thrown back into his couch as the 'Mech collapsed onto its back.

Pale light and a trickle of blessedly cool air filtered through a crack in the cockpit's shell.

"Alive!" Sorenson said aloud. The sound of his own voice, coarsened though it was from his ordeal, reassured him that he was right. Grimacing from the pain that movement sent through his arms, he forced the neurohelmet off and let it clatter to the back bulkhead, then unbuckled the straps and slid his bloody shoulders free. As he climbed from the couch and found that he had no grip, he reached for the overhead grab iron to steady himself. Puzzlement was all he felt as he slipped into darkness for the second time in a matter of minutes.

Sorenson opened his eyes to see the sun sinking into the fens. Backlit before him was the three-quarter-buried shape of his *Grasshopper*. Little more than its torso showed above the fire-blackened sedges and brackish water where it lay. The head, cockpit access hatch gaping, hung limply on a narrow thread of cables, and its right arm jutted from the marsh. Sorenson knew from its angle that the arm was no longer attached to the 'Mech's shoulder.

> *Grasshopper leaps far,*
> *At home in an autumn marsh*
> *Dies like samurai.*

It took Sorenson a moment to realize that the words spoken behind his head came from a living person and not from some frog-voiced marsh spirit. He rolled on his side to see the speaker.

There was Takashi Kurita, sitting calmly. His folded legs showed bare and bruised, as did his left arm. He was smeared all over with mud and dried blood. A soiled, blood-stained white rag was wrapped around his head like a ancient warrior's *hachimaki*.

"Your BattleMech is a total wreck," Takashi Kurita told him. "Sacrificed in your effort to save us from the doomed *Startreader*. For some time, I thought you, too, had moved onward."

Sorenson tried to chuckle, but the sound he made was too

ghastly to express humor. "I'm in too much pain to be dead."

"You have my gratitude and I shall reward you for today's deeds," Takashi said. "At the very least, I shall see that you receive a replacement for your machine."

"A new 'Mech would be appreciated, *Tono,* but I need no reward for doing my duty."

"Spoken like a true samurai. But you will be rewarded nonetheless. All scales must be balanced, and your reward must balance the punishment inflicted on those responsible."

Sorenson contemplated what that punishment might be. The lucky ones would have a quick death or a quiet life in the Black Tower. Somehow he didn't think there would be too many lucky ones involved in this plot. The conspirators' luck had run out when they failed to kill the Coordinator.

Takashi gazed at the sunset until the last rim of the orange sun dropped below the horizon. In the twilight, he spoke again, and his voice had that adamant quality attributed to Emma-Hoo, Judge of the Dead and Lord of the Buddhist hells.

"Those involved have forfeited the right to life. The conspirators and their families, all of the plotters' generation, their parents and their children, shall be put to death. No child shall survive to avenge a parent, nor parent take revenge for a child. I will see this conspiracy ground out completely."

13

Palace Hall, Reykjavik, Rasalhague
Rasalhague Military District, Draconis Combine
23 September 3019

Theodore looked up at the frowning gray stone facade of the sprawling Palace Hall, seat of government for the planet and the District of Rasalhague. Yesterday, he had expected that when he passed through its iron-bound, studded doors, he would be wearing a formal black kimono, his long nape hair oiled and bound into a topknot. Yesterday, he had expected to be on his way to his wedding.

He mounted the steps at an awkward pace, irritated at their shallow rise and exaggerated width. The strides he took would not have been possible in a kimono, but the trichloropolyester trousers he wore offered no restraint. The pants were the same dark gray as his jersey and matched his grim mood.

A full company of infantry from the auxiliaries of the Eight Rasalhague Regulars guarded the doors, but they passed Theodore without question.

He found his father in the Governor's office, seated behind a massive oaken desk. Aides and generals looked up at Theodore's sudden intrusion. Takashi bade them leave. In a clatter of comp pads and murmur of hushed comments, they gathered their materials. Takashi swiveled his chair to one side and eased a bandaged leg gingerly onto a stool. The departing attendants kept their eyes low as they filed past

Theodore, who stood in the center of the room, hands clenched at his sides.

Last to leave was Subhash Indrahar, who touched Theodore's shoulder as he passed. An electric feeling of confidence shocked Theodore. He controlled his surprise and only nodded to the Director. Indrahar's smile was warm, but Theodore did not let it touch the icy resolve he had nurtured during his walk from the military camp at the starport. As the doors closed softly behind him, Theodore raged, "How can you sit there and let this go on?"

Takashi closed his eyes and took a deep breath. "To what exactly do you refer?"

Theodore strode up to the desk, slamming his palms against the wood and leaning forward. "The executions of innocent people. How can you do it?"

"How can I not?" Takashi replied, gently massaging one of the many plastiflesh patches covering the lacerations on his face.

"It is barbaric—criminal."

Takashi lowered his hand and turned baleful eyes on his son. "You pride yourself on your knowledge of the classics, so I assume you are familiar with *Heike Monogatari*."

"Of course," Theodore returned sharply. He was bothered by the change in subject, but knew his father would not proceed until he had satisfied his pedantry. "What self-respecting scholar or warrior does not know of it? The tale recounts the war between the Taira and the Minamoto. That war resulted in the first ruling shogunate of old Japan."

"*So ka*," Takashi grunted. "Are you also familiar with the antecedents of the final struggle between those clans?"

Theodore was truly annoyed. Tetsuhara-*sensei*'s voice urged him: *Answer with the expected words, even when they belie your heart's true reply, and your enemy will open his mind to you.*

All right, I'll give him the answer he wants to hear. Then maybe he will let me see what he really wants. "The Taira had all but eliminated the Minamoto in their struggle for influence over the Emperor. But two young Minamoto boys escaped the purges of the victors. They were the brothers Yoritomo and Yoshitsune. When they grew to manhood, they revived their clan, led it against the Taira and destroyed their enemy. Yoritomo became the first shogun."

Takashi smiled with satisfaction. "Thus, you see that what

I do is necessary. I can leave no survivors of the conspiracy and I cannot leave possible seeds of a new one."

"What about Marcus?" Theodore countered.

"There is no solid evidence. He was elsewhere when the communique you received was sent from his offices. It cannot be proved that he wished you present for the fatal crash. There is only the word of a traitorous assassin that he was involved in the sabotage of the *Startreader*."

"Surely you don't believe that he is innocent," Theodore said incredulously. Takashi said nothing. "If we had both been killed in the crash of the *Startreader,* he would have taken the office of Coordinator."

"You forget your cousin and my nephew, Isoroku. He would have been recalled from his monastery to take up the office of Coordinator."

"He would have been dead before he reached Luthien," Theodore snapped. "If Marcus was ready to go after us, he would have had no qualms about a mouse like Isoroku. That monk would never have a chance against such a predator."

"That is irrelevant," Takashi said, with a shrug. "Matters have turned out otherwise. Marcus has withdrawn to a fortified redoubt in the mountains north of the city, and cannot be reached without extraordinary effort. He is strong here in the District, too strong to confront openly. He must not be allowed to hold his position and threaten the realm.

"Effective this day, Vladimir Ivan Sorenson is Warlord of Rasalhague."

Theodore was shocked. "Marcus will revolt. He has chanced too much already to sit quietly and let you strip him of his rank."

"I think he will accept it. Marcus cannot refuse a promotion." Takashi languidly pointed at a document, rolled and sealed, which lay on the desk. "I have made cousin Marcus my Chief of Strategies for the DCMS. He will sit above the Warlords on my council. But to do so, he must leave his hole and come to Luthien."

"Yes, he will come to Luthien," Theodore agreed. "Then you will execute him."

"Then we will see."

Theodore considered Takashi's publicized promise of death to the conspirators and their families. Should Marcus be implicated in the conspiracy, Takashi would have to order the deaths of his Aunt Florimel and Uncle Undell, Marcus's father, for they were of the previous generation. Having brought Marcus into existence, they were responsible for bringing treachery into the universe. Takashi would also have to execute all of Marcus's children, including Constance, for the taint of traitor's blood they carried.

Such executions would gut the ruling family of the Kurita clan, leaving only Theodore and his parents. There were other Kurita lines, of course, notably that of Malcolm Kurita, whom Takashi had appointed to replace the recently deceased Sjovold as District Governor. But Malcolm was old and sickly, and his son Mies was no warrior. None of the cadet lines had as pure a blood line as Takashi's own family; none had a clearer claim. There would be civil war. Weakened by internal strife, the Combine would fall prey to the predations of the other Successor States.

Takashi would not let that happen, Theodore knew. He would not destroy his own Great House. He would squirm as much as necessary, make any compromises in order to find an appearance that would suit.

Theodore realized that his father had done just that.

One would hardly appoint an assassin to reign over one's military strategies, but that was exactly what Takashi had done. Therefore Marcus could not be an assassin, at least not to outward appearances. His life was safe. The family was safe.

But other families were not so lucky. When a salvage crew seeking the *Startreader*'s lost BattleMechs had returned from the fens with his father and Warlord Sorenson, Theodore had been secretly relieved. He did not want to be Coordinator yet. In his relief, he had told Takashi of Ottar Sjovold's plan and his own rejection of it; of the Governor's reaction and Duke Ricol's timely intervention. Takashi had not yet made public his vow, and Theodore had unknowingly sealed the death warrant for Anastasi Sjovold, his betrothed.

His own part in implicating the Sjovold family disturbed him, though he was not sure why. Theodore had no doubt that the traitors should die. Death was their proper reward. But Anastasi was a mere pawn to her father's ambition, a poor fly caught in the web of treachery.

He also knew that death was a part of life. It came to all, even the innocent. He himself had killed on the battlefield, but that was different from an execution. Anyone on the battlefield knew the risks. The pilot of a BattleMech embraced the concept of war.

Yet, had he known of Takashi's vow, he could have explained Sjovold's death in some other way and saved Anastasi from the firing squad. Compassion toward the innocent was also part of the code of *bushido*. He decided to try again to dissuade his father.

"You have gone to great lengths to preserve Marcus," he began. "What about Anastasi? She is totally innocent. Her grasp of politics is nonexistent, and I doubt that she could conceive of treachery. She could not have been involved. Why not show mercy? After all, *you* arranged for her to marry me."

Takashi looked at his son with naked contempt. "Aside from the pertinent political considerations, the arrangement was designed to produce children."

"Children that you want," Theodore reminded him.

"Would you make Kurita into Taira?" Takashi asked. "A child could grow up to desire the destruction of those who killed his family. Such a child, born of the union between you and that woman, would be in a unique position to destroy our clan."

"He could be educated otherwise."

"You are naive." Takashi shook his head. "Perhaps you should have taken another name instead of the tongue-twisting Theodore at your *gempuku* ceremony. With the attitudes you profess, Kiyomori would suit you. He destroyed his Taira clan with the same weakness you are asking me to show.

"The next marriage I arrange will not be to a mother of vipers."

Stung by Takashi's suggestion that he lacked concern for his clan, Theodore decided to hit back. "Your sudden fatherly conscientiousness is surprising. Had you shown such feeling at the time of my coming-of-age ceremony, I might have bowed to your wish and chosen a traditional name. You had no use for me; I had no use for your wishes."

"Pity the man cursed with an unfilial son," Takashi intoned. "Your mother . . ."

"My mother has nothing to do with what is between us," Theodore shouted. "Leave her out of it!"

"Your mother has more to do with it than you know,"

Takashi said in a hard-edged voice. "If you ever speak of her with raised voice again . . ."

"What? You'll have me executed?"

Takashi's eyes narrowed as color flared up his neck and onto his cheeks. "Get out!"

Theodore smiled inwardly, pleased to have gotten a rise out of his father. He executed a sharp, formal bow.

"I accept my dismissal," he said in a silky voice. "Long live the Coordinator."

Turning on his heel, Theodore strode from the room. He was halfway back to the barracks when he heard a volley of gunshots. The synchronism of the reports was that of a firing squad, reminding him suddenly that his trip to Palace Hall was a failure. Anastasi was still to be executed. His shoulders slumped. He walked on slowly.

14

Draconis Military Starport, Reykjavik, Rasalhague
Rasalhague Military District, Draconis Combine
23 September 3019

The sun had set over an hour ago, but the room was still comfortable. Theodore was even warm enough, especially where Tomoe's flesh met his own, that he did not yet wish to draw up the quilted covers. That time would come soon enough. For now, he was pleased to fold his free arm under his head and let his eyes roam her length. He smiled in pleasure that it was she who still shared his bed.

His thoughts turned to the previous days' events, making him wonder if perhaps his father should have died in the crash. If he, Theodore, were in charge now, only the guilty would face the firing squads. He knew that the group was responsible for the actions of its members, but failed to see how a child could be held responsible for the actions of its elders.

When he had returned from the meeting with Takashi, he had railed against the executions, calling Takashi's reprisals brutal and excessive. Tomoe had listened patiently, letting him talk himself out. Once he had exhausted his outrage, she led him to bed, soothing and calming him. Her talents as a listener and a bedmate were remarkable. He did not want to lose her.

"To-*chan,* I want to marry you."

She went very still as he spoke, and it was several heartbeats before she replied. "Do not tease me."

"I'm not teasing," he insisted. "I'm serious. My wedding has been cancelled, and now my father talks of arranging another. The realm still needs heirs. Why shouldn't *we* make them? We are in love."

Tomoe squirmed out of his embrace and sat up. "You are still angry at your father. You just want to spite him by marrying your warrior doxy. Tomorrow you will see more clearly."

"Then marry me tonight," Theodore said, before she could marshal further arguments.

"It is not proper."

"We are in love. What could be more proper?"

Tomoe's only response was silence. Feeling that he had found a chink in the armor of her resistance, he went on. "It's not just to spite him. If it were, I'd want to throw the marriage in his face, wouldn't I? We can keep it a secret; he won't know."

"Ever?" she questioned incredulously.

"Well . . ." he stalled, caught out in an obviously ridiculous scheme. "Indrahar will help us keep the secret for awhile. He'll keep my father from becoming a matchmaker again. We could let Takashi know when our children are old enough. By then, it will be too late for him to do anything about it. The dynasty will have its heirs, legitimate ones. He'll probably say that the secrecy was his own plan all along. It makes for a better appearance that way."

Tomoe said nothing, but reached out to lay a hand on his leg.

"Say yes, To-*chan.*"

She ran her hand along his side while Theodore tried to reinforce his arguments. Finally, seeing that she was not paying attention, he too lapsed into silence. With her mind on other things, he knew that his arguments, however rational or forceful, would have no effect. He watched as she caressed the scar on his left hip, the one from the night that Indrahar had inducted him into the Sons of the Dragon. "You wouldn't have that scar had you not fought again so soon afterward," she said in a soft voice, distant with old memories.

"I never told you how I got that," he said, suddenly wary.

"But I know."

"How? How could you know?"

"I gave it to you," Tomoe said.

Theodore sat upright. He grabbed her shoulders and pulled her up to face him. She was unresisting in his grip.

"On the night Indrahar tested you," she continued. "I was there. I was the one who cut you."

"What?" He could not believe what he was hearing. How could she have been there?

"I am a *jukurensha* of the O5P. Trained in *ninjutsu* as well as battle technology."

Theodore blinked in surprise. *A Pillarine? An adept?* He would never have considered the possibility.

"That night was my own test. I was to intercept you and retrieve some item from you. I took your pouch, but cut you in the attempt. Your own mastery of the Yagyu forms was too great for me to strike cleanly. I thought that I had failed but the *Jokan* Florimel said that I had passed. I did not understand, but I bowed to her wisdom. She gave me a new assignment; I was to get close to you, to protect you.

"I have failed in this assignment worse than in the last, because I became so close that I fell in love with you. I no longer have the detachment to maintain clarity of mind and fulfill my assignment."

Theodore was stunned. He had known Tomoe for four years at the Wisdom school. He had battled with and against her in the mock combats. She had been cold and distant, but he had seen nothing of the training of a Pillarine monk. She was a warrior, even if the gossips said otherwise.

Then he remembered her sudden thaw on graduation day and where it had led.

"Besides," she continued, oblivious to his thoughts, "I have no lineage. What is in my military record is a lie. I am not the daughter of a lesser house on the edge of the Pesht District. My father was a trade agent on the planet Volders in the Rasalhague District. He worked for Isesaki Shipping. When I was three, my parents were killed in a Steiner raid. The Pillarines took me in and raised me. They had me trained as a MechWarrior, among other things. They falsified my history to place me in the DCMS. When I showed promise, they arranged for me to advance, ultimately to the Wisdom of the Dragon school. I am insufficiently exalted to be the wife of the future Coordinator."

Theodore released his grip on her arms. She slumped a little but otherwise seemed not to notice. She was a wonder. He thought he had known all about her, yet he was not angry at her revelation, only surprised. He hated intriguers and deceivers, but could not find it in himself to hate Tomoe. Her essence was pure and honest, fiercely loyal. Gently, he caressed her hair.

"I am not a slave to appearances like my father. I don't care if your parents were leatherworkers or gamblers. The O5P may have gotten you into Wisdom, but you were good enough to make your way through. We both know that old Leather Face Zangi would never accept a bribe to alter a student's scores.

"You are strong and capable, beautiful and loving," he said. "I want you as my wife."

Tomoe turned her dark eyes on his. He could feel her searching him, testing the strength of his emotions. Seeming finally satisfied with what she found, she bowed her head. Though she tried to mask her smile with the fall of her hair, Theodore caught it.

"I would be honored to be your wife, Theodore-*sama*," she said demurely.

He tossed her over onto her back, revealing her radiant smile, and saw his own wide grin reflected in her eyes. They made love to seal their pact, not once but twice, before stealing out of the barracks to rouse a sleepy Buddhist monk from his cell and cajole him into legalizing their vows.

=== 15 ===

Constance Kurita tugged at her formal *obi,* straightening it until the proper smooth line of her kimono was achieved. She looked over her shoulder into one of the full-length mirrors scattered around the hall to see if the large and elaborate knot had been disturbed by her fussing. In so doing, she saw that an ornament had become caught on one of the pearl strands looping her formally coiffured wig. Reaching back to untangle it, she pulled her *obi* out of line again. Sighing, Constance straightened it once more.

Surely Great-Aunt Florimel never has so much trouble with traditional dress, Constance thought. *She is always in control of herself and her environment. May the blessed Buddhas someday grant me such aplomb. I do not want to disappoint her.*

Two months had passed since Florimel had stepped down as Keeper of the House Honor, naming Constance in her stead. Two long and hectic months in which Constance had learned how many duties Florimel had handled as Keeper. Even her six years as Florimel's aide had not fully prepared Constance for the demands and pressure. Thank the Buddhas that Florimel was still there when Constance needed counseling. The grand old lady was a rock, a shield. Sometimes Constance suspected that she was a sword as well, secretly helping from behind the scenes.

In the dark of earliest morning, Constance fretted at that help, worried about her own ability. Yet Florimel had turned over the office to her, pronouncing Constance a fit and able successor. Despite Constance's great faith in Florimel's judgment and despite her great-aunt's encouragement, she felt inadequate for the job.

Even her recent successes in negotiations with the Coordinator had not raised her confidence. The Coordinator had granted the charter for the new academies and approved the ivory trade plan, while she had made no concessions. Both items meant substantial gains in power and prestige for the Order of the Five Pillars, especially on certain key prefecture capital worlds and trade-route planets. It seemed too easy a victory. She suspected that Takashi was humoring her, allowing the little girl her harmless toys.

Her success had, at least, quieted *Shoducho* Oda for the moment, making it harder for him to keep up the pressure to remove her as an ineffectual leader. Over the years, he had grown less guarded in Constance's presence. She knew now that he was an ambitious man, one who felt uncomfortable in the shadow of a woman. He wanted full and complete control of the O5P, and did nothing to conceal that ambition from her. Oda did not seem to consider her a factor in the Order's future at all.

She wondered if Takashi knew of Oda's opinion, if he was making her look good to divide the Order's leadership, setting one against another as he did the Warlords who were the de facto rulers of the Combine's five main districts. The day would no doubt come when he would ask for something. On that day, he would remind Constance that he had helped to consolidate her position, of the debt she owed him.

Had that day come?

The invitation to take tea with the Coordinator had arrived this morning, polite but peremptory. Like those she had received from her masters in the order, the message specified no time. Unlike those summons, she knew there was some small time allowed to prepare herself. Her maids were quick and thorough, their expert attentions readying her in an hour, in spite of elaborate formal robes and hair style.

Now Constance stood and waited, unwilling to sit or kneel lest she wrinkle her kimono. She wandered to the window and rested her hands on the weather-stained teak railing as she stared out at the snow clouds gathering in the northern mountains. *The winter comes early this year,* she thought. Lowering her gaze, she looked over the palace walls and into the confined court two levels below. By the shadows of the rocks among the raked gravel, she estimated that she had been waiting for two hours. Takashi was demonstrating his estimation of her importance.

Finally, a servant arrived to lead her to a small, wood-paneled room where the Coordinator waited. The rich aroma of the tea herbs almost masked the sweet scent of the blossoms in the room's traditional alcove, a properly subtle enhancement to the serenity of the chamber. Takashi's reception was cordial, but he reserved his words for the conventional dialogue of the tea ceremony. Constance replied in turn, trying to slip into the almost trancelike state of peace fostered by the soothing ritual. But she was too nervous for more than a superficial show of tranquility.

After Constance pronounced the tea well-made and Takashi humbly thanked her, there was silence. Knowing Takashi's eyes were on her, Constance kept her own lowered. At last, Takashi's resonant voice broke the stillness.

"Something disturbs you, Constance. Your mind was not on the ceremony. What is it?"

"Nothing, *Tono,*" she lied, hoping that he would believe her.

Takashi breathed a gentle sigh. "You may be honest. We are cousins as well as leaders of our clan. I had thought you would be more open with me."

Constance's mind raced. He knew she was upset. What could she tell him? She could not bare her concerns about the Order. She needed a safe subject, something that he would believe concerned her, yet not something that touched on her office.

"The . . ." she started to say.

"Theodore," he finished for her. "You and he were quite close when young, were you not?"

"Yes," she answered in sudden relief. His son and heir was clearly on his mind; otherwise he would not have picked up the name from her hesitation. Discussion of his son would certainly steer him away from the O5P. *Shimatta! What if he knows how we are helping Theodore,* she thought with rising fear. *This is not a safe topic, after all.*

"I have seen little of him since Rasalhague," she continued.

"Yes," Takashi said thoughtfully, "He has been moving about quite a bit since the Wedding Plot."

From Takashi's inflection on the word "wedding," she knew she had started in the wrong direction. Constance decided to shift the focus of the conversation. "Theodore now serves on the staff of Warlord Cherenkoff, does he not?"

"That is his assignment, but he is here on Luthien."

That was not news to Constance, but she felt it best not to reveal her knowledge. "How wonderful! You have kept him away for so long."

"I have not summoned him here," Takashi said ominously.

So much for that being an innocuous angle, Constance thought. There seemed to be no safe area of discussion concerning Theodore.

"Has there been another problem with the Warlord?" she ventured.

"Probably, but that is not the issue."

"Perhaps it is just time for a new assignment," Constance suggested.

Takashi said nothing, and Constance let her mind race over the last several years.

Theodore's marriage to Tomoe had surprised her and Florimel when a fearful but uncontrite Tomoe had reported it to them before their departure from Rasalhague after the abortive conspiracy. Florimel had been less enraged than Constance expected, and had finally decided to support Theodore's plan to keep the marriage a secret. Maintaining secrecy was easy enough; steering Takashi's plans away from other arranged marriages was somewhat harder. But the O5P had managed. She knew that the ISF also had a hand in scuttling more than one arrangement. What lever could Theodore have with Director Indrahar that the spymaster would support the son rather than the father, his childhood friend?

Constance had not seen much of Theodore these last few years, but she knew his service record quite well. After the Wedding Plot was unraveled, his assignment to the Rasalhague Regulars had been canceled, and he had been shipped out to the Benjamin District. In the year that followed, he had been shuttled through three regiments of the Benjamin Regulars, including the Third, Warlord Yoriyoshi's own command. He had ended the year with a stint in the Second Sword of Light Regiment, one of the Combine's elite military units. Through all those travels, Tomoe and the rest of his command lance had accompanied him.

She remembered a note from him received at the end of 3020. In it, Theodore reported that his father had raged at Theodore's latest refusal to consent to another marriage. The heir's attitude had insulted the woman's father, who had withdrawn from the arrangement. In reaction, Takashi had ordered Theodore's lance out of the Sword of Light. Theodore had been philosophical. While pleased at the chance to work with that elite unit, his assignments had all been similar since Rasalhague. None were near the front, where he might earn glory.

His next assignment was with the Arkab Legion, apparently a punishment that would make him long for the Japanese customs that permeated most of the Combine. The Arkab Legionnaires were primarily soldiers native to the strongholds of Islamic culture in the Combine. They lived by folkways alien to the Kurita norm. Yet Theodore's letters had revealed him to be more intrigued than repelled by the differences of those Islamic warriors. His only complaint was their attitude toward Tomoe.

The whirlwind rotation had continued. Theodore had served with seven regiments of the Dieron Regulars, none for more than four months. His letters still mourned the lack of opportunities to prove himself as a warrior, and Takashi had finally responded to his continual requests for a frontline post by transferring his son to the staff of Warlord Yoriyoshi. Much as Theodore hoped to see action on the Davion border, it was relatively quiet. And when things did heat up, Theodore's assignments always seemed to lead him elsewhere.

The easy duty came at a fortunate time. The Order, by virtue of a request from the non-existent Lord Sakade, was able to arrange for Tomoe's absence without arousing suspicion. She passed her time in the safety and security of Benjamin, eventually presenting Theodore with a son.

After Theodore had been on Yoriyoshi's staff for nine months, Takashi advanced another likely candidate for marriage to Theodore. Constance knew far better than the Coordinator how the girl in question became involved in compromising circumstances that forced Takashi to repudiate the deal. Perhaps in frustration, Takashi transferred Theodore yet again. This time he sent his heir to serve on the staff of the fat and obnoxious Warlord Vasily Cherenkoff, General of the Armies. With the transfer, Theodore had received a promotion to *Chu-sa.* "For appearances," Theodore had claimed in a letter. "He really has done this to punish me. The Warlord is overbearing and utterly stupid. The only initiative he shows is in claiming credit for any good ideas his staff hands him." Theodore and the Warlord argued constantly and Cherenkoff reported nothing good to Takashi.

Still, Theodore had now served in the staff position longer than anywhere else since the Wisdom of the Dragon school. *Maybe he is growing up,* Constance thought. *Perhaps the son Tomoe gave him has made him a man.*

Constance looked up at Takashi. His face was sour, his eyes downcast. Perhaps he, too, was reflecting on his son's career, for he seemed not to have noticed her silence. She wondered what he thought of her suggestion about a new assignment for Theodore.

"Theodore was always restless as a youth. A change of scenery might make him more amenable to your wishes."

"It has not so far," Takashi began. He clearly had more to say, but stopped suddenly, head cocked in listening. In a moment, Constance, too, heard the approaching footsteps.

16

Unity Palace, Imperial City, Luthien
Pesht Military District, Draconis Combine
22 December 3024

The *shoji* door shrilled as it was forced violently through its tracks.

Theodore Kurita stepped into the room, the white of his dress uniform jacket strangely bright in the shadowy room. As he slid the door shut behind him, Constance noted the changes almost unconsciously. His shoulders had broadened with the strong muscles of a grown man. He was still lean, a *karateka* rather than a *sumotori,* and as handsome as ever. She swiftly suppressed a flash of envy for Tomoe.

Theodore's blue eyes were icy as he advanced to where he towered over the Coordinator. "I have heard that you have done the unthinkable."

Takashi simply stared through his son's belt buckle and calmly moved his tea cup to one side.

"I cannot believe it," Theodore exclaimed. "Tell me that it is only a rumor."

Takashi settled back on his heels, a look of long-suffering forbearance on his face. "Be seated, my son, and we will talk."

Constance started to stand, but Takashi shook his head, "Please stay, Constance. Your presence may keep this more civilized."

Theodore spared Constance a glance as she resettled herself. She read no distress at her presence, but she detected a definite look of apology in his expression. He settled to his knees, back stiff.

"Do you think her presence will keep me from saying what is on my mind?"

"Hardly," Takashi answered. "But my hope of keeping this discussion calm is not unreasonable."

Theodore bristled at Takashi's choice of words, and Constance knew why he reacted with such anger. Takashi had long complained that his son's stubbornness was unreasonable; Theodore's strong will had been a point of argument many times. She saw from Theodore's reaction that he, too, had heard the rumor that his father believed him ambitious, too eager for the throne.

Theodore turned to her. "Do you know what he has done? He has named your father as head of the Otomo. Marcus Kurita, the man who wants his throne, as his bodyguard."

Constance had heard that Takashi might make the appointment, but this was the first confirmation. She did not doubt that the Coordinator's intent was to increase the scrutiny on his cousin. She knew that her father coveted the Coordinator's office. Filial loyalty prevented her from revealing that, just as clan loyalty kept her from aiding him in any way.

"You have come here to speak to me, boy. Do so," Takashi said harshly. "Do not distress Constance with your ravings."

"It's true, then."

"I have named Marcus Kurita as head of the Otomo."

Theodore slammed his black officer's cap onto the *tatami*. "How can you be such a fool?"

Constance lowered her head, unwilling to watch as Theodore insulted his father. She could do nothing to divert him. If she acted now, she would not be in a position to help him later. Openly coming to his defense would be too revealing an act. She hoped he would not enrage Takashi too much.

"Marcus was the best choice for the post at this time," Takashi stated calmly.

"What about me?"

"What about you? You warn me of ambitious men, then ask for an important post. You still have much to learn."

"You were head of the Otomo at twenty-seven. I'm twenty-eight."

"You are not settled. When I headed the Otomo, I was married. I had an heir."

"So we come to that again. Haven't you had enough failures? Let me alone. I'll give you an heir when I'm good and ready."

"Your attitude validates my decision," Takashi announced, the harshness returning to his voice. "You are still too callow, too flighty, too unconcerned with the needs of the state. You have had it too easy."

"It's not been easy with you as a father."

Takashi reached under his tea tray and pulled out a compdisk. "Look over this file. The girl is an excellent match. Her connections will benefit the realm."

Theodore took the disk, his knuckles white as he held it before his face. He stared unseeing at the iridescent object. Suddenly he threw the disk to the side, where it shattered against the fine oiled wood of a support beam, scarring the finish. Theodore glared at his father.

"Reconsider your decision," Takashi said. His face was expressionless, but his voice betrayed the leashed violence of his emotions.

"No."

Constance wished she were elsewhere, anywhere. She could feel the two powerful wills in contest before her. Neither would retreat. Neither would lower his guard enough to discuss the real issues.

"Very well." Takashi reached under his tray again and brought out a sealed envelope. Constance recognized the form and colors of a document from the Bureau of Substitution, the military office that handled transfers. Takashi had been prepared for his son's response.

"*Tai-sa* Kurita, you have a new assignment. You are to report to the Eleventh Legion of Vega on Marfik. They are misfits and malcontents; you should feel at home."

Theodore said nothing as he reached out to take the envelope, but Takashi did not release it at once. "When you understand your place, you may return," he said, opening his fingers.

Theodore stuffed the envelope into his tunic, eyes locked with Takashi's. Constance well remembered a similar moment six years ago on Kagoshima, but this time there was no pride on Theodore's face. Instead of a smile of pleasure, clenched muscles twitched in his jaw and his eyes were slitted with rage.

Theodore heaved himself to his feet and stomped toward

the door. He shoved the door open with such violence that it jumped from its track and clattered to the floor, tearing the delicate rice paper. Theodore walked on.

Constance picked up the cap Theodore had left lying on the mats, the action recalling her to Takashi's attention.

"I apologize for my son's behavior, *Jokan* Constance," he said gravely. "It seems our talk is no longer necessary. I am sorry to have taken your time."

"Your apologies are unnecessary, *Tono*," she said. *Unnecessary to me,* she added to herself, *but long overdue to Theodore.*

"Excuse my curiosity, *Tono,* but you called your son *Tai-sa* as you handed him the orders. How could you promote him at the same time that you banished him to the Legion of Vega?"

"It would not be fitting to have a *Chu-sa* in command of a regiment, let alone the whole Legion."

17

Legion of Vega HQ, Massingham, Marfik
Dieron Military District, Draconis Combine
1 April 3025

Theodore tossed the rag down and turned away. The "Revenant" had come through the three months of transit with minimal freeze-up. He looked for Kowalski, intending to commend him on his diligent maintenance, but the Senior Tech was nowhere in sight.

He scanned the hangar. It was strangely quiet, the only noise coming from the bays housing the 'Mechs of his command lance. He rubbed sweat from his brow with his forearm and frowned.

Theodore had seen the sorry state of the Legion's 'Mechs when they brought the lance's machines in last night. He had told Sandersen to post an order suspending the regular work schedule, accompanied by a request for voluntary maintenance work. When the Legionnaires arrived, he planned that they would find him already present, working on his own *Orion*. Theodore had hoped it would show the men he was on their side, and not some tight-assed, spit-and-polish martinet. He also believed it would be a good way to get to know the men of his new command.

In a way, he had been right, but the lesson he was getting about his men was a sad one. Rows of Legion BattleMechs stood silent and unattended in their bays, a frozen carnival of shapes and colors. There was no pride here, he decided. No discipline, either.

He walked to the next bay, where Tomoe's black *Panther* stood. She was fussing over an actuator linkage in the foot assembly. Though the pose did not show her to her best advantage, she was as beautiful as ever. And as alluring. When he reached out to caress her buttocks, she did not start in surprise, but simply slapped his hand away distractedly.

"Have you seen Kowalski?" he asked her south end.

"Not recently," came the muffled response from within the armored foot assembly. "Thought I saw him heading over to the supply shed to scrounge up a part."

Theodore wondered how lucky the Tech would be. The documents Theodore had studied on the trip to Marfik had indicated the supply situation for the Legion was bleak. He remembered one particular complaint that claimed that the Procurement Department had forgotten the Legion's existence. If the documents were correct, Kowalski would need all his fabled scrounging skill to get whatever he needed.

Taking a firm grip on Tomoe's hips, he tugged her from the dark confines of the *Panther*'s foot. "We've put in enough time for today, especially with all the support we're getting. Let's knock off."

She took in the quiet hangar, a slight furrow appearing between her brows. She shrugged off her reaction without sharing it and said, "I'm getting hungry. How about you?"

"Now that you mention it, yes. Let's pull out the other two and head for the mess. Maybe we'll run into Kowalski on our way. Let's not take too long, though. I promised Hohiro we would be out to see him tonight."

Hohiro. Theodore reflected fondly on the last night's parting. The boy was too young to understand the necessity of a nighttime landing at the Massingham starport and a hurried trip to a prepared safe house, but he had been a brave soldier when Theodore said goodbye. Already the boy was used to partings from his devoted, but far too often absent, parents. At least, Tomoe had been able to spend almost a year with him after his birth. The deceptions were complicated, but with the aid of the O5P and a few favors from Subhash Indrahar, they were managing to keep the boy's existence a secret.

Theodore squeezed his wife's hand before walking down to the next bay. His call was greeted by the plastic smile of Ben Tourneville. Theodore smiled back as though he didn't know that the man was an enemy, a spy for the Coordinator.

Tourneville continued to be the biggest threat to their secrets, but Theodore saw no good way to replace him without arousing suspicion. The man's proximity to their daily lives was a constant danger, but the ever-loyal Sandersen, privy to the secret, helped immensely in distracting Takashi's spy.

Hirushi Sandersen had heard the call as well and appeared from behind the half wall separating the bays. The tall man grinned pleasantly as he said, "'Bout time you decided to break for food, Theodore-*sama*. Those sandwiches Kowalski hauled in for lunch weren't enough to fill the belly of one of the local microlizards."

"You always say you never get enough food," Tourneville griped. "Even when you eat twice what I do."

Theodore just shook his head and continued toward the hangar door, where the little group came to an abrupt halt when he nearly stumbled over a huddled, sobbing shape.

"Kowalski?"

"Sir," the Tech mumbled as he struggled to his feet, pain obvious in the way he moved. Kowalski was bruised, his uniform torn and smudged. Dried blood crusted his hairline, making his normally immaculate gray hair stick up haphazardly on one side.

"What happened?"

"They said I didn't have the authority to requisition parts. When I told them I was your personal Tech, they laughed. They said my word wasn't enough. They offered me a chance to establish my authority. I didn't do very well."

"Who were they, Kowalski-*kun*?"

Kowalski turned away from Theodore's gaze, his shoulders slumping. "I can't say, sir."

Theodore's eyes narrowed. "I'll find out who was responsible."

"No," the Tech protested, twisted back to face Theodore. "Sir, please don't. That's not the way it works here."

Theodore could not ignore the naked plea in the Tech's eyes. "All right, Kowalski-*kun*. I'll do nothing for now, if you'll report to the infirmary. You are off-duty till further notice."

Kowalski bowed awkwardly and limped away.

"He's right, you know."

The four Kuritans spun to face the new speaker. The tall, strongly-built man leaned against the wall of the shed. A thatch of red hair bushed out from under his black uniform cap to shade a freckled face wearing a relaxed grin. The man wore a MechWarrior's jumpsuit with a *Tai-i*'s blue katakana "5" on his left collar. His cap insignia identified him as belonging to First Company, Second Battalion, of the Second Legion of Vega.

"Ninyu!" Theodore exclaimed, recognizing the face he had first seen in a dark alley on Kagoshima. "I haven't seen you since that commando scare on Al Na'ir."

"It's been too long, my friend. Still keeping up your kendo?"

"Not as much as I would like. It's hard to find an opponent of Subhash-*sama*'s caliber," Theodore said as he stepped up to shake his friend's hand. "What are you doing here?"

"This is my station," Ninyu replied, tapping the insignia on his cap. "Loyal MechWarrior among the scum of the Combine."

Theodore nodded. He knew Ninyu was a fellow member of Indrahar's Sons of the Dragons, and unlike himself, well-versed in subterfuge and the dark side of the military. If Ninyu was here, there would be a reason, quite possibly one not to be pursued before witnesses. To cover what was becoming an awkward pause, he said, "Let me introduce you to my lance."

Theodore indicated each of his companions with a gesture and each made a formal bow of greeting to Ninyu. "*Tai-i* Tomoe Sakade, my exec. *Chu-i* Hirushi Sandersen, operations specialist. *Chu-i* Benjamin Tourneville, comm specialist."

"*Chu-i* Tourneville and I are old acquaintances," Ninyu said.

"*So ka,*" Theodore acknowledged, understanding by Ninyu's remark that he knew of Tourneville's other occupation. "This is Ninyu Kerai, an old friend." *Sotto voce,* he added, "Be careful around him. He's ISF."

Ninyu grimaced in mock annoyance, from which Theodore gathered that the man expected the others to know that already. "You'll find that quite a few people here are ISF," he said. "Watching the malcontents, and each other."

"We were headed for the mess hall," Sandersen reminded them, patting his belly.

"A man with his mind on important business," Ninyu laughed. "Come on. I'll show you the way. I wouldn't want you strangers to get lost trying to get to the most wretched hive of scum and culinary disasters in the Combine."

Theodore was glad to have Ninyu for a guide. In the daylight, the scramble of buildings and huts did not seem to correspond to the orbital photographs he had studied. The walk to the messhall was mercifully short; Sandersen's continual grumblings about the lack of food were beginning to get old.

The hall was crowded, the noise and smoke combining to give it the air of a seedy cantina on some backwater planet. Most of the men and women were already seated, many halfway through their meals. Theodore wondered briefly what they had been doing all day.

The trip through the chow line was frustrating. The servers and the few others still in the line met Theodore's attempts to be comradely with ill-concealed hostility, answering his questions with the absolute minimum response and perfunctory politeness. Comments were ignored in the surly atmosphere.

"What's going on?" Theodore asked Ninyu quietly as they left the chow line.

"You're new, an unknown quantity," he replied. "They only know what they've heard and most of them think you're a wimp, a disgrace to the Dragon. It's true most of these hardcases don't give a fart for the Dragon, but neither do they like papa's boys. You've got yourself a kettle of hot water, hotshot. Let's see you make tea."

Ninyu drifted off in search of a place among the crowded tables.

Theodore spotted two open spaces and nudged Tomoe toward them. They put down their trays and sat down while their new table companions traded shifty glances.

"I don't feel very hungry anymore," a sallow-faced woman announced, standing up with her half full tray. The others at the table grunted agreement, and in a moment, Theodore and Tomoe sat alone.

Two tables down, a man stood and said something to his companions. Coarse laughter followed as he strode across the space between the tables.

"Here comes the welcoming committee," Tomoe whispered.

"Let me handle it."

The man approaching them was huge, over two meters tall and heavily muscled. Despite the fact that the fellow wore a shabby MechWarrior's jersey, Theodore found it barely credible that the man's massive body would fit inside the cramped cockpit of a BattleMech. His lower face was covered with dark, bristly stubble, except for a line running from chin to his left temple. The scar stood white against his swarthy skin and did nothing to improve his sinister look. That look was obviously cultivated, as indicated by the gold stud through the lobe of his left nostril and the blood-red scharacki feather dangling from his right ear.

"Olivares is my name," the man said in a voice that rumbled up from his broad gut and through his barrel-chest to erupt from his full-lipped mouth. He plunked down his tray on the table, pulled up a stool, and sat. "*Sho-sa* Esau Olivares. I'm ramrod here. You get along with me, you get along with them."

"I was under the impression that *I* had been given command of this regiment."

"Listen, pretty boy. This here's the frontline. Them Elsies could come dropping in any old time. When Steiner 'Mechs are falling on our heads, we ain't got no time for a wet-eared academy boy getting in our way. I been fighting Elsies for ten years. I know 'em. We get company, you just curl up at HQ with your books and your bimbo. I'll take care of business."

Theodore raised a quizzical eyebrow. The gesture was lost on the *Sho-sa,* who continued on.

"We hear you think you're real hot, been burning up the sim tanks with your tactics. But you ain't in the classroom now. This here's the real world. It ain't anything like you think. Your Kurita name ain't gonna make the Elsies bow down and kiss your behind. So if them Steiner MechJocks come to call, stay out of my way. You can sashay back to HQ, and stay safe and sound with the other pretty boys. You should have lotsa fun."

"An interesting comment from someone with a feather in his ear."

"You calling me a poof?" the burly man roared.

"Could be."

Olivares snarled as he stood, kicking his stool over backward. The man threw his shoulders back, a motion that emphasized his massive muscles, and raised his clenched fists.

Still seated, Theodore drew his gun and fired. The scharacki feather floated to the table, its gentle motion almost audible in the sudden shocked silence that pervaded the hall. Olivares stood, mouth open, in shock.

Calmly, Theodore holstered his gun. "On the other hand, maybe I was wrong. After all, you don't have a feather in your ear."

Olivares reached up a beefy hand to feel his ear. He looked astonished to find no blood on his fingers. He collected his stool and sat.

"Some more soy sauce, *Sho-sa*?" Theodore said casually, offering the bottle.

As Olivares took the bottle, the clatter of conversation, cups, and plates, resumed around the hall. Theodore felt Tomoe relax. He snagged a morsel with his chopsticks and popped it into his mouth. Ninyu was right, the cuisine was wretched. *That too,* Theodore vowed, *would change.*

18

Unity Palace, Imperial City, Luthien
Pesht Military District, Draconis Combine
1 December 3026

The two armored men circled cautiously, weapons held before them. Each searched for an opening in his opponent's guard. The taller suddenly shifted to high speed and advanced, his point seeking the other's throat. His target swayed slightly to the left, leaving his point to strike only empty air. A sharp, rattling crack filled the air as his opponent's *shinai* struck home on the taller man's *do.*

"Well-struck," said Takashi Kurita, stepping back to salute his opponent with his own slit-bamboo sword. Pulling off a glove by trapping it under his arm, he reached up and flipped his *men,* combined fencing mask and throat protection, from his head. "It is good to test your *shinai* against mine once again, old friend."

"Most pleasant," Subhash Indrahar agreed, removing his own mask. "With more practice, you may improve your *men* thrust."

"Improve?" Takashi questioned suspiciously. "You are not able to deflect it when I focus."

Subhash inclined his head, smiling the while. "But you do not always focus."

Subhash could see Takashi considering the second meaning in his words. Occasionally, as now, Subhash found it useful to speak in phrases whose second meaning was a gentle rebuke to the Coordinator, inciting him to improve in the performance of his duty. It was almost a game between them.

"And today's focus is the strategy session, is it not?"

"It is as you say, *Tono*. Yet you are distracted. Theodore again?"

"My constant trial," Takashi conceded. "He has spent more than a year with the scum of the Vegan Legion. One might think he prefers those ruffians to the courtiers on Luthien."

"You have given him little chance to know the court here on Luthien."

"It is not safe. There are too many intrigues, too many unscrupulous villains who would dupe him into their treasonous plots as he was duped in Rasalhague."

"He is not a boy anymore, my friend," Subhash ventured. "He needs to learn how to survive here at court."

"He needs to rid himself of his battlefield fantasies first," Takashi snapped with sudden heat. "The only communications I receive from him are wild plans for the conquest of the Lyran Commonwealth and curt refusals to consider any woman I suggest as a suitable wife. The reports from Marfix show him to be content with pretending he is in command of soldiers, happy to play with his concubine. After all these years, he still does not understand the demands of the realm."

"Those demands are great indeed, *Tono*," Subhash said in a placatory manner.

There was little else he could do. Takashi still refused to accept that Theodore would never be the man the Coordinator wanted him to be. Certainly the heir could be guided, but not with Takashi's strong-arm tactics. The Coordinator's pigheadedness was itself a threat to the continuity of the House Kurita's rule, and therefore to the Draconis Combine. But Subhash knew that open opposition to Takashi would only weaken his own position and make it harder for him to protect the Combine.

The Draconis Combine stood in increasing peril. It needed the undivided attention of its Coordinator, and Subhash intended that nothing would prevent that.

"Have you read my reports, *Tono*?" he asked, doffing his armor.

"Yes. This morning," Takashi replied, removing his own *do*. "You are sure this Davion adventure is over?"

"It would seem so."

For most of the past three months, there have been massive troop movements along the Davion border. Ten Battle-Mech regiments and a hundred conventional units had been involved in something called Operation Galahad. It had not turned out to be the beginnings of a war, as Subhash had feared. Only a few minor raiding forces had crossed into Combine space. House Davion had gone to great expense "to demonstrate the Federated Suns' preparedness to repel hostile invaders." He knew that Prince Hanse Davion, whom many called "the Fox," must have something more in mind, but his ISF agents had so far come up empty.

Takashi finished arranging his armor on its stand and headed for the showers. Subhash followed, willing to let Takashi determine the conversation's next step. They had washed away the sweat from their exercise and begun dressing before Takashi spoke again.

"Your assessment of our allies is uninspiring."

"I do not report strength where there is none. If Prince Davion starts a war, we should not expect much of our Kapteyn allies."

They both knew that the lack of reliable allies was a serious weakness. A man of vision could no longer ignore the ever-stronger alliance between the Federated Suns and the Lyran Commonwealth, the Combine's bitterest enemies. Any sane ruler would fear such a combination.

"We must be strong if the Fox decides we are his prey," Takashi stated.

"Our strength increases. The Ryuken experiment has proven its worth. I recommended expansion."

"That seems reasonable," Takashi conceded. Subhash knew that the Coordinator would not make a final decision until after he consulted the Warlords, but Takashi seemed inclined to take the step.

"They and the Genyosha will become very important if Wolf's Dragoons cannot be retained."

"Yes, the Dragoons. Your report was not specific. What is the real situation there?"

"Our plans are in motion, *Tono*. Their debt increases daily, and we prepare in case they do not fall to the 'company-store' ploy. Where the Dragoons fail to provide us with material for blackmail, I have arranged to manufacture it. We have been fortunate in finding a most convincing Natasha Kerensky."

Takashi nodded solemnly as he slipped into the simple soldier's jumpsuit he affected on military occasions.

"I do not want the Dragoons to leave the Combine," he stated firmly.

"I will convey your wishes to our agents, *Tono*."

"In the meantime, we must attend to the more pressing business of the Combine's strategy for the coming year."

"Indeed, *Tono*," Subhash agreed, pleased that, for the moment, Takashi had forgotten his problems with his son. Now the Coordinator would apply his considerable wiles to important problems. "The Warlords await you."

"Then let us get to work."

Subhash was even more pleased at the resolution in Takashi's voice. His own work had been successful. As they started for the main building of the palace, he said, "Allow me to precede you, *Tono*. It would be better if the Coordinator were not seen to favor the ISF over the Warlords by arriving in the company of the Director."

"As usual, my friend, you are right."

Indrahar bowed and proceeded across the court, satisfied that Takashi was well-prepared to meet with his Council.

19

The red banner snapped in the stiff breeze. Rattling pulleys caught Theodore's attention, drawing his eyes to the Legion's symbol boldly emblazoned on the flag. The scruffy, cigarette-smoking rat, seated in front of the red disk, returned his gaze with the serene indifference of the two-dimensional.

"Another fine day under Takashi's eyes," Theodore mused to the massive man at his side.

Olivares rubbed at his scar with a grimy finger before responding. "The rat ain't got no eyes, *Sama*."

"That seems to have been a problem all my life."

Olivares' face contorted into a grimace of confusion as he shook his head slowly. "You is fine in the field, *sama*, but sometimes you sure do talk strange."

Theodore chuckled. "Don't worry about it, Olivares-*kun*. Hadn't you best get down to the landing field? The DropShip with our new recruits is due within the hour."

"Recruits?" the big man rumbled as he walked off in the direction of the landing field. "That's a good joke."

Theodore listened to the *Sho-sa*'s laughter fade into the distance. Almost three years on Marfik, and he still didn't understand Olivares' sense of humor. But that seemed only fair; neither did the *Sho-sa* ever seem to grasp the ironies that Theodore perceived in existence.

Marfik was a fine world, an unlikely dumping ground for the refuse of the Combine military. It was a far pleasanter posting than Vega, where the Legion's other two regiments were stationed.

Theodore gazed past the city of Massingham at the distant forest of brella trees, a magnificent sight to start a morning. Thirty meters of massive, naked trunk rose from the leaf-mold of the forest floor before the branches began, arching out and interlacing in an intricate web. Those limbs were bare now, but when spring came, their deep blue leaves would cast the forest into deep shadow, making it a bewildering maze for those who did not know the paths. The forest was a wonder, one of the many on this pleasant world.

Refreshed, Theodore mounted the steps to the one-room hut ostentatiously labeled "Comanding Oficer." The misspelling did not bother him; the sign was a gift from his officers and he treasured the respect it signified. He entered the office to find Ninyu Kerai stretched out on the faded couch, feet propped up on the radio table. Ninyu appeared to be asleep, hat pulled low over his eyes, but Theodore knew better.

"Must you adopt their slovenly habits?"

"Protective coloration," Ninyu mumbled from beneath his cap. "Very important in my business."

Theodore crossed to his desk, threading his way past the pair of straight-backed chairs, and dropped into his rickety armchair. It groaned but held. "Shall we pretend that you are still in the military, and try to get some work done?"

Ninyu sat up, grabbing his cap before it could hit the floor. He rubbed his free hand back and forth over his bushy red hair and said, "You've been testy since Tomoe left on her furlough. Maybe we should take a trip to the Pleasure Quarter."

Theodore shot him a disapproving glare, to which Ninyu responded with a shrug. "You know that I'm worried about her. She's having more trouble this time."

"Brother Nitti is a fine doctor. Mother and child will be fine."

Theodore could not disagree. "Still, I miss her."

"That's obvious. But at least Hohiro is getting some time with his mother."

"Something I don't get to do while I have to look after my other children," Theodore said petulantly, waving a hand toward the window through which the barracks of the Legion could be seen. "If they were real soldiers, I wouldn't have to babysit them."

"They may not be Sword of Light, but they're not babies," Ninyu observed. "They were trash when you took over, but things are different now. And you're the reason, my friend. Whether you believe it or not."

Theodore gave him a skeptical look.

"It's true," Ninyu asserted. "You took the first big step when you cowed Olivares instead of letting him bully you. That made you alpha male. These mongrels are used to fearing the boss dog. You've always told me that fear was an unsatisfactory motivator, so you're not satisfied.

"Take a good look around. Their attitudes are changing. You lifted their morale by dubbing them *buso-senshi*. Armament warriors. Some of them didn't appreciate the pun at first, especially the non-Japanese. But they could hardly be expected to know that the character for 'armament' had a cognate that meant 'matchless.' You gave them heart. The real turning point came when you called the rat on the banner 'Takashi.' It struck a chord with them, crystallized your kinship with them as a fellow outcast.

"Didn't Tomoe and I help you spot the real trash infecting the Legion? The squealers with no morals or loyalty and the gutless wonders are gone now. With the false-front office I set up, even the reports of the ISF spies in the unit go across your desk, to be altered or passed on intact. Lets you keep the Coordinator's nose out of your business.

"Fundamental changes don't happen overnight. You're getting results. The 'Mechs may still be a patchwork and look like a pack of gypsy vagabonds, but the troops are working with them, improving what they can. They're starting to operate as units, too. It seems to be rubbing off on the conventional troops as well."

Theodore chuckled. "Yeah, in ten years they might be able to face Steiner. Thank Buddha we're not on the Davion border."

"Rome in a day, Osaka Tower overnight, and all that sort of thing. Patience, my friend."

"Thank you, font of wisdom," Theodore said drily. "Can you solve the supply problem as well?"

Ninyu shrugged. "I'm an acclaimed wise man, not a miracle worker."

Theodore sighed. "The Legionnaires are still a bunch of rowdy hellions, ready to brawl at a moment's notice. Their discipline is almost as sloppy as the way they dress."

"This ain't the court on Luthien," Ninyu reminded him needlessly. "Come the day, they'll fight—that's what's important."

"We'll see when the day comes." Theodore flipped the switch on his compdeck and slipped in a disk. He scrolled the screen for several minutes, studying the data as it flowed past his eyes. "That day may be near."

Ninyu stiffened with sudden attention. "Orders for a raid?"

Theodore shook his head. "No such luck. This unit isn't likely to be sent into action as long as I'm in charge. It's a matter of principle with a certain person.

"No, I'm talking about the reports the ISF has gotten concerning Davion officers advising Steiner units. The Lyran troops have shown noticeable improvement over the last years. After Davion started his saber-rattling with Operation Galahad, the Lyrans copied him with their own Operation Thor. The storm is coming to a head."

"Will they push it to all-out war?"

"It seems only a matter of time. Hanse Davion's wedding binds more than two political units. It weds a strong economy to a dangerous military. We're definitely looking at trouble."

"You think they'll take us on?"

"Who else is as dangerous to them? Surely not the muddled Free Worlds League, or the outgunned Capellan Confederation. The Periphery states are too small to be a real threat, and the lesser houses are unimportant. The Dragon is their rightful concern.

"We shall be pressed to the utmost fighting against both Houses. It will be a glorious war."

Theodore smiled, his thoughts on the possibilities that a war would bring. At last, he would have a chance to prove himself as a warrior, a commander. Takashi would no longer be able to deny him his place. Theodore would prove himself a worthy heir.

A sudden, dark thought intruded on his dreams of glory. War would bring danger to his own son and heir.

"Ninyu-*kun*, I want you to do something for me."

"Ask," Ninyu said warily.

"I want my family moved to a safer world. We are too exposed here on Marfik. Too close to the Lyrans."

"Tomoe can't leave until after she delivers," Ninyu reminded him.

"I know that. As soon as she can travel, I want them gone."

"It will be hard to cover."

"I have faith in your skills, my friend," Theodore said with a smile.

Ninyu returned to the couch and stretched out. "This will take a lot of planning," he said. "I might as well get started."

Theodore watched his friend replace the cap over his eyes and settle down. He shook his head. Had anyone else reponded to his orders in such a way, he would have been incensed. But he knew from past experience that no matter how relaxed Ninyu looked, his mind was always working. Satisfied that his friend would come up with a solution, Theodore turned his attention to the compdeck. He called up the latest unit-readiness reports and began to study them.

20

Legion of Vega HQ, Massingham, Marfik
Dieron Military District, Draconis Combine
11 December 3027

Olivares' bass voice interrupted Theodore's concentration. From the bellowings, he knew that the *Sho-sa* had herded the new arrivals to the building to meet their commander. Quite a far cry from the nonexistent reception committee gathered for his own arrival.

Before Olivares had them in order, Theodore walked out into the sunlight. Ninyu roused himself and slouched along in Theodore's wake.

Stopping by the flagpole, Theodore looked over the men and women slowly shuffling into ragged lines. A wide variety of uniforms and partial uniforms were present: MechWarriors and footsoldiers, tankers and AeroJocks, mechanics and cooks. They came from all branches of the Combine military. Many wore patches of units that had been involved in the disastrous Galtor campaign. One non-uniformed clump stayed stubbornly together. Theodore presumed that they were what was left of the mercenary Kelly's Killers, destroyed as an effective unit when Davion raided New Mendham. The unit's debt to the Combine was being paid off by service with the Legion.

Olivares looked over to Theodore, who nodded.

"Damp it, you slimelickers," Olivares bellowed. "*Tai-sa* Kurita has got a few words for ya. Dig the wax outa your ears and listen up!"

Theodore was impressed by the eloquence of Olivares' introduction. The *Sho-sa*'s long speeches were usually unprintable. Theodore cleared his throat, pitching his voice to carry over the field.

"Welcome to the Legion of Vega.

"I know what you've heard, because I've heard it, too. That this is the cesspit of the Draconis military. That your careers are over. That no one ever returns from the Legion.

"You can believe it if you want. You can make it true, by becoming the scum others believe you to be. I won't stop you. And I won't stop you because I can't. If you have no honor left, you will be what they say. Marfik will become your personal hell.

"It doesn't have to be that way. Ignore what you heard before coming here, and look to your honor. It is the strength that will sustain you and the armor to shield you. The Legion offers you a new start. I challenge you to prove that you are warriors, men and women of worth. Earn my respect, if you can. It won't be easy.

"It's up to you. Think about it.

"I'll be speaking to each of you individually. For now, head to the barracks. *Sho-sa* Olivares will show you where to stow your gear. Check the roster for your interview time.

"Dismissed."

A tall black man caught Theodore's eye. Something about him was familiar, but Theodore could not recall having seen him before. His service cap was no help; the unit badges had been torn from it.

"You," he called, pointing at the man. "Come over here."

As the soldier approached, Theodore observed the left side of his collar. The fabric was frayed in places and a slightly darker color outlined the shape of a different insignia from the *Chu-i*'s triple blue bars that glinted in the sunlight. The man had been demoted from the rank of *Tai-i.*

Theodore noted the curly black hair and the carefully tended mustache and goatee. He searched the lines of the man's face that was so naggingly familiar.

"What's your name?"

"Fuhito Tetsuhara, sir," the man replied in a deep, clear voice.

"I thought you looked vaguely familiar," Theodore said with a smile. "Minoru Tetsuhara was one of my tutors. You must be his grandson."

"His son, sir," Fuhito said, shifting uncomfortably. Whether his discomfort was from having to correct his superior or due to the mere mention of the old warhorse's name, Theodore couldn't tell.

"Strong *hara,*" Ninyu commented from behind him.

"Ease off, Kerai-*kun,*" Theodore said, giving his friend a glance that meant he was serious. Ninyu looked offended.

Theodore reached out a hand to Fuhito's shoulder. "Come inside. I just rescheduled your interview for now. Leave your bag. *Tai-i* Kerai will stow it." He ignored Ninyu's annoyance, knowing he could square it with him later.

"Tell me, Fuhito-*san,* how is your family?" Theodore asked as he led the *Chu-i* into the building.

"Father and Mother are well, *Tai-sa,*" Fuhito began haltingly. He was clearly not used to discussing his family with a superior officer. "Eldest brother *Chu-sa* Minobu has recovered from his accident and commands the Ryuken-*ni* on the Galedon border. My other brother, *Tai-i* Yoshi, has received the red-and-back banner. I am here."

Theodore heard the rising bitterness in Fuhito's voice. He waved a hand at the couch to indicate that Fuhito should be seated, and then perched himself on the edge of his desk.

"Please accept my condolences on the death of Yoshi. He must have died valiantly to have received the banner. It is a great honor for a minor officer's name to be inscribed on the Great Wall of the Fallen Samurai. Your family is honored."

"We are ever servants of House Kurita," Fuhito intoned mechanically.

"I remember once seeing your eldest brother, Minobu, when he visited the court at Luthien. I was ten years old and quite surprised to see a black samurai, especially one with a Japanese name. I didn't know then that one did not have to be Japanese to embrace the code of *bushido.* Nor did I know that being Japanese did not automatically make one a believer in the code. I've learned much since my youth, including how to judge each man individually and to be wary of what others say about him."

Fuhito said nothing.

"Minobu is doing well for himself. His Ryuken experiment is a success. The regiments have none of the problems we face with the Procurement Department, and he has the blessing of the Bureau of Administration as well. Even here on Marfik, we felt the sting of the orders to supply the

'Mech pilots he requested when he formed the Ryuken. I had to send *Chu-i* Sandersen from my own command lance. The Legion hasn't lost a man that way since the Genyosha was formed."

Fuhito remained silent. Theodore, wondering if he were getting through, picked up a folder from his desk. He thumbed it open and perused the contents. "I've got a slot open for a good recon lance commander, Fuhito-*san*," he said casually. "Do you know of any among the transferees?"

"I have heard that Hanson is good, *Tai-sa*."

"Hmmm. You commanded a recon company, didn't you?"

"*Hai*, on Galtor. The company no longer exists."

"Tell me about it," Theodore ordered. "You may speak freely."

Fuhito hesitated a moment and then began to pour out his story. Theodore sighed inwardly. Tetsuhara-*sensei*'s caution had not taken deep root in this son. Despite himself, Theodore was soon caught up in Fuhito's tale of the misplaced loyalties and political infighting that had contributed to the debacle on Galtor. Warlord Yoriyoshi's ego had been bruised by the continual insults of his rival, Warlord Samsonov. When Samsonov's strategy placed Yoriyoshi and his troops in an untenable situation, the exasperated Yoriyoshi had abandoned the planet. His departure had left Samsonov facing overwhelming Davion forces and forced him to leave as well. Yoriyoshi was relieved of command and demoted, blamed for the Combine's failure and branded a coward and incompetent. A false picture, according to Fuhito. He claimed that the Warlord had known that the campaign was already lost, and had simply saved his men to fight another day. Theodore's own study of the campaign tended to confirm that assessment.

Fuhito had defended his commander, loudly, to the inquiry board. When the decision went against Yoriyoshi, Fuhito was caught in the fallout.

"I spoke from my heart, and told the truth as I saw it," Fuhito concluded. "In doing so, I made some powerful enemies. I thought they would cashier me. That's what they did to the others who spoke out."

"But now, having learned your lesson, you would act otherwise?"

"*Iie, Tai-sa*," Fuhito blurted indignantly. "I have my own honor to guard."

Theodore smiled sympathetically.

"I think that you are the man to take over First Battalion's recon company. You are certified in a *Griffin, Tai-i.*"

"Tai-i?" Fuhito repeated, puzzled. "But I was demoted to *Chu-i.*"

"Men in the Legion find their own ranks, *Tai-i.* I can't have a lesser rank in command of a company."

Fuhito was clearly overjoyed for a command again, but something hid behind his joy. He hesitated, chewing on his lower lip.

"There is a problem," Theodore prompted.

"I am certified for a *Griffin, Tai-sa,* but 'Katana Kat,' the family *Panther,* was shipped to Marfik with me."

Theodore understood at once. "How can I stand in the way of family honor?"

Gratitude shone in Fuhito's face.

"But before you take the assignment, I'll want to see if you have the Tetsuhara touch in a 'Mech. Meet me on the practice field in twenty."

"Hai, Tono!" Fuhito shouted.

21

Unity Palace, Imperial City, Luthien
Pesht Military District, Draconis Combine
17 March 3028

Constance Kurita looked at her face in the mirror. Though she had borne the responsibilities of the Keeper of the House Honor for only four years, she felt keenly the weight of responsibility. She searched for signs that the stress was beginning to show, but found none. *That's a relief,* she told herself. *There is no time now to hide them with cosmetics.*

When the servant called her name, she made one last check of her appearance before exiting through the door he held open. Walking along the veranda of the mansion, she unconsciously smoothed the line of her kimono.

The rhythmic beat of her heavy, double-tied ponytail against her buttocks was like a metronome to help Constance calm her thoughts. Only a few years back, just the idea of a meeting with the Coordinator had filled her with apprehension. She was glad now that time had strengthened her confidence enough that she could maintain the proper inner control. She had grown in her role as the conscience of the Coordinator. Though her cousin Takashi was her elder by twenty years, he no longer treated her like a child playing at being a grown-up. He even listened to her . . . sometimes.

Constance found Takashi seated in the raked gravel garden at the end of the veranda. His black senior officer's uniform blended with the basalt bench where he sat. He was meditating, gaze fixed firmly on the dwarf cryptomeria tree standing against the low bamboo fence opposite his seat. As she stepped from the wooden porch onto the first slate of the pathway, he rose and faced her, bowing a formal greeting.

"You wished to speak with me, *Jokan* Constance," he said as she returned the bow deeper, as befitted a servant of the ruler.

"I did, *Tono.* Thank you for taking the time." Constance hesitated a moment in token acknowledgement of the Kurita custom of beginning all conversation with only the most insignificant preambles. She and Takashi, cousins as well as functionaries of the state, had long passed the point where they needed that formality to gauge one another's state. "I am informed that you have not forwarded an invitation to Theodore," she said, going directly to the point.

"That is correct."

"This is an important occasion, *Tono.* The wedding of Hanse Davion, ruler of the Federated Suns, to Melissa Steiner, Archon-Designate of the Lyran Commonwealth and heir to the throne of that state, is an unprecedented event. Every head of state in the Inner Sphere will be there. This is an invaluable chance for your heir to meet them. An unparalleled opportunity."

"He remains adamant," Takashi stated flatly. In the set of his jaw, Constance read the irritation that he kept from his voice.

"As do you," she said sadly. There had been little communication between father and son since Theodore's banishment to the Legion of Vega over three years ago. "You treat him poorly. You are the Coordinator and he is your heir. If you do not prepare him well, you fail the Dragon and the realm."

"I am well aware of my duty to the realm, *Jokan,*" Takashi snapped. "All that I do is with the sole purpose of molding my son into the kind of leader the Combine needs. He must learn."

"Exactly my point." Constance kept her tone calm and even. "He can learn much during the wedding festivities. He can meet the rulers of the enemy states bordering our realm. And it will give him the chance to meet and take the measure of our Kapteyn Accord allies."

Takashi's stillness told Constance that her words fell on deaf ears. This was not to be one of her victories. As she bowed and turned to go, Takashi spoke again in a firm, determined voice.

"He still has things to learn on Marfik. Let him stay there and miss all the excitement."

═══ 22 ═══

Massingham Valley, Marfik
Dieron Military District, Draconis Combine
29 August 3028

"**W**e've got some excitement on the left flank," Fuhito Tetsuhara reported over the optic fiber link from his company's concealed position in DonnerBrau Forest.

Theodore rotated the "Revenant's" head to bring the sensor scan to bear on the disturbance. The compressed images on his 360-degree screen flowed until he had a view of the Legion's left flank in the center, where the image had the least distortion. Billowing dust confirmed *Tai-i* Tetsuhara's report.

Theodore keyed open the link to his 'Mech force commander. "Eleventh Armored is raising dust," he said. "Why aren't they holding their positions?"

"I don't know, *Sama*," Olivares replied, his rumbling voice unmistakable even over the commlink.

"Well, find out!" Theodore snapped, his temper short from lack of sleep. As Olivares ordered Tetsuhara to send out a recon lance, he cut the comm link and turned his attention to the tactical map scrolling across his main screen.

Five days ago, Steiner DropShips had been detected heading for Marfik under high acceleration. Their JumpShips had made a perilously close transit into the system, appearing at a "pirate point" only a few thousand kilometers out from Marfik's orbital path. The proximity of the transit point had drastically reduced the flight time of the piggybacking

DropShips as they burned toward the planet. In using the "pirate point," the Lyrans had risked a large fleet of several JumpShips, not to mention the DropShips and the troops they were carrying. Those owing allegiance to House Steiner were known throughout the Inner Sphere as shrewd merchants, always aware of the balance between profit and loss. Clearly, they saw that the gains possible in the Marfik system were worth the gamble.

When Theodore had first seen the radar tracks, the number of invaders had startled him. There were dozens of DropShips. Fortunately, their masses and radar signatures indicated that the force was primarily composed of conventional forces. Few of the DropShips had been identified as 'Mech transports. To make a major assault using so few of the most potent weapons available under the Ares Conventions of War did not make military sense. Only the need for Steiner BattleMech forces elsewhere could justify it. That could mean only one thing: *War!*

He had been expecting it for some time. The expense of running the Davion Operation Galahad and Steiner Operation Thor military exercises was enormous, even for their wealthy realms. Theodore had been unable to discern the full intent of those massive military maneuvers, even with the Order of the Five Pillars funneling intelligence to him, but the shifting of unit positions hinted at in the reports was ominous. Now, surely, the war had come. When the Steiner DropShips appeared in the system, Theodore had burned incense at the local shrine to thank Buddha that the children had lifted for safety two weeks earlier.

Yesterday, a ComStar Adept had delivered a communique confirming his fears of war. The message disk had contained a full recording of the wedding toast in which Hanse Davion had offered the Capellan Confederation to his bride as a wedding gift. The toast was his announcement of the Federated Suns' assault on the Capellans. The timing was too close to the appearance of Steiner troops in the Marfik system. It had to be that Archon Katrina Steiner was supporting her Davion ally by opening a front to occupy the Dragon while Prince Hanse battered the Capellans. As yet, there had been no communications from the Dieron command announcing an invasion, but it was likely that Lyran troops were assaulting other border systems as well.

As soon as they reached orbit, the Lyran Commonwealth

DropShips had made assault landings on all three of Marfik's major land masses, Yantiban and North and South Galfree. Attacked by almost twice their number, the four regiments of conventional forces defending Yantiban had been overwhelmed at once. The three regiments on South Galfree had held out for two days against the Steiner assaults. Only North Galfree had maintained opposition to the invaders. That was to be expected, for the largest concentration of the Combine's forces were on that continent.

Intel had identified at least ten conventional regiments and one BattleMech regiment among the Steiner forces on North Galfree. The twelve Kurita regiments assigned to the defense of the continent were all conventional except for Theodore's own 'Mech regiment, the Eleventh Legion of Vega.

It surprised him when the Steiner 'Mechs landed near Netaltown, a resort east of Massingham. He had also been thankful, for once, for Tomoe's stubbornness. The Legion was supposed to be conducting summer training on the dunes near Netaltown, but after another argument over her refusal to join the children, Theodore had been too annoyed to deal with the problems of running training maneuvers. Had he not canceled the Legion's exercise, the Lyrans would have come down on the Legion's heads, scattering the Kurita 'Mechs and probably eliminating them as a viable combat force. If the BattleMechs had been lost, all hope of resistance on Marfik would have gone with them.

As yet, the Legion's BattleMechs were not committed to combat. That would not last long. An overflight by Legion AeroSpace Fighters had confirmed that the Steiner forces were finally on the move. Several armored columns were striking out along the valley toward the mining town of Massingham on the far side of the vast expanse of DonnerBrau Forest. The Steiner BattleMechs were massing fifty kilometers to the east of Massingham, starting their march up the undulating plain of Massingham Valley.

A flashing light on the console demanded Theodore's attention, announcing an incoming comm laser message. He engaged the "Revenant's" autotrack system to focus the viewscreen on the source, then flicked the switch to bring the audio to his speakers. The *Orion*'s screen settled on a distant hill, ten kilometers to the southwest. An increase in magnification allowed Theodore to see the *kahuto*-helmeted cat face on the chest of the 'Mech crouching there. It was Fuhito's *Panther*.

The *Tai-i* had moved forward to maintain contact with his recon lance. He had been forced to sever the fiber optic line and was now using a comm laser on a direct line-of-sight to avoid intercept.

"*Tai-sa*, we have enemy BattleMechs coming in from the east. Eleventh Armored is moving to engage and calling for support."

"Are the 'Mechs scouts?" Theodore asked. Lighter BattleMechs usually moved ahead of the main body to determine enemy resistance and disposition. It might be possible to engage the scouting force and deny the Lyrans information about the Kurita position before the heavier forces of the main body arrived.

"No, sir. These are heavies. We've got three assault 'Mechs of at least ninety tons under observation. The remainder of the force appears to be medium and heavy machines."

"An assault force leading the advance?" That made no sense. The orbital battle was still denying full aerial reconnaissance to both sides. To commit one's main force without knowledge of the enemy was foolhardy. *Unless,* Theodore thought, *they've outflanked us.* "Relay a hold order to the Eleventh. Their light armor won't stand up to those Steiner 'Mechs. Put some flankers out wide, *Tai-i* Tetsuhara. Watch for enemy forces along the forest edge. I don't want any surprises from that direction.

"How much in the way of armor and infantry is moving up with the 'Mechs?"

"None, sir. Enemy force is . . ." The transmission cut off while the *Panther* ducked its head as a number of missiles impacted on the hill crest, sending gouts of dirt skyward. "Say again, enemy force is unsupported. Unit markings indicate Fourth Skye Rangers," came Fuhito's calm voice as soon as he had realigned the comm laser.

"Message understood, *Tai-i*. Keep your eyes on them."

Theodore closed the commlink to consider the situation in the humming privacy of the "Revenant's" cockpit. *An unsupported advance? The Steiner commander was either an idiot or extremely confident.* The latter possibility was a serious concern.

Theodore brought up the library program on the "Revenant's" computer, calling for data on his opponents. He did not like what he saw. The Fourth Skye Rangers was a formidable unit composed of elite MechWarriors, highly trained and motivated, with an impressive record. Their commander was listed as Hauptmann-Kommandant Kathleen Heany. The records of her ability were spotty and deprecatory, but that was typical of Combine reports on female officers, especially Steiner officers.

The Rangers were from the Isle of Skye, one of the three founding states of the Lyran Commonwealth. Skye, which included about a third of Steiner space and much of its industrial might, also composed nearly half the Combine's border with the Lyrans. ISF reports claimed that Skye was as troublesome to House Steiner as Rasalhague was to House Kurita, because of a strong separatist movement there. Skye units often refused to participate in Steiner military excursions because the Skye Islanders favored a strongly defensive stance. But here were the Rangers taking part in an assault on the Kurita world Marfik, which was certainly no defensive maneuver.

Another sign that all-out war had begun.

Tourneville's voice broke in on Theodore's thoughts. "*Tai-sa*, our intercept units are picking up their comm channel. I don't understand it, but they're broadcasting in the clear." Tourneville paused as though not knowing how to phrase what he needed to say. "From the chatter, they are here to capture you, *Tono*. They are even betting on how long the Legion will last."

"Arrogant of them," Theodore remarked. The news that the Steiner forces hoped to make a prize of the heir to the Combine explained their "pirate point" gamble. As long as he thought their attack an ordinary, if strong, raid, they knew he would remain to fight them for a chance at martial glory. A normal trip into the Marfik system would have allowed time for word of the war to reach Theodore, giving him more than enough time to realize the danger and to escape their trap. They no doubt hoped to capture him in the opening battle as a way of severely embarrassing the Dragon.

That was something Theodore did not intend to see happen. "We'll just have to teach them a lesson," he said.

23

Massingham Valley, Marfik
Dieron Military District, Draconis Combine
29 August 3028

"I'll lead the 'Mechs out," Tomoe announced.

"Negative," Theodore countermanded. "I want you supervising the conventional regiments. They're still not used to operating together and will need shepherding. Take Shirakawa's lance with you."

"*Hai, Tai-sa,*" she replied. Theodore knew from her tone that Tomoe disliked the assignment, but she was too good a soldier to refuse. She knew as well as he that someone needed to do it, and she was his best choice.

Theodore surmised that Tomoe would like his next decision even less. "I will command the advance of the Legion."

"You'll be playing right into their hands," Tourneville cautioned.

"That's what I want them to believe."

Forestalling any further discussion, Theodore opened his links to all regimental commanders. "All regiments, this is *Tai-sa* Kurita. All armored and infantry regiments, except Twenty-fifth Light Horse, will withdraw into DonnerBrau Forest. Scatter into small groups in the pattern we used in last summer's exercise. *Sho-sa* Olivares will give you your rendezvous points. Twenty-fifth is to swing north, wide of the forest, and move along the coast to prepare the defense of Sitika; the hovercraft will be no good among the trees."

"*Sama,*" Olivares objected. "Fourth Skye is heavies. We

can't beat 'em in a stand-up fight. When their aerospace is done with our air, they'll be crawling all over us."

"Then we must move quickly," Theodore said. "Second and Third Battalions form in skirmish line on *Tai-i* Tetsuhara's position. First Battalion stays in reserve to cover the infantry's withdrawal."

Theodore heard the grumble from Olivares, but the man stifled his usual disagreement. Olivares' battalion had the heaviest BattleMechs in the Eleventh Legion. The machines were too slow to participate in Theodore's scheme.

"Warriors, we have a battle." Theodore pressed down on the "Revenant's" accelerator pedal, and the machine started forward. The 'Mech's mighty legs pistoned, driving it quickly to top speed. Fiber optic commlines stretched taut and snapped as the seventy-five-ton machine rushed forward. The regimental commanders' protests and objections were abruptly cut off, leaving Theodore with only the sounds of his own breathing and the thousand noises of a BattleMech at high speed.

Motion on the 360-degree screen told Theodore that 'Mechs were moving out of the Legion's prepared positions. In moments, the lighter, faster 'Mechs were pacing the "Revenant's" ungainly run. One *Locust* strutted out ahead, its pilot booming out an unauthorized *"Banzai!"* over his external speakers.

As the "Revenant" swept past *Tai-i* Tetsuhara's position, Theodore informed the young officer of the battle plan. Relying on him to coordinate his own company, Theodore led his battalions down the slope into the teeth of the Fourth Skye Rangers.

Missiles roared from the "Revenant's" shoulder-mounted Kali-Yama launcher, exhaust smoke arcing toward the advancing Steiner machines. Autocannon fire joined in, though the ranges were still too great for most of the weapons to lock onto their targets.

The Lyran MechWarriors seemed surprised by the sudden appearance of the Legion 'Mechs. Most of the Steiner pilots hesitated, or continued trying to hit the sniping 'Mechs of Tetsuhara's recon company, which continued to harass the Lyran left flank. A few returned fire, but it was futile against the fast-moving Kuritans.

As Theodore led his forces toward the Lyrans' right, maintaining speed and distance, the enemy finally began to react, turning their attention to the charging Vegans. As the volume of fire increased, Theodore watched one Kurita *Panther* take a particle-beam hit in the cockpit. Before the blue lightning of the charged particles ceased dancing among the ruins of the 'Mech's superstructure, a second beam tore into the *Panther*'s torso. Frozen in a running stance, the *Panther* toppled forward to slam into the ground. Enraged by the loss of their comrade, the *Panther* pilot's lancemates concentrated their weapons on the killer *Warhammer*. The seventy-ton Steiner machine lumbered into cover of a stand of brella trees rather than face the wrathful Kuritans' fire.

The "Revenant" shuddered as several long-range missiles struck. The status board pinpointed the strike locations, but showed that the explosive warheads had failed to penetrate the 'Mech's multilayered armor. It was going to take more than a few missiles to stop an *Orion*.

Soft earth geysered in Theodore's path. Armor vaporized and flowed away in silvery streams as Steiner energy weapons struck the "Revenant." The status board showed more colors as the computer painted in the hit locations, but the penetration warning alarm remained silent.

Theodore's companions were in worse shape. In the growing deluge of fire, the BattleMechs nearest Theodore were taking more than their share. Already, a *Jenner* had gone down, fit only for the scrap heap. Most of the others showed one or more gaping holes in their armor, leaving internal structural elements and myomer pseudo-muscles exposed.

Olivares was right about the Legion's 'Mechs being unable to stand up to the Rangers. Speed was not enough protection on the sparsely wooded, rolling ground of the valley floor.

A fusillade of dozens of missiles engulfed a *Cicada* pacing on Theodore's left. The bird-like 'Mech crashed to the ground, one leg completely torn away. Before the pockmarked hulk struck down, scintillating energy beams laced a deadly pattern around a *Vulcan* fifty meters behind the "Revenant." The *Vulcan* staggered for an instant, then its faceplate blew away as the pilot rocketed out in his ejection seat. The pilotless 'Mech started to topple backward, its torso exploding outward as its ammunition detonated.

Suddenly the pattern was clear. The Lyrans had identified Theodore's BattleMech, and they were trying to strip away the troops nearest him.

"Olivares!" Theodore called over the comm. "You get those people into the woods yet?"

"Almost, *Sama.*" Olivares' reply was swift. "Got a problem with Thirty-fourth Infantry. They won't leave Massingham. *Sho-sa* Willis says he won't lead his men out to be slaughtered in the open."

No, Theodore thought, *he'd rather be slaughtered with walls around him.* "Leave them then. They've made their choice. Take First Battalion into DonnerBrau. Hold at the edge. We may need your covering fire."

"*Hai, Sama!*"

Theodore ordered Second Battalion to fall back on its original position while Third Battalion provided cover. His force lost two more 'Mechs before Second signaled they were ready to go. Theodore flashed an order to Tetsuhara's company to pull back to the north before taking to the woods and cutting away from the melee with the Rangers.

Slower than most of the Kurita 'Mechs engaged in the battle, Theodore's *Orion* needed every layer and plate of its heavy armor to survive the run. He was the last of the Legion to reach Second Battalion's line. Third Battalion, now taking their turn to withdraw, passed his position as he turned the "Revenant" to face the slowly advancing Rangers. Third Battalion continued on toward DonnerBrau Forest, screened by Second Battalion's battle line.

The Lyrans were unhurried, secure in their victory with the Kuritans on the run before them. The Rangers performed a deliberate and orderly advance, steadily covering the ground between them and their opponents.

Just before the Steiner 'Mechs closed to effective range for their medium weapons, Theodore ordered a full retreat to DonnerBrau Forest. All the Kurita 'Mechs abandoned their positions and fled. For the second time, the Lyrans were caught off-guard; their advance faltered.

As Theodore brought the heated "Revenant" into the shadow of the giant brella trees, he halted and turned to survey the oncoming Rangers. The Kuritans had outdistanced their enemies, reaching safety under the deep blue canopy. It seemed now that the Lyrans had finally thrown caution to the winds. Their lighter 'Mechs, freed from their reserve positions by the Steiner commander, were crossing the open ground. The Rangers' rigid formations were breaking up as the MechWarriors gave themselves over to the pursuit of a broken enemy.

It worked, Theodore thought, gazing out at the broken remains of more than a dozen Legion BattleMechs. *If only the price hadn't been so high.* By his rash assault and the fighting skill of the Legion, he had bought time for the conventional regiments to escape. As the Legion BattleMechs pushed deeper into the forest, his external microphones relayed the sounds.

Now, Kommandant Heany, the hunt begins.

Hauptmann-Kommandant Kathleen Heany opened the hatch of her *Atlas,* letting the cooler outside air flood in. She hoisted herself up into the hatchway, thanking the Lord for the relief from the oppressive heat of the cockpit. The commlines trailing from her neurohelmet pressed gently against her left leg as they stretched from their connection to the command board.

From this vantage point, she could see the last of the Kurita 'Mechs escaping toward the forest. Most had already disappeared into the blue-tinged shadows. There was no sign of the conventional troops. They had fled even before the BattleMech forces had engaged.

When the Fourth dropped on Netaltown, they had not found the Legion. It had been an embarrassing moment for the Davion advisors attached to her unit, and a frustrating one for her troops, eager for action. The Fedrats had offered no explanation for the failure of their vaunted intelligence apparatus, prompting Heany to tell them what they could do with the contingency plans they suggested.

She knew that the Fourth was more than a match for a motley collection of Kurita scum. Her MechWarriors didn't need ground-pounders or turtles to accomplish the objective. They didn't need to shelter under air cover. That kind of insecurity was Fedrat style. Her Skye Islanders were real MechWarriors.

She laughed aloud, feeling pleasure at her victory. She had been right. *The Vegans were just what everyone had predicted.* They had come out to meet the Fourth like some ancient samurai spoiling for a fight. What fools! Idiotic bravery was no match for a hundred tons of BattleMech.

The Snakes had turned tail, seeking safety in the forest, as soon as the Fourth demonstrated its superiority. The forest offered them false hope, however. There would be no place to organize, no way to team up against the Fourth's heavy 'Mechs. The Rangers outmatched the Legion 'Mech to 'Mech.

We shall hunt you down, Little Prince. We shall destroy your followers one by one until I get my hands on you. The Legion of Vega is doomed.

Heany opened a line to her comm officer.

"Call our Davion friends, Hauptmann. Tell them that we Skye Islanders know how to conduct an operation without their meddling advice. Tell them we'll own Theodore Kurita in a few hours."

24

Gether's Jewel, Marfik
Dieron Military District, Draconis Combine
29 August 3028

A flight of five missiles howled overhead. Colonel Randy Thompson dropped down in his commander's seat, jamming his elbow against the edge of the cupola. He yelped with pain as the hard metal slammed his bone even through the padded joint protection of his tanker uniform.

"Move out!" he yelled into the intercom. He was rocked violently into his padded chair as the driver obeyed and sent the Rommel jouncing across the field.

"Kelly, link me to all battalion COs. I want to know what in hell is going on."

"Yessir!" Without looking at his commander, the CommTech busied himself with the task.

Thunderous booms from the massive autocannons of the two other tanks in the command lance drowned out Thompson's next order. He snapped on his vision screen in time to see the second volley from his lancemates' vehicles.

Two mid-size BattleMechs were advancing toward the lance, firing as they came. The Rommels were unable to score against the fast-moving 'Mechs. The Kuritans were firing much more effectively. Particle beams ripped at the armor of Beta vehicle until the ravening energy clawed its way through to the tank's innards. Thompson imagined he heard the crew's screams as flame gouted from the wound.

"Forward, dammit! We've got to close with them!"

A sickening crash punctuated his words. A glance at the screen told him that his fears were fact. A Kurita *Panther* had landed directly atop Gamma vehicle. The thirty-five-ton BattleMech had crushed the tank's turret.

Thompson cursed as he watched the *Panther*'s broad feet smash into the Rommel's upper surface. Dust raised by the 'Mech's jump jets obscured his view of the damage left by the machine's violent impact on the tank. The running 'Mechs had been a diversion to set up the *Panther*'s "death from above" attack.

The *Panther* untangled itself from the wreckage of Gamma vehicle even as the turret of Thompson's Rommel traversed to bring its main battery to bear. The BattleMech moved in swiftly, sliding past the outthrust muzzle of the Defiance autocannon. As the 'Mech's hands seized the barrel, it froze in place, the turret's motors no match for the strength of the 'Mech's myomer musculature.

A second 'Mech, a fifty-five-ton *Griffin,* landed in a flare of ion flame to join the *Panther.* Thompson stared helplessly as they combined their strengths to tilt the Rommel on its side. The tank's right tread dug into the earth, canting the vehicle further. Thompson was thrown from his seat as the Kurita 'Mechs began to rock the tank up and down. With a final heave, they upended the Rommel.

Seemingly content to leave the machine turtled and helpless, the two 'Mechs moved off to engage more of Thompson's regiment.

"Sir," Kelly called, hanging suspended in his restraining straps. "Are you all right?"

Thompson ached all over, but knew that complaints would do nothing to enhance his image as a tough tank commander. "I'm alive," he said flatly.

"Very good, sir," Kelly acknowledged. "I have Hauptmann-Kommandant Heany on the comm for you."

"Great." Thompson tried to switch his helmet comm to the command circuit, but all he got was a hiss of static. He ripped the faulty helmet from his head and snapped his fingers at Kelly. The CommTech nodded and handed down a headset. Thompson slid the ear piece in and opened the channel. "Thompson, Seventy-second Skye Armor, here."

"Colonel, as soon as you have secured Gether's Jewel, I want you to move your armor through DonnerBrau Forest to map reference zulu-two-three. We have broken the Legion and chased them into the forest. I have pulled Fourth Skye back to regroup and organize a net to surround the Snakes.

"Get your regiment in place along the ridge at zulu-two-three. I want to hammer them on the anvil of your tanks. Victory is near, Colonel. They are demoralized and disorganized."

"Lost the Legion in the woods, did you?"

"No need to get impertinent, Thompson," Heany retorted indignantly.

The commline hissed with electromagnetic static as a particle beam passed near Thompson's Rommel. He heard the shattering crash of a brella tree even through the hull of his tank. He knew the sound was being picked up by the comm microphone. "What the devil is going on at your end?" Heany inquired.

"Nothing much," Thompson replied sarcastically. "We're having a little visit from the demoralized and disorganized 'Mech force you lost. They're stomping my tanks into snail snot."

25

DonnerBrau Forest, Marfik
Dieron Military District, Draconis Combine
14 September 3028

Fuhito flipped up the visor on his neurohelmet and popped a food concentrate bar into his mouth. *Yuk*, he thought, *when will they stop making these things out of three-day-old fish?* He tried to wash the taste away with a mouthful of water, but the liquid from the 'Mech's recycling system was tepid, stale, and had a faint metallic tang. Such cuisine. Even the slop in the Legion's messhall was better.

The messhall was history now. Two weeks ago, the Elsies had assaulted Massingham and forced the Legion away from its base. Since then, they'd been on the run, dodging Steiner aerospace while playing tag with the ground forces and living off rapidly dwindling supplies. The Legion had fought as well as it could. Even the ground-pounder regiments had held their own along the trees of the great forest. Again and again, the Kuritans had stung the Steiner invaders and then disappeared into the shadows of the brella trees.

Despite it all, all the sacrifices, nothing had been gained and much had been lost. Half of the Eleventh's BattleMechs were crippled or destroyed. The conventional regiments had taken an even worse pounding. Only the Eleventh and Fifteenth Armored remained as fighting forces, and most of their surviving vehicles were stranded for lack of fuel, reduced to immobile pillboxes. The Steiner juggernaut rolled on.

The Elsies were weakened, perhaps even hurt, by *Tai-sa* Kurita's tactics. Now the end was near. Expendables, especially ammunition, were running out, the supply insufficient to last more than a week of fighting, even at their reduced numerical strength. The men were worn down, almost spent.

At the morning briefing, Theodore Kurita himself had been bleary-eyed and haggard with exhaustion. But the *Tai-sa* seemed unbroken, firm in his determination to resist the Elsies to the end. Just as the meeting was breaking up, word had come that the Thirty-fourth Infantry, who had remained in unmolested containment in Massingham, had surrendered to the Lyran forces. With them had gone the spaceport where the Legion's DropShips had stood—and all hope of evacuating the planet. Theodore had not wavered. "A setback," was all he said before ordering the planned hit-and-run tactics to continue. "We must defeat the Steiner forces."

Fuhito had been impressed with Theodore's conviction, his display of the Dragon's virtue of tenacity. He found the *Tai-sa*'s calmness and certitude encouraging. Though Fuhito could see no way out of the Steiner trap, he had confidence in his commander. If there was no hidden solution to be revealed when the time was right, Theodore would lead them down the path of honor to warriors' deaths. Comforted, he had led his battered company out to play their part in the *Tai-sa*'s plan.

Now the waiting was getting on his nerves. Fuhito was used to action, movement. He understood the necessity, but that didn't make him like ambushes. He scanned among the trees, trying to spot his own men. Their concealment was excellent. He could only find Gutherie's *Locust,* and he had known where to look. The reduced heat signatures of the motionless BattleMechs and the screening effect of the giant tree trunks helped protect them from IR searches. Fuhito was pleased; he might not like ambush duty, but he could set a good one. A yellow flag flashed among the sparse undergrowth, attracting Fuhito's attention.

A soldier in the tan fatigues and padded brown battlejacket of a Kurita infantryman stepped away from the bole of a tree. He raised his left arm and pumped it up and down four times. He then held up both hands, fingers spread wide. He closed his hands into fists, then opened them again. He repeated the motion, but raised only nine fingers.

Twice more he opened his hands, showing seven fingers each time.

"Frak!" Fuhito cursed aloud. A full lance of four 'Mechs. If the groundpounder's estimates of tonnages were correct, nothing less than a seventy-tonner. What remained of Fuhito's recon company was outclassed. Their heaviest survivor was Busek's fifty-five-ton *Griffin*.

Fuhito watched the soldier disappear into the shadows. *May we all have good karma, soldier, but your last life had best have been very good. I wouldn't want to be out in the woods as naked as you are when the energy weapons let loose. Old "Katana Kat" may be only a light 'Mech, but he's still carrying a lot more armor than your DCMS tans.*

Fuhito checked his scanners. IR caught the flash of the supporting infantry moving through the undergrowth, taking positions in the meager protection of fallen tree trunks. Magscan was overloaded by the metallic content of the brella trees, so he flicked it over to anomaly detection. The screen flickered as wind ruffled the leaves, sending subtle shifts through the magnetic field. The minor disturbances of the field were suddenly overridden as a huge mass moved from behind a thick brella stand four klicks to the northeast.

Confirming the presence of a 'Mech on passive radar and IR scans, Fuhito ran the profile through his computer, searching for an ID. Just as the massive Steiner machine hove into view, he read the identification.

An *Atlas*!

As he set his computer to monitor the scanners and tied in the ID function, he studied the approaching hundred-ton monster. From its globular death's-head cockpit assembly to its blocky feet, the humanoid 'Mech was heavily armored, imposing. Its weaponry was awesome, ranging from the 100 mm High Velocity 1000 autocannon over its right hip to its pair of rear-mounted Martel 5cm lasers. Even alone, it could probably outfight his whole command.

Another machine, almost as massive, moved up behind the *Atlas*. The "Kat's" computer tentatively identified the 'Mech as a *Banshee*. Fuhito switched on visual scan and zoomed in. The 'Mech looked to be a variant on the standard BNC-3E. A small missile launcher sat on its right shoulder and its left arm was replaced by an energy cannon assembly. This was certainly no standard-model *Banshee*. Among

MechWarriors, the ninety-five-ton behemoth was widely considered to be under-armed for an assault BattleMech.

For an assault 'Mech! Frak! What was he thinking? His company was almost all lights. Those two Steiner BattleMechs alone massed almost as much as his entire command. This *Banshee* carried heavy armament and Dragon knew what else. Whatever modifications the machine had, Fuhito felt sure they would make the 'Mech a more formidable opponent than he cared to deal with.

The rest of the Steiner lance appeared. A pair of ZEU-6S *Zeus* BattleMechs, the Lyran Commonwealth's standard eighty-ton assault 'Mech. The hunch-shouldered humanoid machines lumbered out to either flank of their heavier brethren, arm-mounted weapons swaying as though already seeking targets.

Strips of wayward sunlight flickered over the Steiner 'Mechs as they advanced, sparkling off the heat-scoured weapon muzzles. The insignia of the Fourth Skye Rangers blazed from the chest of each BattleMech, far more prominent than the Steiner fist decorating each machine's right shoulder. The machines showed battle damage and the marks of field repairs, but were clearly functional. Fuhito had no doubt that *they* were well-supplied with missiles and ammunition.

The *Zeus* on the Lyran left flank began to move at an angle, bringing it closer to where the Kuritans lay in ambush. Then it pivoted and took a few tentative steps back in the direction of its fellows, and halted. Fuhito noted the depth to which the *Zeus*'s feet had sunk into the debris of the forest floor, and he realized that the Ranger feared miring his 'Mech or losing his footing in the soft ground.

The *Atlas* swiveled its head to regard its wayward companion briefly, but continued on its way. The *Zeus* began to move again, its pilot searching for a path able to bear the assault 'Mech's weight. The separation of the Ranger lance increased to two hundred meters as the *Zeus* continued to be frustrated by the soft footing. The 'Mech turned in an effort to skirt around the problem terrain and walked up the slope from the soft ground, right into the clearing where the Kuritans awaited their prey.

"There's our mark," Fuhito called over his company's channel as he forced his 'Mech forward, out of its concealed position. "The *Zeus* is prime target. Hit 'em!"

The "Katana Kat's" arm-slung particle PPC cracked forth a bolt of blue lightning. Fuhito watched the PPC's ravening energy catch a fire-blackened scar in the cylindrical left-shoulder assembly of the *Zeus*. Dark shadows evaporated under lambent light as the destructive beam vaporized more of the 'Mech's ceramet armor and melted part of the exposed structural frame.

Laser pulses from the other Kurita 'Mechs gnawed at the giant's armor, exploding incandescent globs of metal off into the trees. Small pocks appeared across the *Zeus*'s chest as the concealed infantry opened up with their heavy-caliber machine guns. Fuhito admired their audacity; those weapons were little more than annoyances to the behemoth.

Busek's *Griffin* appeared at the edge of the trees behind the *Zeus*. Raising his 'Mech's right arm, Busek triggered the machine's Fusigon PPC. The particle beam slashed at the *Zeus*'s wounded shoulder, shattering the armor casing over the joint. White steam mixed with oily black smoke and clouds of sparks as the 'Mech staggered and spun half around under the impact of explosive energy transfer.

Fuhito saw the arm actuators begin to shift as the Steiner pilot tried to bring up the Defiance 75 mm cannon mounted in the *Zeus*'s wounded arm, but the damage was too great. The stress of the movement snapped the titanium alloy bones, sending the autocannon crashing to the forest floor. Coolant fluid leaked out to soak the humus as though the arm had been torn bleeding from the shoulder of a giant.

Distracted, Fuhito almost missed the Steiner pilot's other move. The Coventry launcher in the *Zeus*'s right arm vomited forth a spread of fifteen long-range missiles. The LRMs streaked across the clearing, underlighting the overhead leaves with the hellish light of their exhaust. Only his fortuitous position behind a brella bole saved Fuhito from catching the center of the spread. As it was, three warheads exploded on "Katana Kat's" right thigh, blasting away shards of armor.

Fuhito throttled up, dodging among the tree trunks. Whenever an opening occurred, he sent out a blast from the "Kat's" PPC, never knowing whether or not he had scored. His attention was centered on guiding his warriors; only with careful coordination could they hope to survive this encounter.

Fuhito could see the company's two *Locust*s tearing

wildly among the trees behind the *Atlas* and the other Ranger 'Mechs. He even thought he could hear Gutherie's strange, whooping battlecry echoing from the external speakers of the *senshi*'s 'Mech. The light 'Mechs were distracting the Ranger pilots by running around behind them, placing shots against their weaker rear armor. The company's light 'Mechs had used the tactic in the skirmish outside Massingham. Here in DonnerBrau Forest, they had traded some of their speed for the protection of the massive trunks of the brella trees. So far, to Fuhito's relief, the Elsies had failed to connect.

With the main body of the Steiner lance occupied by Fuhito's diversionary forces, the rest of his team concentrated on the lone *Zeus*. Energy weapons savaged the tottering giant.

Trying to gain time and recover from the surprise, the *Zeus* started back the way it had come. As it lurched through the miring humus, the 'Mech's unexpected staggers made it an even more difficult target than had the pilot's deliberate evasive maneuvers.

Amid the eye-searing pulses of the Kuritan fire, an HK-17 armored personnel carrier appeared, the bedraggled rat of the Legion emblazoned on its dented and ragged side armor. The vehicle's treads churned through the muck, spraying grayish gobs in high roostertails behind vehicle. The APC slipped between brella boles, heading toward the *Zeus*.

The *Zeus* swiveled its torso at the APC's approach, but the Ranger, apparently disdainful of a mere infantry carrier, twisted back and loosed a laser pulse at the Legion 'Mechs. The APC careened in under full power, slamming into the *Zeus*'s left leg. The 'Mech staggered under the impact, and flailing its right-arm missile launcher, toppled face-first into the muck.

As the *Zeus* struggled to stand, the APC driver shifted into reverse, his bravado apparently replaced by good sense. Before the APC could extricate itself, however, the *Zeus* rose at its side, the bulbous shape of the 'Mech's Coventry StarFire launcher held high above its blocky cockpit. Smashing its arm down on the APC, the *Zeus* crushed the tank's passenger compartment. The APC's treads still moved, and so the *Zeus* struck again and again until the vehicle was a twisted, motionless hulk at its feet.

Busek's *Griffin* pounded past "Katana Kat," headed for

the Ranger 'Mech. A short flight of seven missiles erupted
from its shoulder-mounted launcher to crater the armor of
the *Zeus*. Busek fired his PPC as well, but the shot went
wide.

Fuhito loosed a blast in support of his lancemate's reckless charge. Ionized air screamed as the artificial lightning
tore at the wounded *Zeus*'s torso. Then the Ranger 'Mech's
rear-mounted laser suddenly began to fire wildly, the pulses
increasing in frequency until they merged into a solid beam
and melted the lasing crystal.

The *Griffin* closed, and the *Zeus* turned to face it. Busek's
PPC fire was ineffective, his aim poor. The Ranger showed
a more deadly accuracy. He managed two full volleys from
the StarFire launcher, which savaged the Kurita 'Mech's
chest, exposing structural members and starting a geyser of
coolant fluid. The *Zeus*'s 10 cm Thunderbolt laser finally
came into play, ruby bolts slagging metal and boiling ceramic. The *Griffin* crashed to the ground, limbs sprawling
limp.

The *Zeus* strode to its downed opponent and halted by the
armor baffle on the downed 'Mech's left shoulder. In a slow,
deliberate movement, the *Zeus* raised its right leg and
stepped down on the bubble canopy of the *Griffin*.

Fuhito screamed his outrage, his voice lost in the sizzling
crackle of "Kat's" PPC. The bolt slammed the *Zeus* in its already weakened left chest. Flames licked out and a new
cloud billowed from the 'Mech's destroyed shoulder. From
the external speaker of the Ranger 'Mech came the hacking
laughter of its pilot.

Azure lightning shattered the tree at Fuhito's left. Two
more particle beams sizzled past. The other Elsies had given
up chasing Kurita shadows in the woods and were joining
the fight. Growling his rage, Fuhito threw "Kat" into a dive,
seeking the cover of a deadfall.

Busek had been helpless. There was no honor in killing a
helpless opponent. No true warrior would ever consider such
an action. The Zeus pilot deserved a messy execution for his
dishonorable act.

The *Zeus* was badly damaged. Another charge by Fuhito's
company could finish it off. But the other Rangers had arrived, which would make such a charge lethal for the
Kuritans.

There would be another day.

Fuhito brought "Katana Kat" to its feet, heading for the treeline.

"That's it," he called on the company comm line. "Head for cover."

Throughout the area, the Combine 'Mechs turned, dodging behind trees as they ran. The supporting infantry ignited smoke bombs to screen the passage of the 'Mechs before running themselves, hoping that the Steiner pilots would not bother with such paltry targets. As he ran the "Katana Kat" through the forest, Fuhito could hear the Elsies blasting away, shattering the woods in their fury and frustration.

26

The *Atlas* took a last thundering step onto the airstrip at Jilenka. The slam of the cockpit hatch against the upper surface of the head was lost amid the rumblings and creakings of the BattleMech as it settled to rest. Hauptmann-Kommandant Heany stood in the hatch and let the September breeze ruffle her ash-blonde hair. She sketched a salute to the Senior Warrant Officer in charge of the resupply team that had begun to swarm over her 'Mech.

A pair of SYD-21 AeroSpace Fighters roared overhead. Heany looked up at them and smiled to see the blue stetson-in-the-ring symbol of Hauptmann Kreuger's AeroLance. Kreuger's fighters had reported the remnants of the Eleventh Legion of Vega gathering near Sitika. Jump troopers on scout patrol had confirmed the report. The annoying weeks of hit-and-hide were over. The Legion had been brought to bay.

The last months had been too much of a trial, adding to the embarrassment Heany had suffered when the Legion fled her 'Mechs at Massingham and eluded them in the woods. While the Fourth Skye Rangers were stumbling about in the unfamiliar terrain, the godless Snakes had crossed a narrow neck of the forest and bushwhacked the Thirteenth Assault Regiment, causing enough damage to have Colonel Thompson's unit pulled back for refitting. There would be hell to pay when General Nondi Steiner could spare enough attention from the rest of the Götterdämmerung Offensive against Kurita space to inquire into the doings on Marfik. But Heany intended to have accomplished her mission by then. Surely the actual capture of the Heir-Designate of the Draconis Combine would overshadow anything else that happened on Marfik. Thompson's complaints about Heany's alleged incompetence would go unheard.

The weeks of constant harrying by her air command and ground forces had taken their toll on the Kuritans. More than two battalions of BattleMechs had been captured or destroyed. The Legion of Vega was as good as defeated. The previous week's ambush, which had crippled Benoit's *Zeus*, was a last gasp. If any real fight had remained in the Snakes, they would have gone after her *Atlas* instead of the *Zeus*. The contacts with Combine forces in the last few days had been fleeting. They had initiated no strikes, laid no ambushes. Her biggest headache had been the clashes between off-duty troops and the civilians in the occupied cities. The fool Dracos not only didn't know when they were beaten, they didn't know when they were free from the tyranny of Kurita.

Now that didn't matter. Her prayers had been answered; the Legion was gathering in the hills east of Sitika, forgoing their sniping games for a last stand. Heany laughed aloud at the thought. If those samurai wanted a last, glorious battle, she would give it to them. Already the tanks and 'Mechs were moving into position. Tomorrow the Fourth Skye Rangers would descend on the Legion of Vega, and Theodore Kurita, dead or alive, would be hers. This time he would not escape. There was nowhere left to run.

The explosion threw clots of dirt against the leg of the "Katana Kat," but Fuhito ignored it. The Steiner infantry were using antipersonnel charges in their mortar shells; even a direct hit would have little effect on the BattleMech's armor. The Kurita infantry, digging in along the south perimeter of Leftior township, were not so well-protected. Most had scrambled for cover as soon as the barrage began. The rest lay sprawled and dying in the tall grass.

"Gutherie," Fuhito snapped. "Take that lance of 'craft from the Light Horse and run off those groundpounders. Give our people some room."

"Hai!" was the reply as the battered *Locust* strutted out over the tarmac. Four J. Edgar hovercraft whined along in its wake like strange, squat ducklings.

Fuhito didn't bother to watch as the hovercraft and the *Locust* fanned out to drive away the lead elements of the Steiner forces descending on Sitika. If their scouts had arrived, could the main body be far behind?

Half an hour later, the "Kat" was pacing down the highway that ran through the Leftior hills. Ahead on his right, Fuhito could see the remaining 'Mechs of the Legion preparing positions. Silhouetted against the setting sun, they looked like exaggerated cartoon figures, crazed ditch-diggers more concerned about the placement of the dirt they shoveled than about the ditch they dug.

Among the fifteen 'Mechs working there, Fuhito saw the blocky shape of *Tai-sa* Kurita's *Orion*. Just as he had throughout the five weeks of bitter raiding among the shadows of DonnerBrau Forest, the *Tai-sa* was among his men, urging them on. The handless arms of the *Tai-sa*'s 'Mech were of no help in the digging, but the *Orion* seemed always to be there when brute strength was needed to flatten a tree, to open a fire lane, or to bull out a boulder for setting into a defilade position for one of the last few tanks.

The Legion had been battered down, and *Tai-sa* Kurita had decided to make a stand. He had chosen Sitika as the spot for his honorable end, saying that the hills matched a description he had read in *Koyo Gunkan* of the battlefield at Kawanakajima. That had been an epic battle in the annals of old Terra's samurai. "If we cannot win," the *Tai-sa* had declared, "let us die in the epic tradition." Soldiers who had mocked the *Tai-sa* when he first arrived had roared their approval.

Fuhito was proud to be serving under such an officer. The *Tai-sa* treated his men evenhandedly; anyone who broke his regulations was punished, regardless of rank. The *Tai-sa* shared the same trials and dangers as the troops. He held no exaggerated opinions of an officer's sanctity, such as Fuhito had seen among the commanders in Warlord Samsonov's forces on Galtor. If the *Tai-sa* were to die here on Marfik, it would be a great loss to the whole Draconis Combine.

The "Kat" ran on. In minutes, Fuhito had reached the Sitika airport, last stop on his tour of the facilities for the final defense. He jetted the "Kat" to the roof of the terminal building to survey the area. To the east, amid the rolling green hills outside the city, the Legionnaires toiled away, preparing their defensive line. All recon reports indicated that the Lyrans were accepting the inherent challenge of the Legion's stand and were advancing to meet the Kuritans head-on.

To the west lay the placid waters of Sitika Bay. That at least was a secure flank. The Elsies had no naval forces in their invasion force, and an amphibious attack by 'Mechs was also impossible. The floor of the bay was soft silt, a mire trap for any bottom-walking BattleMech.

To the north and south, the flanks were virtually open, screened only by a few mobile units. There seemed to be little threat, for Lyran probes had been light or nonexistent. Even were it a ruse, the Kurita flankers were far enough out that they would give *Tai-sa* Kurita sufficient warning to revise his battleplan.

The city itself was a pitifully small collection of buildings, not really large enough for a 'Mech battle. Its most prominent feature, the spaceport, was also of little use now. The Legion's AeroSpace Fighters were all destroyed or in hiding elsewhere in the system, and their atmospheric craft were reduced to a mere handful, operating from clearings in the forest.

Fuhito decided to check the hangars and support buildings for any meager supplies they might provide for the Legion. The "Katana Kat's" jets lifted it from the terminal roof and carried it in a gentle arc thirty meters to the north. The *Panther*'s legs flexed on contact, easily taking the shock of the landing. Fuhito began his search.

For an hour, the "Kat" strode among the deserted hangars in the failing light. The fenced yards held crates of clothing, chemicals, and consumer goods—nothing of use to the embattled Legion. Using the *Panther*'s strength to force open the doors of buildings whose interiors were not already accessible, Fuhito found no booty, not even with the help of the "Kat's" light-amplification circuits.

He had just exited a warehouse showing the logo of Isesaki Shipping when he spotted a small shack bearing a hand-painted placard. The sign displayed twenty-five connected stars in the shape of the Kuritan dragon, the insignia of the technical branch of the Draconis Combine Port Authority.

So ka. Perhaps the Techs had left something behind. Any tools would please Senior Tech Kowalski. Ever since he'd had to abandon his shop at Massingham, he had been repairing 'Mechs with what he referred to as "baling wire and spit." Fuhito didn't know what baling wire was, but he had understood the meaning. Without the proper equipment, even the Senior Tech's technical genius had its limits. Almost half the Legion's 'Mechs were no longer battleworthy. If the Port Authority mechanics had left even a few of the proper tools behind, the Senior Tech might be able to repair another BattleMech or two.

Hopeful yet fearing disappointment, Fuhito opened the "Kat's" cockpit and climbed down. The shadowed air in front of the shack was cool against his bare arms and legs. The scanty shorts and cooling vest were just right in the hot cockpit of a fighting 'Mech, but not enough to keep a *senshi* warm in the fall air of a temperate climate zone.

The door was ajar, and Fuhito shouldered it wider open as he entered the building. Switching on the lights, he scanned the debris that littered the interior. The Techs had left in a hurry, no doubt abandoning their barracks when first word of approaching BattleMechs had rippled through the city. He saw no precious tools, but Fuhito did find the chief's duty log open on a table. The last entry was a week old.

He shook his head sadly. The Techs were frightened birds to run so easily before a rumor. Hens before a fox. He laughed humorlessly then, realizing the image would have been more suited to an attack by Davion forces. It was their Prince who was nicknamed "the Fox."

Something had brought that image to mind, and it made him remember his father's admonishments that such flashes could be the voice of spirit, which was quicker and deeper than thought. With a troubled frown, Fuhito scanned the chief's last entry again. *Ah, there it was!* The first entry on the list of the day's duty read: "*Arctic Fox* readiness check."

Fuhito tossed the duty log back onto the table and started to turn away before he remembered what the *Arctic Fox* was. He grabbed the log again and flipped rapidly through its pages. There was no location listed.

"Frak!" he said aloud as he slammed the book to the floor. Fuhito knew that the *Arctic Fox* could not be in Sitika; it was too large to hide. He rubbed his palm across his chin, thinking furiously. The Elsies didn't have it; they would have cheerfully broadcast the news of its capture or destruction. The *Arctic Fox* was still out there somewhere. Even if it were not functional, it would have something for the desperate Legion.

Inspiration struck and Fuhito bent to retrieve the abused log. "Ha!" he shouted in triumph as he located the computer disk nestled in its pocket inside the front cover. The fleeing Techs had not taken the technical data file with them.

Clutching his prize, Fuhito raced outside and scrambled up the waiting *Panther.* He slid into the cockpit, skinning an elbow in his haste. Dropping into his command couch, he slipped the disk into the "Kat's" computer slot and tapped in the command to list the disk's files. He called for the one labeled "Arctic Fox" as soon as it scrolled onto the screen. Fingers flashing on the keyboard, he skipped through the data, a wide smile growing on his face.

He reached across to the comm board and opened a line to his superior. "*Sho-sa* Olivares, this is Tetsuhara. I have something you need to see."

"What is it?" Olivares growled, his annoyance clear. "I got a lance of Elsie turtles moving around out here."

"This is more important than a few Steiner tanks, *Sho-sa.*"

"So you say, boy. Ain't got no time for nonsense—wait."

Silence fell on the line for five minutes. Obediently, Fuhito waited, but his frustration grew almost unbearable.

"Call me a purple-bottomed Marfik chickenhawk. They're pulling up." Olivares' voice was full of amused surprise. "They must be gonna let the *Sama* play his honor game. Frak! That's got to be the reason they pulled the birds off our heads."

"Then you have the time to see what I've found. The Elsies'll wait till morning."

"All right, all right," Olivares grumbled. "I'll come have a look-see."

27

Sitika County, North Galfree, Marfik
Dieron Military District, Draconis Combine
27 September 3028

"It would be cowardly to leave."

"It would be foolish to stay," Tomoe snapped.

Eyes narrowed and nostrils distended, Theodore stiffened at her harsh words. Around the chamber, men and women pretended sudden interest in other things: walls, fingernails, folds in their uniforms. Theodore and Tomoe's eyes locked, stubbornness meeting persistence.

The code of *bushido* did not allow a commander to run from a hopeless battle, leaving his soldiers to die. All his life, Theodore had wanted to lead Kurita warriors in battle, and here on Marfik, it had finally come to pass. Even hamstrung by poor equipment and lack of supplies, his Legion had given a good account of itself. Now his forces faced the end, despite Theodore's best-laid plans. *Bushido* demanded that he face that end with them.

Tomoe stood and stalked to the end of the table, almost out of the circle of light. She stopped there, but did not turn around. Light gleamed from the metal fittings on the bulky shoulders of her cooling jacket, but her anger still showed in the hunch of her shoulders.

"She's right, *Sama*," Olivares rumbled. "You do not need to die here."

Heads nodded agreement around the table.

"The *Arctic Fox* is only a *Union* Class DropShip," Theodore protested. "She's not even big enough for the *buso-senshi* and their 'Mechs. Even if we abandoned all our equipment, we could not cram in the rest of our people. Anyone left behind will be slaughtered by the Lyrans.

"Besides, we have no JumpShip. The Combine navy was chased from the system more than a month ago. We would have no way to leave the system."

"*Tai-i* Kerai said he had a solution to that problem, *Tono*," Fuhito offered.

"And where is he?"

Fuhito shrugged and helplessly spread his hands wide.

"Kerai-*kun* may be quite remarkable in some areas, but even he cannot conjure up interstellar transport from nothing."

Fuhito started to object to Theodore's dismissal of the issue, but the buzzsaw whine of a VTOL jet landing drowned out the words. The sentry threw open the door and announced the return of *Tai-i* Ninyu Kerai. Ninyu wore a sneaksuit, the hood pulled back to reveal his tousled red hair. The circlevision visor clattered against the holstered KA-23 subgun holstered on his right hip. His smiling face was a distinct contrast to the sober expressions of the officers gathered in the room.

"What, still talking?" Ninyu asked. "I thought you'd be packed by now."

"I'm not leaving," Theodore replied. "I have a duty to the Legion."

"You're too important to die on this backwater planet."

"I'm not too important to ignore *bushido*. As a Kurita warrior, honor demands that I do my duty. I must fulfill my duty to my soldiers and face what they must face."

"*Baka!*" Tomoe shouted, spinning around. "You are a fool! You're *not* some simple warrior! You are not even just the commanding officer of a regiment. You are the leader of the entire Legion of Vega, not just the Eleventh Regiment. Two more regiments of your precious *buso-senshi* and forty conventional units are fighting on Vega, struggling for their lives against the Lyran invaders. What is your duty to *them*? Will you let them die without a leader?

"You are also the Heir-Designate. If you are captured or killed here, it harms the Combine. The succession will be in dispute, and your father will be distracted from the conduct of the war. Can you believe that your death would serve the Dragon, no matter how nobly you contrive to arrange it?

"You speak of your responsibility to your troops. What of your responsibility to the Draconis Combine? Does your belief in *bushido* allow you to throw your life away when you have important duties elsewhere? Will you allow the personal desire to be a noble warrior lead you away from your duty as a member of House Kurita?"

Tomoe folded her arms over her chest as she drew herself to full height. Her eyes blazed. "A samurai's road is the path of *giri*. It is your *duty* to leave Marfik."

Theodore was stunned by her outburst, embarrassed that she would shout at him before the Legion's officers. But she seemed so sure she had the right of it. Had he been blinded by his concern for the troops here on Marfik and by his sense of personal honor? As commander of the Legion, it was the first time other Kuritans looked to him with respect for reasons other than his position by birth. They had earned his loyalty. But was Tomoe right? Did his other responsibilities, his other duties, outweigh these? It was so hard to know the right path.

"*Arctic Fox* is armed," he began. "Aloft, it will be easy prey for the Steiner aerospace forces. If we keep the DropShip grounded, we can adapt our defenses around it, build a firebase to gut the Lyran attack. The Steiner air power won't be able to do much against it as long as the ship stays in the cover of the forest. We can still win here on Marfik."

"Staying is a hellacious gamble," Ninyu Kerai observed. "The Rangers want your head."

"Senior Tech Kowalski's crew is already preparing the *Arctic Fox* for lift-off," Fuhito Tetsuhara pointed out.

"The troops ain't changing their positions. They won't follow your plan to set up a defense around the *Fox*," Esau Olivares announced. "We got volunteers already dumping what's left of our supplies onto the ship, but nobody, not even the wounded, will be riding it out unless you're onboard, *Sama*. My *Victor*'s waiting there for you. It's even got its circuits tuned to your base readings. I'll jockey the 'Revenant' in the morning. That'll keep the Elsies occupied."

"The heir to the Dragon must leave Marfik," Tomoe Sakade insisted.

Theodore looked at the faces around him, their eyes hard and challenging. Not one yielded before him. His officers were resolute. With or without him, the Eleventh Legion of Vega was going to die here on Marfik in the morning. These people did not want him to die with them. How could he betray such loyalty by running away from them?

"I will take this under advisement."

Two fire lances from Wagner's Battalion moved forward on the left flank, lending their missile and energy weapon fire to the advance of the Twenty-third Armored Infantry. Kathleen Heany watched in satisfaction as her tanks and APCs drove the Snakes from their outlying defenses. It had taken all morning to get this far, and the Vegan Mech-Warriors had yet to put in an appearance.

Two Lyran AeroSpace Fighters dove out of the sun. Skimming at treetop level, the aerojocks opened the valves in their belly-slung tanks. Dense clouds billowed from the crafts' exhaust as the chemical mix ignited in smoky combustion. The long streamers of artificial fog settled on the field, screening the advance of the Lyran tanks.

Heany was pleased by the pilots' precision and adherence to the tactical plan. They were showing better discipline than that crew who had lifted their DropShip at first light, flying too close to Sitika on their way to orbit. As soon as she had time, the entire crew of that DropShip was going on report.

Booming explosions returned Heany's attention to the field. She grinned in savage anticipation. The Drac center was breaking. The Twenty-third had created a corridor through the Kuritan defenses. *The Lord provides for she who prepares,* Heany thought.

She pushed her *Atlas* to a run, signaling the rest of her command lance to follow. The Snakes would have to bring in their BattleMechs now. She and the Fourth Skye Rangers would be there to meet them. The battle's climax was to hand.

Half an hour later, her hopes were confirmed. The Fourth Skye engaged what she estimated as half the remaining Kurita 'Mechs. The fighting was sharp, exhilarating. The Kuritans retreated, falling back on a position defended by the rest of the Legion. She watched the *Orion* that intel had identified as Theodore Kurita's own machine leading the fight.

Under fire from the entrenched BattleMechs, the Skye Rangers advanced. Heany was pleased with their élan. They reached the Kurita battle line with minimal damage. Hunicutt's *Quickdraw* was first to reach the line. That was no surprise. The Sergeant's preference for close-in combat was legendary in the Fourth Skye.

The *Quickdraw* came in on a *Dragon* from the left. The Ranger must have surprised the Snake, for the Kurita 'Mech made no effort to turn and face the *Quickdraw*. Hunicutt ripped off a flight of short-range missiles as he closed. Without waiting to see the results of his attack, he charged in.

Smoke from the detonations of the rockets screened Heany's vision momentarily. As soon as it cleared, the Hauptmann-Kommandant was shocked to see the *Quickdraw* standing in a pile of scrap metal. Impossible! The *Dragon* was a sixty-ton BattleMech. Even Hunicutt's close-combat ability could not destroy a 'Mech that fast.

The *Dragon* was a fake, a decoy! All across the Kurita position, Heany could see Ranger 'Mechs discovering the same thing. Some had punched through sheet metal, shattering light metal structures built to resemble BattleMechs. Within those Trojan horses, infantry gunners and rocket teams had sheltered, simulating the firepower of Battle-Mechs. Only a few of the shapes in the position were real 'Mechs, and those were crippled, unable to escape the Ranger machines and incapable of utilizing more than a fraction of their weaponry.

She had been fooled again.

Heany ran a full scan of the area. Radar picked out a flock of targets moving southeast between the hills, headed toward the cursed forest. She focused the visual scanners on them: ten Kurita BattleMechs led by a drab green *Orion*.

"Oh, no, you Satan-driven Snake!" Heany shouted. "Not this time."

She was ready for that trick, at least. She opened the channel to the Ranger fire base. "*Achtung! Achtung!* Fire mission six-three-three. Execute now!"

Leading the Ranger 'Mechs in pursuit of the fleeing Kuritans, she awaited the results of her order. They would not get away this time.

The first artillery shell streaked in two minutes later, splintering into bomblets as it fell. The ground erupted in front of the Kurita 'Mechs. More shells followed, throwing the landscape skyward to join the atmosphere.

Heany watched the *Orion* go down within the hell of the artillery barrage. *Got you!* "*Achtung!* Cancel fire mission six-three-three. Repeat, cancel fire mission."

Two minutes later, the ground ceased its shaking. In the morass of torn dirt, Kurita BattleMechs lay battered and dismembered. Alloy bones showing through torn armor skin, the *Orion* was sprawled on its back.

Heany was surprised when her comm panel indicated a microwave transmission emanating from the fallen 'Mech. As she tuned in the channel, her video screen brightened with a picture.

The MechWarrior in the cockpit of the *Orion* had removed his neurohelmet, a sign of submission because he would not be able to control his 'Mech without it. His grime-smeared face was scarred and he wore a red scharacki feather in his right ear. White teeth shone amid a halo of black stubble as he grinned at her.

"*Ohayo,* Hauptmann-Kommandant Heany. *Tai-sa* Kurita regrets he could not attend your party. But don't be upset. He ain't got enough hair on his chest to keep you Elsie gals happy, so I stayed to be sure ya got taken care of. Come and get me!"

Heany smashed her fist into the screen, her Sanglamore class ring scarring the plastic surface. *Where in the cursed galaxy was Theodore Kurita? How could he have escaped her again?*

28

"**C**aptain."

Walter Garrett felt Hans Alders' hand on his shoulder and wished he did not.

"Captain, you told me to wake you before docking."

"You did, Hans. You did," Garrett mumbled. "What's the status?"

"We're two hours from zero point on this leg. Haupt-mann-Kommandant Heany's DropShip will intercept that position in 128 minutes. I've delayed the restart on gravity maneuvering until after docking."

"We're going to have trouble if their comm is still screwed."

The DropShip's comm laser had been destroyed in the fighting, and the radio was only working fitfully. Even the IFF transponder was putting out a garbled message, but it was enough to recognize the DropShip as one of their own. Not that there was much chance that it was a ruse; system command had not reported any Kurita DropShips in space since the week after the invasion and all of the Legion's DropShips had been captured at Massingham.

"It's still malfunctioning, Captain. Their Techs can't seem to trace the problem. But I had an idea about that. Sure surprised me when they agreed; I never thought those

MechJocks would agree to let a Navy man touch their controls."

Garrett shook his head in confusion, the motion sending him into the bunk's restraining straps. He was still muddled from sleep, exhausted from the long duty shifts necessitated by the *Kit Carson*'s short-handed crew. He understood the importance of the Pony Express system of which his JumpShip was a part. The system was named after an ancient Terran mail-carrying network that once served the vast western frontier of North America. Instead of horsemen relaying across the plains, there were JumpShips playing tag across the stars, transferring data pulses and DropShips to keep information flowing from the front to the high commander and back again.

The method was expensive, but more secure and dependable than the ComStar-controlled Hyperpulse Generators that carried normal interstellar communications. Though the HPG was quick, a message might sit at a ComStar station for weeks until a batch accumulated. Cutting ComStar out of the loop had also enabled the Steiner-Davion Alliance to achieve the surprise that had so shocked the Draconis Combine. But the system meant short crews. Secrecy had demanded that military crews be shifted to the civilian ships requisitioned for the war. Garrett knew it was necessary, but his body objected. He was getting too old for constant duty watch.

"Just what are you talking about, Hans?"

"I've sent Leutnant Morrison out in the *Lucifer*. He's got Alaric Gerhardt with him. Morrison can put into their Aero-Space Fighter bay easier than they can dock with us. Once Alaric is aboard, he can eyeball the ship in. I thought the *Carson* would be safer that way; we don't have to worry about damage from an incompetent docking."

"A lot of trouble for a ground-bound general looking to hitch a ride to HQ."

"If it were only a colonel, we wouldn't be making the effort, right?"

"Astute, Hans. We must always pay attention to the politics of rank." Garrett slipped free of the bunk straps and glided across the compartment, elegant and nimble in the microgravity despite his age and artificial leg. "I'm going to shower and grab a bite before docking. We should probably have the whole crew on hand. Generals like a proper reception."

"Aye, Captain."

Two hours later, Garrett and Alders stood in the cargo well, near the docking collar hatch. The other six members of the crew fidgeted nearby. Alders only had to shout once to get them to stop their grumbling about unnecessary shows for unnecessary generals. Garrett knew that their lack of respect for the army was traditional rather than personal, but still hoped that they wouldn't embarrass him too much in front of the visiting officer.

The *Kit Carson* shuddered from the impact of the DropShip in the collar. Garrett made a mental note to chew out Gerhardt for his substandard performance. The soles of Alder's grip shoes made sucking sounds as he stepped forward to the hatch controls. There was a slight hiss as the panels of the hatch began to dilate, and the rank odor typical of an old *Union* Class DropShip wafted over the waiting JumpShip crew, a gift of the slightly higher air pressure on the incoming ship.

The growing circle of the open hatchway was only half-size when a black-clad figure shot through it in a dive impossible in gravity. The red-haired man struck Alders amidships, ripping his suction soles free from the decking and sending both men tumbling toward the far bulkhead.

A second figure thrust into the *Carson*. This one expertly banked off the upper bulkhead of the short passageway connecting the hatch to the cargo well. With the ease of a person used to zero-gravity acrobatics, the black-garbed figure landed in a crouch in front of Garrett. The Captain recognized that this one was a woman, and a beautiful one, before his eyes riveted on the shining sword she extended to touch his throat.

"The point is sharp enough to penetrate before the reaction takes you away from me, Captain," she said softly. "Surrender and spare your life."

Garrett heard a rustling behind him as the crew began to react. Before he could think about turning, the woman raised her left hand. Her laser pistol hissed a single pulse and he heard the gurgle of a dying man. Her eyes never left his own.

"Stand fast," he stammered. The woman smiled.

"The Dragon rewards wisdom," she said, lowering her sword. "Walk carefully to the bulkhead with your men."

Garrett complied. Biting his lip, he saw Bernhardt floating lifeless near the center of the cargo well, a slugthrower drifting gently from her outstretched hand. The red-headed intruder stood over Alder's limp body, holding it to the deck with a foot on the man's head. The intruder menaced the survivors with a vicious KA-23 subgun. The Kuritan was braced to absorb any recoil should he fire his weapon.

The man flashed Garrett a smile, then turned to the woman. "*Arigato*, Tomoe-*san*. I didn't see the one with the pistol."

"*Do itashi mashite*," she shrugged. The woman faced the open hatch and called out in Japanese words that Garrett recognized as an all-clear signal.

A tall figure, immaculately clad in a Combine Mech-Warrior jumpsuit, stepped through the docking collar hatch. The apple-green triple bars of a *Tai-sa* flashed on his collar. The officer made a slight bow.

"Good day, Captain. Let me be the first to welcome your ship into the Combine navy. Kindly prepare for jump. I'm in a bit of a hurry."

29

Nevcason, South Nantuo, Vega
Dieron Military District, Draconis Combine
16 October 3028

Theodore checked his ringwatch and put down his copy of Sun Tzu's *Ping Fa*. The dog-eared, leather-bound volume looked strangely out of place among the datadisks and slick sheets covering the work desk. He picked up two of the disks and slipped them into a pocket of his jumpsuit. Undecided, he hesitated a moment, then slid his two swords into his sash. Some formality might be in order, for his subordinate regimental commanders both held higher military ranks than he did. Only his position as Heir-Designate allowed him to command them. He left the small study and walked down the hall to the conference room.

Tai-sho Michael Heise of the Second Legion was already there, field-stripping his personal sidearm while he waited. His black duty uniform was rumpled and spotted by oil dribbling from the rag he used to clean his weapon. Heise looked up as Theodore entered the room.

"*Konnichi wa*, Kurita-*sama*," he said from his seat. "Recovered from our inadvertent reception?"

"Quite, thank you. I had expected Lyrans to be hunting me, not Kuritans."

Heise snorted. "Gotta expect that when you come calling in a DropShip with the Steiner fist on it. Lucky the AeroJocks pulled back and let you land when you didn't return their fire. I would have had a hell of a time explaining to the Coordinator how I ignored his son's broadcasts and had his DropShip blasted out of the sky."

"You acted with understandable caution and suspicion, *Tai-sho*. None can fault you for that."

"I don't think the Coordinator would've seen it that way."

"Then perhaps *you* are the lucky one," Theodore suggested. "Where is *Sho-sho* Nordica?"

"Chris was a little late leaving the Fourteenth, something about turning back a probe from Third Guard. She should be here in a few minutes."

"*So ka.* What's the latest from the field?"

"Pretty quiet at the moment," Heise announced as he activated the holotank that dominated the small room. The milky tank came to life, darkening to the black of space, a globe of Vega floating in the center of its volume. The world-girdling ocean appeared a uniform green, while the three continents were painted in gold. The sphere rotated until the south pole was uppermost and sank through the base. The vast expanse of the enormous South Nantuo continent spread out to fill the bottom of the tank. As it did so, mountains rose from the undifferentiated surface and rivers appeared, cutting valleys and spreading flood plains as if all geological time had been compressed to a few seconds. The isthmus to North Nantuo and the southern tip of Forsiar showed at one edge of the tank, but South Nantuo and its bordering seas filled most of the space.

Heise touched a control, and military data began to appear on the map surface. Light blue shading, representing territory under the sway of the Steiner invaders, covered most of the neighboring continents. South Nantuo was marked as well, a blue swath filling much of the space between the Great Desert of Tears and the Trebason mountains. Darker blue icons marked the dispositions of the two dozen Steiner military units in the field. The most dangerous unit, the Third Lyran Guard BattleMech Regiment, was highlighted in its position just to the west of the Roccer-Halo line. The red icons of the Kurita forces stood before the Guard in an arc, sealing off the eastern end of the bulge that held the planetary capital of Nevcason. Most of the forty regiments of conventional forces were scattered across the continent, holding other vital positions, waiting for the Lyran advance to reach their defensive zones. Only the Legion, one armored regiment, and a half-dozen infantry regiments defended the lowlands around Nevcason. The Second Legion of Vega held the northern flank. To the south, the Fourteenth Legion was spread out among the mining camps of the De Zerber region.

"As you know, we've heard nothing from North Nantuo or Forsiar since the end of September. Our scouts have just identified elements of the Thirty-third Lyran Armored Guard moving through Al Aldurban, southwest of De Zerber. Since the Thirty-third was involved in the initial drops of the Forsiar coast and was later observed during the fall of Qaterrani on North Nantuo, we must presume that all organized military resistance on those continents is ended. We can expect more Lyrans soon."

"This was not unanticipated," Theodore said.

"Anticipation never stopped a tank."

Theodore started to retort that anticipation had, indeed, stopped many a tank. A good commander could halt an enemy by anticipating his actions and rendering them useless before the enemy could carry them out. But it seemed futile to make the point. Heise had seemed overjoyed to see Theodore emerge from the *Arctic Fox,* but the officer's subsequent manner led Theodore to believe that the man's happiness was due more to being relieved of responsibility for the planet's fate than to any expectation of success under Theodore's guidance. Theodore was disappointed in Heise, who had seemed much livelier and optimistic during earlier visits to Vega. He hoped that *Sho-sho* Nordica was not infected by Heise's pessimism.

The loud bang of a wooden door against the wall announced Nordica's arrival. Theodore turned to watch the tall blond woman, skin glistening with sweat, enter the room. She wore a cooling jacket and her normally curly locks were plastered down with sweat, sure signs that she had just exited her 'Mech.

Christine Nordica strode up to Theodore, hand outstretched. "Welcome back to Vega, *Tai-sa.*" she said, pumping his arm as she spoke. "I want to say that I think it was real audacious the way you conned the Elsies into giving you a JumpShip. I always said that you'd more than live up to your advance billing."

"What you said was that nobody could be that bad," Heise scoffed.

"Close your mouth, Mike, or your smart remarks are gonna get you a fist in it."

"At ease, *senshi*," Theodore said, laying a hand on Heise's shoulder to restrain him before he could stand. "This is no time for bickering among ourselves."

"Well, anyway," Nordica insisted. "I thought you did real good."

"I was fortunate. The Lyrans were so secure in their arrogance that we were able to gull them into believing we were one of their own DropShips. Convincing the captain to take us to the Konstance system was easy compared to getting him to recharge the JumpShip's Kearney-Fuchida drives from the fusion plant in order to complete the transit to Vega. Between the stress that put on the hyperdrive and the pirate point transit point I demanded, he was sure we would be lost to hyperspace. The ship was damaged, but we made a timely arrival here at Vega." Theodore shrugged. "That is history now, and we must deal with the future. I've already been over the situation with *Tai-sho* Heise."

"Well, he ain't got no manners, but he's got it together. Between him and the stuff I heard you got from the Elsies, you should have a pretty good idea of the situation."

"It's true we were fortunate enough to capture one of their 'Pony Express' JumpShips and recover a substantial amount of military data from its computers. But unit dispositions are not enough. I want to know what you think of the opposition."

Nordica laughed despairingly. "You've read the reports and seen what they've done here on Vega. You've seen our supply situation as well. We're on the slide down, unless you've come up with something brilliant."

"I do have a few ideas, but first I want your evaluation of Leutnant-General Finnan. He is the overall commander as well as leader of the Third Guard, and I've been informed that you know him."

Nordica stiffened, hooding her eyes. "I don't know what you're talking about."

"Yes you do," Theodore said softly. "As I said before, we must deal with the future. Your past is unimportant." Seeing that Nordica was still reluctant to speak, Theodore added, "You are of the Dragon now, *Sho-sho*, and the Dragon protects its own. Your knowledge of his character could help me know what to expect from him as commander of the enemy." Nordica raised a hand to her mouth, biting gently into the web between her thumb and fingers. With a sigh, she raised her eyes and stared into Theodore's. After several heartbeats, she dropped her gaze again.

"All right," she said. "He's a real hard-liner, fanatically loyal to House Steiner and blind to anything said against them. He takes the Third Guards' nickname very seriously. They're called 'The Ever-sworded Third,' and he wears an antique broadsword all the time, even in his 'Mech. He's a little weird that way."

Her voice dropped on the last words. Theodore followed her eyeline to the swords in his sash.

"No offense taken, *Sho-sho*," he said. "Please continue."

"He must have come here straight from Tharkad. He's gonna be real uncomfortable with the weather here, but he's a vet and won't let that affect his judgment. He calls his troops 'Teutonic heroes,' and they're as fanatical as he is. They're Steiner mainline all the way."

"*So ka.* You would assess him as a traditional Steiner leader?"

"Well . . ." she began. "Yeah, sure."

"Very good," Theodore said, satisfied. He slipped a disk into the holotable and tapped at the control keyboard. Red Kurita icons shifted to new positions, and faint orange arrows appeared, spearing outward toward the Steiner dispositions.

"These are the sites where we attack tomorrow."

The Legion officers studied the map, Heise licked dry lips and Nordica chewing on a finger. She asked for a replay of the planned attack and asked terse questions while Heise computed figures on his handset. After a few minutes, Heise furrowed his brow and raised his head from his computations.

"The attacks you propose will burn all the expendables we have left," he objected.

"That's true," Theodore conceded easily. "But soon or late, those supplies will be gone, whether we attack or not. *Toujours l'audace, mon General!* We should be able to acquire some more from the Lyrans as we push them back."

"It's a big gamble," Nordica said, running the tip of her tongue back and forth across her upper lip. Her face showed her worry.

"You're the one who called me audacious."

"Yeah, I did."

"Well, audacity is a virtue of the Dragon. Do you have the courage to go along?"

Nordica bridled. Theodore guessed that she assumed he was slighting her courage because she was a woman. He knew better; Tomoe had taught him much about a woman's capacity for courage.

"I'll match you stride for stride, buster," Nordica ground out.

"Dekashita!" Theodore said with a grin. "We'll give the Lyrans a run."

═══ **30** ═══

Steiner Supply Depot, Cochus, Vega
Dieron Military District, Draconis Combine
17 October 3028

Fuhito cursed the weather, shivering as a cold trickle of rain found its way past his collar to run down his back. Thunder answered his words, reminding him that the weather was his friend. He calmed his mind, seeking to ignore the cold and wet. He had just put the discomfort from his mind when a Striker light tank rolled by and deluged him as its wheels hit a deep puddle.

Fuhito stepped back directly into a Steiner soldier marching alongside the column. The Lyran, the leutnant in charge of the guard detachment, shoved Fuhito away with a rough oath and said something in German. Fuhito only caught the name Kurita and the ill-tempered tone, but he recognized it as an insult.

A poke in the back from one of his companions reminded him to act cowed. He snatched a glance backward and caught a slight head shake from Ninyu Kerai. Though Fuhito generally found Kerai disturbing in some obscure way, he knew the man was right now. Needing cheap labor, the Lyrans had called on the populace with threats and empty promises to get it. Fuhito and the other disguised Kurita soldiers were supposed to be part of this group of people rounded up from the countryside by the Steiner invaders. To continue to hide safely among the laborers, they had to avoid suspicion. If one of the Lyrans got nosy and searched them, all would be lost. The patriots who had thrown in with the Kuritans for this mission would be shot as spies. The soldiers, even though they wore their DCMS tans under their rain ponchos, would likely receive the same reward.

"Move it, you malingerers! I don't plan to spend my night with you wetbacks," the Lyran leutnant snarled, his temper as foul as the weather. The officer shoved his laser carbine into the back of one of the locals, urging the frightened woman forward. "Come on, come on! The sooner you get to the compound, the sooner you get out of the rain."

The ragged line of miserable men and women trudged on.

Finally, they reached the gate to the Lyran supply compound at Cochus. It was a good site, ideally positioned to support the advance of the Third Lyran Guards against the capital. Supplies could be landed safely on Forsiar and ferried across to the city piers. From the coastal city, the Lyrans would send the supplies out by truck along the main highway, by monotrack to railheads at strategic locations, or by military carrier to almost anywhere else.

Huddling in rain, the Kurita soldiers and the conscript labor among whom they hid waited for their masters. The footsoldiers gathered under the leaky canopy that served as a gatehouse to conduct their business in relative comfort. Fuhito heard the compound guards complaining about the tardiness of their relief. He listened in surprise as the guard against whom he had stumbled suggested that the complainers take matters into their own hands and go kick their replacements' butts out of the barracks.

Fuhito found the concept of abandoning one's duty post because of personal discomfort to be treasonous, unthinkable. But these Lyrans were soft, always thinking of their own comfort. And they were cocky, too assured of being safe so far behind the lines. Only a pair of Strikers, buttoned up against the weather, stood sentry. Apparently, their crews were unwilling to get wet simply to watch over a bunch of submissive laborers. *Soft.*

The guards returned to lead the conscripts to the shacks where they would spend the night. As the group left the gate, Fuhito looked back to see the men on duty at the gate take the leutnant's suggestion. En masse, the guards left their post and headed for the main barracks. Fuhito wondered if the Steiner MechWarriors were equally lax.

When they reached the shacks, the Lyrans separated their

charges into groups and assigned them to huts. When only one group remained, the officer dismissed his men, urging them to warm up on some schnapps for him. The last group was almost completely composed of Combine soldiers, and Fuhito felt a sense of impending danger as the leutnant stood by the door, flashing a light into each person's face as he or she passed into the dimly lit interior of the hut.

"Oh, ho," the soldier exclaimed as he pulled one of the hunched figures from the line. He tugged the poncho's rainhood down, exposing the woman's head. Fuhito held his breath when he saw that it was Tomoe Sakade.

"Very nice. Maybe I was a bit hasty in deciding who I would spend the night with. There are quite a few privileges for those who are friendly," the leutnant told her, slipping a hand under her poncho.

In the faint gleam from the open door, Fuhito saw the Lyran's eyes go wide. He surmised that what the leutnant found in his groping for soft flesh was the hard metal of Tomoe's subgun instead. The man took a step back, but not fast enough to escape Tomoe's flashing hand. Her stiffened fingers drove into the man's throat. He collapsed with a broken trachea, choking on his own blood.

All the Kuritans froze, waiting to see if they were discovered. There was no sign that anyone had heard. The rest of their guards continued noisily toward the barracks. On the far side of the camp, a lone guard 'Mech prowled, its searchlight gleaming as it swept the perimeter.

"No more time to lose," Tomoe announced. "Kerai! Tetsuhara! Get your team together. You two, drag this garbage into the hut. Let's move!"

The Kuritans tossed off their ponchos. Fuhito counted heads, and found that some of his team had already been herded into the shacks. Quickly, he gathered them, twenty soldiers and twice that number of brave locals eager to do their bit for the Dragon. At the head of his thirty raiders, he headed for the Lyran barracks. Tomoe and Ninyu had already vanished into the night, gone to their own tasks.

Fuhito dispersed his men to cover all sides of the building, careful to assure that they were not visible should some Lyran glance out a window. He found himself a good vantage point overlooking the main avenue of the camp and waited.

Ten minutes later, twin explosions announced the success of Tomoe's team as the Strikers succumbed to limpet mines.

First of the Steiner troops out of the barracks were the negligent gate guards. Fuhito straightened from his crouch and fired his KA-23, cutting them down before they had gone twenty meters. Around him, spurts of flame appeared as his squad opened up. Bullets pocked the surface of the building, seeking and finding flesh whenever Lyrans attempted to leave the barracks.

Short-spaced crashes filled the air, the massive footsteps of the approaching Steiner guard 'Mech. The beat of those footsteps slowed as the machine neared the barracks court. Then it appeared from around the corner, striding slowly forward as the flames from the burning Strikers underlit the twelve-meter 'Mech, giving it the aspect of a hellish demon. Fuhito recognized the machine as a thirty-five ton *Firestarter,* a dangerous anti-personnel BattleMech. The light 'Mech stalked across the court, searching. Its head-mounted searchlight probed the shadows. One of the recruits panicked, dropping his weapon and running away from the *Firestarter*. The 'Mech's torso swiveled to face the man, and heavy slugs from the torso-mounted Deprus machine guns shredded him.

Fuhito stood motionless as the *Firestarter* passed his position. Knowing too well that his motion might be visible on the pilot's 360-scanner, he threw a flare ahead of the machine and to its left.

The 'Mech blasted the spot where the flare burned as soon as the magnesium ignited. After a moment, the *Firestarter*'s guns fell silent and it stepped into the alley behind the barracks, seeking prey.

Watching its passage, Fuhito noticed a dark lump on a radio tower near which the machine had stopped. The shape moved, resolving itself into that of a clinging man, arm poised for a throw. A sputtering object arced across the space to impact at the side of the *Firestarter*'s head.

The bomb burst in a shower of flames, its jellied petrochem plastering the 'Mech's head. The heat and gummy liquid blinded the *Firestarter*'s sensors and apparently disoriented the pilot. Stumbling into a wall, the 'Mech knocked itself off-balance and fell.

As the *Firestarter* struck the pavement, one of the canisters clustered around its right shoulder ruptured. The liquid inside erupted in a fiery paroxysm that engulfed the entire upper body of the 'Mech.

Fuhito was appalled. Those canisters usually carried extra coolant, necessary to protect the machine's actuators as the fusion heat of the reactor was channeled from the engine to the arm-mounted flamers. Instead, this 'Mech had carried incendiary chemicals that it could project as a clinging mass of fire to cripple and burn any enemy, including another BattleMech. A fiery death was the deep-seated fear of every MechWarrior, a terror born in the sweatbox cockpits where they piloted their nuclear-hearted monsters. This man had wished that death for his opponents; now he roasted in his own cockpit, a victim of his own desire.

The loss of their giant guardian took the heart out of the remaining Lyran troops, who were waving a white rag from a door.

Fuhito left acceptance of their surrender to his sergeant. He stood watching the conflagration of the *Firestarter,* thinking dark thoughts, when Ninyu materialized out of the darkness behind him.

"Well timed, Tetsuhara-*kun*. You suckered him into position like it was some parade-ground exercise. It's almost as much your kill as mine."

Fuhito turned to him, feeling heat that did not come from the burning 'Mech. "No MechWarrior should die that way."

Ninyu shrugged. "He was a Lyran."

"He was a human being. Have you no heart?"

"My heart belongs to the Dragon. It holds no sympathy for those who stand against the Dragon." Ninyu's stare was as hard as his words. "Let's go. The hovercraft have arrived. All hands are needed at the warehouses."

Fuhito followed the black-clad man, mind numb.

The following hours of labor only numbed him more. As a MechWarrior, he was able to handle one of the industrial exoskeletons, and that put him in constant demand all along the waterfront. He was too busy to think.

Periodically throughout the day, Fuhito observed as Tomoe fielded supply requests from Steiner units, assuring anxious officers that their requisitions were being processed and that supplies were on their way. In point of fact, the Kuritans were taking those supplies for themselves.

The volume of Lyran demands indicated that Theodore's attacks were well underway. Combine forces were striking all along the front, hitting them hard and diverting attention from Cochus. As the day wore on, the Kuritan supply-raiders worked harder. They pushed themselves beyond fatigue, unsure of how much time they had. Every case of supplies would be vital to the continued resistance on Vega.

The cargo ships that had followed the hovercraft finished loading at dusk, the hovercraft themselves held in reserve for the expected arrival of Steiner troops. Fuhito had a few moments' rest as the last ship wallowed from the pier and before the first hovercraft could be brought in to be crammed with all it could carry.

It was late night, with only a dozen hovercraft left to load, when the scouts reported a detachment of Lyran tanks and infantry carriers headed for Cochus. Some Steiner officer had finally decided to look into why his supplies had never shown up.

Tomoe supervised the last, rushed loading, ordering Fuhito aboard with his exoskeleton before she took her own onto a hovercraft. Turbines whined to full power, lifting the craft for their run out of the bay and down the coast to Nevcason. The Combine raiders had nearly stripped the supply camp.

The flotilla was nearing the headland of the bay when a lance of *Scorpions* arrived on the beach. As the light tanks halted and fired a few rounds at the rapidly vanishing hovercraft, Fuhito found the strength to raise the exoskeleton claw and wave goodbye.

31

Edge of the Sea of Tears, South Nantuo, Vega
Dieron Military District, Draconis Combine
30 October 3028

The *Dervish* loomed out of the blowing sand. Ruby death pulsed from its blocky forearms and 60mm demons screamed from its bloated chest. The thunder of its steps was lost in the howling wind that seemed to carry half of the Sea of Tears through the sky.

Half-blinded and choking on the dust, Leutnant-Colonel Brian Kincaid stumbled out of the path of the behemoth just barely before one of the 'Mech's massive feet demolished the work shack he had just left.

Trying to shield his face with one hand, he wrestled his sand goggles into place with the other. Eyes still stinging and watering from the abuse, Kincaid was able to discern a wall of the hut still standing, its door slamming violently in the wind. He fought his way to the lee side and grabbed one of the filter masks still hanging undisturbed on the remains of the wall.

He was trying to remember the layout of the base, but without much success. The airfield was already socked in when his battalion command lance had pulled in for repairs. There had been little to see in the rising storm. He knew that the shack was somewhere south of the terminal building near where he'd parked his *Zeus*, but the confusion of the sudden Kurita attack and the raging sandstorm had disoriented him.

Flashing fire split the darkness that ruled the storm's depths. Tracer rounds from a heavy-caliber autocannon sought out a target, finding the terminal buildings. Vitryl and masonry exploded free to be taken up by the roaring gale.

The originator of the barrage, a Combine *JagerMech,* appeared briefly through the swirling sand. Kincaid watched helplessly as a pair of Steiner ground troopers struggled to bring their missile launcher to bear on the 'Mech, only to be vaporized under a pair of coherent light pulses from the machine's lasers.

The storm's whimsy shielded the Kuritan, cloaking the *JagerMech* more effectively than it did the four or five other shadowy shapes that clumped past the ruins of the shack where Kincaid crouched, hugging the still-standing wall, knowing the crumbling masonry was no protection against the enemy BattleMechs. Kincaid cursed his helplessness. He was in command of two-thirds of the Third Lyran Guards BattleMech regiment, as well as half a dozen conventional regiments, but he was separated from his *Zeus* and out of communication with his command. Carrying only his M & G service automatic, there was nothing he could do to stop the rampaging Kuritans.

The wind began to drop suddenly, heralding the passage of the storm's eye over the base. Visibility improved, but in every direction, the horizon remained invisible behind walls of airborne sand. Thick clouds still boiled overhead. In the gray twilight, Kincaid could see the appalling destruction the Snakes had already wreaked in their sudden raid.

Caught by surprise, the Lyran vehicles and 'Mechs had been destroyed where they stood. Barracks and service buildings were a shambles, many completely flattened. His back to the sheltering wall, Kincaid looked across the field at the Combine attackers.

Two lances of Kurita 'Mechs stood scattered about the tarmac. Sand-crusted lubricant fluid oozed from their joints and dripped sizzling to the paved surface. Their weapons were mostly silent, pilots venting heat to bring the machines' temperatures down to safer levels, but machine guns and the occasional autocannon cut down any Steiner troops gutsy enough to face the marauders.

A shrill hooting emanated from a sand-colored *Panther* whose chest was emblazoned with a *kabuto*-helmeted feline. Kincaid recognized the grouping of the sounds as a battle code, a rally cry. Answering hoots came from the northeast. Kincaid looked over the upper edge of his wall in time to see another lance of Combine 'Mechs crash through the hangar area, destroying those buildings as thoroughly as a man scuffing through a child's cardboard castle.

The four joined the other Combine machines already gathered on the runway. The 'Mechs sorted themselves out into a loose wedge, the *Panther* at the head. The 'Mechs on the left flank swiveled their torsos to the left while those on the right twisted right. Gathering speed, the hulking machines began to pound along the runway.

Energy lanced out from laser crystals and PPCs while deep-throated autocannon vied noisily with the shrill whine of machine guns as the 'Mechs raced along. Their targets, Lyran AeroSpace Fighters grounded by the weather and tarped-over for protection from the sand, erupted in flames. The oily black smoke that rose from their blasted remains was shredded and dispersed by the winds still raging high above the base. The Combine BattleMechs continued on when they reached the end of the runway, weapons silent now. The 'Mechs were shadows in the sand, becoming progressively more obscure until they disappeared into the storm's embrace.

Kincaid was standing alone on the runway amid the burning wrecks when the Lyran reaction force arrived.

"Where are they, Colonel?"

"Gone. Again."

It would be no use to pursue them. Even during the first week of the Kuritan offensive, the damned Snakes had somehow been able to strike and vanish almost with impunity. Now, under cover of the storm, they would be more elusive than ever.

The "Katana Kat's" myomer-powered fingers clung to the rockface, anchoring it in the hundred-kilometer-per-hour winds. Fuhito watched the funnel cloud whip down the wadi, sucking sand from its hard-packed bed. The dark whirlwind slid over McCoy's *Cicada,* knocking the long-legged 'Mech to the ground and pulling it to pieces.

"Frak!" Fuhito swore. McCoy and his 'Mech were the third they had lost to the wild tornadoes in the two weeks since the seasonal weather front had closed in on South

Nantuo. The Legion had taken fewer battle casualties while hamstringing the Lyran invaders during the same period.

The killer funnel passed on, and Fuhito and his detachment continued on their way in the diminished storm. An hour of hard travel brought them to the cliff face that sheltered the Second Legion of Vega's base camp. In the caves honeycombing the cliff, away from the sand and wind, the Legion had set up their little-used rest-and-recovery facilities. Looking forward to the quiet, Fuhito led his men through the makeshift windscreens into the relative quiet of the caverns.

He dumped his record of the sortie over the microwave link to the unit's battle computer and eased off the heavy neurohelmet. The four-day patrol had stiffened his body, making the climb down the "Kat's" exit ladder an exercise in agony. He found Michael Heise waiting for him.

"Good hunting, Tetsuhara-*kun*?"

"Good enough, *Tai-sho*. The full report's in the comp," Fuhito said wearily. He ran his tongue over his gritty teeth; somehow sand had leaked into his purification system. "The weather is deadly. We lost McCoy to a funnel."

"Unfortunate. But not unexpected for this time of year. Vega is not known for its gentle summer weather." Heise shrugged. "It's been a boon to us this year, though. The damned Lyran AeroSpace force has been grounded for two weeks. *Tai-sa* Kurita's strategy of mounting attacks under cover of the storms has paid off incredible dividends. Between the storms and our attacks, more than half the Lyran fighters are ruined. Which means that when the skies clear in a week or two, our air forces will be evenly matched. Then we shall have a glorious fight."

"With all respect, *Tai-sho*, you sound like one of *Tai-sa* Kurita's inspirational speeches."

Heise chuckled. "And why not, Tetsuhara-*kun*? I am inspired by him. He has turned the situation entirely around. When the weather breaks, we will destroy the Elsies."

"We shall certainly fight them, *Tai-sho*," Fuhito agreed, unsettled by the unfounded optimism replacing Heise's previous unfounded gloom. "But, again with respect, destroying them is another matter."

Undaunted, Heise waved his arm to indicate the Kurita forces gathered in the caverns. "These are inspired troops. They cannot but achieve victory. When the weather clears, we will take to the wadis again, running along our secret highways to attack the Elsies where they least expect it."

The Steiner forces had been fooled so far, but despite their reputation, they were not totally dim. They would not remain oblivious to the Combine ploy. Once the Lyrans figured out the *Tai-sa*'s strategy, the Legion would have to face the elite Third Guards 'Mech to 'Mech. The Second and Fourteenth Legion Regiments had not had the benefit of *Tai-sa* Kurita's attention as had the Eleventh Vegan. Even though they probably outnumbered the Elsies, these Legionnaires were not yet ready for open battle with the Lyran veterans.

"Soon the Lyrans will realize that we are traveling on the wadis, and our element of surprise will be lost," Fuhito said. "We will have to face them directly."

"With *Tai-sa* Kurita to lead us, we shall triumph!"

Fuhito hoped he was right.

32

Kerschengian Factory Complex, Cochus, Vega
Dieron Military District, Draconis Combine
13 December 3028

The *Victor* shuddered under the impact of armor-piercing shells from the Lyran *Marauder*'s autocannon. Theodore stomped down on the throttle, running for cover behind the gutted factory building. Blue lightning from one of the Lyran's PPCs ripped the ground at the accelerating *Victor*'s feet.

That Lyran strike team had pierced the Legion's lines and cornered him and his command lance in the Kerschengian Factory Complex on the outskirts of Cochus. Tourneville had transmitted a warning of the Lyrans' arrival before cutting behind a row of storage tanks, leaving Theodore and Tomoe to face a quartet of Lyran heavy 'Mechs. Tomoe's outclassed *Panther* had been gutted in the first rush, but she had punched out as the 'Mech collapsed. He had seen her chair's parachute and assumed she had landed safely. He dared not consider any other result.

Without warning, azure fire burned across his path. Theodore twisted the *Victor* to the left, and as he did so, the origin of the bolt was revealed: Trouneville's *Vindicator*. Theodore checked his wide scan and refocused the visual scanner on his rear quadrant. Tourneville's target, a Lyran *Crusader*, was visible there, still reeling from the damage it had taken from the *Vindicator*'s PPC. Sputtering fires burned in the wounded 'Mech's left belly.

Theodore ripped off a burst from his Pontiac 100 autocannon. The high-velocity shells clawed through the *Crusader*'s torso, shredding ceramet armor. Secondary explosions sent shards of titanium-alloy internal braces rocketing from the wound. The *Crusader* doubled over and sat down heavily. A massive explosion stretched it out as the fusion reactor blew, spewing a fountain of liquid metal and hot gases into the air.

The *Marauder* rounded the corner behind Theodore, who fired the *Victor*'s jump jets, hoping to escape the enemy warrior's sights before he could get a weapons lock-on. The eighty-ton machine rose rapidly, as twin PPCs ionized the air beneath it.

Looking for a safe landing place, Theodore watched Tourneville dodge away as a Lyran *Warhammer* cratered the tank behind which the *Vindicator* had sheltered. The Kurita medium 'Mech fled for cover, unable and unwilling to stand against the seventy-ton monster.

Theodore searched for the fourth Steiner 'Mech, an *Ostroc*. He found it, the smooth shape of its egg-shaped body standing out plainly from the angular tangle of I-beams jutting from the rubble of a workshed. Angling his flight, he tried for a landing to the *Ostroc*'s right, well out of the field of its shoulder-mounted missile launcher.

The Lyran saw him coming, turning as Theodore recovered from the landing. The *Ostroc* unleashed a full fusillade of laser fire. One of the weapons missed the hulking *Victor* completely, but the other three savaged the 'Mech's duralex sheathing. Armor plates flowed, revealing further layers, shiny from partial melting.

Theodore fired his jump jets again, trying to overlap his enemy and catch him from behind. The Lyran reacted, the stubby snouts of all four lasers tracking the flight of the *Victor*. Ruby pulses sought the Kurita 'Mech's vitals, but the heat build-up in the Lyran machine must have affected its targeting computers. The pilot missed what should have been an easy shot.

The *Victor* grounded a scant ten meters behind the *Ostroc*. Theodore fired the Pontiac, then closed without waiting to see the results. Fragments pattered against the *Victor* as 100mm shells shattered the weak back armor of the Lyran 'Mech. Armor vanished, exposing the machine's internal superstructure. It, too, cratered and disappeared under the explosive fury of the shells. The *Ostroc*'s chestplate and right arm leaped into the air as the 'Mech's rocket storage ignited in a violent chain of explosions. The Steiner machine toppled, a disjointed puppet bereft of guidance.

Theodore aborted the kick he had intended to cripple the *Ostroc*'s left leg.

Victory was short-lived. Theodore's 'Mech rocked under renewed assault by the persistent *Marauder*. The Lyran's PPCs gobbled the *Victor*'s back armor, exposing its inner workings. The *Victor* toppled under the violence of the attack, crashing to the ground before Theodore could compensate.

The impact jarred him, costing him precious seconds as the alien shape of the *Marauder* stalked closer. The advancing 'Mech pulverized concrete blocks under its clawed feet as it scrambled over a wall of rubble. Its carapace swiveled to point in Theodore's direction, lining up under the dorsal autocannon, which spat explosive death at the downed *Victor*.

Lyran shells crawled destructively across the breast of the *Victor* and crashed into the 'Mech's head. The cockpit rang under the pounding, pitching under the release of kinetic energy. Theodore was tossed violently about. When his neurohelmet connections ripped free, Theodore was slammed back against the command couch, stunned.

Lacking the neural feedback from Theodore's system, the *Victor* went limp, lying defenseless before the *Marauder*. Wary of a trick, the Lyran advanced cautiously. At thirty-five meters, it halted. One massive, blocky forearm rose and extended toward the fallen 'Mech's leg. Cyan energy howled out to caress the limb, flaying armor plates under its hellish energy. The Lyran pilot fired again, dissolving the rest of the *Victor*'s protective covering. Exposed actuators and myomer pseudomuscles melted and flowed under a third blast. Coolant fluid from ruptured lines flash-boiled in an explosive burst of steam.

Satisfied that the *Victor* was crippled, the Lyran paced his 'Mech forward to stand towering over his fallen enemy.

Dazed, Theodore wondered if the Lyran intended to boil him within the 'Mech or to ask for a surrender. There was nothing more that he could do. He was trapped in his cockpit, the right side of his body pinned under a massive tangle that used to be his system function board. His right arm, limp and broken, rested on the comm board. Theodore had fought as well as he could against a superior foe; there was no shame in this defeat.

The hiss of particle beams heralded another twist in the flow of the battle. One of the azure bolts creased the *Marauder*'s right leg, furrowing globs of molten armor from it. Multiple missile impacts cratered the 'Mech's turbine-shaped air exchanger system high on the left-rear torso. The *Marauder* crouched down under the impact, then straightened, shrugging off the damage. It swiveled its carapace to the left, directing a blast from the Magna Hellstar PPC in the left forearm at an unseen target. An autocannon roared out its own response to the *Marauder*'s right. The Lyran 'Mech held its ground.

Did the Lyran know who lay at his mercy? Theodore wondered.

Another flight of missiles screamed in to chip away at the thick plating on the *Marauder*'s upper carapace. The Lyran, exhibiting admirable fire discipline, paced his shots by alternately firing the Hellstar PPC and 5cm laser in the left weapon arm, then those in the right. The autocannon howled constantly.

Theodore, desperate to bring the *Victor* back into the battle, found that his neurohelmet was shattered beyond hope and that the autonomic feedback systems that allowed free play of the *Victor*'s arms were gone. He steadied his breathing, reaching for his *hara*. The faint voice of Tetsuhara-*sensei* whispered in his head, *Pain is a thing of the mind, and the mind is the servant of the spirit.*

Hai, sensei. I will control my pain. He reached out with his shattered arm, watching the bone ends slide past one another as he straightened the limb. Clinically, he observed the fresh blood flow as his fingers tapped out the code to elevate the *Victor*'s right arm.

Through the shattered viewport, he watched the wide muzzle of the Pontiac 100 cant toward the sky, surprised to see the machine respond. His karma was good, then. He reached for the grip and depressed the firing stud.

Deep booming echoed through the cockpit as the Pontiac's cassette round emptied, sending 100mm shells tearing into the underbelly of the *Marauder*. The Lyran 'Mech jerked upward from the impact. Theodore fired again. One of the *Marauder*'s legs stiffened spasmodically as its myomer pseudomuscles contracted under a faulty command. Trailing smoke and sparks, the 'Mech collapsed onto the *Victor*.

Darkness filled the cockpit as seventy-five tons of incapacitated BattleMech crashed to the ground. Theodore sighed, releasing his control and letting the darkness fill his mind as well. Warm and welcoming, it caressed and took him far from the stink and heat of the battlefield.

Well done, said Tetsuhara-*sensei*'s ghostly voice.

33

South Nantuo, Vega
Dieron Military District, Draconis Combine
Late December 3028

The soft susurrus of the military command center in the next room called Theodore from his foggy dreams. Awakening to the concerned faces of Ben Tourneville and Fuhito Tetsuhara, he tried to raise his right arm to wave them back. When his arm did not respond, he looked down to find it encased in a preserving sleeve. He also recognized the itch of peeling plastiflesh on his forehead. The memory of his last battle came back.

"The physicians say that you should recover full use of the arm, *Tai-sa*," Fuhito assured him. "You will have a scar on your head, though."

"You must have complete rest," Tourneville insisted.

Theodore shook his head. While Steiner forces infested Vega, he could not rest. A samurai would never be kept from his duty by personal injury.

"There was some trouble with Heise and Nordica while you were unconscious," Fuhito said cautiously. "They did not understand your plan and wished to jeopardize it by running in different directions. Using her authority as your executive, *Sho-sa* Sakade has placed me in command."

"It is most irregular," Tourneville observed sourly.

"But has it worked?" Theodore asked, turning to Fuhito. "I've tried to see that the spirit of your plans was followed, *Tai-sa*," Fuhito answered with a shrug. "It's not for me to say if I have succeeded."

Typical Tetsuhara modesty. If Fuhito had not handled the situation, things wouldn't be so calm. Tomoe had done well to appoint him as overseer. Heise would not have accepted her, and no one else had enough experience in command to execute his orders. "Where do we stand with the Lyrans?"

"Your plan is a success, *Tai-sa*, despite this fellow's dabblings," Tourneville assured him. "We have split the Steiner forces, and our link-up with our forces from the west of the Trebason Mountains is complete. Our capture of Cochus will force them to rely on longer, overburdened supply lines. The Lyrans are in serious trouble.

"Second Legion and twenty of our conventional regiments are pushing most of the Third Lyran Guard and six of their armored regiments north toward the edge of Great Desert of Tears. They will soon have a sea of sand at their backs.

"Fourteenth Legion is leading another fourteen of our regiments against the remainder of the Third Guards under Leutnant-General Finnan. The Lyrans have four regiments of conventional forces with them. Their 'Mech force is fighting well, but even our non-'Mech forces are fighting excellently. The Lyrans are abandoning the Roccer-De Zerber line. We shall drive the invaders from Vega soon."

Theodore nodded. "Do you concur, *Tai-i* Tetsuhara?"

"We have had successes, *Tai-sa*, and many of Commonwealth's forward supply depots have fallen to us during the advance. The Lyrans are facing the severe shortages that once were our lot. They are in trouble, but they are far from beaten."

"I see. Set up a full staff conference immediately. I want situation reports from all fronts for review. And send in *Sho-sa* Sakade."

Fuhito and Tourneville exchanged glances. Theodore narrowed his eyes suspiciously as Tourneville cleared his throat.

"*Sho-sa* Sakade encoded a message disk for you before she left."

"It's true, Leutnant-General Finnan. The Legion won't hit Roccer for another two weeks at least. The Fourteenth only has a skeleton force left along the Roccer-De Zerber line.

There're just three burned-out armored regiments on the front and a couple more in reserve."

The Steiner officers in the command hut exchanged skeptical glances. Kommandant Werner Jones stood to face the speaker. Leutnant-General Patrick Finnan had already reviewed what the Kuritan defector had brought with him. This session was for the command staff. Finnan let his security officer take the lead, approving of the hard stare Jones fixed on the Kurita *Chu-i.*

"How can we trust you, Leutnant Tourneville?"

The man he addressed rubbed his eyes, then ran his hand through his curly red hair. He was clearly tired from the interrogation session, but his manner remained composed, confident. He was still holding a card in the hole. "I don't expect you to take my word. You've seen the datadisks I brought. The Legion's in trouble. You people have got them on the ropes. I don't want to go down with them."

"So you sell them out?"

The Kuritan gave Jones a sour look and turned his attention from the security officer to the head of the table where Finnan sat. "Leutnant-General, I served the Combine like a good little soldier for ten years, but I opened my mouth at the wrong time to the wrong people and got sent to this hellhole of Vega. Five years here, watched all the time. I wanted out, but in case you ain't heard, nobody leaves the Legion on two feet. Your invasion was the first chance I had to run."

"You took quite a risk, coming across the lines," Finnan commented.

"Sure it was a risk, but if I'd stayed with the Legion, I was a dead man when you attacked. They ain't got much longer, even if they can't see it. Well, I want to stay alive, so I've come to you."

"And we welcome prisoners, Leutnant," Jones said.

"I don't intend to be a prisoner," the Kuritan stated. "You haven't seen all the data yet."

"What do you mean?" Finnan asked, sensing that the man was ready to reveal his secret.

"Disk three, Leutnant-General. Put it in your computer and call up the 'Conference Gray' file."

"There is no such file on the disk," Jones scoffed.

The red-haired Kuritan smiled. "Don't be so sure, Kommandant. Call it up."

Jones didn't move until Finnan nodded his assent, then he

retrieved the file. After scanning its contents, he announced, "It's the minutes of a staff meeting, sir. Colonel Kurita was wounded in our counterthrust at Cochus. He is recovering, but currently immobilized at an unspecified location, which the staff feels is underguarded."

"That," the Kuritan said triumphantly, "is my ticket off this hell-ball. You assure me of amnesty and a free ticket to the world of my choice, and I give you the location."

"We could force it out of you," Jones warned.

"What do you think you are? The ISF? By the time you break me, it will be too late to do you any good.

"Right now, the Combine leadership is confused and divided. General Heise wants to throw all their strength at First and Third Battalions, to take them out while the Legion is still strong enough to do it. Nordica wants to dig in and wait for reinforcements and supplies."

"They must have captured some of ours."

"Some, but not enough. You hid them too good. Tell me, Leutnant-General, have any of the Combine 'Mechs you've been fighting used any missiles lately? No? Didn't think so. They're hurting and you know it, Leutnant-General."

"Gentlemen and ladies, I think Leutnant Tourneville is on the level. All of our own data coincides with his story. It sounds as though the Legion of Vega is indeed on its last legs," Finnan announced with a predatory grin. "With the information that Leutnant Tourneville has brought us, and with Kincaid's forces distracting the Snakes' attention, we can launch a devastating attack at the Legion's rear.

"Leutnant, where did you say Kurita is?"

"We have a deal then?"

"We have a deal."

"Jalonjin. A mining camp about ten klicks outside of De Zerber."

"Near enough for us to mount a surgical strike and do what Heany failed to do on Marfik. Nagelring over Sanglamore as always," Finnan gloated, savoring the opportunity to succeed where a graduate of a rival service academy had failed. He beamed at his assembled officers. "Theodore Kurita and his Legion of Vega are in our hands."

Finnan stood and walked to the door to his office. Ignoring the assembled officers as they leaped to their feet and saluted, he spoke to the Kuritan.

"Come along, Leutnant Tourneville, I have some questions about the Legion's dispositions that I would like answered before I plan our attack."

"Roger, LCAF-hire *Starsled*," CommTech Loris acknowledged. "Telemetry transfer complete. Prepare to receive gantry connections."

"Roger, Roccer Control. Standing by."

Loris directed his gaze out the Roccer control tower's main window. Twenty-five hundred meters away on the landing field the Lyran DropShip *Starsled* stood, still hot from atmospheric entry. Gantries rose from sheltered bays on the tarmac, skeletal fingers reaching for the spheroid shape. As he watched the tower probes enter the waiting recesses on the vehicle, the DropShip's pilot spoke again.

"Roccer Control, this is *Starsled*. Gantries locked in. Permission to commence unloading."

"Permission granted, *Starsled*. Welcome to Vega. We've been looking forward to your supplies."

The pilot started to ask for the latest groundside gossip, but Loris was distracted by a flashing priority signal.

"Hold on, *Starsled*. I've got a situation here."

Loris cut off the pilot and routed the priority signal to his station. His screen tagged the origin and flashed the alpha retransmission code that the Lyran command used to facilitate passage of messages from field units to the more powerful transmitter at the Roccer landing field. Roccer's communicators had the power to cut through enemy jamming and bounce signals off the planet's comm satellites. Loris listened to the message with increasing worry.

"Sir."

"What is it?"

"I've got a relay here for Leutnant-Colonel Kincaid on the Desert of Tears front. Leutnant-General Finnan is ordering him to retreat the First and Third Battalions of the Guard to orbit and prepare for a combat drop behind the Fourteenth Vegan Legion's positions north of De Zerber.

"What should I do?"

"Acknowledge the order, CommTech Loris," Theodore said.

"Sir, you don't want me to transmit Finnan's order."

"Of course not," Theodore chuckled. "Acknowledge receipt of the order by Kincaid's command. Leutnant-General

Finnan does not need to know that his order has been received by us instead of the intended recipient. Besides, it will assist us in our own plans if that is what he believes.

"Route any further transmissions through the Twelfth Legion's intelligence section. We will let the Lyrans believe they are still talking to each other."

"Take it easy, Leutnant. You've had a rough time."

"Had to get here, sir. Had to tell . . ."

"You will," Brian Kincaid assured quietly. The leutnant's haggard, sunken eyes did not conceal the beauty of her Eurasian features. Kincaid submerged that thought. The leutnant was in rough shape from a run through the Kurita lines in a half-destroyed 'Mech. She needed a professional attitude from him, not a personal one. "Drink that coffee down. I've got time."

She shoved the offered cup away. "That's just it. You don't. We all don't!"

"What are you talking about?"

The woman paid no attention to the other officers. She searched Kincaid's face, her head moving back and forth in a tiny, disbelieving shake. "Then I'm it. The only one to make it."

She buried her face in her hands. Her body shook with breathy sobs. Kincaid felt it tremble under the hand he laid on her shoulder. As he hoped, she steadied under his touch.

"Tell me what happened, Leutnant."

"We were surrounded outside Jalonjin," she began, voice muffled by her hands. "Leutnant-General Finnan had taken in a Kurita deserter and listened to him. Planned an attack based on the scum's information. It was a trap. The Legion was waiting for us. We didn't have a chance.

"Finnan gave the order to break into pairs and fight our way out. Just before my team went out, his *Atlas* caught a barrage of Snake rockets. He . . . he went down. I think he's dead."

Kincaid exchanged a worried look with his executive officer.

"Colonel Donovon took over. She seemed sure that we could beat the Dracs. Don't know why she was so sure. We was getting stomped.

"She ordered my lance out to make contact with you. It didn't make any sense to me. Last I heard the rest of Third

Guard was fighting way up north. We went, though. We lost Chaney right away when we cut through the lines. Whitney bought it when we ran into a Kurita reinforcement column. Me and Bradley, my partner, kept going. We thought we were in the clear when a pair of *Dragons* caught up with us outside of Halo. Bradley's *Commando* lost a leg, and the damned Snakes hunted him down after he punched out. They squashed him like a bug."

"Take it easy, Leutnant. Get on over to the barracks tent and get yourself some rest."

She rose shakily and left. As soon as the door closed behind her, the gathered officers of First and Third Battalions turned anxious faces to Kincaid.

"This is real bad, Brian," Kincaid's executive officer, Willy Williams, declared. "We're nearly surrounded here, and we've got that damned sand sea at our backs. Sounds like Second Battalion is cut up pretty bad. With Finnan down—even if he's just wounded—the southern front is in big trouble. Donovon in charge . . ." He shook his head. "If the Legion is going to be able to concentrate on us here, we're finished, too."

Kincaid knew he was right. The Second Legion was bad enough. If they had the Fourteenth coming down on them as well, it was all over.

"It looks like we have no choice, Willy. Call in the DropShips. We've got to evacuate. But they're not going to like it on Tharkad."

Theodore and his officers crowded around the main radar screen in the Roccer command tower.

"That's the last one, then?" he asked.

"Yessir, outward bound on a solid burn for the jump point," the CommTech replied.

"We've seen the last of Finnan and his Third Lyran Guard."

Theodore smiled at Tomoe's comment. He put his left arm around her, reassuring himself that she had returned safely from her mission of deception into the Lyran camp. She nestled in close, careful of his injured arm. "What you did was very dangerous. You too, Kerai-*kun*."

"It saved lives," she pointed out. "By convincing the Lyrans that their position was hopeless, we made them retreat. With one force withdrawing, the others had no reasonable option but to follow. We were fortunate that Finnan was wounded. Had he still been in command, things might have gone differently. We cut the campaign here by weeks, possibly months."

"Sure it was dangerous," Ninyu said with a laugh. "But it was fun, too. You should have seen Tourneville's face when I told him that I used *his* name in the Lyran camp. He was fit to blow a coolant seal."

With Tourneville absent from the group, they all joined in with Ninyu's laughter. When they calmed, Fuhito said, "The Lyrans will compare notes when they're together again. They'll see that we manipulated information and made them believe in circumstances that were not reality."

Ninyu shrugged. "So what? We fooled them, and they'll be shamed by it. They probably won't even admit to their masters on Tharkad that we conned them."

"Finnan has certainly been embarrassed by the actions of his subordinates. When he recovers, he will face serious questions from his superiors. Perhaps he'll attempt to fix the blame on his junior officers. Already they are squabbling. In the last transmission we intercepted, Colonel Donovon was calling Leutnant-Colonel Kincaid a coward, which, of course, he denied vehemently while suggesting that she had no idea what she was talking about.

"It will be some time before the Lyrans sort matters out," Tomoe predicted.

"I'm sure it will," Theodore agreed. "We have done well here. Vega is safe. But we have a lot more to do elsewhere. This war is far from over."

34

Ninyu slouched into the room and threw himself down into the massive floral armchair facing the oaken desk, heedless of the damage his grimed jumpsuit would do to the hotel's furniture. He peeled off his tight black gloves and dropped them into his lap. Flexing his fingers, he carefully tested the flexibility of each digit. His survey complete, he rocked his head back into the soft cushions.

Looking up from his book, Theodore was appalled by the haggard, worn look of his friend. A year of war had hardened Ninyu and stolen much of his jovial manner, just as it was wearing down everyone around Theodore. Even Tomoe seemed so exhausted when she left in response to Constance's message that Omi needed her. Was it affecting him, too?

A glance in the mirror on the wall separating the outer room from the bedchamber told him it was so. His shoulder-length hair was shaggy from lack of proper trimming. The silly, affected mustache he had worn during his tour in the Benjamin District was gone. He didn't even know if the style was still in vogue on Luthien. His face was thinner, almost gaunt, and his eyes were as haunted as Ninyu's.

"Tourneville is taken care of," Ninyu announced wearily.

"What do you mean?" Theodore was puzzled.

"He's dead."

Theodore sat back in surprise.

"Yesterday I learned from one of my people that he was ready to blow the whistle on your plans to invade the Commonwealth," Ninyu continued. "I was waiting for him outside the ComStar compound when he arrived. He had a coded message marked for delivery to the Coordinator. *Chu-i* Tourneville has had an unfortunate accident."

"Couldn't you just have distracted him? Bought us some time?"

Ninyu shrugged.

Theodore was confused. "Subhash-*sama* is helping us by altering Tourneville's reports. If you could merely have delayed Tourneville, it would have given the Director time to take care of this message. Surely he would not have ordered the man killed just to stop this one communication."

"The Director didn't order it," Ninyu stated.

"What?" If Ninyu had not acted under his ISF superior's orders, this show of initiative might be the sign of a dangerous loyalty shift. Even if the change were in Theodore's favor, altered loyalties were a sign of an unstable personality. The last thing Theodore needed now was a rogue ISF special agent, especially with Tomoe gone. She would not be able to counter Ninyu's actions with her special O5P talents.

"Then why?" he asked.

"I acted in the best interests of the Dragon. We have too many worries to keep that slinking tattletale on our list of problems. Subhash-*sama* trusts his Sons of the Dragon to act as they think best." Ninyu's face held the hint of a smile. "All of them."

Ninyu picked up one of his gloves, turning it right side out. He inspected it carefully before returning it to his lap. He seemed satisfied, as though his act had restored the universe to proper order. "Don't be squeamish, my friend," he said casually. "It's no worse than your shooting Sanada."

Theodore hid his outrage, but not fast enough. Ninyu's smirk told Theodore that he had caught the emotion and was pleased to have provoked the reaction. It was true that Theodore had shot *Tai-sa* Sanada, but it was an impulsive solution to a problem, not premeditated murder. Besides, Sanada had been a dangerous, incompetent commander who had put his own vanity and honor before the needs of the Combine.

"That was different. Tomoe told me just before I went

into the meeting with the generals that Sanada was in Warlord Cherenkoff's pocket. The fat fool may be impossible, but he's still a warlord, and dangerous because of it. He would never approve my invasion plan. Cherenkoff would quash Operation Contagion simply to annoy me. He would be happy to reward anyone who helped him make my life more difficult. Like calls to like, I suppose.

"This is too important. I cannot allow the invasion of Skye to be halted because of one man's petty desire to avenge an imagined insult or to curry favor with the Coordinator. If Cherenkoff learns of the troops we have assembled, he will issue orders to stop me. He will redeploy our troops and requisition the JumpShips for less important duty.

"The Warlord wishes to steer a course of dangerous indolence. He wants to sit and pick at Davion, as he has for years. Sometimes I wonder if he realizes that we really are at war. How can my father allow Cherenkoff to maintain control over Dieron?" Theodore's voice had risen as he spoke, his long-leashed anger and frustration running free. Catching himself, he paused to regain more control before continuing.

"The Combine needs this attack. We must strike back at Steiner.

"All through the meeting that thought gnawed at me. We discussed the plans openly, Sanada listening and taking careful notes. I knew that a good officer would do that in order to prepare properly, but I suspected his real motive was to gather evidence for Cherenkoff. Could I let one self-interested fool cripple the Combine's chances? I had been planning to embarrass Sanada before the other generals by repudiating his action in the Jinjiro Thorsen incident. I thought it might bring him into line, force him to abandon his selfish attitude.

"But then I saw the look on his face when Thorsen entered. I could feel his contempt and hatred, and I realized that public airing of my displeasure with him would only push him over the edge, and drive him fully into Cherenkoff's camp. I had no doubt that as soon as Sanada left that meeting he would go straight to the Warlord, who would have scuttled the invasion and the Combine's best chance to stop the Steiner attacks. Shooting Sanada was the only way I could think of to stop him."

"Stow the justifications," Ninyu snapped. "I never said I disagreed with what you did. Shooting Sanada put the fear of *you* into the rest of the generals. That's good. Nobody's talked to the Warlord, and with the landings on Dromini VI, they're in too deep to try that now. They'll stick with you."

"I don't want them with me. I want them with the Combine."

"Same thing."

"I am not yet the Coordinator."

"It's only a matter of time."

"Would you kill my father to suit your ideas of what the Dragon requires?"

Ninyu shrugged.

Unsettled by his comrade's ambiguous response, Theodore stood. He wanted to be alone.

Ninyu simply closed his eyes, ignoring the implication that he should leave. Annoyed, Theodore stalked to his bedroom. He was halfway across the inner room before noticing the object lying in the center of the bed. He halted in surprise. It had not been there when the orderlies had left, and no one had disturbed him until Ninyu had arrived. Fifty stories above the street, the windows were permanently sealed. There was no way into the bedroom except through the door to the outer chamber. How could it have gotten here?

He stepped to the bed and lifted the lacquered mask. Beneath it lay an origami cat. "Frak!" A folded paper sculpture in the shape of a cat was the signature of the nekogami. They were reputed to be the best at what they did. Assassins, spies, and saboteurs. Though the subjects of innumerable entertainments and books, few knew their real capabilities. None knew their identities. Ninyu appeared at the door, alert and ready for trouble, with a short, flat throwing knife in his hand. His eyes went wide when he saw the origami sculpture on the bed. Walking softly and scanning the room, he crossed to Theodore's side.

Theodore held out the mask. It was full-size and complete with the silken cords to tie it to the wearer's face. Theodore recognized it as one of the types worn in the Noh drama, but he did not recall the character it represented. The mask's staring eyes and grimacing mouth were menacing, an odd contrast to the long, bright red nose. With exaggerated care, Ninyu took the mask and examined it.

"It is a *tengu* mask," he pronounced.

"*So ka*. The winged swordmaster spirits of the forest. They were great tricksters. Is this a joke?"

Ninyu held the mask high to let light illuminate its black lacquered interior. He pointed to the two needles jutting out beneath the eyeholes. Each tip was coated in a dull brown substance.

"No joke," he said. "Anyone who wore this mask would die a painful death. This is a hint.

"In some traditions, the *tengu* were the original tutors of the ninja. In my year of training with a nekogami *sensei*, I learned something of the many ancient customs and beliefs that the nekogami observe. They take the *tengu* as their ancestors, venerating them as they do the generations of ninja who tie them to ancient Japan. The Spirit Cats are very traditional." Ninyu handed the mask back to Theodore. "They are not happy with you."

"What did I do?" Theodore asked innocently.

"You said they were your agents on Dromini VI."

"I thought it would give the officers more confidence. The nekogami are feared throughout the Inner Sphere. If the generals knew we were relying on our own sleeper agents and half-trained volunteers . . ."

"Just because a strike team wears black suits doesn't mean they are nekogami, no matter what you call them. Frak! It doesn't even mean that they're ninja. You could have said the ISF would take care of it."

Theodore thought he detected a note of hurt pride in Ninyu's voice. "The generals are simple military men. They've little faith in the agents of the ISF and believe commando raids should be left to their own specialists, such as the Draconis Elite Strike Teams and professionals like the nekogami. They would not have believed that I had arranged for a DEST attack without alerting the Coordinator or the Warlord. Since no one really knows how and where to contact the nekogami, I thought they might believe I had somehow gotten access to them."

Ninyu shook his head. "Using the nekogami's name without their permission was a bad idea. One of the bigger clans like the *Kageyoru* or the *Dofheicthe* would have been a better choice. They may not be as good as the nekogami, but they aren't quite so fanatically possessive of their reputation.

You could have gotten almost as good an effect without angering the Cats."

"I'll be more circumspect in the future."

Tapping a finger on the mask in Theodore's hands, Ninyu said, "You'd better be."

35

"**Y**ou bastard! How could you sit here and listen to me prattle on about honor and agree with me when you were planning such treachery?"

Enraged at the news he had just received, Theodore swept the visiphone across the taboret. The comm device smashed into the fine crystal decanters and took them crashing to the hard marble floor. Even before the shards of crystal bottles and ancient ceramic *sake* bowls landed, Theodore had drawn his sidearm. Driven by fury and frustration, he leveled it at the man kneeling in the center of the room.

Duke Frederick Steiner, ankles manacled and left arm still linked to the hobble by a short length of chain, stiffened. Rising as erectly as possible under the circumstances, he lifted his chin and met Theodore's gaze defiantly.

"I have no idea what you're talking about," he said calmly. The Duke's eyes never wavered to the pistol whose single, black-eyed stare was directed between the Lyran's blue eyes. Theodore could not help but admire such cool acceptance of the death before him.

The Duke's serenity touched Theodore despite his rage. Perhaps Frederick Steiner was, indeed, a true warrior. Perhaps he did not know. Ever since the Duke had landed at the head of a Steiner raiding force to cripple Theodore's invasion plans by destroying his carefully hoarded supplies,

Frederick Steiner had conducted himself well. He had fought fairly and with great courage, and nearly led his single regiment of BattleMechs to victory against the three Kurita 'Mech units already onplanet. The fervor he had inspired in his men was a testament to his leadership.

Unable to sense a hint of treachery in the man before him, Theodore banked his anger. The Duke had to be a dupe of his cousin and ruler, Katrina Steiner, Archon of the Lyran Commonwealth.

"No. *You* would not have resorted to such trickery," Theodore said, speaking his conclusion aloud. "Your cousin sent Loki agents to cripple the JumpShips of my fleet. Four have blown helium tanks, two have had their solar recharging exchangers destroyed, and the last has lost its station-keeping engine. That one is currently falling toward the sixth planet, though other ships should be able to stabilize its orbit." Theodore's voice rose in anger as he described the damage done by the Steiner saboteurs. "What you fail to do in honorable combat, *she* accomplishes by trickery."

"Get used to it, Theodore. It is the way of things. Politicians will forever betray warriors because what we observe as the conventions of war they exploit as our weakness," Frederick said with a smile.

Theodore's anger flared again, the Duke's smile enraging him. Frederick's acceptance of such an intolerable condition was disgusting, unbecoming. How dare he be so smug while Theodore's dreams to save the Combine turned to smoke around him? His finger tightened on the trigger.

Through the walls of his anger, Theodore sensed satisfaction and a feeling of completion coming from Frederick. Despite all that had happened to him, this man was ready to die to see his state continue.

As much as Theodore wanted to lash out because of the destruction of his own ambitions, his dreams for *his* own state, Theodore knew that this was not right. This man was not responsible for the dishonorable deceits of his ruler. Frederick was an honorable warrior, and Theodore could not shoot down such a samurai while he knelt in chains.

Theodore's finger had been increasing its pressure on the Nambu's trigger while he struggled with his thoughts. Honor overcame rage, but only in time for Theodore to redirect his aim. The Nambu boomed, obscenely loud within the confines of the room.

The slug slammed Frederick in the side of the head. The Duke jerked backward, toppling to the floor. His free hand pawed feebly at his wound, smearing the blood. Then, with a sudden shiver, the Duke went limp.

Theodore took a half-step forward, afraid his decision to spare Frederick had been too late. Blood gushed from the Lyran's fingers to foul the elaborate pattern of the carpet where he lay. Theodore let out a sigh when he saw that Frederick still breathed.

Guards exploded into the room. Eyes wide and weapons ready, they searched for any danger to the Prince. Reassured by Theodore's ready weapon and obviously uninjured condition, they subsided into cautious watchfulness. Three slung their weapons in preparation for removing the Lyran. Their manner indicated that they assumed Frederick to be dead. Theodore halted them with a raised hand.

"Send for the Brotherhood physician." He holstered his pistol. When the confused guards were slow to respond, he snapped, "Quickly!"

Two guards collided in the doorway in their haste to do his bidding.

The doctor arrived to find Theodore attempting to stanch the flow of blood. Surrendering his patient to the expert, Theodore stood back and watched. After a few minutes, the doctor stood up. "There is no more that I can do here," he announced blandly. "He must be taken to the infirmary."

"See to it," Theodore ordered sharply, pointing to a pair of guards. He turned to the physician, who flinched back from him. Feeling the tightness of his facial muscles, Theodore realized how grim must be his countenance to make the other man react so. "Your prognosis, Doctor-*san*."

"The man should live," the physician began tentatively. "Though he might not wish to. I am not sure how much damage there is to the brain. There is only so much that I can do."

"I understand. *Domo arigato*, Doctor-*san*."

The physician bowed and left the room hurriedly. The guards, sensing Theodore's mood, followed him out. "An eye," Theodore mused aloud to the empty room. He remembered a snatch of a Germanic legend in which the deity Wotan had traded an eye for wisdom. An odd trade, eyesight for insight.

"I shall see that you are treated well while you are in

Kurita hands, Frederick Steiner," Theodore vowed. "Though I have closed one of yours, you have opened my eyes and I am grateful.

"You have pointed out what I have chosen to ignore for far too long. Being a simple warrior, even a *buso-senshi,* is not enough. Likewise, it is insufficient to be a good field commander. I am the heir to my clan and to the Draconis Combine. I must be more than an ordinary samurai.

"For the honor of my clan and for my own honor, I swear to become all that I must. I will do whatever is required. The Dragon must triumph!"

BOOK 2

Tenacity

36

"**C**ousin!" Theodore called as he rose from his cross-legged seat on the greensward. Even where he stood within the shadow of the trees, Constance Kurita could see the pleasure on his face. His mood was far different from the one that had ruled him the last time they'd met together. That had been the day Takashi banished his son to the Legion of Vega.

She was as happy as her cousin. It was too long since they'd been able to enjoy each other's company. But Constance was conscious of her dignity as head of the Order of the Five Pillars, and she maintained her steady pace. Showing haste to meet Theodore would set a poor example for the half-dozen Adepts who accompanied her. Once, she would also have been concerned at how smoothly she walked over the undulating ground of the Kanzijankin Reserve. Today she glided comfortably, her skirts smooth and undisturbed by her step. Her saffron kimono was set off by the red robes of the *jukurensha* like a goldfinch among cardinals.

Drawing nearer, Constance was surprised to see the scar that ran from Theodore's central forehead down to the outer edge of his left eyebrow. He had not mentioned it in his letters, nor had Tomoe spoken of it during her short debriefings at the hidden villa where trusted Pillarines oversaw the upbringing of Hohiro and Omi. The scar marked him as a mature warrior, even more than the Katana Cluster he had been awarded in 3028. Nor was the scar the only mark the war had left on him. She noted his thinness. Any trace of fat had long ago surrendered to the rigors of the field. While his increased bodily strength was easily visible, her practiced eye also noted something more intangible in his stance. Gone was the cockiness and brash arrogance of youth, replaced by an assurance of strength and confidence of position.

Seeing Theodore now, she had no doubt that he was a samurai, and a strong one. She wondered how Takashi could have doubted the reports that his son had destroyed so many enemy 'Mechs. The Combine had needed a hero in those dark days of the Steiner offensive when so many planets were threatened by the invading forces. Lost in his obsession with Wolf's Dragoons, the Coordinator had approved the award, but he had confided to Constance that he was sure the numbers were inflated by toadies hoping to flatter Takashi's own vanity. Takashi had left the Katana Cluster awards ceremony to Warlord Cherenkoff of Dieron. He had refused to see the son who had for months communicated with his father only through the routine battle reports of a field commander to the Coordinator. Takashi's actions, or rather his lack of them, had only fueled the bad feeling between them. Father and son had not seen one another since the confrontation on Luthien almost five years ago.

Since that painful day, the relationship between Takashi and Theodore had remained static. Not so the universe around them. Even before the war broke out, a series of events had occurred to plunge the Combine into turmoil. Warlord Samsonov of the Galedon District had bungled the attempt to retain Wolf's Dragoons, and had failed even more miserably to execute the contingency plan that called for the Dragoons' destruction. The result was that several fine DCMS formations were mauled or destroyed in battles with the mercenaries as they escaped to Davion space. Enraged, the Coordinator had ordered Samsonov's execution. The cowardly Samsonov had bolted for the Periphery, taking officers and men from his Fifth Galedon Regulars with him. The ISF had managed to hide the disgrace from the news media, promulgating a story of Samsonov's assassination by a member of Wolf's Dragoons and the *seppuku* of the Warlord's inner circle of officers who had been shamed by their failures. Constance believed that even the frightfully efficient intelligence apparatus of House Davion had been taken in by the tale.

To replace the missing Samsonov in Galedon, Takashi had transferred Warlord Kester Hsiun Chi from Pesht. That competent officer had found it difficult to restrain his new district's warriors from pursuing a blood feud against Wolf's Dragoons. The war-within-a-war against those mercenaries had crippled efforts along that section of the Davion front until Chi finally managed to assert himself and coordinate efforts with Warlord Shotugama in the neighboring Benjamin District. Despite that, the Combine forces made little headway. Not even Takashi's waking from his dream of revenge and taking direct interest in the Davion front had been enough. There were few successes.

In what Constance believed to be an error in judgment, Takashi had filled the gap in the quiet Pesht District by naming her father, Marcus Kurita, its Warlord. Certainly, Takashi could not afford to have the ambitious Marcus waiting for an opportunity to strike at the Coordinator's back, but making him a Warlord again was dangerous. Yet the move had taken Marcus from close proximity to the Coordinator's person, and intrigue on Luthien had shown a dramatic decrease since his transfer to Pesht. Knowing that units of Pesht Regulars had gone to aid the fighting in the Rasalhague District worried Constance. Rasalhague had been her father's old power base.

The removal of Marcus as head of the Otomo bodyguards had rendered moot the putative cause of Theodore's exile. The way should have been clear for him to step into the traditional post of Heir-Designate. But then the war had begun, and Takashi breveted a little-known *Tai-sa*, intensely loyal to the Coordinator but a cipher in imperial politics, to the office. There had been no word from Theodore on the issue. He had no time to worry about family quarrels and empty honors.

That would change soon. As would so very much else.

Signaling her monks to remain at the edge of the trees, Constance continued on alone to where Theodore stood waiting. They exchanged bows.

"What is the news that you could not send by messenger?" he asked.

"The war is over," she stated simply.

Theodore froze, lids shuttering his eyes to a narrow, suspicious glare, but Constance ignored it. "My agents on Tharkad report that Archon Steiner has called off the Commonwealth's offensive," she went on calmly. "She plans to consolidate her gains and concentrate reserves on contested worlds. The DCMS's counterattacks have proven too strong for the Lyrans. All indications are that she has advised her Davion allies to do likewise."

"This is unexpected news." Theodore's voice was carefully neutral. He turned half-away, fingering the edge of his battle jacket in a gesture that Constance knew well from media footage of the warrior in the field. "Your Order has provided me with invaluable intelligence throughout the last six years. Often your assessment was more reliable than the ISF's. Don't think me ungrateful or that I doubt your Order's abilities, Constance, but can you be sure? There's been no hint on the front and no comparable reports from the ISF. The Coordinator's order to cease our own offensive activities should have strengthened the enemy's resolve."

"My sources are impeccable."

"So ka."

"The river of Steiner resources runs deep, Cousin, but the pool of their resolve is shallow," Constance said. "Their Davion allies are made of sterner stuff, but they lack the resources, and the ComStar Interdiction has crippled their economy. The alliance between the two Houses is still young; they are not unified. Like us, they have been stretched to the breaking point. They are incapable of further offensive action."

"What more do they need to take?" Theodore asked incredulously. "The Lyran armed forces now garrison more than fifty of our worlds. My Operation Contagion was blunted by treachery, and we have gained but two of their planets. So far, we have not done well. But I was so close . . . most of the units along the front were taking orders from me. Even Warlord Sorenson acknowledged my command.

"We had hope of prevailing against the Lyrans, at least. Against Davion, the Dragon seems impotent. Cherenkoff still squats in his bunker awaiting a mythical Davion attack while he mounts 'major assaults' that are little more than raids. Shotugama and Chi have been active, but we have gained little—a few insignificant rimward worlds and the recapture of the systems in the Galtor Thumb. Since my diligent father took command there, we have had nothing more than increased casualties all along that border. With Hanse Davion focused on the Liao offensive, we should have been able to do much more. And I *could* have done more, if allowed to." Theodore shook his head ruefully.

"Despite their propaganda about Tikonov and St. Ives becoming independent states, Davion now rules most of Liao space. Hanse Davion has gotten most of what he wanted. The Capellan Confederation is crippled, ready for Davion's coup de grace. The political balance has taken a drastic shift. With Liao out of the equation, Hanse Davion is one step closer to becoming First Lord of the Inner Sphere."

"Closer he may be," Constance agreed, "but even the mighty war machine of the Federated Suns is not unlimited. It grinds to a halt, its communication and transport capabilities stretched beyond usefulness."

"We face only a temporary lull," Theodore warned. "I expect that it'll be longer than that of last spring, but hostilities haven't ended, despite the sanctimonious words of the Steiner and Davion rulers. Hanse Davion has unveiled his true intent to secure rulership of the Inner Sphere for himself and his descendants. The Fox will be looking for us next. As soon as he is able to move, he will be at our throat. He will harness his new gains to his purpose and recover enough of his losses—in about five years, I'd say. He won't wait longer, because he will fear our own recovery."

Constance flinched at the fire in Theodore's eyes.

"How can you be so sure?"

Theodore smiled, a sudden flash of light in the darkness of his intensity. "Now *you* question *my* veracity. I'm as sure as any commander can be without being inside his opponent's head. I read his mind and will in his actions, and I discern his intent behind the words he speaks. I learn what he teaches by example. But most important, I am not blinded by my obsessions." Theodore clasped his hands behind his back and looked up into the sky. "I am not the only one who sees the Fox's greedy designs. Many others are concerned as well."

"You mean ComStar?"

"So you know that I have received a courier from the new Precentor," Theodore commented, raising an eyebrow in mock surprise.

"Only that a messenger arrived," Constance admitted. It

was best not to give Theodore unwarranted expectations of the intelligence-gathering capability of the O5P. "I have no knowledge of the message."

"Primus Myndo Waterly wishes to meet with me."

This was startling news. ComStar always professed neutrality in the affairs of the Inner Sphere. Yet ComStar agents had contacted Theodore eight months ago, warning him that they were about to interdict House Davion's interstellar communications. After discussing the news with Constance, he had decided to pass the information on to Subhash Indrahar in the hopes that the Coordinator would make better use of it if he believed the warning had come through the ISF. Though ComStar had asked for nothing at the time, Constance's instincts had told her that the followers of Blake would one day expect something in return for their timely revelation.

"Do you think that ComStar wishes payment for their warning about the interdiction of Davion?" she asked. "Or do they want you involved in peace negotiations?"

"Both," he replied. "But I think there's more to their agenda. They sent Waterly's replacement as Precentor Dieron, Sharilar Mori, as their messenger. A member of the First Circuit governing board is too high a functionary to serve as a mere courier."

Constance arched her brows at the messenger's name. That did put a different cast on the situation. Theodore was certainly correct in his assessment that ComStar had a very serious interest in the matters at hand. The new leadership of ComStar seemed to wish a larger, more active role for their organization. They would have to be watched closely.

"ComStar appears to be moving out of the shadows," she commented.

"It'll make little difference. They're weak, weaker than they would have us believe. Their communications interdiction wasn't enough to stop the Davion warmongers. The Federated Suns and their Steiner lackeys continued with their war of conquest."

"The alliance did have its 'pony express,'" Constance reminded him.

"Such a chain of JumpShips is very expensive, and too limited in the planets it can reach. By itself, it wouldn't have been enough to provide the communications needed by such a far-reaching military operation. They must have had *other* methods of communication."

"Do you mean the black boxes your Kowalski has been studying?"

"Kowalski-*san* is sure they are communications devices."

Theodore looked away and up into the cloudless sky. "We must learn the secret of the black boxes and duplicate them. I wish you to lend some of your Order's technicians to the task."

"That will not please ComStar. It threatens their monopoly."

"It is already threatened by the waning of their philosophical influence. Their order's position and prestige have been steadily weakening in the Federated Suns. Given that, I think that an Inner Sphere unified under the Davions sun-and-sword will disturb ComStar more than the Combine's access to a limited interstellar communications ability. We'll need that technology and more if the Combine is to weather the storm that is to come."

"Rest assured of the support of the Order of the Five Pillars. The Draconis Combine must remain strong."

Theodore's dark brows arched over suddenly widened eyes. "From anyone else, I might take that as an incitement to overthrow the Coordinator."

Frightened by his perception, Constance hastened to cover herself. She laughed lightly. "From another, it might be so. But I am the Keeper of the House Honor, and Kurita's spiritual well-being is in my hands. Despite Takashi-*sama*'s recent . . . ah . . . excesses, we must not divide the clan. Civil war at this time would destroy the Combine."

"Indeed it would. But you have not denied that the Coordinator should be replaced."

Constance was taken aback. Over the years, she had learned to perceive the hidden intents underlying courtly speech. In the chaos of the war, Theodore must have had his own revelation. This was not the young man who had blustered before his father. Theodore had, indeed, grown in more than body.

"You have done much to save the body of the Dragon," she said, still trusting to courtly speech. "Now you must fight to save its heart."

"*So ka,*" Theodore said with a nod. "Though it cost me my soul, that is my intent."

37

Izumi Shoin, Shandabbar, Awano
Benjamin Military District, Draconis Combine
10 January 3030

Moonslight flooded the courtyard of the monastery with harsh, cold brightness. Hoarfrost sparkled from the metal roof decoration and the gilding of the great arches. Alone and stately on its platform in the center of the yard, the great temple bell hung in its swath of glittering ice crystals.

Dechan Fraser's breath expelled in a steamy huff of surprise as his companion strode out into the open yard. Hours of slinking through the city and surrounding suburbs on their way to the monastery, and now the armored man just walked out into the open as though he owned the fief. Dechan shook his head in wonderment, and followed. From past experience, he knew that his companion sensed somehow when there were no watchers to mark his passage.

They headed for a darkened building, then turned to walk along its length. The armored man stopped and tilted his head toward one door, confirming Dechan's own count—this was the one they wanted.

Dechan nodded and stepped forward to rap on the rough plank door. After a moment, he heard a soft rustling inside. Another moment, and the door creaked open to reveal a woman in a nightrobe. Her head was shaven bare in traditional Buddhist fashion.

"*Jokan* Tomiko Tetsuhara?" he inquired.

Her eyes flicked over him. Dechan was acutely aware of

his scruffy appearance. He stood rigid, as though under inspection by a full *Tai-sa*, wishing he could hide the ragged, dark patches where once the proud insignia of Wolf's Dragoons had been. A brief frown crossed the woman's face as her bright eyes released him and shifted to the man at his side.

If I fail to meet her standards, Dechan thought, *how can he pass?* Dechan made his own inspection of the man standing quietly at his side. His stance was relaxed, barely betraying the weight of the metal case he held in his left hand. He wore a full helmet, which concealed his features. Rigid plates of body armor, pitted and scuffed with long abuse, and bulky vambraces of arcane shape distorted his body's outline. The massive shoulder-arm slung on his left side made the holstered pair of pistols, and Dechan's own sidearm for that matter, look like the weapons of a child. *No, not someone I'd open my door to in the middle of the night,* Dechan concluded.

"I am Anshin," the nun said softly with a graceful bow, as though to superiors. "I am no longer Tomiko Tetsuhara. My lord Minobu has joined his ancestors."

She stood expectantly. Dechan knew she was waiting for them to introduce themselves. That, he decided, he would leave to his companion. The trip was a bad idea and he had argued so from the start, but he had failed to dissuade his comrade.

The armored man stood silent under the gaze of the nun.

"I know you," she said. "You are . . ."

"I, too, am no longer who I once was," the armored man said, cutting her off. The helmet made his voice harsh, almost guttural, as the words passed through the external speaker. "I bring a gift."

The refrigerator unit whirred softly on the box he raised. With his free hand, he released the catch on the front panel. Soft green light spilled from the box as it opened. Lying within, ghastly in the bilious glow, was a severed head, an expression of profound surprise frozen on its features.

"This is the head of Grieg Samsonov, one of those who conspired to trap your husband," the armored man explained. "It was my task to acquire it."

"I do not want it!" The nun shrank back into the shadows of her cell. Her serenity shattered, her voice quavered.

"Send it to his father. The old man will appreciate the sentiment."

The armored man knelt to refasten the box. As the green light vanished, the nun spoke again with a hint of her former serenity.

"I have sought my own peace here, and found it in some measure. Please do not disturb it further."

"As you wish."

Dechan's companion executed an awkward bow. Dechan bowed, too, but his awkwardness came from the situation and his lack of practice rather than the armor that encumbered his fellow. The two men walked slowly back across the courtyard. As they did, Dechan heard the nun's door close quietly. The wooden barrier did little to muffle the sound of her sobbing.

38

Peace Park, Newbury, Dieron
Dieron Military District, Draconis Combine
30 September 3030

Theodore watched the woman in the gray cloak turn onto the path that led to the cul-de-sac where he sat. A flash of light from the trees signaled that she had entered the park alone. He nodded his receipt of the message to Fuhito Tetsuhara, hidden among the shadowed boles, before standing to greet the woman.

"*Ohayo,* Precentor."

"Good morning to you, Prince Theodore. Please ignore my rank and call me Sharilar."

"You are kind to allow me such familiarity." *And prudent, too, to be concerned that someone might overhear your title,* Theodore observed silently. "Allow me to extend the same offer. Such familiarity was normal among soldiers on the frontlines in the recent unpleasantness, and I have learned the virtue of dispensing with formalities when necessary. Please call me Theodore."

He indicated the nearest in a row of ferrocrete benches. While she sat down, he moved to the other side of the gray mushroom of a table, and took a seat. The table's surface was inlaid with a red-and-black checkerboard of duraplast. Theodore produced a flat case from beneath his long overcoat. He opened it to reveal the ivory tokens within, each painted with the calligraphic symbol for its name. "A game of *shogi* while we wait for your mistress?"

Sharilar shook her head, and Theodore shrugged, returning the case to concealment.

"Perhaps, then, you would care to enlighten me as to your mistress's concern."

Sharilar fidgeted and glanced about warily, but Theodore read her action as a show. He could feel that, underneath, she was not at all nervous. *Why does she wish me to think so?*

He suddenly wished for the advice of old Tetsuhara-*sensei*. He was wise in the ways of people and could discern their true feelings, often before they were sure themselves. *Sensei*'s control of his *hara* was more than enough for such a minor feat. But *sensei*'s voice was silent, as it had been since the capture of Cochus in '28. His other teachers were equally silent.

When Theodore had complained of their absence to Tomoe, she told him flatly that he didn't need them anymore, that he had outgrown them. When his resolve was strong, he believed her. But most days, he knew that couldn't be so. He didn't feel as assured as he acted. He felt out of his depth, in need of guidance, but had no one to lean on but himself.

People passed the row of benches and game tables. Intent on themselves or their business, they paid scant attention to the couple speaking quietly to one another across the gray mushroom. After a few minutes, a woman wearing a caped overcoat much like Theodore's took the seat next to him.

"Ninyu says she's entered the park," Tomoe said. Her words were for Theodore, but her eyes were fixed on Sharilar.

The ComStar Precentor returned her stare. *She-wolves,* Theodore thought. *They are measuring each other, assessing their positions in the pack. Friend or enemy?* Theodore found himself wondering if ComStar emissaries would be friends or enemies.

A woman strolled into sight. She was dressed in elegant but understated clothes, their muted colors appropriate to the drab morning. Nothing the woman wore betrayed her rank or origin; she might have been any well-off matron taking a morning constitutional through the park. As she drew nearer, Theodore realized that she could only be Myndo Waterly, Primus of ComStar.

All the participants in the clandestine meeting had concealed their identities. Of them, only Theodore showed any symbols of affiliation. A large disk held his overcoat closed just over his solar plexus. The plate showed the Kurita Dragon, though an observer might assume it was merely a badge of allegiance, feigned or true, to the Draconis Combine. Tomoe's similar disk was blank.

Greetings were brisk and swiftly completed. All four sat down, to outward appearances merely a group of chance-met friends. But nothing had been left to chance in arranging the meeting. They might all seem friendly at the moment, but for how long?

Apparently glimpsing worry in Theodore's expression, Myndo said, "I assure you that no one will overhear our discussion, Prince Theodore. We of ComStar have certain technological resources."

"A bold assertion, Primus," Theodore challenged.

Myndo bristled. "Fact, Prince," she stated firmly, showing none of the concern about eavesdropping that Sharilar had displayed earlier. Indeed, Theodore noted that the Precentor herself looked more relaxed now.

"No hostility intended, Primus," Theodore said in a conciliatory tone. To himself, he chuckled. *I have learned a few tricks from my black-clad friend, Ninyu. Your ruffled feathers direct your attention to me and away from Tomoe. We shall see if your security is as strong as you say. If we can penetrate it, others may as well.* "All know that ComStar strives to keep lit the flame of the old knowledge."

"It is a struggle," Myndo conceded. Theodore sensed that she was still angry, though he could not tell whether it was because of his lack of faith in ComStar's capabilities or the light tone he had used in quoting the ComStar maxim. He was impressed that her voice gave no hint of anger, but that should be no surprise. Myndo Waterly had been a citizen of the Combine before she joined ComStar. Anyone who had progressed so rapidly must obviously be shrewd in many of the ways of the Dragon.

"The Draconis Combine is in serious danger," Myndo said bluntly.

"That's so." Theodore saw little point in denying it. He was sure Myndo had access to all the communiques that passed through ComStar's hands. From such a trove of data, any dolt would be able to tell what dangers the Combine faced. "I'm not in need of an oracle on this matter."

"I do not pretend to be one. ComStar does not wish to see the Draconis Combine fall."

Theodore could almost hear the words "at this time" that the Primus must have appended silently to her statement. "And what of your neutrality in political matters?"

"We have no wish to see Hanse Davion rule the Inner Sphere, either, for he is no friend to our Order."

"So you feel threatened as well."

"There is some truth in what you say," Myndo conceded. *Much,* thought Theodore. *If only I knew exactly what you perceived to be the real threat.* Aloud, he said, "You wanted this meeting for a purpose. May we get to that?"

"Very well." Myndo leaned forward across the table. "We of ComStar are well aware of the Combine's military and industrial capabilities at this time. We know that you cannot raise and train a sufficiently powerful force before the Steiner-Davion alliance turns on you.

"We offer you a solution. In doing so, we trust you with a confidence and rely on your honor to keep it. Through the years, we have trained and established a force of arms. Originally, these warriors were intended to defend our blessed Terra from aggression by treacherous lords, a secret last line of defense. We have come to see the necessity in these dark days of protecting our own interests and facilities throughout the Inner Sphere. As you know, we have already secured the right to garrison our compounds on all planets in Davion space. We also maintain substantial numbers of mercenaries under contract, both MechWarriors and conventional forces.

"Under the guise of manning our stations in the Combine, we propose to provide a military force that you may use to repel any invasion against the sovereign territory of the Draconis Combine. Such forces would come equipped with considerable stores of vehicles and supplies. We can also provide, at substantially reduced rates, the contracts of a large number of mercenary units.

"Also, in the event of another outbreak of war, we shall provide interstellar communications to the Combine at reduced rates. Good communications have done more to win wars throughout history than well-armed battalions.

"You cannot afford to refuse our offer."

Theodore hid his surprise behind what he hoped was an interested and thoughtful expression. The Primus was offering what he needed to save the Combine—an army. But who would really control those forces? Only a fool would believe that ComStar would totally relinquish control. The troops would be an outsider's army coiling within the Dragon's bosom. ComStar offered a promise of salvation, but posed a definite threat to the Combine's safety. They were too much of an enigma to be trusted. They had already gotten an agreement to place similar troops in the Federated Suns. Had they made the same offer of defensive aid to Hanse Davion? There was still much to learn. There had to be a catch. "How do I know I cannot *afford* to refuse your offer? I have not heard the price."

Myndo sat back, measuring Theodore with her gaze. "We wish to see the District of Rasalhague as a free and independent state. We expect you to support the Tyr movement in their bid for independence."

"That would cut valuable worlds from the Combine."

Myndo scoffed. "Most of the systems are already in Steiner's grip, even though peace negotiations are continuing. Do you expect to regain them at the table? The Lyrans have always been tight-fisted traders, with little inclination to give up what they already hold.

"Your support, even if only tacit, will encourage the Tyr movement. They will cry as loudly to be free of the Lyran Commonwealth as they will to be quit of the Draconis Combine if they see a chance for full independence. Besides, Rasalhague has ever been a thorn in the Dragon's side, draining resources better spent elsewhere. Without Rasalhague to defend, you would free up more forces to concentrate against your opponents. You would also have a buffer zone extending over half of your pre-war border with the Lyrans.

"You are very aware of strong separatist sentiments in the Isle of Skye. We are assured that they would take Rasalhague's freedom as a sign. Their leaders could easily decide it was time to declare independence from the Lyran Commonwealth. Think about that."

Theodore knew too well what that could mean. Driving Skye from the bosom of House Steiner had been one of the goals of his aborted Operation Contagion. During Frederick Steiner's final days on Dromini VI, he had been most talkative about the separatist movement, confirming Theodore's evaluation. If Skye went independent, Davion would be cut off from Steiner, and the Federated Commonwealth would die aborning. And House Steiner would lose a large portion of the industrial heartland upon which their economy depended. With two isolationist border states between the Combine and the Commonwealth, that entire border would be secure.

"You could turn all of your attention to Hanse Davion," Myndo prompted.

Theodore found that thought very seductive. He could succeed where Takashi had failed. Once Davion was ... Wait! He suddenly realized what was wrong with the Primus's offer. "Why haven't you gone to my father?"

Myndo looked at him as though the question were foolish. "We have. The Coordinator was blind to the benefits of mutual interest."

"But I don't have the power to do as you wish."

"ComStar does not live in the past, or even the present. We are the future, and thus know much of what is to come. When the time is right, you will have the power."

Theodore did not bother to hide his skepticism. "Mystic prognostication, Primus?"

"If I thought you would believe it, I would say yes. You are too well-informed for that. We have learned that you are soon to be named *Gunji-no-Kanrei*. The post of Deputy for Military Affairs could be quite powerful. You will oversee the reshaping of the Draconis Combine's military. Some of that might could come from unconventional sources."

"*So ka.* And I am to turn a blind eye to Rasalhague, ignore reports of secessionist movements, redirect military strength, and in general make your political play easier."

"You have excellent vision."

Vision enough to see that I have no wish to be your pawn, Primus, Theodore thought. He ran his fingers along the dragon image graven on his coat plate. The Combine needed the strength ComStar offered, but the necessity for outside help made him burn with shame. If there were a way to minimize the influence, and threat, of ComStar, he would find it.

"You've given me much to think about, Primus."

Myndo smiled in satisfaction. "Do not think too long, Prince. The stars move onward in their course."

39

Deber City, Benjamin
Benjamin Military District, Draconis Combine
8 October 3030

From his vantage point across the busy street, Dechan Fraser watched the three men walk in jovial companionship. Sheltering under the roof of a noodle shop, he waited until they turned down a side street. Dechan signaled Jenette Rand with a tug of his cap as he left his stool and walked swiftly to the corner. A glance around told him that the targets were proceeding unaware. He breathed his relief to see the lane empty of innocent traffic. Behind him, a sudden ruckus drew the attention of the crowds in the street.

Dechan slid around the corner just as the trio stopped before an unmarked door inset in a shabby ferrocrete structure. As they hesitated, confirming the address scribbled faintly on the wall, an armored figure stepped from the shadowed alley at the building's side. Wan sunlight glinted on the over-size muzzle of the weapon he held ready.

The three were quick to react. The tallest, already in motion before the gunman cleared the alley, stepped sideways. The short and stocky one at the back of the group reached beneath his overcoat, clearly going for a weapon. The third, a redhead, cut across in front of the first. His arm moved in a blur as he threw something and shouted, "The Bounty Hunter!" Any further words were drowned out by the brief banshee wail of the armored man's Ceres Arms Crowd-buster.

The three dark-clad Kuritans crumpled to the refuse-strewn pavement.

Dechan moved in, rapidly stripping the bodies of weapons. Swords and pistols clattered into an untidy pile. The armored man plucked a dull black throwing knife from his ballistic cloth jumpsuit before joining his partner in searching the bodies. Dechan knew the weapon was likely to be poisoned.

He completed his search of the redhead. "This one doesn't have the papers."

His partner acknowledged the comment with a nod, intent on getting the stocky Kuritan's body to roll over. Dechan busied himself with the tall one, hoping that Jenette's diversion would keep the crowd away from their back-alley business long enough for them to get clear.

"Panati." The armored man's tone was flat and final, making the name into a sentence of death. "You will not escape this time."

Dechan looked up in shock. It seemed impossible that they had at last brought down a long-sought quarry. His partner seemed reluctant to take action. *Very well, my friend,* Dechan approved silently. *Savor your good fortune.* He turned back to his task. Dechan's surprise at his companion's discovery was replaced by awe as he recognized the man he himself was searching. "Unity!"

He straightened from his crouch, dropping the Kuritan's arm. As the fallen man's hand hit the pavement, a groan escaped his lips. Dechan took two steps back and bumped into his armored companion, who stood staring at the man he had identified as Panati.

"Forget your assassin. We've bagged Theodore Kurita!"

The armored man elbowed Dechan away and stepped over to confirm the identification.

"What a break!" Dechan exclaimed. "We've got Takashi's son in our hands. You can get your revenge against Kurita now."

"No."

Dechan was surprised by the monosyllabic answer. "I thought you believed that the whole family was responsible for the actions of one member."

"It is true that the group is responsible for the actions of an individual member."

"Then we can kill this one and finish it now. A Kurita life

to fulfill your revenge. We won't have to risk our necks going after the Coordinator."

"It is not that simple. This is a vendetta. Only the responsible individuals are eligible targets."

A groan from the subject of their conversation brought it to a halt. The armored man's gun snapped down to cover the reviving Theodore as he rose unsteadily. Dechan moved to restrain the groggy Kuritan.

"He must have been screened from most of the charge by the redhead."

"You're scum, Bounty Hunter," Theodore croaked. "A murderer. You have no claim to vendetta."

"It is not my wish to kill you, Prince Theodore. The man Panati must die whether you surrender the papers or not."

"I have no idea what you are talking about. If you kill Panati-*san,* you will be hunted down like the dog you are."

"I have the right of vendetta to kill him," the armored man insisted.

"You have no such right. You're slime! A hired murderer!"

The armored man stood stock-still for a moment. Then he removed his left hand from the forward grip of his weapon and slid it up under his helmet. Dechan recognized the sound of the suit seals ripping open. In a smooth motion, the armored man lifted the helmet clear of his head and dropped it ringing to the pavement.

Dechan felt Theodore start as his partner's face was revealed. The armored man no longer had the fair regular features of his youth. A ragged scar ran up his left cheek, across the orbit, and disappeared beneath his raven hair, now slicked to his skull with sweat. The eye had been savaged by the vicious wound. Its milky white iris was a shocking contrast to the deep brown of his other eye.

"I am Michi Noketsuna," the armored man said. "Most of my past is of no consequence. For years, I served Minobu Tetsuhara as a staff officer. He was trapped into a situation from which there was no escape. I stood at his side in the *seppuku* forced upon him by his honor. Dishonorable men brought him to that end, and I swore that they would pay.

"I hunted the Warlord Samsonov who betrayed him on Misery. I wished also to hunt the Warlord's agents who arranged the events leading to that final betrayal.

"Regrettably, the principal agent of my lord's unnecessary death, Jerry Akuma, died on An Ting. But he was aided in his schemes by two men: Quinn and Panati, assassins who maimed and would have killed my lord in an effort to frame Wolf's Dragoons as traitors. The man holding you had the honor of causing the deaths of Akuma and Quinn. Panati, however, has eluded me until now. It was he who planted the bomb that crippled Tetsuhara-*sama,* and I require his death."

Michi fell silent. Time stretched, long enough that Dechan began to wonder if his partner had decided to conceal the last of his prey. Then Michi took a deep breath and continued.

"My vendetta has one more target: Takashi Kurita. He was the one who set into motion the plan to discredit the Dragoons. It was he who ordered Tetsuhara-*sama* to command the forces assigned to destroy the Dragoons. He knew that my lord had befriended Jaime Wolf, and that to face off with his friend on the battlefield would be intolerable. Had Tetsuhara-*sama* won that bitter battle on Misery and killed his friend as his duty required, he would have been shamed. Tetsuhara-*sama* knew that Jaime Wolf and his Dragoons were innocent of the heinous crimes laid to their name. There was no honor in bringing a friend, a man he considered closer than a brother, to ruin. Even so, he obeyed his orders as best he could.

"I need not elaborate on the penalty for a samurai who disobeys his lord. However the battle on Misery might have ended, Tetsuhara-*sama* was faced with *seppuku* as the only honorable solution."

"I apologize," Theodore said. "You have cause for vendetta. Panati is yours."

Michi bowed, then stepped over to the unconscious assassin. He cocked his wrist, and a blade slid from his vambrace to lock in place with a soft snick. Michi knelt by Panati and whispered, "The death I give you is too good for the cowardly murderer you are. You will not suffer pain, as you should, in payment for what you have caused."

He slid the razor edge into the soft tissues of the man's neck. The blade hesitated only an instant before slicing through the cartilage between two cervical vertebrae. Panati's head fell free from his body, and blood spurted out, befouling both corpse and pavement. Michi snapped his wrist, flicking the blood free from the shining steel. The weapon hissed back into its concealed sheath.

Dechan, absorbed in his partner's actions, was surprised by Theodore's sudden move. Almost as soon as he felt the Kuritan's hands upon him, he was flying through the air. Theodore snatched at the pile of weapons, grabbing the uppermost, a *katana*. The blade hissed free. Michi whirled, the muzzle of his Crowdbuster rising to cover the newly armed Theodore.

"Go no further, Noketsuna. I must oppose you."

Dechan struggled to his feet, pistol in hand. Unwilling to risk a shot past Michi, he waited for his partner to make a move.

"Do you believe that Takashi Kurita is innocent?" Michi asked the defiant Theodore.

"I don't know. But I must stand against you for my honor and for the sake of the Combine. I cannot allow you to go free so that you may attack the Coordinator."

"You have no chance against my weapon," Michi said quietly. "I can cut you down and walk away."

"I must attempt to stop you here if you insist on pursuing your vendetta at this time. If you walk away from here and leave me alive, I will hunt you down."

Michi stared up into the taller man's eyes. Neither moved for a full minute. Dechan shivered. He hated it when the malking Dracs went mystic.

Michi lowered his weapon, then slung it into carrying position on his left shoulder. He bowed, stiff and formal.

"I salute your resolution."

Theodore reversed his grip on the sword. He relinquished his right hand's grip and let his left arm fall to his side. The sword rested loosely in his hand, edge toward the sky. He returned the bow.

"The Combine cannot be deprived of the Coordinator at this time," Theodore insisted.

"I will stay my vendetta if you can prove that Takashi Kurita is innocent in this matter," Michi offered.

"That is impossible right now. I have other, more pressing business: the continued survival of the Draconis Combine."

"The Combine must survive," Michi agreed. "Allow me a day to discharge an obligation and I will aid you in your business."

Theodore nodded once. "I would be honored, Noketsuna-san."

Dechan scratched his head, bewildered at the sudden turn of events.

≡ **40** ≡

Dechan Fraser glanced over to the campfire near the DropShip where the crew and the Techs were finishing their evening meal. From the bursts of laughter and occasional snatches of speech, he knew they would soon fall into their habitual dice game. He turned back to stare at his own barely touched food.

The four BattleMechs that made up the Bounty Hunter's strike force stood silent sentry, arranged in a rough triangle. One apex was Vic Travers' tiger-striped *Orion*. At the second, the two smallest 'Mechs of the lance stood side by side, Jenette Rand's *Dervish* and Dechan's own *Shadow Hawk*, their dark-blue paint schemes blending into the night sky. The tallest of the four machines, the Bounty Hunter's bright green *Marauder*, made the last point. Between its deep, birdlike legs, the campfire burned, throwing its ruddy light onto their faces. Across the fire, Michi Noketsuna sat eating his supper, the Bounty Hunter's helmet resting upright at his feet.

"You were late getting back to camp. You been laying plans for what we do next?" Dechan asked.

Michi carefully set his plate on the fallen tree that served as his seat. "*We* do nothing. *I* go on alone."

"What?" Seated beside Dechan, Jenette was incredulous.

"My friends, you have no common cause with the

Draconis Combine. In fact, your own friends and families war with the Dragon. I, however, am still loyal to my homeland. In this matter, my feud with the Coordinator is unimportant. Though Takashi has forfeited my loyalty to his person by dishonorable behavior, I cannot let his faults and failures turn me from the Combine.

"Early this evening, I met and spoke again with Prince Theodore. What he told me of the dangers facing the Combine was chilling. He does not believe his father guilty in the matter of Minobu-*sama*'s death, but he can offer no proof at this time. He is sincere, an honorable man who seeks to save the Dragon from desperate straits. When the Combine is safe, he will see that justice is done.

"Right now, there is a great danger to the Combine, and all true samurai must come to his aid." Michi paused briefly, looking up at the stars. "I may be *ronin,* in the sense that I have no master, but I am still a loyal servant of the Dragon. When the Dragon is in need, I will stand to its defense. I must put aside my quest for vengeance until the realm is safe. When that day comes, I will kill Takashi Kurita with my own hand."

Dechan sat quietly through Michi's speech, trying to understand the complicated hierarchy of loyalties that ruled his friend. Though Dechan never wished to be tangled in as intricate a web of allegiances as bound a Kuritan, he had his own strong feelings about loyalties. In Wolf's Dragoons, it was much simpler. A man stood by his friends. "After all we've been through, you expect us to let you walk into the Dragon's den alone? Who's gonna watch your back?"

"I cannot ask it of you. The matter has become more complicated. Prince Theodore had informed me that the Coordinator was never scheduled to visit this planet. Therefore, the papers allegedly detailing his itinerary never existed. I believe that whoever was behind our now-deceased informant deliberately directed us at the Prince. Perhaps that person knew my true identity and expected me to kill any Kurita on sight. Perhaps not. Either way, the villain knew my target was the Coordinator."

"This is not your cause."

"It wasn't my cause on Milligan's World either," Dechan insisted. "I told you I'd see this through. You're not rid of me so easily."

"Or me, either," Jenette affirmed. Dechan showed his lady

the pride he felt with a smile. She slipped her hand into his and gave it a squeeze. "We can look after ourselves."

"You honor me beyond my due, my friends," Michi replied as he bowed.

Dechan felt awkward; formality never sat well with him. To cover himself, he turned to Travers. "What about you, Vic?"

Michi and Jenette turned expectant faces to their fourth companion. Travers swallowed, rubbing his hands nervously along the tops of his thighs. The bristly black hair on his arms stood out starkly against his pallid skin as he added to the accumulated grease on his coveralls. "It's not what I signed on for."

"I understand," Michi said, face expressionless. Dechan, however, frowned, and Jenette's look of disappointment seemed a mirror to his own. Awkward silence fell over the group, and they returned to their supper.

When Michi tossed his empty plate into the cook-pot and rose, Travers stood as well. He seemed troubled, embarrassed.

"Ah ... before you leave," Travers said, fishing a crumpled paper from his pocket. A small, enameled lapel pin speared the folded sheets together. "I have a name and a letter. It'll help."

"Yakuza?"

Travers nodded.

Michi held up his hand in refusal. "I have my own connections."

"Not with this gang. You'll need these," Travers insisted, thrusting the gift forward.

Dechan didn't believe that. Travers' contacts with the criminal underworld had been useful in the past, but now Michi was dealing with politics. Besides, Dechan had never liked dealing with that kind of people. He always came away feeling soiled.

Michi gave a sharp nod of sudden agreement and accepted the offered letter. *"Domo arigato."*

Unity! Dechan thought. What's gotten into this boy?

"I have a gift for you as well," Michi told Travers, pointing to the bright green *Marauder*. "Please take it. I will not be able to use it where I am going."

"I couldn't," Travers protested, shaking his head. His

stubble-bearded face was awash in confusion. "That's the Bounty Hunter's 'Mech, and you're the Bounty Hunter."

"No longer. I have worn the armor while it served me. It allowed me to safely reenter the Combine. Where I am going, the identity will be more of a hindrance," Michi said. He picked up the helmet and held it out to Travers. "You are the Bounty Hunter now."

"Take the 'Mech. Cellini can handle the *Orion*. I leave you the DropShip, the armor, and half of the war chest. I will need some of the money we have collected." Michi popped open a compartment on the side of the breastplate he wore. From its darkness, he removed a battered book. The solidograph on the volume's cover was scratched and scuffed. Papers, many stained and yellowed with age, and plastisheets of various colors jutted from the open sides, held in by a cord the color of dried blood. He tossed the packet to Travers. "The tradition is yours as well."

Travers caught the book and held it to his head as he bowed deeply to Michi, surprising Dechan with this show of etiquette.

Michi turned to Dechan and Jenette. "If you still wish to accompany me, we must leave within the hour."

41

Kanrei's Residence, Deber City, Benjamin
Benjamin Military District, Draconis Combine
15 January 3031

"Then you won't come along," Theodore said, hoping to end the fruitless discussion.

"*Iie.* I've told you too many times that I think this plan is foolish," Ninyu snapped. "The Combine doesn't need criminals in its army. Besides, I don't trust this adventurer, and you shouldn't, either."

Michi, leaning in the corner he had appropriated upon entering the room, stood silent under Ninyu's accusation.

"He was a loyal retainer of my brother," Fuhito objected, stepping in to defend the silent man.

Theodore let Fuhito speak. Perhaps his words would succeed where Theodore's had failed, persuading Ninyu to accept Michi as the newest addition to his inner circle, those he called his *shitenno.*

In ancient Japanese history, that name had been applied to the loyal companions of Kiso Yoshinaka, the husband of another Tomoe. Yoshinaka's wife had been the celebrated Tomoe Gozen, a female samurai like his own Tomoe. Giving his companions the same name as Yoshinaka's seemed apt. Theodore also had it on good authority that his use of the term bothered his father, who remembered the fate of Yoshinaka. Theodore, of course, had no intention of ending up the same way.

Ninyu dismissed Fuhito's argument with a slash of his

hand. "This fellow served your brother a long time ago. Noketsuna went rogue after Misery. He's a renegade who consorts with other renegades. He cannot be trusted."

"If, by renegades, you refer to Fraser and Rand, you are mistaken, Ninyu-*kun*," Tomoe said. "They voluntarily left Wolf's Dragoons to join Michi-*san* in seeking vengeance for Minobu Tetsuhara. Their loyalty to him has been exemplary."

"*Hai!*" Fuhito agreed forcefully.

Ninyu snorted his disgust as he turned to Theodore. "If you wish to be surrounded by the naive," he said, shrugging his shoulders to indicate that he refused to take responsibility for the results. "At least, don't give them any power. Keep them as advisors if you must, but don't follow them blindly. Abandon this renegade's plan to recruit soldiers from the yakuza. The yakuza are criminals, worthless scum who stand apart from our ordered society. They are untrustworthy. The Combine doesn't need soldiers who would disgrace their uniforms. If you need warriors, look to our ordinary citizens. When their belief in the Dragon is strong, they are more than good enough. If you think they are insufficiently capable, and that the Combine still needs manpower, draft ISF civilian agents. Their loyalty is beyond question."

"All the loyalty in the worlds is insufficient to stand up to a BattleMech and defeat it," Tomoe countered.

"She's right," Theodore agreed. "We need warriors, trained fighters. I believe we'll find many among the yakuza. Michi-*kun* has informed me that some gangs even maintain MechWarriors. We need that strength."

"Noketsuna again," Ninyu said through clenched teeth. He heaved himself up from his seat and leaned over the table to stare into Theodore's eyes. "You are blinded by your *bushido*, tricked by the illusion of nobility. Do you think he's some kind of noble paladin just because he kills people for revenge and calls it a vendetta of honor? Perhaps you think you are play-acting in some galactic version of *Chushingura*. Well, you know what happened to the forty-seven ronin. They died."

"Wasn't their greatest virtue supposed to be loyalty, Ninyu-*kun*?" Tomoe asked. Her voice was light in tone, deliberately innocent.

Ninyu straightened and glared at her. He let out his breath

through distended nostrils. His voice was brittle as he stomped to the door. "Go on then, be a fool. Go on to hell!"

The door slammed.

With stance and expression broadcasting his outrage at Ninyu's poor manners, Fuhito offered, "I'll bring him back, Theodore-*sama*."

"*Iie,*" Theodore said. "Let him go work it off."

"You are better off without him, *Tono*," Tomoe averred. "His attitude would be a hindrance to your efforts, making the issue of his skills irrelevant. I shall replace him."

"Always looking to get into the action, To-*chan*," Theodore said with a smile. He had no doubt her skills could replace those of his nekogami-trained friend. Their workouts left him with no doubt that she retained all her finesse, though she had borne him two children. But he needed something else from her now. She had valuable assets far beyond her dark-night talents.

"You know I have a greater need of you in the sunlight. While I am trying to gain these allies, someone must cover my absences and handle the day-to-day business. Someone must oversee the reconstruction plans and guide the development of the regiments as we rebuild."

"What about Asano and Earnst?" she protested. "Armstrong?"

"All good officers, but I trust no one as much as you to see that the old, wild attitudes do not corrupt the rebuilt army. Those you suggest are vital to our future, but they do not yet have the vision. Only you have the strength to guide my plans when I am elsewhere." Theodore reached across the table toward the hands she held tightly clenched before her. At the tentative touch of his fingers, her tension relaxed. He felt her surrender to his argument, submitting to necessity, though her heart wished otherwise. For all her teasing that he was unreasonably bound by *giri*, she, too, understood the iron call of duty.

"Trust Fuhito-*kun* before the others, though," he said. "He's matured into an excellent officer with a superior tactical sense. More important, he understands our goals and has a firm grasp of my intent." Theodore ignored the look of surprise that washed over Fuhito's features. "Dechan-*kun* and his lady Jenette will help you as well. You cannot trust them with everything, of course, but I believe you can rely on them to train soldiers. Their Dragoon experience will be invaluable.

"I cannot be in two places at once. While I search for new soldiers, someone must guide the old. I need you to do that, To-*chan*."

She nodded. He sensed the fear that she felt for him. That was understandable. He certainly wasn't blind to the danger. The criminal underworld of the Combine was a dangerous place, a world unto itself whose rules he didn't understand. From what Michi had told him, his position as Heir-Designate might not be sufficient armor. The yakuza, or some other underworld denizens, might be just as happy to see Theodore die as talk to him. But this was a job that only he could do, for only he had any hope of commanding allegiance from the outlaw yakuza. He wanted to hold Tomoe, to kiss away her fear and thereby lose his own. He could not. Even here among his closest friends, propriety forbade it.

Michi stirred. "Time to go," he announced.

42

Sound struck Theodore with almost physical force as Michi opened the door into the bar. The pounding, cardiac beat overwhelmed all noise from the milling inhabitants of the dim chamber, which was darker by far than the neon-strobed night of the street. Spotlit on platforms suspended by gossamer threads above the crowded floor, scantily clad dancers gyrated provocatively. Not until one of the women misstepped and nearly plunged from her platform did he realize that the dancers were not holographic projections, but were real. Of course. Live entertainers cost much less and had other capabilities no holo ever would.

Theodore started down the five steps to the main floor, following his companion. While Michi paused at the bottom to scan for a path through the milling bodies and crowded gambling tables, Theodore observed the grim-faced pair of rogues reflected in the mirror-like, metal wall just opposite where they stood. One was significantly taller than the other, but their garb was almost identical. They could have been any two of the thousands of restless soldiers who roamed the Combine, unwilling or unable to return to their homeworlds after their regiments were shattered in the recent war. No one would guess that these two were the Heir-Designate and a former officer of the Ryuken.

Michi's faded tan overcoat swathed his body from neck to

ankle. The caped shoulders flared out, widening his silhouette at chest level. The Kurita dragon dyed into the leather of the right shoulder padding was a pale serpent, almost invisible. The battered disk clasping the coat rode somewhat higher than on Theodore's, allowing an observer a clearer look at the distressed battle jacket and heavy sidearm belted on it. While Theodore carried his own two swords, Michi had a single, long sword slung on his back, the grip protruding over his left shoulder. The hilts of all three weapons had scuffed, nondescript fittings and braid.

Turning from their reflection, Theodore observed a woman weaving toward them through the crowd. Deftly avoiding or countering hands that snaked out to grope her or delay her passage, she was clearly used to receiving such attention. Michi stepped into her path, blocking Theodore's view of the woman's red-sheathed form. Unable to hear their conversation, Theodore was surprised to see Michi pull out a folded piece of paper. A large denomination C-bill was held to its underside. The woman smiled at Michi and took a step back. His offering vanished into the soft crevice between her breasts, which heaved visibly in the circular cutout of her dress. The woman waved a nonchalant hand toward the bar and turned away.

Michi nudged his companion with an elbow and tilted his head in the direction of the bar. Theodore nodded and followed willingly. Two stools emptied as they approached.

Michi slid onto one, pointed at the dirty cups already present, and held up a hand with the last three fingers extended. The paunchy ugly behind the bar nodded and poured two cups, holding them in one greasy paw until Michi slipped several C-bills into his other, outstretched hand. Theodore sat next to Michi and picked up his drink. His nose wrinkled at the foul stink of the booze, but he downed it, for the sake of his disguise.

They waited.

The bartender had just extracted the payment for a third round when Theodore felt a familiar unease. He scanned the room for the source until his eyes settled on five men emerging from a doorway that led to the inner reaches of the building. Soft light emanated from concealed fixtures beyond the doorway, backlighting the men and making it hard to distinguish their features.

The first two were clearly *kobun,* soldiers of the yakuza.

They were big, muscular men with hard faces. Both wore jackets of shegila leather, the iridescent scales glittering in the light from the inner room. The next two were dressed in dark business jackets over the open-necked plaid shirts popular with corporate types in the inner Combine. But one look at their faces told Theodore that these were no simple businessmen. Their hard eyes and scarred visages pronounced them as much *kobun* as the first pair.

The fifth man was different, though he wore a businessman's jacket as well. The other *kobun* showed such deference to the older man that Theodore was certain it was Yasir Nezumi, the *oyabun*. He was the gang boss they had come to meet.

The *kobun* nodded and bowed to acknowledge their instructions from the *oyabun*. As they started around the bar, their leader took a half-step back and leaned against the door frame. The light from the inner chamber now illuminated his face. Theodore noted the thin-lipped mouth, relaxed expression, and perfectly trimmed gray hair, not a strand out of place. Theodore was surprised to find him so distinguished-looking. Despite what Michi had told him, he had been expecting someone more like the classic Lobinsonu, whose coarse mug had inhabited many a gangster holoflick.

The four *kobun* walked the length of the bar, stopping when they reached Theodore and Michi. As they did, the music cut off, making the room seem suddenly silent despite the continued noise of gambling and bawdiness throughout the chamber.

The shorter of the two in business jackets rolled his shoulders, then tugged at his lapels to settle the garment into a straighter line. His rough voice grated on Theodore's ears. "Nezumi-*sama* can't see you. He is very busy."

"That is unfortunate, friend," Theodore said, slowly revolving on his stool to face the man. "Opportunity is passing you by."

"Don't need no soldiers," the man said, with a plastic grin that never touched the steel in his eyes. "If you really want to join the family, we got toilets that need cleaning."

Theodore recognized the insult. Traditionally, new members of a gang did menial and trivial work, including housekeeping chores for the boss. Often it would be years before a new yakuza was allowed to participate in the real work of the gang. But toilets! This *kobun* was offering them work reserved for women.

"Wouldn't dream of taking your job, *Jokan*."

The yakuza soldier's nostrils went wide with rage. He snarled and reached out to grab Theodore's lapels, but Theodore deflected it with his forearm. Converting his own motion into an attack, he brought the rigid edge of his hand down hard on the man's sternum. The *kobun* staggered back, coughing.

Michi had swiveled his stool and stood up as soon as the *kobun* moved on Theodore. He drove his fists into the bellies of the two brawny toughs. They doubled over, wide-eyed expressions of shock on their faces. Michi pulled his hands back, blood dripping from the blades that protruded from his vambraces. As the yakuza crumpled to the floor, Michi rotated his forearms with a snap, flicking the blood from his weapons. The wet slaps of the drops, spattering the floor and fallen *kobun*, were loud in the suddenly silent room.

The fourth yakuza saw that he had the undivided attention of the two men his group had outnumbered a moment before. He took several halting steps backward, nearly stumbling to the floor when he hit a patron too slow in clearing the way. Theodore reached back toward his sword, and the man turned, running for the door. Theodore changed his reach for the sword into a motion to scratch his left ear.

Michi tapped him on the shoulder, then pointed a thumb toward the back of the room. "Our host has vanished."

Theodore noted that Michi's blade had vanished as well, as he turned to confirm that the doorway was, indeed, vacant. The light was gone and only the dark wooden panels faced the barroom.

"Shall we let ourselves in?" he asked.

"*Iie*. We haven't got the firepower."

"All right. We'll at least leave him a message."

Theodore tossed a folded piece of plastisheet onto the bar, and followed it with a black plastic credit key and a small wad of C-bills. Then he turned to the man he had struck. The man's face was contorted with the pain of his coughing, as he tried to breathe with a cracked sternum. Theodore hooked his hand under the *kobun*'s jaw. The man struggled to stay on his toes to avoid choking.

"Most of the stuff on the bar is for your boss. I trust you

can manage to see that he gets it." Theodore dug his fingers into the flesh of the man's neck. "The C-bills are for you. Take some etiquette lessons, friend. You have very bad manners."

Theodore released the *kobun,* who fell into a sobbing heap. Theodore looked down at him and shook his head. Too fragile. He had expected the yakuza to produce tougher soldiers. Perhaps this plan was flawed.

"An inauspicious start."

"Perhaps less so than you think," Michi commented. "But I believe we are no longer welcome here."

Theodore let his eyes rove the room. Hard-faced men turned away, returning to their pursuits, but not before Theodore read the hostility in their eyes. "You're the guide."

Michi led the way back through the sea of tables. Behind them, voices resumed as the rattle of dice and the shuffle of cards broke the silence. Gambling was in full swing as they hit the door. The music picked up the beat again, its bass rumble expelling Theodore and Michi into the harsh neon glare of the street.

"I thought you'd given up those blades along with the Bounty Hunter armor."

Michi shrugged, a half-smile of embarrassment on his face. "Some things are harder to give up than others."

43

Unity Palace, Imperial City, Luthien
Pesht Military District, Draconis Combine
10 June 3031

Takashi Kurita strode into the Black Room, and the door hissed shut behind him. The closing door signaled the start of the meeting, and no one else would be admitted until the Coordinator left. Vasily Cherenkoff, the only Warlord yet present for the council meeting, looked questioningly across the table to Subhash Indrahar. The ISF Director smiled politely. He was as puzzled by Takashi's early arrival as the fat warlord, but he would not show it. Subhash and Cherenkoff started to stand in order to make their formal bows, but Takashi waved them down. He stepped behind his chair and rested his hands on its back.

"Where are Wolf's Dragoons now?"

Subhash removed the archaic gold-rimmed spectacles he affected and rubbed the bridge of his nose. He felt tired. Was it possible the Coordinator would resume his futile fixation on those mercenaries? Takashi had already squandered precious Combine resources on his obsession with destroying the Dragoons. Why? Because Jaime Wolf had shamed him on Terra? Because the Dragoons had shamed the DCMS on Misery, then again at Harrow's Sun and on Wapakoneta, and yet again on Crossing? Takashi had taken the words and actions of Wolf's Dragoons too personally, placing his own needs and goals before those of the state. Subhash had not been able to deflect him.

Then came the disappointing verdict from the ComStar Mercenary Review Board. Declaring a no-fault, the mediators denied Takashi's demands for restitution and condemnation of the Dragoons for their actions prior to and immediately following the end of their contract with the Draconis Combine. Had the Coordinator found this decision too damaging to his honor and so returned to plotting against the Dragoons? "Regrettably, *Tono,* we have not been able to determine their whereabouts."

"Incompetence! I will not have it!" Takashi shouted, launching into a tirade. The taunts and imprecations were nothing new to Subhash, having become all too familiar in the last two years. Subhash drew on his *hara,* replenishing his serenity and strength. He settled back to let the Coordinator's irrational anger wash over him. Takashi stalked the room from one wall to the other, bellowing his outrage. Finally exhausting his vitriol, he slumped into his seat at the head of the holotable. "Perhaps you are incapable of doing your job. Will you fail me like the others?" Takashi asked, breathing heavily after his tirade.

"You worry unnecessarily, *Tono,*" Subhash replied softly. *Your words do not touch me, Takashi, but your lack of control is very disturbing. I have not failed in my duty to the Combine, however much you think that I have failed you. Have I not hidden your instability from our enemies?* "I seek to serve the Dragon to the best of my ability, *Tono.*"

"Then get me that information!"

"I will try, *Tono,*" Subhash said. He keyed the table to display a stellar map of the Draconis Combine. "Consider, please, the situation in Pesht. Warlord Marcus is gaining strength. He is strengthening his ties in what Archon Steiner has left us of the Rasalhague District, playing on the fears of our loyal subjects. And he has contacted Warlord Chi again."

"That is no threat. Chi is too canny to fall in with Marcus." Takashi laughed. Suddenly he stopped and commanded, "Put a watch on Chi. He has ordered Galedon too well."

"Quite right, Coordinator," said Cherenkoff, his jowly face bobbing in approval. "The old goat must be watched."

Subhash noted the order on his datapad. Warlord Chi was unlikely to be part of any plot to topple the throne because he was too loyal to the Combine to endanger it. Marcus was a far more dangerous threat. "Pesht, *Tono?*"

"Marcus is a fool and a weakling. He had years here on Luthien to overthrow me and he couldn't do it. The closest he came was that sabotage of my *BattleMaster* in '25. But I was too clever for him. Too strong! I hold the reins of the Combine. It is mine!"

"Quite right, Coordinator. And so it must be," Cherenkoff boomed. In a softer voice, he added, "Until the day your heir takes over."

Takashi stood and slammed his palms against the table. Reports scattered. The Coordinator glared at his Warlord. Cherenkoff gulped air, clearly afraid of his lord's reaction.

Subhash wondered what the fat fool had in mind. Certainly, Cherenkoff hated Theodore for his successful defense of the Dieron District's border with the Lyran Commonwealth while the Warlord had remained on Dieron, failing miserably to mount any effective attacks against the weakened Davion border. To make matters worse, Theodore had acted behind Cherenkoff's back to win the glory that had eclipsed the Warlord's efforts.

"Coordinator, I meant no disrespect. I have always been your loyal supporter." Cherenkoff's voice dripped sincerity, but he would not meet Takashi's eyes. "Prince Theodore is wily. Perhaps he is using his office as Kanrei to operate behind your back as he did mine in the war. His people are always snooping around, poking, prying. And the company he keeps! That woman of his was bad enough. Now I hear he has given shelter to two of the infamous Wolf's Dragoons."

Takashi's lips drew back from his teeth, but he said nothing. Though the Warlord seemed oblivious to Takashi's reaction, Subhash knew that Cherenkoff had gone too far. "The persons you refer to are not Dragoons, Warlord. They are rebels who left Wolf's Dragoons after Misery."

Cherenkoff waved his hand in dismissal of Subhash's words. "They are not the real issue. Prince Theodore and his ambitions are what must concern us. Though he gained little for the Combine against the womanish Lyrans, he was awarded the Order of the Dragon. Then, when the ceasefire came, he was made Deputy for Military Affairs." Cherenkoff raised his eyes to the Coordinator's. "You create your own rival, *Tono*. Do you not see that he plays for your throne? Daily, his popularity grows . . ."

"Enough, Warlord," Takashi ordered, straightening and turning his back to the table. "I am quite aware of the doings of my son. The ISF is well-informed."

Subhash bowed his head in acknowledgement of the hand Takashi thrust in his direction. *If only you knew how well, my friend, you would not care for that knowledge.*

"Do not seek to question my will, Warlord. All that I have done was with a strong purpose in mind. Our realm needed a hero in the early days of the war. Thus did I award my son the Katana Cluster, though I knew he could not have destroyed as many 'Mechs as reported. This gesture also underscored the Lyrans' failure to capture him. I shamed our enemy.

"You cry about his actions in Dieron, yet I did not replace you, did I? Many thought he should have had your position as Warlord. Instead, I awarded him the Order of the Dragon. A pretty ribbon to soothe his common soldier's ego.

"I know better than to give his ambitions a power base. What do you think he can do with the Office of Military Affairs? He has no political instincts. He will play with his toy soldiers, and be content. Because I see that he does have some *little* aptitude on the battlefield and in the matters of military organization, I satisfy him, cut off his ambitions, and serve the Combine at the same time. He is a hero to the people and the soldiers. They will rally for him. And they will become a new army." Takashi spun to face Cherenkoff again. "But the army he builds will still be *mine!*"

The Warlord gave a ragged bow from his seat, a hesitant smile on his face. "As you say, Coordinator. It still disturbs me to see how the Genyosha and the regiments of the Ryuken are being rebuilt. They receive training only from Prince Theodore's hand-picked officers. Consider what such a force could mean in the hands of a rebellious general, even one without political acumen."

An injudicious push, Subhash observed silently. He expected another outburst from Takashi, but the Coordinator merely sat down again, calmly arranging the reports he had scattered in his earlier outburst. Takashi mused for a few minutes. A smile split his now-placid visage. "I shall order the training regiments dispersed, their troops to be scattered

among the units of the DCMS. With no core of loyal regiments, my son will never have a military power base. So
you see, Warlord, there is no need to fear an armed coup.
Even if Theodore could put together the political or popular
support, he will never have the military strength."

44

The cavernous hall was filled with five rows of the massive, twelve-meter ovoids, and their gimbal-jointed frames. Technicians scurried among them, checking connections and monitoring coolant levels. They were careful to avoid touching the inner shells, lest a hand or finger be trapped and torn off by a sudden shift of orientation within the skeletal frame. They were also wary of burning themselves on the recessed patches of shell that glowed orange from the laboring heat simulators.

From his perch in the control booth, Dechan Fraser watched with satisfaction. He didn't envy the Techs on the floor, for they did not have the advantage of the heating that kept him warm. Despite frosty breath and numb fingers, they were preforming well. They were two hours into the run, and there had been no equipment failures. He swiveled his chair around to the console and checked the readouts. All was going well.

Across the small booth, Chief Tech Kowalski bossed his team of supervisors and fussed over the fine-tuning of the computer system managing their simulator run. At his side were Tomoe Sakade and *Tai-sa* Narimasa Asano of the Genyosha, whose troops were undergoing today's testing.

"Problem three," Tomoe announced. "Initiate on my mark."

Dechan bent over his keyboard, starting the preliminary artillery barrage on her signal. In a nearby building, the boxy shapes of vehicle simulators had come to life, rocking and jolting on their pistons and spinning on their turntables as they impersonated a battalion of armor moving to the attack. The troopers inside would experience it as a real charge into battle. After five minutes, Dechan was pleased at the tactical expertise the Genyosha were showing against their computer opponents.

"Your new Genyosha MechWarriors have shown a remarkable improvement, *Tai-sa* Asano," he complimented.

"These are only simulators, *Tai-i* Fraser," Asano said, his lined face expressionless beneath his thatch of white hair. "It is very different when one is in a real BattleMech."

"We don't have the real thing for training the warriors," Tomoe lamented. "And even if we did, we couldn't afford to run wargames to give them practice."

"It's a good thing you were able to acquire these sim tanks, then," Dechan concluded.

"It's just too bad they're not a single lot," Kowalski complained, having crossed the room to place a stack of computer disks in front of Tomoe. "The computer is having fits trying to keep the parameters balanced between the different models, let alone the different manufacturers."

"You mean you're having fits, don't you, Mister Kowalski?" Dechan said.

"Same thing," Tomoe chuckled. "Kowalski-*kun* is half-computer, or so the other Techs in the Legion claimed. They used to say that his mother was a MultiMac 2700."

Kowalski frowned in annoyance. "That's a bad old joke, *Sho-sa* Sakade."

"You are right, Kowalski-*kun*," she said, contritely. "I apologize."

"Accepted."

"But you're having trouble?" Dechan asked insistently.

"How could I not be?" Kowalski rubbed his right hand back and forth across his head, rumpling his short hair into new patterns of disarray. "I'm only a mortal man, woefully ill-educated in these days of *lostech*. There's so much we don't know about what we've lost. I feel adrift in specifications and blueprints.

"The rebuilding program's technical teams are giving me all the help they can, but their members are just as overworked, and the resources never seem to be enough. There's too many programs, and we've too little knowledge to draw on. There are so many things the Kanrei wishes developed at once. Battle technology, communications work, agriculture. We spend weeks or months recreating research that a Star League scientist could have simply called up from his computer. I'm a Tech. What do I know about rice?

"I am as much a scientist as anyone can be in these latter days, but I cannot know everything, or be everything. The Kanrei put me in charge of research, but I'm not a bureaucrat. I belong in a lab. Still, I might be able to monitor progress on at least some of the projects if it weren't for all this moving about. I haven't been in one place long enough to do anything properly."

"We will do something about that soon," Tomoe promised him. "This training system must be fully functional. We need to take the sim tanks with us when the training command moves on."

"Moving again," Kowalski sighed, then pointed at the stack of disks. "At least this project is done. These compdisks should enable you to run the system with minimal interference from the Techs of the units to be trained. Please keep it out of the hands of any fumble-fingered MechWarrior who thinks he understands technical matters. The training team has worked too hard on this to see some well-meaning monkey undo it."

Kowalski had more to say, but Asano interrupted.

"Trouble on the floor."

Asano pointed to two figures running between the last rows of the tanks. One was a black man in a Kurita MechWarrior's uniform. The infantry-style battlejacket he wore over his jumpsuit flapped loosely as he pounded across the floor. The jacket had been adopted by the Ryuken and the Vegan Legion in imitation of Theodore, and marked the running man as belonging to one of those regiments. The other figure was a woman whose clothes were a motley collection of uniform pieces. Her hair was bound back into a tight braid that bounced as she ran. Dechan recognized her instantly. Her presence also identified the Kuritan for him.

"That's *Sho-sa* Tetsuhara and Jenette Rand," he announced.

"Weren't they supposed to be down at the ComStar compound overseeing that first shipment of parts?" Asano asked.

"Hai," Tomoe confirmed. "Something must have happened."

Tension built within the control booth as they waited for the two to climb the stairs. Dechan envisioned a wide variety of disasters, from ComStar reneging on the deal to a new outbreak of war. A glance at Tomoe's worried face reminded him that there was another sort of news that Fuhito might feel he had to bring in person. Something might have happened to Theodore.

Fuhito and Jenette tumbled through the door Asano opened for them. Dechan caught Jenette by the shoulders to steady her, and she slipped an arm around his waist. From their exhaustion, they must have run all the way from the airfield. In the moment it took them to catch their breaths, Dechan stole another glance at Tomoe. She had controlled her emotion and hidden her concern behind a mask of calm. "*Sho-sa* Tetsuhara, report!" she ordered.

Fuhito tried once, to no avail. He closed his mouth, swallowing to control his diaphragm. His tongue flicked out to wet his lips before he spoke. "The Coordinator has ordered the training regiments broken up. We are to be scattered across the Combine."

"Has the training command been dissolved?" Tomoe asked.

Fuhito shook his head.

Dechan was relieved. He looked across to smile at Tomoe, and she returned his grin. Fuhito's brow wrinkled at the reaction to his words. Asano looked as puzzled as Fuhito.

"It's all going according to Theodore's plan," Tomoe explained. "He expected this to happen sooner or later, once his father realized that we had a strong corps of loyal soldiers building up. The spread of the troops will allow the spread of his program that much faster."

"This explains your requirement that the troops teach each other once one lance had mastered a problem," Asano said.

"Exactly," Dechan said. "We want them to get the other regiments of the DCMS infected with our tactics. The training command can't get all of the DCMS regiments, so we send out the next best thing—loyal, educated soldiers. As soon as he can manage it without attracting undue attention, Theodore will arrange for the promotion of our scattered trainees. We have been training sergeants here, not privates. We know we can't get to every soldier, but at least we will get the lance commanders and line officers on-line with the program."

"But with our regiments split up, Prince Theodore will have no strong force in readiness," Fuhito objected.

"The regiments will not stay dispersed forever," Tomoe assured him.

"*So ka,*" Asano said, nodding. "Our Prince Theodore plays a deep game."

45

Beneath Pauchung, Xinyang
Benjamin Military District, Draconis Combine
18 June 3031

"Too deep," Michi coughed as Theodore pulled him back onto the narrow ledge at the tunnel's edge. His overcoat hung soggily over his compact frame as he regained his feet. Michi pulled his scabbarded sword out of the carry loops on the coat's back. He flicked open the catch behind the fastening plate and shrugged his shoulders free of the heavy garment. "Only slow me down now," he said to Theodore's questioning look, stuffing the sword through his belt.

"You said you had the right code phrase to contact this gang," Theodore accused.

"I did, but it was two years old." Michi released the empty magazine from his Nambu. It splashed into oblivion in the scummy water around their knees. He slipped a fresh clip into place. "How was I suppose to know that the gang would splinter, and our contact end up on the losing side? That Chokei fellow must have done something really awful for those guys to be so hot on the tail of anybody who claims to be associated with him."

A laser pulse struck the water near them, steam rising in an evil hiss as the water vaporized. Michi shoved Theodore to get him moving and snapped off a pair of shots at the unseen gunner.

They cut into a side tunnel to avoid any more immediate fire. Two alternate tunnels later, they were back in the main tunnel, splashing through waist-deep water at a junction, when a shout announced the arrival of their pursuit. Ten yakuza soldiers were splashing along the submerged catwalk against the tunnel wall. Michi knelt, heedless of the filthy water that lapped at his chin, and took careful aim. He squeezed off a single shot, chipping the wall near the head of the lead *kobun*.

The man shied from the ferrocrete fragments that stung his face. His foot slipped from the path as he stepped back, and he windmilled his arms to maintain balance. His weapon splashed into the water before he did. As the man's head disappeared beneath the scum, his thrashing foot caught the next *kobun* in line and tripped him cursing into the muck.

Taking advantage of the confusion, Theodore and Michi ran on. Half an hour of twisting tunnels and backtracking brought them to a tunnel that angled upward. The *kobun* were gaining. As the two moved up the tunnel, the water level gradually dropped until it was only ankle-deep. Though less cumbersome to run through, it was more noisome. Foul odors rose with each squelching footstep. After five minutes, they came to a halt before a massive metal grating that spanned the tunnel.

"Control?"

"None."

Theodore could hear the pursuit drawing nearer.

"The last cross-tunnel is too far back. We'll never reach it before they do."

Michi nodded.

"I didn't want to kill them," he said, pulling the slide on his Nambu to ensure that the action was free of sludge. He caught the ejected shell before it hit the water, and pocketed it. "Too much blood will make a wall you won't be able to cut through."

"They're the ones who won't let us leave peaceably. What happens is on their heads. *Shigata ga nai*," Theodore said fatalistically, checking his own weapon.

There was no cover, so they pressed against the walls to take advantage of what little protection the conduits might afford. The first *kobun* appeared, and Theodore took him down with two shots. Michi dropped one and wounded two more before the survivors stumbled back around the curve of the tunnel.

The wan yellow light from the overhead panels that had

lit their way so far began to dim and fluctuate. Moments of utter darkness alternated with seconds of pale illumination. Theodore crouched, awaiting the assault that should follow the yakuza's tampering with the lights.

A sudden crash and scream echoed through the tunnels. Firing started around the curve. Theodore recognized the angry whine of ricochets from metal. He had seen no armor, metal or otherwise, among their pursuers. Had someone else cut themselves into the situation?

The noise stopped. Theodore looked over to Michi, who shook his head. They waited.

Their rescuer appeared down the tunnel. In the fitful light, it seemed that a fantastic armored beast shuffled toward them. Red beams lanced the flickering darkness from its headlight eyes. Metal squealed with each step the lumbering monster took. Its huge claws were outstretched, reaching for them. Had their rescuer only acted in order to claim their lives for himself?

The machine squalled to a halt, and the tunnel lighting stabilized. In the low glow, Theodore finally recognized the shape of a cargo-loader exoskeleton. Crude armor of welded metal plates protected the operator, and shielded the more delicate parts of its superstructure. In a more open environment, it would have been easy prey for a trained rifleman with a good eye to find its weak points; but here in the cramped, ill-lit tunnels, it was as potent as a BattleMech.

The makeshift 'Mech's torso clamshelled open to reveal the driver removing the neuroband from his head. He was older than Theodore had expected, his gray hair and lined face a stark contrast to his well-muscled body. He wore only shorts and a stained, makeshift cooling vest, with a battery pack over his lower abdomen.

"Looks like I saved you boys a good bit of trouble. Lucky for you I was on my way home. My name's Frank Chokei," the man announced, holding out his hand. Neither Theodore or Michi moved. Chokei grimaced indifference and dropped his hand. "I see you've heard of me."

Chokei turned back to his machine and flicked a toggle. The grate that had barred passage rose silently into the ceiling. "Come on in anyway," Chokei grumbled as he brushed past them. Ten meters down the line, he stepped up into a dry side passage. Theodore and Michi followed.

Chokei led them to a large chamber, well but crudely outfitted for living. Theodore counted twelve bedrolls. The amount of personal gear scattered looked right for that number of inhabitants. To his surprise, a table in the corner held a partially disassembled neurohelmet of the style used in BattleMechs. On a rack behind the table hung a half-dozen DCMS-issue cooling vests. So the rumors were true—Chokei was a MechWarrior and had other MechWarriors in his employ.

"We have indeed heard your name, Chokei-*san*," Michi said politely. "But we do not understand why you are here in the sewers. Just what did you do?"

Chokei gave him a sidelong glance before walking over to a table and opening a silver humidor. He took out a long, black cigar, snipped off an end, and stuffed the uncut end into his mouth. Just when Theodore thought Chokei intended to ignore the question completely, his gravelly voice slid out around his cheroot.

"I broke the code of the yakuza."

Chokei lit his stogie and puffed for a minute. "At least, that's what they say. I told the district governor about some of the *Hanei-gumi*'s activities. Quite intricate detail, too. Several very prominent businessmen were very embarrassed. Some of the gang stuck with me, especially my MechJocks. Most of them had spent some time in the DCMS and understood what I was doing. The rest turned on me, swore to kill me. But I'd do it again in a minute."

"That's pretty cavalier for a man under the *Hanei-gumi*'s death sentence," Theodore commented.

"I got my reasons."

"And what are they?"

"You're awful nosy, young fella."

"I have been accused of that."

"You know, kid, I like your style. I'm gonna tell you something that I never told the bosses of the *Hanei-gumi*. Not that I think it would make much difference with them. They're real hard ones when it comes to the yakuza code.

"Those businessmen I embarrassed—they were passing info to the Fedrats. I couldn't stand the thought of somebody making a profit from endangering the Combine. So I figure they earned what they got." Chokei took a long pull on his cigar, then blew the smoke into the overhead fan. He watched as the anemic blades swirled the wafts into intricate patterns. "Then I headed down here. My people hid the

'Mechs while we looked for a way offworld. There's quite a lot a smart man can do to make money with a few BattleMechs.

"I been thinking about getting out of here, finding a cooler climate. I figure my MechJocks and I could get into the mercenary business. Know anybody who's hiring?"

Theodore smiled. "As a matter of fact, I do."

46

Theodore watched the screen relaying the main viewer signal from the bridge of the DropShip. The stars disappeared as the ship's bow entered the docking tunnel. The channel monitoring the ship's progress switched to the debarking bay as the DropShip shuddered to a halt, gripped in the rotation of the asteroid.

The long trail through the Kurita underworld was coming to an end. The nearly two years of tricks and traps and bluffs were over. He and Michi had come to the asteroid belt of the Corsica Nueva system, having finally engineered a meeting with the *kuromaku,* the fixer who could accept their proposals and act as their contact to the federation of gangs, the *Seimeiyoshi-rengo.*

Theodore unstrapped and readied himself. His rough soldier's garb was no longer appropriate. Today, he wore a fashionable business suit of dark cashmere. His silken cravat was held in place with a stick pin of onyx and gold depicting the Kurita Dragon. He checked his appearance in the silvered foil mirror of the tiny washroom, and then keyed open the compartment's door. Michi Noketsuna awaited him in the corridor. Michi, too, was immaculately dressed, though his white-irised eye lent him a sinister air. Without a word, they walked to the hatch.

Three men in dark suits met them as they exited the docking bay. Theodore was pleased to see that each wore a different lapel pin. The years of groundwork had paid off; a coalition of gangs was forming.

Though no names or ranks were mentioned, the three men were unfailingly polite as they led Theodore and Michi through the arrivals complex. Theodore disrupted the smooth march as he stopped to take in his first view of the almost legendary Mizutoshi.

In the center of the hollowed asteroid was the great solarsphere, a Star League-vintage artifact that lit the day cycle of the hidden city. Under its soft glow, Mizutoshi sprawled in a blaze of attractions. All manner of vices were catered to by the yakuza who ran the asteroid. Theodore could see the first emissaries of the city's flesh trade notice his hesitation. Extravagantly dressed men led scantily clad women toward the new arrivals, each group eyeing the others competitively. The nearest began to extol the virtues of his merchandise, but the man went silent at a head shake from the leader of their escort. The others followed his example. The panderers stood restlessly, their greed warring with their fear of approaching the group around Theodore.

Theodore allowed himself to be urged forward. Three more men, with three varied lapel pins, waited by a huge, black turbofan car. Its manufacturer's plates indicated an origin in the Lyran Commonwealth. The model was only a year old, a blatant sign of yakuza power and influence. There had been little trade with the Commonwealth since '28, even less in such luxury goods.

Their escort entered the car, brushing down the main seats as they settled in the waiting jump seats. At their urging, Theodore got in, with Michi thumping down beside him. Two of the three men who were waiting with the car took seats on either side of the visitors, closing the doors behind them and shutting off the sounds of the busy city. The last seated himself in the enclosed compartment with the driver. At his signal, the driver engaged the fans. Dust rose sluggishly around the vehicle as it lifted. Though the whine of the lifting fans went unheard, their thrumming vibration could be felt slightly through the vibration dampers of the Steiner luxury vehicle.

The aircar cut through the clear, recycled air of Mizutoshi, the driver expertly compensating for the effects of the asteroid's tight rotation. As they slowed for their landing on a private platform of what was obviously a luxury hotel, Theodore's practiced eyes noted the bulges and panel lines that marked concealed sensor and weapon ports distributed around the landing area.

The car settled gently, and the waiting groundcrew had the doors open before the fans had stopped. Theodore stepped out, suddenly reminded of his location by the noticeably lighter gravity here on the upper story of the building. He was given little time to admire the view before he and Michi were ushered inside to the executive suite, an elegant room paneled with mirrors and fine-grained wood. One of the mirrors had a control console indicating that it doubled as a viewscreen. Before that wall stood a table on which an antique samovar gurgled as it performed its function. The outer wall of the room consisted of a single window, offering a superb view of Mizutoshi.

Three more men in black suits were waiting for them. Theodore recognized all of them from previous dealings. They were all *oyabun*, gang leaders, of considerable stature in the underworld. Theodore was surprised that one of them was Yasir Nezumi, the man who had refused to see them at the start of their odyssey. The yakuza chiefs and their guests bowed formally to each other.

"It was great kindness to allow us to visit today," Theodore said, offering a small, rice-paper wrapped package. It contained nine thousand K-bills, but the yakuza who accepted the package did not bother to look at the contents before placing it in the drawer of a table by the door.

"Please be seated," another *oyabun* said, indicating a pair of plush chairs separated from an arc of nine straight-backed chairs by a glass-topped table. A tenth chair, an overstuffed monstrosity of garish upholstery and crudely carved wood, sat between the arc and the table. As he and Michi took their places, Theodore observed that none of the *oyabun* sat in the armchair.

"You have no complaints of your reception?" one of the *oyabun* asked, beginning an interview that covered most of Theodore's interaction with the yakuza during the time he was seeking this meeting. The atmosphere alternated between tense hostility and relaxed friendliness. He was grateful for Michi's coaching in the proper attitude to take. He was careful to note which of the *oyabun* spoke often and which rarely. Michi had warned him that a paucity of speech would mark the more highly placed chiefs, though they, as guests, would not be expected to show the same restraint. Yasir Nezumi only asked one question. Finally, Theodore and Michi's answers seemed to satisfy the group.

Though Theodore had seen no signal, the nine yakuza stood up simultaneously. Theodore and Michi also rose when the *kuromaku* entered the room. A short, blocky man with a bull neck, he walked with a slight limp.

"Green tea for our guests," he said, settling into the overstuffed armchair across the glass-topped table from Theodore and Michi. He motioned for them to take their own seats. Behind him, the nine yakuza *oyabun* remained standing. Small talk about the trials of interstellar travel and life in a large city occupied them until the first cup of tea was drunk and a tray of sweets brought.

The *kuromaku* settled back. Theodore placed his tea cup on the table, prepared to listen.

"I grew up poor," his host began. "My family had little, often only pickles and rice to eat. My father was an educated man, a teacher at Luthien University, but he lost all to gambling. I do not have the education he had, but I've done the reverse.

"I started as a strong-arm. Life was simple then. Very simple. I was simple, too. An acquaintance introduced me to the yakuza. When I agreed to join, I had no idea what it would be like. I started by cleaning floors. Soon I progressed. Every day at five in the morning I would wash windows. Cold water, cold weather. It was very severe training. It's not so hard these days.

"My gang is old. Its lineage goes all the way back to Terra. It is a proud heritage. Pride is something you understand, my friend." The *kuromaku* sipped his tea. "I don't require you to tell me your story."

Theodore's immediate reaction was relief. He felt uncomfortable with the tale he and Michi had developed. Then something in his host's tone registered, and suspicions suddenly flared in Theodore's mind. "Do you know who I am?"

"Of course," the *kuromaku* said, nibbling at a sweet roll. "Courtesy of the *Kereikiri-gumi* out of Marfik. They are very enamored of you. Others think that you should be ignored, that you have no real claim on us. If I thought you were who you pretend to be rather than who you are, there never would have been a meeting. But I was satisfied, and impressed, by your persistence. Thus we meet today to talk about what can be done to our mutual advantage."

The *kuromaku* wiped his hand on a napkin. Raising a finger, he sent one of the *oyabun* to the ancient samovar to draw tea for his guests and himself.

"You see, we are in trying times. Young men are less loyal these days, harder to control. I try to take in many, to show them the right path. It is my hope that they will do the same with the next generation. Beyond that, a man can have little expectation of affecting the future.

"I am a traditionalist, a firm believer in the old ways of *giri* and chivalry. Ah, I knew you would approve. But these are difficult times, and we do have to adjust. Sometimes we do things that will make a bad impression, but we are trying to fulfill our role. We would like to be appreciated for the vital part we play in our community."

"*Kuromaku-sama* is a gentleman," Nezumi interrupted. The elder yakuza smiled indulgently.

"He certainly is," Theodore agreed. *At least on the surface. He is a fine dresser with polite manners and an excellent sense of hospitality.*

"*Domo,*" the *kuromaku* said. "You must understand that the *Seimeiyoshi-rengo* is loyal to the Dragon. Our connections let us see much, and we are well aware of the dangerous waters where the Dragon now swims. The powers in Luthien scorn our aid. So we are most pleased that you are receptive.

"We shall drink on it."

He nodded to Nezumi, who left the room briefly and returned with a lacquered tray bearing a steaming *sake* flask and a single cup. A towel was draped over each of Nezumi's arms. As he placed the tray on the table, Michi removed a small wooden box from his jacket. He took out the ceramic cup it held and passed it to Theodore, who placed it on the tray. The *kuromaku* smiled benignly as he poured *sake* into the cups. Theodore noted that he was careful to ensure that the amount of rice wine in each cup was exactly equal, the sign of equality between gang bosses when they drank to seal treaties.

"We drink," the *kuromaku* said, lifting the cup Michi had produced. "I from your cup and you from mine, affirming our loyalty to the spiritual family that is our homeland."

He tossed back his cup. Theodore did likewise.

The *kuromaku* refilled the cups for a second round. This time, he poured slightly more into Theodore's cup than into his own.

"Now we drink to show our loyalty and devotion to the Dragon."

They drank.

The *kuromaku* took the cloth offered by Nezumi and carefully wrapped his cup inside it. He tucked the package inside his kimono. Theodore followed his host's example, wrapping his cup in the offered cloth and placing it in a pocket.

The *kuromaku* settled back in his chair. "Now let us talk business."

BOOK 3

Audacity

Unity Palace, Imperial City, Luthien
Pesht Military District, Draconis Combine
18 August 3033

Theodore raised his eyes to the ceiling of the great chamber. Even lit with hundreds of globular paper lanterns, the dark wood rafters held their shadows and secrets. *Like the Combine itself,* he thought. *Like myself.*

Beneath those rafters, a throng milled. In the traditional fashion, one side of the room was predominantly filled by men, some in formal dress and some in ancient Japanese style. The garments were radically different in cut, but the colors were much the same, blacks and grays and black-striped grays, a stark and formal patterning that offset the varied skin colors of the nobles, officers, and courtiers gathered for the occasion. Across the hall, the women gathered in constantly reforming clumps. With most dressed in formal kimono, they were like a bouquet of summer flowers, far outshining the masses of sunflowers set about for decoration.

The mood was happy and celebratory. Understandably so, for the Coordinator's birthday remembrance was the most lavish festival on the Combine calendar. Even in the worst moments of his feud with Takashi, Theodore had received a perfunctory invitation. There had never been a personal message, but his father could not ignore the importance of the Prince and Heir-Designate's appearance at the function. The three-day-long festivities were one of the few occasions when Theodore was invited to the Combine capital. Even his own birthday celebrations were often held without him. He did not mind overly; in fact, he had preferred to avoid Luthien since that painful occasion of his banishment to the Legion of Vega.

There was little Theodore regretted about his absence from the Court. His foremost sorrow was that he saw little of his mother. Even on those occasions that he visited the capital world, Takashi's shadow always seemed to come between them. He also missed his favorite cousin Constance, but at least they kept in contact through letters, holo-messages, and couriers. His mother wrote, too, but Theodore suspected that Takashi edited all such communications.

Since his appointment as Kanrei three years ago, Theodore had not attended the Coordinator's birthday festivities. He knew that his absence fueled the talk of division within the clan and further incensed his father, but he had more important things to do than pander to his father's vanity. He had, of course, sent appropriate presents and the formal poem wishing the Coordinator good health and long life. They had not been well-received. Constance had described how Takashi ordered the Lord Chamberlain to burn the poems and send the presents to the most remote storehouses. Theodore didn't understand the excessive reaction, but then, Takashi had been given to excesses since the war.

This year was to be different. Previously, he had chosen to be occupied elsewhere, but now, of his own choice and in his own strength, Theodore had come. With his plans progressing so well, he had reached a turning point that made his presence on Luthien the best way to advance the situation. It was time to take a step out of the shadows.

He turned his gaze to where the Dragon Throne stood in splendor on the *tatami*-covered dais. Behind the carved teak chair was a wall of ebony bearing a four-meter disc of gold-rimmed carnelian. Flecks of ruby mapped the suns of the Draconis Combine among the pale mosaic chips of the background. On that field coiled the serpentine dragon of House Kurita, its elaborate shape picked out in scales of enameled metal, each gold-rimmed and patterned. The teeth of the Dragon's gaping jaws were flawless ivory and its eye was an amethyst, the continents of old Terra standing in carved relief above the smooth polished surface of seas.

Takashi sat on his throne like the monarch he was, imperious and domineering. His black-dyed *daigumo* silk kimono flashed highlights from its folds whenever he shifted in his seat. The black-striped gray *kataginu* and *hakama* of his *kamishimo* were of a matte finish, superbly setting off the shine of his underrobe. His once-raven hair was shot through with white, and the white patches at his temples had increased. The war had worn him. The war and his stroke. Once he had scorned the chair and had knelt like a samurai lord of old. Now, with his weakened leg, he could not kneel through a whole day of ceremonies. Any attempt to do so would fail, and the failure would embarrass him. The Dragon would never allow weakness to show; always he sought to give the appearance of strength.

Appearances.

That I have learned from you, Father. Appearances are important. But you must learn that they are not everything.

Subhash Indrahar stood on the dais near the throne.

You, too, play with appearances, my old mentor. You have aided me in keeping secrets from my father. What secrets do you keep from me? Is there something you could tell me about Ninyu Kerai, who stands at your side? Constance says that you have recently adopted him, making him your heir. I had considered him one of my shitenno, *a trusted, if headstrong, companion. Do you seek to turn him from me? Or has he always been your agent among those who stand by me?*

What is real and what illusion, master of the shadows?

Across the room, Subhash turned. His eyes met Theodore's and he smiled. Startled, Theodore broke eye contact, suddenly finding interest in the shuffle of courtiers at the five steps leading up to the dais. The nobles had already presented their gifts to functionaries who meticulously recorded details of each gift and its value. Now, each in turn at the call of the Lord Chamberlain, they came to present the Coordinator with a poem of praise and good wishes. Most read from papers they carried with them, but some few spoke from memory, and one or two clearly composed their odes on the spot. The Coordinator's fondness for poetry was well-known, and Theodore knew that his father put great store in a man's ability to compose poetry extemporaneously. It was only one more area in which Theodore had failed to satisfy him. He had no talent at all for verse.

At last, the line dwindled and the court poet finished reading the greetings of absent lords. The Lord Chamberlain nodded to Theodore. He stepped forward, well aware of the multitude of eyes following his progress across the hall. With absolute correctness, he bowed as he reached the stairs and again when he stepped onto the dais. He made a third bow halfway to the throne.

"*O-medeto,* Coordinator," he said in a voice pitched to carry no further than the immediate area. "My talent for poetry is so poor that I have prepared another sort of presentation for you."

Takashi stiffened, but Theodore ignored the reaction. "You have long hoped for a legitimate heir to carry on the clan after you and I have gone onward along the wheel. Today, I bring you that wish. I have a son for you to meet, an heir for the Dragon Throne."

"I have known of your bastards for some time. They are not welcome here," Takashi snarled. "This is poor joke."

"It is no joke," Theodore returned calmly. "Any bastards of mine are, indeed, of no consequence. But I have a legal heir, born of my legal wife."

"Impossible! You are unmarried," Takashi snapped. "Indrahar would have told me."

"It is true, *Tomo.*" Subhash bowed so that he did not see the fury flare in Takashi's eyes, but Theodore had no doubt that the ISF Director knew what reaction his words would bring. Subhash straightened, his face and manner unperturbed. The Chamberlain and the poet padded down the steps, wisely exiting what could soon become a battleground. Takashi turned on Theodore, hard-eyed.

"Who is this woman?"

"Tomoe Sakade." Theodore held his head high.

"You are foolish as ever," the Coordinator said to his son. "I will have this marriage annulled."

48

Unity Palace, Imperial City, Luthien
Pesht Military District, Draconis Combine
18 August 3033

"You cannot annul the marriage," Theodore objected.

"By the laws of the Draconis Combine, he can," Subhash confirmed.

So you play your own game, Subhash-sama, Theodore thought. The ISF Director's eyes seemed to say that it had always been so.

Takashi smiled, vindicated.

"But the Coordinator will not," Subhash stated confidently.

"So you have betrayed me. You side with him," Takashi shouted, stabbing a finger at Theodore. The hall hushed at the sudden bellow from the throne. A muscle in the Coordinator's cheek began to twitch, turning his white-lipped scowl into an intermittent feral snarl. He dropped his voice to a harsh whisper. "Will you kill me here on the throne and put this puppy in my place? You would like such a puppet."

"I do not side with the Heir against the Coordinator. I strive for the Dragon's welfare." Subhash's voice was weary, as though he had said the words too often. "The Combine must have a strong succession. The state must remain stable at a time when we are surrounded by enemies on all sides and face enemies from within. The Combine must show no weakness."

"She is a nobody," Takashi said to Theodore, as though

Subhash had not spoken. "A merchant's child. Even her credentials to join the military were forged."

"Iie, Tono," Subhash contradicted. "She is more."

Takashi stood and took a step toward Subhash, hand half-raised. Theodore was startled, more by Subhash's statement than by the Coordinator's reaction. Did Subhash know of her connection to O5P? A murmur from the crowd made him shoot a glance over his shoulder. Constance was walking toward the dais from the women's side of the hall. Tomoe was nowhere in sight, but Theodore caught a glimpse of Jasmine standing among her attendants, her expression worried. Subhash, too, had seen or detected the head of the O5P's approach. With a small nod, he directed Takashi's attention to her. The men waited in silence.

"Tono, Jokan Constance can tell you of the history of Tomoe Sakade," Subhash said, as Constance joined them.

Theodore knew that Constance was quite prepared to do that. It had been their plan from the start. She was composed and calm as she began to speak. "Tomoe Sakade is another woman than the one she appears to be. Her records have been forged, but today the real story is here for you; a copy has been deposited to your databanks, *Tono.*

"Tomoe's real family is Isesaki. As you know, they are a merchant family. But they are more than that. She is descended in a direct line from Ingrid Magnusson, a descendant of the founding Prince of Rasalhague. The Order of the Five Pillars learned this after taking Tomoe in as an orphan. As we were not able to prove the connection at the time, she was not told.

"As she grew up, she expressed a wish to serve the Combine as a MechWarrior. We made that possible while we continued to search for proof of her ancestry. We hoped that she could serve the Combine as an example of cooperation and understanding. She found a better way of serving the Dragon by herself, it seems. As wife to the heir, she is a fine choice, for her ancestry is truly noble and offers powerful political potential. There is no slight to the clan's honor in this marriage."

Constance started to speak again, but Subhash gave her no chance. "There's more. Ingrid Magnusson married Karl Sakade of the Isesaki clan, which dates her back more than 500 years.

"When the usurper Stephen Amaris slaughtered Richard

Cameron to take control of the Star League government, he too left a job unfinished. In the massacre of loyal League supporters, Johanna Kurita and Duncan Cameron, absent from their apartments on a tryst, escaped. They fled Terra with the aid of a merchant of the wide-ranging Isesaki Shipping Company. Seeking refuge among the stars, they traveled to the edges of Rasalhague Province, a region known even then for fierce independence. After the horrors they had seen, neither wished to have any more to do with the affairs of the Inner Sphere. They wanted only peace for themselves and the children that they hoped to raise. They changed their names to Sakade, and using Johanna's connections for a last time, were officially adopted into the Isesaki clan.

"The clan elders were not acting entirely out of good will. They leaked the information to Coordinator Minoru who, in gratitude for their aid, granted the company a royal patent for trade anywhere in the Successor States. A patent that has been confirmed by every Coordinator since that day."

"I did not know this when I signed the patent," Takashi said petulantly.

"Regrettably, *Tono*. The secret of Isesaki Shipping was lost in the turmoil following Coordinator Jinjiro's removal from office. The information was only recently recovered." Subhash folded his hands in front of him. In a reassuring tone, he continued, "Had you known, you surely would have praised the match between your heir and this lady of noble ancestry. Thus, you cannot be faulted for objections. You acted correctly, given the information available to you."

"Yes, *Tono*," Constance agreed. Theodore was relieved to see that Subhash's revelations had not stolen her poise. "You have certainly not acted wrongly. She is a worthy wife for the Heir to the Dragon. If any are at fault, it is Director Indrahar and myself for not informing you sooner."

Takashi sat down, frowning. Elbow propped on the throne's arm, he leaned into his upraised hand until the lower half of his face was covered.

"Allow me to call her forward, *Tono*." When Takashi gave no answer, Constance turned and gestured toward the woman's side of the hall. The crowd, already surreptitiously trying to observe and eavesdrop on the argument on the dais, openly turned its attention to what was unfolding.

Tomoe stepped away from the ranks of the women, her

stride far shorter than normal, constrained by her formal kimono. Her elaborate wig and court cosmetics made her appear to be one of the court ladies. She was a vision of grace
and beauty, Theodore thought. Regal. She would fill her new
role as fully as she had all her others. He could not keep the
proud smile from his face.

Holding her left hand, the ten-year-old Hohiro stood as
tall as he could, clearly conscious of his dignity. On the
other side of his mother, his five-year-old sister Omi struggled with the skirts of her kimono. Several times, she stumbled and was saved from falling only by Tomoe's strong grip
on her hand. Tomoe flawlessly performed the bows of presentation before the silent Takashi, whose stern face was half-
masked by the hand in which he rested his chin. Hohiro
fumbled the last one, but no one laughed. Omi refused to
bow, preferring to hide behind her mother's skirts.

"*Tono,* there is another male scion of the Dragon," Tomoe
said. "Minoru. He is almost into his second year. He is in
the care of *Jokan* Florimel on her estates."

Takashi stared wordlessly at his sudden daughter-in-law.
Theodore tried, but could not read his mood. Takashi lowered his hand from his face, revealing that his tic had subsided. Gripping the arms of the throne so hard that his
knuckles faded to white, he leaned forward.

"Am I the last to know?"

"In this, the Dragon knows what the Fox does not,"
Subhash stated.

Takashi barked a rough laugh that dispelled the tension
gripping those assembled near him. "Be seated, *Jokan*
Tomoe."

With those words, Takashi had accepted his son's wife
and children. Theodore took a deep breath when he realized
that he had not taken one for some time. He moved to
Tomoe's side, but was intercepted by an anxious Hohiro,
who demanded to know if he had done well. While Theodore was reassuring his son, Subhash summoned the Lord
Chamberlain and bade him make formal announcement of
Theodore's marriage and the existence of the heirs. After a
moment of stunned silence, the hall erupted in wild jubilation.

Takashi settled back on his throne, face expressionless. To
the assembled courtiers, he surely seemed majestic and

lordly; to Theodore, he looked disturbed. Recognizing the tension in the muscles of his father's face, Theodore knew that the Coordinator was not mollified by the revelations of Constance and Subhash, but Takashi could do nothing. He must accept what had happened. Appearances must be preserved.

For now.

At the edge of his vision, Theodore noticed Subhash Indrahar turn to Ninyu Kerai. The ISF Director was speaking softly, but not so softly that Theodore could not hear his words.

"Tie up the loose ends, Ninyu-*kun*."

49

Yoshin Apartment Building, Blenshireton, Wolcott
Pesht Military District, Draconis Combine
21 September 3033

Kathleen Palmer entered the apartment. A quick survey of her tattletales assured her it had been undisturbed during her short absence. She checked on the boy in the bedroom. He was still asleep. She returned to the door and locked it, throwing the bolts on the additional ones she had installed after renting the flat two weeks ago.

Satisfied, she stepped into the kitchenette, removing her pistol from her sweater pocket and laying it on the counter. Two minutes later, she had a cup of fragrant jasmine tea in her hand. Her dinner would be ready in two more. She turned to the table, ready to read the headline on the telescan while she waited. She froze in mid-motion.

A red-haired man in a gray jacket sat at her table.

"Hello, Kathleen."

"Ninyu."

"I am pleased that you remember me," he said, smiling.

"You are a hard man to forget. How did you get in?"

He shrugged. "Where is the boy?"

"You mean Franklin."

"Do you have another son?"

She stared at the floor. "Why did it have to be you?"

"Whether it was me or some other who found you, it would make no difference. The end must be the same. You should not have run."

"I knew it was only a matter of time when I heard the announcement of the Prince's marriage. The insurance was no longer necessary. It had become a liability."

"I'm sorry, Kathleen," he said, reaching into his jacket.

"So am I."

She heaved her steaming cup at him, kicking out hard with her right foot to snap his shin against the leg of the chair. He was too quick. Pushing his chair over backward, he fell away from the blow. Her foot connected but without sufficient force to damage him. The tea splashed across the table as the cup shattered. The telescan sparked and smoked as liquid entered its casing.

Ninyu rolled clear of his clattering seat and was on his feet in an instant, his rapid recovery preventing Kathleen from retrieving her gun from the counter. If she tried, he would be on her before she could make use of the weapon. She circled him warily, knowing he was by far her superior in unarmed combat. For his part, Ninyu stood relaxed, but that did not fool Kathleen into believing him unready. She recognized the *shizen* posture from her own rudimentary *ninjutsu* training. Her only hope was to get her hands on the gun or some other weapon.

She swept the room with her eyes. Too late, she realized her mistake. Ninyu allowed her no margin. He was coming in at her even before she returned her full attention to him. As he moved past her and blocked her hasty attack, she felt his hand strike her left armpit. She turned to face his new position, arm hanging useless at her side. He had numbed it with a strike to the nerve complex.

"Foolish, Kathleen. You have no chance. You should never have run."

He was right, but she could not stop. If she surrendered, her son would die. She took a step backward and felt her right leg brush the second chair.

Time for desperate measures.

Grabbing the chair with her good hand, she heaved the metal frame high and to the left. Ninyu swayed aside, clearing her way to the counter. As the chair crashed into the wall, she threw herself across the narrow kitchenette. Her hand reached out for the pistol, only to close on empty air as Ninyu's kick caught her under the rib cage. She caromed off the range and onto the floor. The pain tore a short, sharp scream from her.

She writhed on the floor, feeling the tearing of her insides. Another blow was all it would take.

Stepping to the counter, Ninyu retrieved her gun.

"Finish it," she pleaded.

He shook his head.

She had hoped that the memories they shared would move him to mercy. A futile hope.

She realized that the boy would have been awakened by the noise of their fight. She had hoped he would flee, but he appeared in the doorway, instead, emboldened by the sudden cessation of noise. Kathleen tried to raise her arm to wave him back, to shout a warning, but her injuries were too great.

A star whizzed across the room to spin past the boy's neck. His mouth opened in surprise as he raised a hand toward his neck. Bright blood burst from the gash torn by the sharp, whirling edges of the shuriken. The boy toppled without a sound.

He is in shock and feels no pain, Kathleen told herself, a small comfort as she watched his life leak out to foul the apartment's carpets.

Ninyu stepped over the small body and disappeared into the bedroom. In a few minutes, he returned, wiping clean his shuriken and replacing it in a concealed pocket of his suit. A wisp of smoke followed him.

He walked softly to where Kathleen lay and crouched over her. He reached out and applied pressure in the careful way they had been taught by the ISF. Her pain vanished. He touched her throat, applying pressure there as well, and she felt the darkness begin to well up from within her. "A terrible tragedy," he said as he stood. "Mother and child die in an apartment fire."

His words were a statement of fact that just happened to describe a job well done. Through dimming eyes, she saw him bow to her, a last salute before leaving the apartment.

He would leave the building unseen, waiting to be sure that nothing disturbed the fire until it was too late. No one would know what he had done here. He had crippled her without doing anything that would mark her bones. All signs of violence would be erased by the flames. The charred corpses of a boy and a woman would be found in the ashes of the apartment.

He was very good at his job.

She coughed up blood. The bright red splashes changed the pattern of the carpet in front of her eyes. She stared, fascinated, as she slipped toward the darkness. She felt regretful sadness that the boy who had died here would never grow to be a man. But as the darkness claimed her, her last thoughts were of her son Franklin. The DropShip taking him to refuge with Marcus Kurita had lifted at noon.

50

Sanctum Arcanum, Unity Palace, Luthien
Pesht Military District, Draconis Combine
2 January 3034

Constance Kurita knelt on the white canvas mat before the elevated platform of the innermost room of the Sanctum Arcanum, the shrine of Kurita honor. Before her in the darkened room was a *tatami*-covered dais. The venerable *dai-sho*, the paired long and shortswords, of dynastic founder Shiro Kurita rested there on a black lacquered stand. Five pillars surrounded the dais, invisible in the gloom save for the ancient carved Labrean *monodon* tusk that glowed in soft luminescence, a ghostly dragon climbing for the sky. Also unseen were the four Pillarine adepts who knelt at the corners of the canvas mat. Though she could not see them, Constance could feel their strength, latent and protective.

The fifth guardian stood at the entrance to the inner chamber, politely but adamantly refusing to allow Theodore Kurita to disturb Constance until she finished her meditations. Even if Theodore had insisted on his rank, the guard would have stood firm. In this place, Constance outranked the Coordinator himself.

She bade farewell to the spirit of Shiro, clapping her hands once sharply as she bowed. The Adepts bowed to her as she rose. She felt their acknowledgment of her authority and radiated her acceptance and approval of their devotion. As she approached his back, the door guardian stepped aside, allowing Constance to bow to her cousin.

"Did it go well?"

"Very well. All four Vegan Legions looked superb," Theodore said, smiling with pride. "I had not expected such parade-ground precision from them. They may no longer be the dregs of our military, but they are still soldiers of the line. A parade is not something they find enjoyable."

"They are fanatically loyal to you, Theodore. They would do nothing to shame you before the Coordinator."

Theodore shrugged, but Constance knew that he was proud that his legions were strong, and honored that they should express such depth of loyalty to him. She could feel it in his *ki* shell and see it in his elaborate casualness.

"The insurrection on *Tai-sho* Rentoshi's homeworld seems serious," Theodore offered in an apparent change of subject. His facial expression lost its lightness and his manner became more businesslike. "The Coordinator granted him permission to attend to it. His first Sword of Light regiment is to accompany him."

"And the Seventh Sword of Light?" Constance prompted, well aware that the subject had never changed.

"They are to leave for training exercises on Daikoku's fourth moon tomorrow."

"The Coordinator has never been without at least one Sword Regiment on Luthien. Will he not override the order?"

"As Deputy for Military Affairs, I deem it necessary for the Seventh Sword to receive this training. Their last missions in such an environment were years ago and they have not had any refreshers on the peculiar tactical concerns of low-gravity operations. Everything has been done according to proper form. Their orders will appear on the weekly update in three days."

"Too late for the Coordinator to object."

Theodore nodded. "Besides, there is no need to keep them here while we have four full regiments of BattleMechs."

"*Your* Legions. With the Coordinator's favored regiments gone from the planet."

"Surely a coincidence," Theodore stated, deadpan. "I expect that matters will proceed in such a way that the Sword regiments will be needed elsewhere for some time to come. Even the Seventh Sword's recent low-gravity training is likely to be useful."

"Requiring them to leave the system."

Theodore nodded again. "It's a painless, non-violent way to remove the Coordinator's loyal troops from Luthien. The Director is justifiably concerned that such supporters might not understand what is to come. It'll be far simpler if my father has no troops immediately available to him. He has become erratic since his illness. Subhash-*sama* is pleased with the plan."

"Director Indrahar is well-pleased with you now, but he will not be so happy when you act on the information I have given you."

"That is unavoidable. With the war against Davion looming closer, we must take drastic measures that will be unpopular in some circles. The spy-riddled ISF must be purged. It is imperative that the Dragon's next steps be hidden from our enemies. Davion must not learn of our technical gains, nor of our new forces. Already they know too much of our plans."

The ease with which the enemies of the Combine learned their secrets was frightening. Constance had observed the phenomenon during the recent war, but had been unable to do much about it. With the cessation of hostilities, she had set plans in motion. The Order hunted for evidence of spies within the Combine, while expanding its own undercover networks within the other powers of the Inner Sphere. In very short order, the effort was proving fruitful, as the new ventures meshed with slow-developing plans and made judicious use of deep-cover agents.

Theodore was correct that the safety of the Combine required a weakening of the ISF. Enemy spies had to be removed or neutralized and Indrahar might not be willing to let it happen. He was certainly devoted to preserving the safety of the Combine, but he was also a man obsessed with his own power. He was unlikely to surrender it easily. Indeed, she suspected that his concern with maintaining that power contributed to the blind eye he turned toward corruption within his organization.

"The Director will see this cleansing as an attempt to weaken him as you have weakened your father," she warned.

"He will understand."

"He will hate you."

Theodore looked pained. "He won't let hate blind him to necessity. Subhash will see that I do what must be done to preserve and protect the Dragon."

51

Unity Palace, Imperial City, Luthien
Pesht Military District, Draconis Combine
14 March 3034

Subhash Indrahar studied Hassid Ricol as the Duke entered the room. Ricol looked tired, worn by the trials of the last few years. His forces and estates had suffered greatly during the recent fighting, now widely known as the Fourth Succession War. The Duke's private army had fought well in the Combine's counterattacks against the invaders, but they were unable to stop the Steiner juggernaut. It was not because of his limited success in the field that he was present at this impromptu meeting of the council of Warlords, however. Normally, a civilian noble would not be invited to such a meeting, but Kanrei Theodore Kurita, initiator of the meeting, had summoned him.

Only three of the *Tai-shu,* or warlords, were present: Cherenkoff, Shotugama, and Chi. Absent were Sorenson of Rasalhague and Marcus Kurita. Marcus had pleaded insufficient time to reach Luthien, as he was engaged in a tour of units stationed along the Periphery border. ISF monitors had pinpointed the origin of Marcus's message: Alshain, a world far from the Periphery and not even in Marcus's own district of Pesht. Subhash did not yet know Marcus's motive, but he knew that it was likely some new intrigue for the Coordinator's throne. Alshain was in the Rasalhague District. Perhaps Marcus's intrigue involved the other missing Warlord as well.

Subhash had no time to consider the possibility, because the Coordinator swept into the room. Takashi called the meeting to order, barely waiting until he had limped to his seat before signaling his son to begin. Theodore acknowledged the brusque wave with a polite bow.

"*Ohayo,* gentlemen. The Coordinator wishes us to be brisk with this morning's business, and I agree. Our guest is not cleared for the Black Room, but Director Indrahar has certified this room to be safe. You may speak freely.

"Yesterday, Haakon Magnusson declared himself Prince of the Free Rasalhague Republic, claiming rulership of most of the Rasalhague District," Theodore stated calmly. "As important as this news is, it is not why we have met today. I have . . ."

Takashi rose from his seat, fury contorting his face. His chair crashed explosively to the floor, scarring the high polish of the intricate parquet. His eyes were wild as he shouted, "Rebellion will not be tolerated!"

"We shall crush the ingrates," Vasily Cherenkoff echoed. "Say the word, *Tono,* and my Dieron Regulars will smash the traitorous dogs."

Theodore raised his voice to cut through Cherenkoff's bluster, but there was no anger in his tone. "Negotiations concerning the disposition of the Rasalhague District have been underway for some time."

"Sorenson will not allow this," Takashi declared, slamming his fist into the table. "He is loyal to the Combine! Loyal to me!"

"He is dead," Ricol informed the Coordinator.

The Coordinator snapped his jaw shut.

"He stood in the way of the Dragon," Theodore observed.

Subhash considered Theodore's words. The Kanrei had informed the ISF of his plans regarding Rasalhague, but there had been no mention of assassinations. Even Ninyu had told Subhash nothing, and he was Theodore's most likely candidate to do the job. This was a new and interesting view of the boy Subhash had shepherded through childhood. The Theodore he knew so well would never countenance assassination as a political tool. *What other surprises does he have today?* Subhash wondered.

"Each of you will find new datafiles in your compdecks," Theodore continued calmly. "They include the text of ComStar's official recognition of the new state of the Free

Rasalhague Republic and a series of conditions agreed to by the rulers of that state. Coordinator, your file also includes the text of the Combine's official recognition of the Republic. It awaits your signature."

Takashi raised his head in indignation.

You have prodded him the wrong way, Theodore, demonstrating that you still lack good sense in handling delicate political situations. Subhash knew that Takashi was difficult to direct on the best of days. His entrance into the room should have been a clue that this was one of his unstable ones. At least, it was not a public occasion. Those were the hardest to cover up.

"I will not sign it!" Takashi declared, stabbing his right forefinger down to blank the screen of his compdeck. Theodore ignored him.

"Many of you may believe this news represents a severe blow to the Combine. It is not. Rather, we are cutting off the limb off to save the body."

"You would have us cut our own throats," Takashi accused. "Your plans will come to nothing!"

The Coordinator stalked from the room, brushing past the surprised guards as they attempted to come to full attention. Subhash realized that the Coordinator expected the other members of the council to follow him out. *Not a reasonable expectation, Takashi, my old friend.*

The other members of the council remained where they were. The Warlords were clearly upset by Takashi's display, yet reluctant to leave the meeting Theodore had called. They were unsure which of the two powers in the Combine they could afford to offend. Seeking an answer, Cherenkoff questioned Ricol about events in Rasalhague. In his typical insulting manner, Cherenkoff implied that the Duke had fled from his responsibilities. Ricol refused to rise to the *Taishu*'s baiting, but answered the queries as fully as possible while maintaining a stiff politeness. At their end of the conference table, Shotugama and Chi were whispering anxiously to one another. Subhash watched as Theodore waited calmly. At the instant Subhash would have chosen, Theodore rapped his ringwatch on the hard wood of the table, catching the Warlords' attention.

"We've formed a buffer state in the FRR, one that will, to a large degree, insulate us from the Steiner enemy. This nascent state is too weak to stand on its own, and so we must offer support if it is to serve our ends. I think that you will all agree that we do not wish to see a repeat of the Tikonov Free Republic farce, where the Fox's lapdog Sortek rigged elections so that the Federated Suns could swallow up the former Capellan State.

"Rasalhague will have our support as an independent entity. Though the FRR will be autonomous, it will be deeply indebted to the Combine. We will not lose all our influence in the region.

"We gain by this sacrifice as well. The Davion-Steiner aggressors will have to abandon their peace-loving facade if they wish to dominate our new neighbor. The entire Inner Sphere, and most especially their own people, will see that the Davion and Steiner prattle of peace is just another of the lies their masters feed them."

"You have betrayed your lord and your father, you unfilial whelp," Cherenkoff growled as he heaved his vast bulk to his feet. "I will not stay while you spout words that betray my beloved Combine. No right-thinking officer could." He swept his sneering gaze over Shotugama and Chi. "*I* won't stand for it. I will reclaim what you have given away even if I have to do it alone."

Cherenkoff stomped ponderously out the door, bowling over one of the guards as he passed. Theodore was unperturbed. He cleared his throat and continued to explain his program.

"We are not surrendering all the worlds. Some twenty will remain under our control. By allowing Rasalhague its independence, we have forced the Steiners to demonstrate the truth of their supposedly peaceful aims. Most of the worlds they took in their recent battles will be claimed by the new state. Steiner must give them up or appear to abandon their position that each state should be free to determine its own destiny. We cannot control those conquered systems at the present time. With this arrangement, we can, at least, deny them to the enemy.

"The worlds remaining under our control will be reorganized into a new district to be named Alshain. It will be composed of the remnants of our Rasalhague District and ten worlds of the Buckminster Prefecture, and will be divided into three Prefectures named for their capitols: Buckminster, Garstadt, and Rubigen.

"Gentlemen, I wish your advice on whom to appoint as

Tai-shu for the new district. It has already been determined that the Governor shall be Duke Ricol. He was dispossessed of his estates by the Steiner invasion. Despite this, his loyalty to the Dragon is strong. This will make him diligent. I believe he will perform admirably."

Subhash noted Ricol's nervousness. The Duke was fingering the metallic cylinder of a computer core that he had put onto the table. Ricol was clearly unhappy about the situation, a man trapped into surrendering an advantage. Subhash knew of the ambitions that Ricol had cherished. For him, this must be a most distasteful course of action. From the Duke's attitude, Subhash anticipated Theodore's next statement.

"Duke Ricol has brought us a Star League library core. This core is a valuable addition to the Dragon's arsenal. A preliminary survey of its contents has led our staff of scientific councilors to believe that this library will advance our reconstruction and rearmament efforts by years. Sections concerning agriculture and military technology have been earmarked for rapid and intensive study."

The library core would indeed be a boon to the Combine, Subhash knew. It was likely the one recovered by the notorious mercenary Grayson Carlyle and his Gray Death Legion from the Star League facility on Helm. Since that time, the mercenaries had attempted to spread copies of the core around the Inner Sphere, with the notable exception of the Draconis Combine. Their efforts had met with curious obstructions, as if some powerful organization were attempting to suppress the information contained in the core. Subhash suspected that ComStar was behind that effort, but did not understand why they should do so. His agents within their organization had been unable to achieve sufficient rank to give him an ear in ComStar's upper echelons.

Ricol had met with Carlyle on Helm in 3028. Most likely, he had obtained a copy of the core at the time. A truly loyal man would have offered the core as soon as it had come into his possession, but Ricol had waited six years. The Duke offered this copy to the Combine now as an attempt to buy his way back into the Dragon's good graces. He was certainly one man who would bear watching very closely.

Theodore continued to praise Ricol while Subhash reflected on the curious history of the library core. The ISF Director did not for a moment doubt that Theodore was well-aware of what Ricol's behavior showed about the man. The Kanrei concluded his paean and shifted to a new subject.

"Now I wish to discuss our military position. Please take a few minutes to study the briefing my staff has prepared."

Theodore tapped at the keys of his compdeck. While the other members of the council turned their attention to the data that Theodore was transferring to their screens, Subhash became suspicious of the time the Kanrei was spending with his compdeck. The Director activated his spyhole program.

Windows opened on Subhash's screen, revealing miniature versions of the Coordinator's and the Kanrei's screens. Each had a copy of the recognition document on it. As he watched, the code for the Coordinator's signature appeared, and the Coordinator's screen flashed recognition of the command for transmission.

A quick clatter of keys traced the document's destination: the ComStar HPG facility. It would be out in the mid-day transmission.

You are bold, Theodore. And very confident.

Subhash removed his antique spectacles and massaged the bridge of his nose. Surreptitiously, he continued to observe the Kanrei. Theodore appeared relaxed, waiting for the Warlords to digest the information he had provided.

You had best watch your step, boy. My fondness for you diminishes as your independence increases. Worse, you listen too much to Pillarine amateurs.

You walk a narrow line. Do you not realize that because you now have a legal heir, you are no longer indispensable? Watch your step, Kanrei, for I will not allow you to endanger the Combine.

The Dragon will endure.

52

Dabbateur Plateau, Alshain
Alshain Military District, Draconis Combine
24 May 3034

Missiles screamed out past the Ryuken positions, arcing in on the renegade camp. Fuhito Tetsuhara raised the right arm of the *BattleMaster* he piloted and unleashed the man-made lightning of the 'Mech's particle projection cannon. Smoke and flames burst from among the target BattleMechs. They wavered as one of their *Panther*s lost an arm in the fusillade.

Satisfied, Fuhito ordered an advance, specifying a left-flank-refused formation for his lance. On receipt of the order, two of his lancemates moved forward on the right. They were piloting those curious *Charger* variants that Kowalski-*san* wanted so badly to see tested in battle. His other lancemate was in position to the *BattleMaster*'s rear, moving up on its left flank. The fire from its heavy-duty laser confirmed that without Fuhito needing to check his 360-screen.

All was proceeding according to the Kanrei's plan.

This operation had a bigger goal than cutting off the supplies of the renegade Combine forces attacking the Free Rasalhague Republic. Those forces, under the leadership of Marcus Kurita, had been branded *ronin* by the Kanrei. They were not operating under the auspices of the Combine and had been officially disowned. Theodore had ordered the DCMS to appropriate all their supply bases within Combine territories. Any resistance by the *ronin* was to be crushed.

More important, the operation was a test of the new order.

Only formations from the recently recombined Ryuken and Genyosha regiments and a select few regular units were involved. Theodore's new doctrine was showing itself superior to the ordinary DCMS training exemplified by the *ronin* troops. Equally important was the opportunity to blood the new *buso-senshi,* giving them a chance to show that they truly were competent MechWarriors and AeroSpace Pilots. The yakuza soldiers and the eager new recruits were not disappointing the Kanrei.

Fuhito halted his machine, knowing it was his responsibility to observe and report on the conduct of his battalion—a more important task than obtaining a little personal glory. A 'Mech paced up beside the *BattleMaster*. For a moment, he did not recognize the fifty-five-ton *Kintaro* piloted by his lance second, Will Randall. Fuhito was still not used to the ancient Star League designs that had appeared in the shipments from the ComStar arsenal. Some of the 'Mechs, such as the *Kintaro,* had not been seen in the Successor State armies since the First Succession War.

ComStar had secretly hoarded the machines for some unknown reason. Yet, as they doled them out now, the robed followers of Blake still kept secrets from the DCMS. Any half-trained MechWarrior could tell that ComStar had stripped most of the BattleMechs of certain kinds of equipment before turning them over to the DCMS. Some weapons and other systems had been replaced by ComStar, though none of the Kuritan technical staff could be sure exactly what was missing. The records from the end of the Star League era were jumbled, and the library core was frustrating in its bounty. There was simply too much information to assimilate quickly, even where the scientists could understand the technicalities of the Star League texts.

The most obvious evidence of ComStar's tinkering was the fact that the machines came with heat sinks of recent manufacture, hardly Star League quality. Even so, the ComStar 'Mechs were superior properties, built in the days when men fully understood the mighty war machines, not the products of half-functional automated factories or the patched-up survivors of generations of warfare.

Yet ComStar was not infallible. Their technicians had been diligent but not thorough in their replacement program. A few 'Mechs had come to the Combine untouched by the robed scavengers. Fuhito believed that the machines in those shipments has been intended for the use of the ComStar HPG station garrisons slowly appearing across the Combine.

The *BattleMaster* Fuhito piloted was one of those machines. It was a BLR-1C and was officially assigned to the Kanrei himself. Fuhito had been given it, with orders to get the feel of the machine, when Theodore had placed him in command of Operation Guillotine. That operation was proceeding smoothly despite a few stiff-necked senior officers who resented taking orders from a junior. Fuhito was thankful that he was only temporarily in command. He understood Theodore's desire to make a point, but hated being the one he used to do so. But this trial would soon be over. With success here, and the Genyosha's assault on the station in the Jarett system, all known stockpiles of supplies for the *ronin* would be eliminated. The Combine would have fulfilled its commitment to the Free Rasalhague Republic. Any rebel troops remaining within their borders were their own problems. The Combine would not cross the border.

The lack of motion from his companion's BattleMech aroused Fuhito from his musings. "*Senshi* Randall, is there a problem with your 'Mech?"

"*Iie.*" There was a soft hiss of static before the MechWarrior spoke again. "I do not like this, *Sho-sa* Tetsuhara."

"Surely you do not fear a trap from these rebels?"

"Hardly that, *Sho-sa.* The best of these *ronin* are certainly not here on Alshain. We have nothing to fear from these troops.

"I am uncomfortable attacking fellow Kuritans. It seems wrong to be fighting warriors who seek only to return Rasalhague to its rightful place within the Combine."

"You should have brought this up at the command session if it bothers you so much. That was the time for questions." Annoyed at the man's untimely reservations, Fuhito snapped, "You're in the field now, facing troops the Kanrei has declared *ronin* and the enemy. Obey your orders or face the Assembly of the Grand Inquisitor."

Fuhito heard the man's indrawn breath over the commlink. "I do not question the Kanrei," Randall blurted. "No need for the Inquisitor, *Sho-sa.*"

The *Kintaro* lurched into a run, moving in on the scattering *ronin*.

53

Tai-shu's *Field HQ, Stalholm, Predlitz*
Free Rasalhague Republic
24 May 3034

Ninyu Kerai, lying in the ventilation shaft, watched the man he had come to kill. Marcus Kurita was relaxed, his uniform jacket open at the collar. Regrettably, the man's sons, junior partners in the *Taishu's* adventure, were not present. If they persisted in the rebellious scheme, they would also become targets on another day.

Marcus had dismissed his officers half an hour ago, but continued to study deployment maps on his datascreen. There were symbols that Ninyu did not understand, including one that seemed to be a Kurita dragon with a cadency mark, around the Lucerne system. Ninyu was certain that it did not mark the location of Theodore or any of his children. Whatever it was, there were no military units there, and so no danger to Operation Guillotine. The plan to cut off the *ronin* from their bases in Combine territory was not threatened. From the unit dispositions displayed on the screen, the *Tai-shu* had not yet learned of the attacks on those bases; ComStar was cooperating. As Ninyu eased open the grill and slipped to the floor, Marcus continued to peruse the data, unaware of his visitor.

"Your security is quite good, *Tai-shu*. I was unable to enter the compound without tripping an alarm."

Marcus wheeled, reaching for the holstered pistol and belt that he had draped across one of the room's chairs at the end of the staff meeting. He froze when he saw the black-clad man already holding a gun on him. His blue Kurita eyes narrowed, calculating his chances. Obviously deciding that he could not reach his weapon, Marcus visibly relaxed his muscles, but Ninyu could see the inner tension. This man was not surrendering.

"Obviously not good enough to prevent you from disturbing me."

"Obviously."

"If you have tripped an alarm, as you say, they will be here for you shortly. You will not escape alive," Marcus assured him.

"You asked to be undisturbed. Your men will honor that wish until they have more conclusive proof of an intruder than a single sensor trace. Your, shall we say, impatience with subordinates who bother you with trivia is well known. As to my escape, we will see. Or rather I will see. You, *Tai-shu,* will be dead by then."

"Perhaps there is a solution that will leave us both alive."

"Unlikely." The man's audacity was impressive. Perhaps he was fooled by the Lyran Intelligence Corps Commando uniform. If so, that would not last long.

"I have some messages for you," Ninyu went on. "Your blundering ally in the invasion of Rasalhague, *Tai-shu* Cherenkoff, has gone to his ancestors. His *Atlas* was beheaded in the first assault on the defense forces of Orestes.

"His second in command, *Tai-sho* Kingsley, took over and ordered a retreat. It seems he does not have the same faith in your ultimate success that you do. Kingsley has asked forgiveness from the Kanrei for the rash actions of the Dieron military, citing his withdrawal as evidence that he supports the Kanrei. I expect that Theodore will be gracious and grant them clemency.

"That's bad news for you, though. You can't expect a thrust from Dieron to support your own actions here."

At the casual mention of the Kanrei and his plans, Marcus's eyes took on a new light. Ninyu caught the scent of fear. The man suddenly realized he was not dealing with a money-grubbing Steiner thug.

"The Kanrei wishes he could be as gracious with you, but he cannot. You've become too great an embarrassment." Ninyu elevated his weapon slightly. "This is a Mauser and Gray rapid-fire flechette pistol, standard-issue to covert agents of the Lyran Intelligence Corps. It strips its ammunition from a block of ballistic plastic at a marvelous rate, producing a stream of high-velocity projectiles that obliterate any flesh they meet. A very nasty weapon, but virtually silent in its operation.

"After you are dead, I will give you back your pistol. Blood will be scattered about the area where I drop this weapon. You will have wounded your assailant, causing him to drop his weapon—a warrior's death for a member of the Kurita clan. This is the Kanrei's wish.

"Your wounded assassin will panic and flee, but will escape your vigilant security. Another success for the Lyrans as they meddle in the sovereignty of another state. A most deplorable action, don't you think, Marcus?"

The irony was lost on the *Tai-shu.* Sweating profusely, he stumbled back into the table. His mouth worked, but no sound came out.

Pitiful, Ninyu thought. "This is your last service to the Dragon."

Eighteen pounds of pressure on the trigger released the swarm of plastic needles to rip across the torso of Marcus Kurita, spattering blood onto the datascreen and drowning his plans of conquest.

Then Ninyu did just as he had promised. He was a kilometer away before the alarm roused the camp.

⎯⎯⎯ 54 ⎯⎯⎯

Dragon Roost, Tatsuyama Mountain, Dieron
Dieron Military District, Draconis Combine
19 July 3034

"Have I not served the Dragon well?"

Dexter Kingsley's face was full of expectation. Theodore realized that the man had come to Dragon Roost anticipating reward for his perfidious action on Orestes. The thought roiled Theodore's stomach.

"You served yourself first, *Tai-sho*. That is a totally unacceptable ordering of priorities."

"But I acted in your interests, *Kanrei*," Kingsley protested. "I've held Dieron in your name."

Theodore drew in a deep breath and slowly released it. "If what you've done was carried out in my name, you have mortally insulted me."

Kingsley looked shocked.

"A ruler whose workers are oppressed cannot bring forth the full fruits of his land," Theodore continued. "You have crippled the economies of several of this district's worlds, plundering their wealth without a thought for the future. You have not done this for me or for the Dragon. You acted only for yourself. And so you have betrayed the Combine."

Michi Noketsuna stepped forward, intruding into the space separating Theodore and Kingsley from the crowd of officers in the great hall. "Seppuku is the only honorable solution," he said.

Kingsley blanched. His eyes flicked to Michi, then back

to Theodore. Neither man offered the *Tai-sho* any sympathy. Kingsley started to speak, but apparently thought better of it. He drew himself up to his full height and saluted, striking his chest with his clenched right fist in the Kurita fashion. He executed a swift bow and turned on his heels, leaving the chamber through the open doors. He looked neither left nor right, ignoring the calls of his fellow officers.

Theodore put his hand on Michi's shoulder and led his friend from the chamber. They passed through a small side door into a private room. Amid the dusty shelves of bound books, Theodore relaxed his posture, relieved to be out of public view.

"Michi-*kun,* do you think he will go through with it?"

"He is afraid," Michi observed. "But, yes, I believe he will."

"That's not good. I had hoped he'd bolt, leaving no doubt in anyone's mind that he was in the wrong. It's an open secret that he engineered the explosion that killed Cherenkoff, and everyone knows that the Warlord and I were at odds. By using my name as he ruled in Cherenkoff's place, he has implicated me in the murder he performed.

"If Kingsley lets it be known that I demanded his *seppuku,* I lose. Some will believe that I ordered the killing of Cherenkoff and am now disposing of my tool. Others will see me as a two-faced ogre who preaches initiative, then punishes it. Either way, resentment will build. If only there were time to gather the evidence to have him tried. A formal execution would be the best solution." Theodore slapped his thigh to express his frustration. "Kingsley's self-interest cannot go unpunished."

Violence is not the way of the Coordinator, Takashi's voice echoed in his mind. *Our destiny demands that we act through others.*

Theodore had heard those words long ago when only a child. They had seemed odd then. They had seemed odder still when Theodore began to understand the tenets of *bushido* and the responsibility that was the warrior's lot. He had grown up believing his father's views to be flawed. Now, though he was not Coordinator, he was more than a simple warrior, and the words no longer seemed so strange. Now *he* acted through intermediaries, and let others do the dirty work. *When,* he wondered, *did I change?*

Michi must have taken Theodore's sudden drift into

thought as a suggestion that a response was expected. "I understand," he said. Michi bowed, his boot heels clicking sharply as he snapped them together. "An accident, then."

As he turned to leave, Theodore reached out to catch the cloth of Michi's white dress tunic, halting him. "Wait. I don't want you associated in any way with Kingsley's death."

Michi stared Theodore full in the face. "I may not be your pet ISF ninja, but I have had sufficient practice, Theodore. There will be nothing to link matters to you."

"I didn't mean to disparage your skill, my friend. Besides, that's not what I mean. I'm thinking that you will have enough trouble in the near future. You don't need rumors that you killed your way to rulership of the district the way Kingsley did. You don't need it and the Combine doesn't need it."

Michi drew away from Theodore, forcing him to relinquish his grip. "What are you talking about?"

Theodore paused, taken aback by the suspicion in his friend's voice. *This isn't the way I wanted to do it.*

He fished a small box from his pocket. He snapped the black lacquer case open as he extended it. Nestled against the white silk were a set of apple-green insignia: two stylized *katakana* numerals and a pair of segmented bars, their second division highlighted in gold. "I'm appointing you *Tai-shu* of Dieron."

"I am not a good choice," Michi insisted. "There will be dissent."

"But nothing you can't handle. I need you here."

Michi walked to the window that overlooked the mountain chain that harbored Tatsuyama City. Without turning to face Theodore, he spoke. "By the friendship between us, and the trials we shared while searching for soldiers among the yakuza, do not ask this of me."

"I must." Theodore was confused. Why did Michi treat this as such an imposition? He was offering the man a post of great power and honor. "This District is the cornerstone of the defense of the Combine. I can trust no one else to handle it the way I want it handled."

"There are others who would be less ... politically unsound."

"To certain persons, anyone who associates with me is politically unsound. You have the skills and the necessary force of will. I need you in the post. The Combine needs you."

Michi sighed. "When we first met, you told me of the threat the Combine faced. I believed that you understood and could halt that threat. I agreed to put aside my personal quest and serve until the Combine was safe again. I will accept the post."

Michi turned and took the insignia from Theodore. No words were said as he replaced the insignia on his collar. Theodore was disturbed by the hostility coming from Michi. He had thought his friend would be pleased by this proof of trust and good will.

A sharp rapping on the door disturbed their privacy. Without waiting for a response, a *Sho-sa* entered the room. Bowing, she announced the arrival of the ComStar Precentor's party. Theodore dismissed her with a petulant wave, but before she retreated, he had second thoughts about keeping the Precentor waiting. He commanded the *Sho-sa* to escort the ComStar officials into the small office.

"I will leave now, Kanrei."

"No. I want you here for this," Theodore said. The new *Tai-shu* stopped in mid-stride. Michi's blind side was facing Theodore and his white-irised eye glinted hard and cold. "It is part of your new job."

"As you command, Kanrei."

55

Primus Myndo Waterly swept into the room, her golden robe of office glittering in the chill late-morning sunlight slanting through the window. In her wake strode the long-legged Sharilar Mori, who wore the scarlet robe and gold trimmings of her position as Precentor Dieron and member of the First Circuit. As soon as the Primus and Precentor had entered, the Kurita *sho-sa* who had led them to the room stepped across the doorway, blocking the way of any further ComStar personnel. She bowed and closed the door, cutting off the protests of the rest of the ComStar delegation.

Theodore smiled at his guests. "Greetings, Primus. Precentor. I trust your flight up the mountain was comfortable."

"As much as could be expected, given the winds on the mountain," Myndo remarked. Her eyes held a question concerning the brooding presence of Michi Noketsuna, his plain gray *buso-senshi*'s jump suit at odds with the rank insignia shining at his collar.

"This is *Tai-shu* Noketsuna of Dieron. He will be part of our discussions, for I wish him to serve as my liaison with ComStar."

Myndo's eyes widened briefly in surprise, then narrowed in sudden calculation. "The Roost seemed little changed from the days when I visited Warlord Cherenkoff here."

Theodore chose to ignore her deliberate choice of the past

tense in her comment. "As you know, we Kuritans are great traditionalists."

He pointed out chairs for the ComStar visitors. When they were seated, he selected one for himself, its back to the window. Michi took up a position behind the chair, to his right, as he had in their days of searching through the Kurita underworld. Their faces were shadowed in the glare from the white-topped mountains outside the vitryl panel. "It's too cold a day for a clandestine meeting in a park," Theodore said, indicating the view with an upraised finger. "I'm glad you feel we can meet openly now."

"Why should we not? You rule the Combine."

"Not so," Theodore contradicted. "I'm merely a servant of the Coordinator, his Deputy for Military Affairs."

Myndo smirked, mocking his protests, but she said nothing.

"I understand that you have some complaints about our agreement."

Myndo inclined her head slightly, acknowledging Theodore's directness. "You have withheld worlds from the Free Rasalhague Republic."

"True. It was necessary in order to placate some of the more radical elements of the council."

"Radical elements! It would seem that you were unsuccessful. Combine military units invaded the Republic, threatening all we have worked for. That is hardly restraint."

"The invasion was a regrettable deed performed by renegades. The Draconis Combine had no part in it. In response, we aided the Republic by destroying the rebel bases."

The cold anger that had risen in Myndo's dark eyes overflowed into her voice. "You have not lived up to your end of our bargain."

"And you have?" Theodore countered calmly. "What about the crippled BattleMechs, AeroSpace Fighters, and tanks you send? My understanding was that the Combine would receive Star League-vintage equipment. You were quite explicit about that. I didn't expect refitted shells."

Myndo was unmoved. "You have received as you deserve."

"As have you," Theodore retorted. "The support of the Combine for the Free Rasalhague Republic has had much of the effect you wish. The Isle of Skye is a cauldron of unrest."

"Not through any act of yours." Myndo held up a solidograph map. Even across the room, Theodore recognized the star systems highlighted on it. "You must free these worlds from your Alshain District. They are to be given to Rasalhague."

Theodore admired her audacity in commanding someone she believed to be the ruler of hundreds of star systems, but he would certainly not bow before it. "That's impossible," he said flatly.

The Primus tightened her lips into a hard white line. "Perhaps you will find that other things are impossible as well." She gave Theodore a moment to react. When he did not, she added, "Communications, perhaps. Or our troops may not arrive to man the equipment that you disparage."

"Is that a threat, Precentor?" Theodore inquired mildly.

"ComStar makes no threats." The fury in her voice belied her words.

No threats? Theodore echoed silently. *I'm not deaf, Primus. But your threat doesn't matter because we have a way around your communications monopoly, thanks to Kowalski's success with the black boxes and the library core. Not as swift, but it will work.*

I have the soldiers I need, and more reliable than the troops you offer. They may be from the dregs of our society, but at least they are ours. *They truly believe in the destiny of the Dragon, and that belief makes them strong, stronger than your hirelings.*

The Skye revolt will disrupt Hanse Davion's timetable. Even if he succeeds in suppressing the rebellion quickly, he won't attack. He will see that we are too vigilant. Sentiment in Skye will still be running too high for him to position his troops there for an assault on us. Even Steiner troops will be uncomfortable there for some months, perhaps years. With this gift of time, I will not need your troops.

"You must act as you see best, Primus. If there are no ComStar-sponsored troops to aid our forces, we will find a way to survive on our own. *Shigata ga nai.*

"If you find it inconvenient to honor your part of our deal, I'll understand. You must follow your karma."

"Karma is not the issue here, Kanrei. Fulfilling one's obligations is. When I was growing up in the Combine, I was taught that a samurai always kept his word."

"Were you also taught, Primus, that fate often prevents

the most determined samurai from fulfilling his word, and that such a failure entails no loss of honor? A samurai is still a man, after all, and many things are beyond the control of a single man."

Myndo sat silent, a sour look on her face. After a moment, she whispered, "Perhaps no loss of honor, but a failed duty. We were both taught the result of that."

"I see that you appreciate my position, Primus. I have greater duties to attend to before I may dwell on minor failures." Theodore folded his hands together and leaned forward. "Despite your order's recent gains in influence within the Free Worlds League, the Draconis Combine is still the only viable threat to the Davion-Steiner alliance. Thomas Marik does not even have the support that his father Janos boasted, which was pitifully little. The Marik family may have pulled together since old Janos's stroke, but they have shown little progress in resolving the disgraceful squabbling within the borders of their own state.

"The Periphery states remain minor players, at best, and the remnants of Liao's holdings are hardly significant. They have no industrial base, and their pride was smashed along with their military forces. The most powerful fantasies of their madwoman ruler will not change that.

"Neither of us wishes to see an Inner Sphere under Davion rule. Since you have decided to step out of the shadows, you must let the light show you that our interests coincide here. You may not have gotten all that you wanted from the Rasalhague situation, but then neither have I. I think that if we can put the past behind us, we can still work to prevent the disaster of Davion domination."

"ComStar works for peace, Kanrei," Precentor Mori stated firmly. "We will have no dealings with an aggressor."

"I find that comforting, Precentor." Theodore returned his attention to Myndo. "ComStar is renowned for its peaceful intent as well as its neutrality and reverence for the sovereignty of national states. You yourself were born in the Combine. Could you sit idly by and watch an invader swallow your homeland?"

"I may have been born in the Combine, Kanrei, but I was reborn among the followers of the Blessed Blake. The Combine means no more to me than any other state of the Inner Sphere. And no less. We exist to serve mankind and our communications network is our greatest service. We will not deny that service, save to those who are threats to the stability of the Inner Sphere."

"Well spoken." *And a relief,* he added to himself. *Even with Kowalski's boxes, an HPG blackout could still hurt the Combine efforts. As would the diversion of intelligence assets, should we be forced to make covert war against your ComStar ROM apparatus, as Davion now does.* "I'm glad to hear that, Primus. I've no wish to face the hostility of ComStar. Let me give you a gift to show that I do not repudiate what remains of our agreement." *Though I have no intention of relying on your good will.* "I believe that you'll find it of use in your own dealings elsewhere."

Theodore clapped his hands. The door opened to admit the *sho-sa*. She carried in her arms a folded packet of clothes, which she placed on a table next to the Primus. Myndo gave it a brief, disdainful look.

Theodore waited until the *sho-sa* exited before speaking. "Do you recognize it?"

"A general's uniform. This is of no use to ComStar."

Theodore feigned a frown of disappointment. "The uniform is empty and of no real consequence. I had only intended it as a calling card." He clapped again.

A man wearing a plain gray jump suit entered. He was tall and gaunt, but despite the white hair and beard, he strode like a young man across the polished wood of the floor to stand before the Primus. He gazed coolly at her with his single, steely gray eye; his right socket was covered by an eye patch. A small white scar crept from underneath the black leather patch to join the weather-etched lines of his face.

Myndo reacted with open shock and surprise. Theodore was pleased that he had caught her off-guard. Even as she stifled her response and slipped back behind her poised facade, he recognized that he had won the battle. There would be no more talk of unfulfilled promises. He could see that she was already considering the possibilities.

56

Kanrei's Palace, Deber City, Benjamin
Benjamin Military District, Draconis Combine
3 January 3035

Theodore tossed his youngest son into the air. Minoru giggled with joy, shouting "Again!" each time Theodore tried to stop. Finally arms sore from the repeated effort, he lowered the child to the floor.

"We of the Kurita clan are MechWarriors, not AeroSpace Pilots."

The youngster nodded solemnly, then with an impish grin announced, "I be both!"

Theodore laughed and hugged Minoru to him. "You are ambitious, my son. A true Kurita."

The boy nestled happily in his father's arms. Minoru's squirming slowed and his breathing became deeper. Theodore brushed a spike of his son's silky black hair down with a kiss. He raised his eyes to find Tomoe had entered the room.

"You should see them more often," she said softly. "They miss you terribly."

"I see them as often as I can."

"It is not enough."

Theodore could hear no accusation in her voice, but he felt the pang just the same. "Duty presses heavily. With all that must be done to ready the realm, it's all the time there is."

"The Dragon's compelling call," she said resignedly.

Theodore, arms full of his son, could not reach out to her. He searched her eyes, but could not find the meaning behind that curious comment. She had locked her feelings somewhere that he could not touch.

"Zeshin," he called. The old monk raised his head. His bright eyes took in the situation as he rose and crossed the room with his distinctive rolling gait. He was already reaching out when Theodore said, "Take him. It's time for his nap."

The monk enfolded the boy in the soft, voluminous sleeves of his Pillarine robe. His deep voice rumbled reassurances to Minoru as the boy fought half-heartedly to return to his father. The sudden sleepiness that takes overactive children when they stop moving was too strong for the young Kurita. He subsided with a yawn, content in the comforting arms of his guardian.

Zeshin took his charge off toward a sleeping room as Theodore stepped next to Tomoe. He placed his hands on her forearms, feeling the muscles stiffen slightly, then relax. She slid her own arms around his waist and held him tightly. Feeling suddenly awkward, he returned her embrace. For several minutes, they held each other without a word.

"Father!"

The strident voice was that of Theodore and Tomoe's eldest son. Hohiro ran past the door of the room, bare feet slapping hard on the polished wood. He skidded to a stop and returned to the door.

"Father! Look what I found!"

Tomoe and Theodore separated as their son approached, but her hand remained at the small of his back as her husband bent to see what Hohiro held out to him.

"Isn't it marvelous?"

The boy held an intricately folded piece of rice paper. The origami cat crouched threateningly on Hohiro's palm, its tail curled up, frozen in mid-lash.

"Where did you find it?" Theodore said urgently. "Is Omi all right?"

Hohiro was startled by the tension in his father's voice. His brows furrowed in confusion. "Sure. She's playing in the garden."

Theodore's eyes locked with Tomoe's. She moved to the door, cautiously peering outside. Her affirming nod released a sigh of shared relief.

"Now," Theodore said calmly, taking the cat from his son's hand, "where did you find this?"

"In the hall near your swords."

"And there was nothing else there? Nothing out of place?"

"I don't think so."

Hohiro was looking more worried. Theodore smiled to reassure him. "You have done well to bring this directly to me. It's a secret message," he added conspiratorially. "If you find any more you must bring them to your mother or me."

Hohiro nodded vigorously.

"All right. Go get your sister, and take her to Tetsuhara-*sensei*. Tell him that it is time for your *kendo* lesson. Your sister is to watch."

"But my lesson's not till three," Hohiro protested. He was clearly upset at being left out of the intrigue he had uncovered.

"Your lesson is now. Go!"

Hohiro's face hardened into a pout, but he left dutifully, making it clear that it was his own idea by taking a circuitous route to the garden. Theodore and Tomoe watched until their son and daughter had disappeared into the shadows of the *dojo* where Tetsuhara-*sensei* waited. Theodore handed the origami cat to Tomoe.

"Is it?"

She examined it carefully. "Definitely nekogami."

Taking it back, he held it to the light from the garden, looking to see if a message was written on the paper. He had thought the cat looked like the one Ninyu had identified at the headquarters on Moore in '29, but he wanted her to confirm it. The nekogami were few in number and rarely acted, but they had a fearsome reputation and were often blamed for the acts they did not commit. They were the premier spies and assassins of the Combine, masters of deceit and subterfuge. His own brushes with intrigue and assassinations over the years had not made him like them any better.

"What does it mean? We've no secrets here to be stolen. No one and nothing seems to be missing."

"It is most likely a message," Tomoe concluded. "You felt the characters embossed onto the paper?"

He hadn't. Rubbing the paper, he traced the strokes now. They were in the formal Chinese syllabary.

"Loyalty?"

"They offer you their services . . . I think. They serve the Dragon's best interests, as they see those interests. It appears that they have decided that you embody the Dragon."

"I suppose I should be honored. This will require a good deal of consideration."

Theodore paced across the room to a console and tapped in his ID code. Tomoe stepped up behind him, laying her hand on his arm. He turned to her. Gazing into his eyes, she gave a slight shake of the head.

"I leave my other life outside this place. Let it go for now."

"I can't."

"You won't," she accused.

"When I'm here, I want to forget what goes on outside. Truly. But I never seem able to. Outside concerns come intruding of their own accord," he said, holding up the origami cat.

"I don't want to lose you," she breathed in his ear, throwing her arms around him to hug him tightly. Theodore felt her strength, strength he knew could snap his spine if applied with the cunning grips of her martial arts training. But there was no danger for him in her arms, only desperate love.

The paper cat crumpled in his grip, dropping forgotten to the floor as he stroked her hair.

=== 57 ===

Kanrei's Palace, Deber City, Benjamin
Benjamin Military District, Draconis Combine
28 December 3038

Dechan Fraser and Jenette Rand bowed to *Tai-shun* Kester Hsium Chi. The Warlord had headed over to them as soon as the strategy meeting broke up. The white-haired *Tai-shu* beamed happily, his wispy beard bobbling as he spoke. "I am pleased that you two will be serving in my district of Galedon."

"It was not our first choice," Jenette grumbled.

Dechan elbowed her in the ribs at the lapse in manners. In return, she scowled in annoyance. *Tai-shu* Chi laughed, relieving the tension. Dechan knew at once that this man was very different from the last Galedon warlord he had known.

As soon as his mirth subsided, Chi clamped a cigarette between the fingers of his artificial hand. The stark white of the cigarette contrasted sharply with the black bioplast of the prosthesis as he held it out for an aide to light. He treated himself to a long drag before fixing them with his shrewd eyes. "I appreciate your dedication to duty, then. Your previous experience should prove useful if I am not mistaken. You do know the District?"

"Too well," Dechan agreed.

"Even disagreeable experiences can be enlightening," Chi counseled, with a wink. "I met your Colonel Wolf once."

"They're no longer affiliated," Theodore reminded him as he stepped up. The Kanrei towered over the diminutive *Tai-*

shu, but Chi showed not the slightest sign of being intimidated by either Theodore's rank or his imposing physical presence. Whether that was due to familiarity with the Kanrei or to Chi's own easygoing nature, Dechan could not discern. The *Tai-shu* simply smiled enigmatically, leaving Dechan to wonder what the Warlord had heard of the circumstances of his and Jenette's departure from the Dragoons.

"As I was saying," Chi continued, "I met Colonel Wolfe on his last visit to Luthien. He is a remarkable man, very adept at his craft. I must say that I admire him greatly. What followed was most unfortunate."

"I am sure the old Wolf will be tickled to hear that," Ninyu quipped as he and Fuhito joined the circle. "Theodore-*sama,* surely you could have found a better use for me than wet-nursing that pirate and his cronies in Dieron?"

Chi exhaled a long puff of smoke, causing eyes to water and cutting off the Kanrei's response by forcing a cough from him. "I knew that Noketsuna had an unusual past, even more so than my monkish confederate Shotugama, but he seems to have ordered his District well. I had not heard that he was a pirate. Is it true, Theodore, that you allow barbarians to run one of our important districts, instead of confining them to the ranks of the ISF?"

"You are impertinent, *Tai-shu* Chi," Ninyu said, warning clear in his voice and tightened jaw muscles.

"Yet you prove him correct with your bad manners, Ninyu-*kun,*" Theodore chuckled. The others followed the Kanrei's lead, pretending to find the comments humorous and thereby avoiding conflict. Dechan found the reaction very Kuritan, but he observed that Ninyu's slow-growing smile did not extend to his eyes.

"With regard to your assignment, Ninyu-*kun,* there is no change," Theodore said. "You'll go to Dieron because I have need of your special expertise along that front. You'll just have to get along with *Tai-shu* Noketsuna as best you can."

Dechan thought that he would rather be the third passenger in a *Locust* with a bad gyro and a faulty leg actuator than be around those two. Ninyu had taken an instant dislike to Michi as soon as he had joined Theodore's *shitenno,* and Michi, though less vocal about it, had returned the sentiment. Jenette dismissed Michi's antipathy as the remnants of anger over events leading to the death of his mentor, Minobu Tetsuhara. Dechan wasn't so sure. He had known Michi longer and had a growing feeling that there was more behind his friend's reaction.

Much of that feud had spilled over onto Jenette and himself, connected as they were to Michi. Ninyu took any opportunity to ridicule them and remind anyone who would listen of their origins. The whole situation had not made their already precarious position in the Combine any easier. The years had gone by quickly, though, lost in training and tactical exercises. Dechan had discovered a liking for the job. The new recruits were eager and many showed great promise; teaching them was easy. Their belief in *bushido* gave them a drive Dechan had only seen previously among the Dragoons.

But despite the pleasure he found in imparting his skills, the years had been lonely ones. He and Jenette, shadowed by their association with Wolf's Dragoons, had encountered little sympathy among the often suspicious Kuritans, and they had no real friends here. Without Jenette, Dechan knew, he would never have lasted. There were few people with whom he was comfortable, beyond Kowalski the Tech, Asano, and Tetsuhara. Dechan still found it hard to believe that Fuhito was the brother of the old Iron Man himself. Theodore was cordial, but Dechan had never really warmed to him. His wife Tomoe was another story. She had been full of kindness, but they saw little of her.

Dechan searched for Michi among the dispersing officers, but he was not there. *Probably already left for Dieron,* Dechan thought ruefully. *So much for spending some time with old friends.* Since his appointment as *Tai-shu* of Dieron, Michi had been uncommunicative, answering their communiques with cold brevity or ignoring them entirely. Michi had abandoned them, leaving them trapped in a promise to help Theodore protect his realm. They had little choice but to follow through. Dechan had expected to be done with that promise by now.

The invasion of the Davion-Steiner alliance that Theodore had predicted should have come and gone for good or ill, but even the Kanrei's uncanny instincts had been thrown off by events in the last few years. The formation of the Free Rasalhague Republic had triggered secessionist sentiments across the Inner Sphere. The Free Worlds League had lost the powerful Duchy of Andurien, and Duncan Marik had seized the Captain-Generalcy and launched a campaign to regain Andurien. The Isle of Skye had threatened secession as well. In response, Hanse Davion had mobilized troops to hold his fledgling empire together by force. His harsh measures proved to be unnecessary when Ryan Steiner managed to bring the matter to a peaceful settlement, thereby embarrassing the Fox. Many in the Combine had expected Davion to throw those same troops into an assault against them, but it had not happened.

Kanrei Theodore had assured his commanders that Davion would not yet attack, for the Fox would wait for the Dragon to relax its vigilance. They had a reprieve, but he warned that Hanse Davion would come, lasers blazing, as soon as he believed he had the advantage.

Now that attack loomed on the horizon. The Free Worlds League was licking its wounds. Thomas Marik had picked up the pieces left behind by Duncan Marik's death in battle, and had successfully reintegrated Andurien into the League. Romano Liao's opportunistic attempt to assert herself had been slapped back. Steiner troops were massing in Skye, and several key units of the Armed Forces of the Federated Suns had vanished from their duty stations, much as they had before the outbreak of the Fourth War. Davionist sentiment was growing stronger in the worlds of the former Galtor Thumb, while Kurita's own attempts to stir nationalist sentiment in the former Tikonov Free Republic were less successful. It would not be long before Davion attacked.

"If Steiner can be intimidated, we will be able to concentrate on Davion."

The snug fit of the comment into Dechan's thoughts wrenched him back into the conversation.

"Don't speak of them so casually as separate opponents," Theodore cautioned the young aide who had spoken. "There's little to separate them now. Steiner troops are configured into the Regimental Combat Teams of the Davion AFFS. Their officers are cross-trained and some of each House's units actually contain troops of the other House. It's one army we face."

"Veneer only," Ninyu scoffed. "It's too soon for the changes to be more than cosmetic."

"What about our own troops?" Fuhito countered. "Isn't

adherence to the Kanrei's new military doctrines also young? Could it also be only a veneer?"

"To a degree," Theodore admitted. "We face certain rivalries among our troops and among our officers as well. But we are bound together by our devotion to the Combine. Our enemies, in their haste to unite their realms, are blind to the depth of the differences that separate their peoples. Nor do their societies understand the necessity of order and the strength of the group. Their leaders see what they want to see: cooperation and good cheer. We'll use their blindness to our advantage."

"Such as the message you sent to the Archon Katrina Steiner," Chi inquired.

Theodore turned an evaluating gaze on the *Tai-shu*. "Yes. That is one tool."

"But you said our enemy is a combined force," Fuhito objected. "Why do you speak to only one leader?"

"To distract them. I wish them to believe that I don't understand their organizational changes." Theodore smiled slyly. "Let them underestimate me. My message should help them do that."

Dechan spoke up. "But what is this message?"

Theodore hesitated, perhaps reluctant to reveal the information. "I simply warned the Archon to stay out of any conflict between the Draconis Combine and the Federated Suns. I pointed out that we had no interest in a conflict with the Commonwealth at this time, but told her that we would consider any intervention on her part as a violation of the conventions of civilized warfare. I warned her that such an act would mean that the Combine was no longer bound to deal with her according to those rules of war."

"You can't be serious." Jenette's expression was one of disbelief and shock. Dechan wondered if his own mirrored it. The Kuritans were infamous for atrocities, going back for centuries. Was the Kanrei preparing to live up to his ancestral heritage? Even though he and Jenette had given their word to help Theodore, he would no longer feel bound to the sacredness of a promise should the Kanrei descend into barbarism.

"But I *am* serious," Theodore vowed. "As she may learn to her sorrow."

58

Greggville Province, New Mendham
Benjamin Military District, Draconis Combine
16 April 3039

"Shadow One to Tango Base, do you read?"

Davion Leftenant Roscoe Walker waited patiently for a reply. There seemed no need to worry; no one in his recon lance had seen a Kurita unit all morning. But that wasn't surprising. The High Command's strategy was based on overleaping the Kurita border planets to avoid their frontline units in the first invasion wave. This thrust into the Combine's Benjamin District was under the command of Duke James Sandoval, commander of the Draconis March. Two other thrusts were hitting the other districts on the Davion border. Federated Suns units were landing on more than twenty planets, striking deep to capture supply and communication centers, to isolate and confuse the Kuritan forces.

Only light resistance was expected at this stage, and so far the High Command was proved right. The burn in from jump point had been unopposed; the assault had caught the Dragon sleeping. Davion Light Guard Regimental Combat Team fighters had found few defenders in their path as they guided the DropShips into position for the orbital drop. The Guard 'Mechs had made planetfall hard and fast, scattering the still scrambling Kurita defense forces. The non-'Mech forces had landed safely. It had been a textbook assault.

Then Marshal Riffenberg's caution had come to the fore. Walker figured that the old man was worried about things going so well. The Marshal had ordered the AeroSpace Fighters pulled back into reserve, as a defense for the grounded DropShips and the landing zones, as well as to await a strike from hidden Kuritans. Reconnaissance was left to the swift 'Mechs of the Light Guards, including Walker's lance.

Walker keyed open the circuit to his lance. "Let's move up, people. Keep your sensors out. We're getting near target."

As the acknowledgments came in, Walker depressed the foot pedal, throttling his *Hatchetman* to a fast trot. Twenty meters to his left, Alison's *Hatchetman* matched his pace. Walker knew that his forty-five-ton machine bobbed as much as hers, but the stabilized picture transmitted to his cockpit screens was steady, undisturbed by the motion of his 'Mech.

The other two 'Mechs of the lance were thirty-ton *Valkyries,* considerably faster than their partners. They were also more humanoid, despite massive shoulder assemblies and right forearms, which housed their Sutel IX lasers. The Davion 'Mechs were in the mottled greens-and-sand camouflage mandated for the open grasslands of New Mendham's savannah. Only the bright foxtails that Reed's machine sported, one on each of four antennae, allowed Walker to distinguish it visually from McCullough's 'Mech.

In ten minutes, they covered almost as many kilometers. The lance was still forty klicks from the Draconis town of Kempis when Walker transmitted the code for a halt. Trusting his command to scan the area, he tried again to contact Tango Base. Again, he got no response.

"Listen up, people. I still can't raise the base."

"Let's go in." Alison urged.

"It's too quiet," McCullough objected. "We should've seen some Snake troops by now."

"Don't overload your reclamation tubes, Bobby boy. You cadets spook too easy. The Snakes are more scared of us than you are of them."

"Ease off, Sergeant Alison. I'm sure you were nervous your first time out, too."

"Come on, Leftenant," Alison griped. "I dropped on St. Andre fresh out of the academy, right into a nest of Capellans. Now that was hot! The Capellans didn't go hide. They hit us before we'd even jettisoned our thruster packs.

Hellfire! Some of the Jocks were still shucking ablative shell."

"Save the war stories, Alison," Reed cut in. "If you were so hot, you wouldn't still be a Sergeant."

"I'm not *still* a Sergeant, Newboy. I'm *again* a Sergeant. And it's not because of anything that happened in the field, unless it was the green-bottomed newboy I skinned for calling me a liar."

Walker shook his head, bemused by his lance's banter. He considered trying Tango Base again, but figured that if they hadn't answered two minutes ago, they wouldn't answer now. It was time to make a command decision. "All right. Damp the chatter. We've got a schedule to keep, so we're going in."

"Good choice, Leftenant."

Alison's *Hatchetman* stalked ahead of Walker's own. Its long-crested head swung from side to side, a stoop-shouldered alien hunter searching for prey. Its right arm twitched, beating a rhythm in the air with the depleted uranium-edged blade that gave the 'Mech its name. Cross-streets gave Walker glimpses of the *Valkyries* prowling a parallel course through Kempis. There were few signs of life. The Kurita civilians had mostly deserted the town or gone to ground in shelters. The Davion troopers saw only a few fleeting shadows in side alleys. None wore the tans of Draco soldiers.

Without warning, an *UrbanMech* in dark gray splinter camouflage suddenly burst through a brick wall a hundred meters ahead. Its domed, cylindrical body swiveled and its stumpy, broad legs scattered rubble as the 'Mech stepped clear of the building that had screened it from their sensors. The *UrbanMech*'s side-mounted Imperator-B autocannon spewed shell casings as it hosed a stream of projectiles at the advancing Guards.

Alison fired her 'Mech's jump jets, rising on ion flame to evacuate the path of the enemy 'Mech's fire. The maneuver simultaneously cleared Walker's line of fire. The Leftenant's thumb mashed down the firing stud on his right joystick as soon as the golden crosshairs of his targeting system slid onto the stubby enemy machine. The Defiance Killer autocannon in the *Hatchetman*'s chest coughed out armor-piercing shells.

Chunks of Durallex armor blew explosively from the *UrbanMech*'s barrel body. Smoke rose from the wounds and joined the billowing cloud of brick dust in obscuring the target. The Kurita Dragon on the 'Mech's dome was revealed to Walker as it shifted to bring its weapons to bear on him. Before the Draco could fire, Alison's *Hatchetman* appeared from an alley thirty meters behind it. The Guard 'Mech raised both arms and loosed twin laser pulses. The ruby energy flooded the drifting dust cloud with incarnadine light, but in spite of the diffusion effect, retained sufficient energy to melt away armor on the Kurita 'Mech's leg and upper dome.

Walker ripped another burst into the Kuritan. Depleted uranium slugs tore through the remaining armor of the *UrbanMech*'s torso, seeking its fusion heart. The Kurita 'Mech tottered under the assault. As it canted over, its dome blew free and spun away like a child's toy. The Kurita pilot rocketed clear, his chair disappearing over the surrounding roofline. The abandoned BattleMech crashed to the ground, bringing the rest of its former shelter cascading down around it.

Alison raised her 'Mech's hand weapon in salute before pivoting her *Hatchetman* back down the alley from which she had emerged. "Tally ho!"

"Keep it cautious, Alison. We don't know what they've got here," Walker warned, knowing it was unnecessary. Despite her lower rank, Alison had seen more combat than he had. She could handle herself. The young Jocks in the *Valkyries* were his real concern. He opened the comm circuit. "Reed. McCullough. Switch to mag scan. You'll have a better chance that way to spot concealed Snakes. It'll be easier to pick up their metal masses than to spot a good camo job."

They chorused acknowledgment.

"And don't push it. You run into trouble, call for help. The Guards don't want any dead heroes."

The Davion 'Mechs moved efficiently through the town. Within ten minutes, they rousted a Kurita *Locust* from a trucking center. The bird-legged 'Mech snapped a laser pulse that scarred the surface of Reed's *Valkyrie* without causing serious damage. The Guards pursued, only to be ambushed by two more *UrbanMechs*. Concentrated fire from the Davion lasers left the first *UrbanMech* a pitted hulk, and the second crumpled under a blow from Alison's

Hatchetman. Overmatched by the unbloodied Guards, the *Locust* fled the town. It, too, had been unscathed until a flight of LRMs from McCullough's *Valk* cratered its armor and tore off the stubby wing-mount machine gun on its port side. Walker forbade pursuit.

McCullough whooped victoriously on the lance circuit.

"Good show, kid," Alison conceded magnanimously. "I told you that this'd be easier than when we popped the Caps on Hunan."

Half an hour later, the jump troops flitted into Kempis, right on schedule. Under the watchful guardianship of the BattleMechs, they combed the town in a fruitless search for the supply dump they had been detailed to secure. They failed even to turn up any of the three Draco MechJocks who had ejected from their doomed machines. Walker put his frustration on hold as the comm circuit crackled with the voice of the regimental controller.

"Tango Base to Shadow One, report please."

"Shadow One here, where the hell have you guys been?"

"We had a little trouble with a kamikaze Snake. The sucker got inside the compound as impressed labor, then drove a hoverflat of explosives right into the commcenter. Took us a while to rig replacements."

"You want us back to guard you, Tango?" Walker jibed.

"The Marshal wants your report, Shadow One."

The snap in the comm officer's voice told Walker his levity was unappreciated. He decided to play it formal. "Light opposition, Tango Base. Target secured, but we came up empty."

"Don't sweat it, Shadow One." The reply was in a friendly tone once more. "You'll find it out there somewhere. Just stomp any Snakes that get in your way. Stomp them good and proper."

59

Dragon Roost, Tatsuyama Mountain, Dieron
Dieron Military District, Draconis Combine
21 April 3039

Ninyu Kerai held the five-pointed shuriken between the thumb and forefinger of his left hand. He passed his right hand over it, and the small throwing star vanished. He picked another star from the stack on the seat beside him. He repeated the operation, this time holding the shuriken with his right hand. When all five stars were stowed about his person, he twisted around to look out the window that was the reason for the niche in the castle's walls.

Below him in the courtyard, a VTOL rotorcraft was landing. Aides and mechanics hurried forward. The first group moved to attend to the officers deplaning, and the second, even more attentive, to the aircraft itself.

He shifted his gaze down the mountainside. Three more aircraft were headed up toward the ancient fortress that served as the headquarters for the Warlord of Dieron. The VTOLs were moving carefully, the pilots wary of downdrafts and sudden, eddying gusts that could sweep their machines to a fiery collision with the gray and black igneous rock of Tatsuyama Mountain. The city lay in the valley below the flickering dots of the climbing aircraft, seemingly quiet.

Ninyu knew better. The town had been bustling during his visit yesterday, as people stocked their shelters with whatever supplies they could afford from merchants whose prices had suddenly doubled. Soldiers had moved in squads, nervously following officers' directions to improve the city's defense works. The small landing field had been even busier, as a constant stream of DropShips arrived and departed. One was lifting as he watched. Its thunder muted by the distance, the *Overlord* rose toward the heavens on a tail of flame. If anything, Tatsuyama City would be more frenzied today.

Ninyu left the niche and sauntered toward the command center. He was in no rush; his presence was not required there since he was no longer in the strict military chain of command. While he waited for the go signal, he was a free agent. When the time came, he would move quickly. For now, he conserved his energy.

The command center, a multi-tiered hall cut into the living rock of the mountain, was aswarm with military and technical personnel of all ranks. Great, flat screens alive with maps and dataflows flickered fitfully in the red-lit hall. On the dimly lit levels, zealous officers clustered around consoles and map tables, forming obstructions to the bustling traffic flow. Most of the junior ranks wore standard DCMS tans, though a few could be identified as BattleMech officers by their red-striped gray jerseys and trousers. A few of each type had their sleeves rolled up in the heat of the chamber, revealing lurid tattoos. Senior officers wore black, like Ninyu's ISF uniform. Unlike the utilitarian ISF rig, with its pockets and straps, the officers' tunics were severely tailored and decorated only with epaulets, collar tabs, and the ubiquitous Kurita dragon.

Tai-shu Michi Noketsuna wore *senshi* grays and a padded battlejacket over them. The Warlord's split-toed 'Mech boots lacked the mirror shine of a proper officer's footwear. He stood in a cluster of similarly garbed men and women. *His damned Ryuken-ni crew,* Ninyu observed. *No surprise there.*

Ninyu decided to drop in on their conversation. He wove his way through the bustling center from tier to lower tier, dodging black jackets and letting the tan-clad junior officers and red-capped Techs clear his own line of advance. The gray-jerseyed *senshi* he treated with respect, the safest approach with warriors who considered themselves samurai. *Even those non-conformist Ryuken,* he reminded himself. Just as he neared the knot of rough-garbed *senshi*, a *Chu-i* interrupted them with a choppy bow. "Comprehensive data feed from Kessel is in, *Tai-shu.*"

"Shunt the situation map to tank four and update the force profiles," Michi ordered.

"Hai!"

Michi said a last few words to his Ryuken officers that Ninyu was still too far away to catch. All but one turned to head for the exit. He recognized the remaining Ryuken officer as *Tai-sa* Ysabeau Johnson, commander of regiment *ni*. The departing officers split their group as they reached Ninyu, careful to avoid him. He found the hostile glances accompanying their perfunctory salutes pleasing, but affected total ignorance of their existence. He had no need of their good will.

He stepped closer, and Johnson greeted him in her pleasant contralto. "Sightseeing, Kerai-*san*?"

"Merely attending to the duties assigned to me by the Kanrei, *Tai-sa*."

Johnson smiled hesitantly and her eyes flicked to Michi. He made no response that the ISF officer could see. Instead, he turned his face to Ninyu.

"Your advice is welcome, Kerai-*kun*," Michi stated stiffly. "But please refrain from disturbing the officers at their duty stations."

Ninyu held Michi's eyes long enough to express his annoyance at the older man's condescending comment, but said nothing. He turned his attention to the center of the chamber where a small elevated section held the principal strategic displays.

Five small holotanks made a rough circle around a larger one, twice their size. Four of the small ones displayed planetary surfaces, blue and red icons glowing to represent tactical dispositions of the forces engaged on the depicted planet. One of the four flickered as Ninyu watched, its image blacked out to be replaced by a new geographic configuration that stabilized as unit icons began to wink into existence. The fifth small tank was a system display, with the characteristic globes of planets and bright dots of JumpShips, DropShips, and fighters. All five were labeled with ghostly glowing characters naming the system: Athenry, Ainasi, Kervil, Kessel, and Vega.

The large tank held a stellar map of the Dieron District. Red fires haloed six suns, including the systems displayed in the smaller tanks. Scarlet flickered in and out of existence around another four systems. The solid tones were accompanied by miniature unit crests to represent the forces identified among the invaders. Some were still blank gray disks, like those that accompanied the intermittent red zones symbolizing enemy attacks short of full invasion, indicating that the exact enemy unit had not yet been identified.

A flush-faced aide bustled up and handed Michi a ComStar packet. The *Tai-shu* ripped it open, read it swiftly, then crumpled it into a ball. He strode stiff-legged to the elevated command chair from which he could survey the center. Without sitting, he keyed on the loudspeaker mike. "All regimental commanders and general staff to assemble on the tank deck. *Sugu!*"

Ninyu tapped his fingers against the top of the holotank where he leaned, suddenly interested. He observed the approach of the officers, noting that several were not very prompt. He recognized protest and disapproval in their tardiness. They were all senior generals, each of whom was said to believe he should have been appointed Warlord after Kingsley's accidental death. Michi's sudden jump in rank had appalled them as much as his former renegade status. If anything, Michi's years as Warlord seemed only to strengthen their dislike and distrust.

As soon as the officers arrived, Michi spoke from the steps leading to his command chair. "Officers of the Combine, I have just received a direct communique from the Coordinator."

Ninyu watched excited expectation ripple through the assembled officers. Most expected word of the Coordinator's response to the invasion, but some, no doubt, were expecting Michi's removal.

"You are all aware of the situation here. Things are little better in Benjamin and Galedon. Davion forces are conducting a full-scale invasion of the Combine. Just as here in Dieron, they have bypassed our entrenched units on the border, passing deeper into our homeland. We have lost all communications with garrisons on Sadalbari, Huan, and Alrakis.

"From the presence of elite formations, military intelligence has estimated that the invaders are thrusting directly for the other District capitals. It appears that the invader intends to isolate Dieron before reducing it. ISF agrees with this assessment.

"The Coordinator orders us to hold at all costs. We are not

to surrender a single planet. Dieron is to be fortified and held to the last man." Michi took a deep breath before adding, "You will be pleased to know that Takashi Kurita expresses complete confidence in our ability to repel the invaders.

"I expect modified defense proposals within the hour."

The gathering dissolved into a dozen different discussions and the bellowing of generals calling their staffs. Some started back to their command tables, but before they could disperse, *Tai-sa* Johnson's voice cut sharply through the babble.

"Can't we appeal this fortress order to the Kanrei? A static defensive posture will be too limiting. We need some leeway to maneuver."

"The communique is countersigned by Theodore Kurita," Michi announced solemnly. "We are now Fortress Dieron."

Johnson ran her tongue across her upper lip. "We'll be fit for the scrap heap if we just sit and wait for them."

"Agreed."

"Let us hit them back. Release the Ryuken to raid behind the lines."

Michi paused as if in thought, but Ninyu was suspicious. The *Tai-shu* would normally put off any such request with a comment about taking it under advisement. Michi's response confirmed Ninyu in his suspicions.

"Very well. I suggest Caph, Procyon, and Saffel as initial targets. I want an operational plan in an hour."

Ninyu suspected that the plan would be in the computer in minutes. This decision had already been made; Johnson's plea was a show for the other officers. The Ryuken officers would be lifting for rendezvous with their units within an hour.

What's the game, Pirate?

Michi turned to face Ninyu. The *Tai-shu*'s face was grim. "*Sho-sa* Kerai. We have confirmed Steiner forces on eight of our worlds, and on seven of those, Lyran forces form the bulk of the hostile forces. It is time for you to implement the *Kanrei*'s contingency plan."

"I don't need you to tell me my duty." Ninyu brushed nonexistent lint from his sleeve. His action belittled the *Tai-shu*'s words, adding to the lack of respect shown by his impolite failure to address Michi properly. "My people are moving into position. They will act on *my* word."

Some of the gathered officers murmured at Ninyu's display of disrespect. He could tell from their eyes and half-hidden smiles that they approved. *Tai-shu* Noketsuna was not well-liked among most of the military.

Better stay on Theodore's good side, Pirate. That's all that's keeping you from the jackals.

60

Manschemman Dune Field, Beiseit Continent,
  Marduk
Benjamin Military District, Draconis Combine
14 June 3039

"It's glorious! Isn't it, Jimmy?"

Static fuzzed some of Sir Michael Hallbrock's words, but his exhilaration was clear. James Sandoval, newly minted marshal of the AFFS, Duke of Robinson, and heir to his father's position as commander of the Draconis March, found himself in full agreement. He only wished that his father could be here to take part in the humbling of the Kurita Snakes.

When the Federated Suns had lost worlds to the Combine during the Fourth War, Aaron Sandoval had nearly revolted and made his own war. But wiser advice had prevailed, and he had adopted a more indirect course to achieve his ends. Five years ago, he had abdicated his Ducal throne in favor of James. With judicious application of pressure and the calling in of favors, the old Duke had arranged to have his son put into the command chair for the Draconis March. James, already rising quickly through the AFFS despite his lack of an NAIS education, had returned to the March to take command of the First Robinson Rangers.

Aaron had moved to New Avalon. It was not merely to clear the field for James, who people were calling the Young Duke, but to take his political fight where he could start the necessary fires. Among the politicians and courtiers, Aaron's borderer's topknot, though gray with age, had been a constant reminder to those stay-at-homes that they had an enemy on their doorstep. The Old Duke had badgered and cajoled and threatened, pushing constantly for the extermination of the Dragon. The Prince himself had not been immune. Whenever they met, the Old Duke had reminded Hanse Davion of his coronation pledge to regain the planets lost to the Draconis Combine in the First Succession War. Whenever possible, Aaron had pointed out that additional worlds had been lost to the Combine during Hanse's reign.

When it looked as though the Prince had been unmanned by the losses of the Fourth War and distracted by the troubles in neighboring states, Aaron had stepped up his program of pressure. The Old Duke was always ready to emphasize the latest intelligence about the Combine's rearmament and to point out, with multiple historical precedents, the likely result of the Dragon's actions. Finally, the distracted Prince had been made to see that the time for a preemptive strike against the still-weak Combine was running out. The plans for invasion had been drawn up.

The Old Duke had done his part; he had set the Federated Suns and their Lyran Commonwealth allies at the Dragon's throat. He had also managed to get James appointed Marshal to lead the thrust into Benjamin. It had been a political coup. Now it was time for the Young Duke to reward his father's confidence.

James was determined to add another Dragon Slayer's Ribbon to the cluster that adorned the parade standard of the First Robinson Rangers. The Rangers had acquired quite a few from their successes against the Combine. He wanted another, but was determined that this would be the one that counted. The last one. The one that meant the Dragon was really slain.

The command lance moved across the sparkling surface of the Manschemman Dune Field. Piloting his *Zeus,* James let the tactical chatter from the maneuvering hovercraft of the Rangers' associated regiments wash over him. The operation was moving well. The Kurita hovertanks were stubborn, but gradually yielding ground. Distant thunder marked scattered engagements to the north.

Just as he was about to order the command lance to move in that direction, a dune eighty meters to his left erupted in a diamond spray of silica. An ochre-painted BattleMech burst up from where it had lain concealed, hidden from the Rangers' sensors by the sand and heat. James's computer tagged the enemy machine as a *Panther* while he tried to bring his targeting crosshairs to bear on the silver trident emblazoned on its left breast. The Kurita 'Mech side-stepped before James could get a lock-on.

The *Panther* accelerated toward him, its right-arm Lord's Light PPC corruscating as the weapon built up charge. As James tried to track the target, the Kurita pilot unleashed his particle beam. The ravening blue lightning licked the *Zeus*'s hip, melting armor wherever the charged particles touched. James stood firm, confident of his 'Mech's capacity to absorb such punishment.

From the lance's right flank, a flight of long-range missiles corkscrewed in to bracket the charging Kuritan. The rockets came from the *Zeus* of Hauptmann Benoit. James saw fragments of armor ripped free by the warhead's explosive power before the smoke of explosions from the rocket barrage obscured the *Panther*.

James sent a burst from his Defiance autocannon into the cloud, hoping the shells would find the target. Hallbrock moved his *Wolverine* closer, cutting the line of fire between James and the Kuritan. Benoit's *Zeus* lumbered in heavily from the right. Even without Devlin's *Enforcer,* currently on liaison duty with the hover regiment, the lance far outmatched the lone enemy 'Mech.

The dust began to settle. James was puzzled when the *Panther* did not appear. The puzzle was solved as the Kurita 'Mech came crawling out of the cloud to raise its arm, firing another blast at the Marshal's *Zeus*.

The cyan energy scythed into the *Zeus* almost exactly where the previous bolt had gouged it. Armor flowed under the energy beam's caress to drop hissing into the gash. In the cockpit, James watched warning lights flash amber for a microsecond before flaring a steady red. He cursed as the *Zeus*'s hip joint froze, flash-welded by the enormous heat.

Hallbrock pumped a stream of armor-piercing shells from the *Wolverine*'s Whirlwind autocannon into the Kuritan. Benoit unleashed his 'Mech's cannon and added ruby pulses of coherent light from his Thunderbolt A5M laser. The *Panther* writhed under the assault. Its shattered armor gaped, and James could see its ferro-titanium bones through the swirls of flame and smoke. Benoit's *Zeus* stepped closer and swung its massive, squared-off foot in a short, flat arc. The kick crashed into the side of the fallen *Panther*'s cockpit, tearing the entire head assembly free as it crushed the side walls together.

"Hot pilot, that Benoit," Hallbrock commented on his private frequency with the Marshal.

"It's not like I need a bodyguard," James snapped. "I could've taken him out myself."

"Never pass up a gift, Jimmy boy. And don't ever be sorry you've got a good MechJock on your team."

"You're right. I should be grateful." He had been scared, frozen by an unreasoning fear when the damned Snake had come crawling out of the dust, still ready to kill. He was glad that Hallbrock and Benoit were there. Still, he had to tough it out. BattleMech commanders were supposed to be as tough as they come. But they were also not supposed to be stupid. He keyed open the lance frequency. "Gonna have to get this baby back for repairs. Thanks for the save, Hauptmann."

"*Bitte,* Marshal."

"Jimmy boy, Devlin reports the Dracs are running."

"Damage to them?"

"Minimal."

"Whatever happened to samurai fighting to the death?"

"Still happens, Herr Marshal." Hauptmann Benoit's *Zeus* kicked the fallen *Panther*. "Whenever we catch them."

And that's been the problem, James mused.

"Ease off, Rangers," he ordered over the RCT command channel. "Let them go. If you get spread out in pursuit, you get into trouble. We don't want a repeat of what happened to Tenth Deneb last week."

James led the command lance back to the field headquarters. The trip back in the wounded *Zeus* was bumpy, and he was relieved when they crossed the perimeter. He parked the 'Mech by the Tech shed, leaving orders that it be rearmed with expendables as soon as the hip was functional. The expeditionary force might not have as many shells and rockets as they wanted, but as commander, his 'Mech would have full ammo racks. Sir Michael Hallbrock was waiting for him when he reached the hotel they had appropriated for the Rangers' headquarters. The old retainer's gray topknot was sodden with the sweat that sheened his flesh. He had a cold beer ready for James. His own bottle was half-empty.

"Getting tougher out there, Jimmy. Them Snakes are looking pretty good. The damn groundpounders are putting up more fight than I've seen in a long time. The bloody planetary militias are even standing up to our armor. It's got me a little worried."

James drained the bottle and tossed the empty over his shoulder. "You're overreacting, Sir Michael. We've been slowed down a little here, but we're doing no worse than most of the other planetary assaults. The first wave is still proceeding well enough, and we still haven't seen the 'death before dishonor' that we were supposed to get from the Dracs. The great ferocious Dragon is turning out to be made of paper."

"I think you're being a bit hasty, Jimmy."

"Prince Hanse will cut loose the supplies for the second wave soon. We have what we need to mop up here and get on with it. We'll take the Rangers rimward and meet the coreward arm of the Galedon thrust, encircling the Galtor Thumb. By then, the rebellions we instigated will be in full swing. I wouldn't be surprised if our friendlies kicked the Dracs out without any help from the mercs the Prince has sent in. We're going to take back all the Snakes have ever stolen from us, and more."

A runner dashed up, sketching a salute as he panted his message. "Tenth Deneb First Battalion reports an attack by Kurita armor, Marshal Sandoval. They've beaten it back, but Deneb commander counts a dozen 'Mechs down, at least three beyond repair."

James dismissed the runner and turned to find Sir Michael's brown eyes regarding him curiously.

"An omen, Jimmy?"

The Marshal laughed. "You a superstitious man, good knight?"

"Maybe so. We've been fighting a lot of their armor here, and lot of other groundpounders, too. But we've seen damned little of their BattleMechs.

"So where are the 'Mechs?"

61

*AgroMekTek Shipping Warehouse, Port Paix,
   Le Blanc*
*Le Blanc PDZ, Draconis March, Federated Suns
6 July 3039*

Noise filled the long, open space that was the AgroMekTek shipping center. That was not unusual for this manufacturer of industrial and agricultural 'Mechs. The corporation often did some minor disassembly of its product here in order to meet the crating needs for the interstellar shipment of their product. That kind of work was noisy. What was unusual was that the machines being worked on in the warehouse were not being broken down; they were being assembled. They were also BattleMechs.

Workers climbed among the scaffolding to free delicate assemblies from anti-shock packing and to reinstall the various pieces of weaponry and electronics that had been shipped separately, for security purposes. Respirator-masked painters scrawled stripes and splotches of color over the white base of the machines, taking special care to cover the long-tailed stars of the 'Mechs' left legs. A sharp petrochemical smell pervaded the warehouse as chem-suited men and women used solvents to strip the last of the protective gel from weapons and moving surfaces. Hard-eyed men with lurid tattoos on their stripped torsos sweated and grunted as they wrestled crates marked "Sounding Rockets" into stacks at the machines' feet. One box escaped its handlers to crash to the ferrocrete floor and shatter, spilling its contents and revealing them to be high-explosive missiles instead. Cursing vigorously, the *kobun* gathered their wayward charges.

Yasir Nezumi walked up to Tomoe Kurita as she stood alternately surveying the progress of the workforce around her and studying a map of Port Paix. The yakuza *oyabun*'s swarthy face was lit by the toothy grin that he considered a friendly and winning smile.

"It goes well, yes?"

Tomoe looked up from her map. "*Hai, Oyabun.* They are almost ready."

"We are pleased to be of service to the great lord Theodore. May he prosper." He leaned forward to indicate confidentiality. "I am glad the Kanrei has not held the unfortunate circumstances of our first contact against my organization. It would have been more pleasant had I known who he was."

"He felt it better to be cautious then, *Oyabun.* He understands and holds no grudge. You and your organization have served him well."

Nezumi felt relief. He was never very comfortable around Theodore, always afraid that the incident on Benjamin was never far from the Kanrei's mind. The words of Theodore's wife and lieutenant eased that concern. "I am glad that I could be of aid, however small, in introducing him to the *Kuromaku.*"

"The Kanrei and the Combine are grateful for your patriotism."

Nezumi bowed. Anything he could do to ingratiate himself with Theodore would not hurt. The Kanrei might simply be waiting for the end of this unpleasantness before settling old scores.

"Perhaps some of my men can be of use to you in taking the city."

"It's unnecessary for you to expose your operation here to such danger, *Oyabun.* This world should not be difficult to secure. Le Blanc is normally an open planet, its money-grubbing rulers seeking to rival Galatea as a haven and hiring hall for mercenaries. They only accept the presence of Davion troops reluctantly, and have no real loyalty to the Federated Suns. The locals will not interfere. With the House troops gone to the front, there is nothing more than a skeleton force stationed at the garrison fort on the outskirts of the city."

"Forgive my ignorance, *Jokan,* but why, then, have you infiltrated so many MechWarriors into the city? Chokei's company has been here openly for weeks, supposedly seeking employment. They are strong. Could they not have taken the garrison themselves?"

"They could," she conceded. "And they will, if the Buddhas smile. But that is only a diversion. My *senshi* and these fine BattleMechs, which have been lost in transit to the ComStar compound here"—at this Nezumi bowed—"are to take advantage of Port Paix's merchants. We will capture their DropShips at the landing field. Once the ships are secured, we will use them to board and take their JumpShips."

"*So ka*. Then they will join the chain of vessels that make our bridge across the stars."

Tomoe laughed. "You have a poetic way about you, Nezumi-*san*. That's hardly what I would call the hodge-podge of JumpShips we've got out there. They're mostly tramps, pirates, and smugglers." At Nezumi's slight frown, she added, "And merchants." He accepted her emendation with good grace. Many of the JumpShips hiding among the uncolonized suns between the Combine and Theodore's targets had come from companies run by the yakuza. Some of those ships had never been involved in illegal activities. In all, the yakuza assets far outnumbered the very few military vessels in the "bridge across the stars."

That "bridge" was a chain that would allow rapid transfer of Kurita assault units into the heart of the Draconis March. As one vessel jumped into a system, it would transfer its DropShips to a waiting vessel with its Kearny-Fuchida drive charged and ready. The passengers would not have to wait while the original ship recharged its drive, a process that could take a week or more. The technique was commonly used for couriers and to transport the rulers of Great Houses, but merchants usually found that the reduction in transit time was not worth the expense.

"Even merchants honor the Dragon, *Jokan*. You will find our captains experienced and efficient."

"I'm sure we will, *Oyabun*," she said with a smile.

A young secretary called to Nezumi from the catwalk outside the office suspended fifteen meters from the ferrocrete. He acknowledged her with a wave, then bowed to Tomoe.

"It is time for the signal broadcast."

"Let's go."

They took the lift up to the office suite, arriving in time to see the ComStar logo fade from the room's news monitor. A yellow-robed Adept greeted her invisible audience and gave a rundown of the daily receipts of newsworthy messages received at the HPG station.

Tomoe and Nezumi waited patiently through the war news, as they had each day of the week since she had arrived. Nezumi sweated, though the office was cooler than the busy workfloor. A glance assured him that the window's broad, frosted pane was slanted open to let air into the room. *Nerves,* he told himself. *Somehow I think that today is the day.*

The general news crawled by, to be followed by the standard list of messages awaiting pickup or private broadcast. Nezumi scanned them avidly and found it. A transmission from Mister Gan of Port Paix to his sister, Rose.

Nezumi looked to Tomoe for confirmation. She nodded.

He stepped behind the desk and tapped out the code for the ComStar station on his comm deck. As he waited for the connection to go through, he readied the speech synthesizer that would be the voice of Rose Gan. Soon they would verify the order to move by checking the seemingly innocuous contents of the traveling salesman's message to his sister.

Nezumi gazed out the window as he waited for the link to open. The synthesizer spoke, beginning its conversation with the ComStar Acolyte who answered the call. He noticed smoke rising in the northeast. Soft and muted by the distance, the sounds of battle drifted through the opened window.

"That will be Chokei," Nezumi decided. "He always was overeager to get to the action."

62

Government Center, Nevcason, Vega
Dieron Military District, Draconis Combine
12 July 3039

Hauptmann-General Kathleen Heany scowled as the group of laughing officers entered the room. It was not that their light humor was offensive. The Good Lord knew that the current success of the invasion was likely to foster such cheerfulness among the young soldiers.

No, it wasn't the young officers who bothered her, but the way Field Marshal Nondi Steiner treated them. These youngsters and their counterparts throughout the Lyran Commonwealth Armed Forces were the fair-hairs, the golden children who received preferential treatment from the promotion boards as well as the quartermaster corps. What made it worse was the way General Steiner and the rest of the High Command listened to their ideas—ideas tainted by Davionist thinking.

Ymir's sword! Even having all Nagelring grads like Patrick Finnan in the High Command would be easier to bear.

Nondi and her clique ignored the sound and time-proven advice of officers like herself. Instead, Heany and many of her contemporaries were relegated to staff positions and given hollow honors. A poor thank-you for talented and loyal people who had served with distinction in Davion's war against the Capellans, soldiers who had borne the brunt of Operation Götterdämmerung and then been betrayed by the politicians who had thrown away hard-won gains.

Ah well, she told herself with a sigh. *The Lord works in mysterious ways.*

Heany swept her gaze across the room. The bright light of the planet's sun, though reduced by the tinted vitryl panel that dominated the outer wall, provided more than enough illumination for the large square chamber. She paid little attention to the posh furnishings and fine-painted screens that decorated the chamber; her interest was in the officers who had gathered. They stood talking in clumps or sat on the room's original upholstered armchairs or newly gathered straight-backed and folding seats.

Across the room, her old rival Patrick Finnan sat alone, looking as sour as she felt. He, too, had taken his lumps from that sneaky Kurita kid. The media wags made much of the mistakes he had made against the fledgling heir to the Dragon. She understood that treatment, for she'd suffered the same herself. It almost made her sympathetic to the hard-nosed Nagelring graduate.

Her thoughts were derailed as the great double doors of the room opened, and Nondi Steiner entered. The Field Marshal waved the assembled officers back to their seats as they rose to salute her. She walked to the fine imported mahogany table where Heany and the rest of the senior staff waited, and placed her compdeck down before addressing the assembly.

"Good morning, gentlemen, ladies. I'm pleased to see that you are all looking rested and fit. You'll need to be." Her face was stern for a second before a grin began to spread over it. "This morning's fax transmission contained the go-ahead for the second wave."

The room burst into enthusiastic cheers and martial shouts. Heany felt a rush of excitement that momentarily let her forget that she would have little part in the offensive.

A single sharp sound reached her ears through the tumult. A gunshot? Incredulously, she turned to look out the window. Many others had heard the noise as well. Heads craned, searching for an explanation.

An infantry helmet of Steiner style tumbled past the window on its way to the ground. A moment later, three lumpy objects splatted softly against the window, sticking where they struck. Heany spied the thin wires trailing toward the roof and was on her feet in an instant. Others were moving as well, but many officers had only just recognized the disturbance among their fellows when the globs of explosive detonated, shattering the vitryl panel. Shards rained in a crystal storm across the room, shredding uniforms and flesh with callous indifference. By the grace of God, she was untouched, but a wide-eyed Kommandant fell at Heany's feet. His mouth worked soundlessly, a vitryl splinter protruding from the back of his torn throat.

Another explosion blew the room's double doors from their hinges. The concussion tumbled furniture and people in a direct line from the blast. The room filled with smoke and screams.

Motion in the corner of her eye caused Heany to pivot back to the window. A half-dozen black-suited figures swung through the jagged-edged opening in the outer wall to land cat-footed in the chaos. The cords they had descended on snaked out the window to hang limply as the intruders' subguns coughed out death to those nearest them. Through a rift in the hazy air, Heany saw a dozen more DEST troopers pound through the demolished doorway. Their guns added to the cacophony.

Suddenly, Heany found herself face-to-featureless mask with one of the invaders. In that frozen moment, she imagined the cold eyes behind the red-tinted mirror faceplate. She felt them take her measure before the muzzle of his gun rose slightly. A cough and stir at Heany's side broke the tableau. Nondi Steiner struggled to rise from behind the overturned table. The DEST trooper pivoted to turn his gun on the Field Marshal. Without thinking, Heany threw herself to the side, knocking Steiner down as the intruder fired. Hot pain flared in Heany's leg as she collapsed atop her superior.

"I'm too old for this," Heany moaned.

Laser pulses clawed through the dissipating smoke, cutting down three of the DEST troopers. Around the room, intruders were breaking free from melees with Steiner officers. Two stood their ground, laying down suppressive fire against the Lyran troops who had finally arrived. Regrouping by the window, the Kuritans locked the dangling lines into devices at their belts and hurled themselves out the window. A high-pitched whine filled the room as they ascended to the roof. Lyran guards cut down the two remaining intruders and hurried across the room to fire up at the vanishing shadows.

As suddenly as it had begun, the attack was over.

More troopers poured into the room. To Heany, their gray

field uniforms and battle vests looked strangely clean, inappropriate to the carnage of the briefing room. As soon as their officer had assured himself that none of the DEST troopers were playing possum, he ordered his men and women to assist the wounded.

Heany rolled off Field Marshal Steiner. The Marshal was ashen pale under the blood that splashed her face. Her own breathing coming quickly, Heany fumbled at Steiner's throat, feeling for a pulse. She huffed with relief when she found one. That comfort evaporated as she noticed the bright blood pumping from the Marshal's thigh. Heany shed her tunic, wadding it into a pad to hold against the wound. Blood soaked through to slime her hands, but the bleeding slowed.

"Medtech!"

When her first call only mingled with the other shouts for help, she added, "Field Marshal Steiner's been hit."

The medics hustled in, relieving her. They assured Heany that, with intensive care, the Field Marshal would live. But her wounds were serious. She would not be commanding any armies for awhile.

Heany stood and caught herself against the wall before she fell. Looking down at the leg that had betrayed her, she found her trousers werë awash in blood. She said nothing. There were more seriously injured officers to be attended to. She leaned against the upturned table and surveyed the room, feeling her stomach rebel at the sight and smell of a conference room become abattoir.

So many! She counted heads, looking for faces she knew. Finnan was nursing a slashed arm, insisting that the medtech trying to bandage him ignore his rank and deal with the more seriously wounded. Brian Kincaid and Willy Thompson were among those who had merely taken gashes from flying debris. Uliosha Donovon lay in a pool of blood, face half torn away by bullets and her torso ripped into a mass of undifferentiated meat and fluids. Too many bodies did not move. Too many of the dead were young officers. She regretted her earlier antipathy. They were too young to die like this.

With a start, Heany realized she was the senior officer.

Kurita could not be allowed to profit from this atrocity. She would have to take command. The offensive was too important and the Snakes needed to be taught a lesson.

Such a humbling of the office corps could only be a sign

from God. He had made his will known in leaving her the senior survivor. She was given this opportunity to show not just the High Command, but the entire Inner Sphere, that the failures during Operation Götterdämmerung were flukes. She would show them that the old way was the best.

"Get yourselves together, people. Everybody who's ambulatory, downstairs to whatever the Snakes have left of the operations center. We've got a war to fight."

63

West Cerant County, An Ting
Galedon Military District, Draconis Combine
9 August 3039

Marshal Ardan Sortek bit off another chunk of the dark brown ration bar, which tasted to him like old sweat, having picked up the overall ambiance of his *Victor*'s cockpit; the 'Mech had been run too long without a system flush. Stifling a yawn, he decided that he had been too long without something as well: a good night's sleep. *Ah, the joys of life in the field.*

If war's only price were the discomforts, he would gladly pay it to be free of the endless political intrigues of the Davion court. Years of having to play the court games had improved his ability, but could not make him like it any better. He was relieved to be back in command of a line unit and pleased that the unit was the First Davion Guards. Even with its death and tactical deception, war was cleaner than court intrigue. It left a man feeling less soiled.

There had been too much of the bad side of war, too much death and pain and suffering, here on An Ting. Contrary to intelligence estimates, the Kuritans had been waiting for the assault. Their conventional regiments had been in prepared positions, ready for the Davion attack. The Drac 'Mechs had so far only put in a brief appearance, striking to blunt Davion breakthroughs and then disappearing. In spite of that, the fighting had been ferocious, each day putting them further behind Prince Hanse's schedule.

Word had come in from scouts in the western foothills that the Kuritans were stirring. Wanting to see for himself, Sortek had set out in his *Victor*, feeling secure enough thirty kilometers behind the lines to travel without escort. That sense of security faltered when he spotted a Vedette tank crawling over the crest of the hill in front of him. The armored vehicle was not emitting any IFF signal that the *Victor*'s equipment could read.

He had not had his missile racks brought to full load and the *Victor* was running hot, its heat exchanger system still malfunctioning from the hits he had taken in last week's battle. The last thing he wanted right now was a fight. As a precaution, he armed his lasers and opened the ammo feed to the Pontiac 100 autocannon that made up the *Victor*'s right forearm. Optimistically, he kept the 'Mech on its heading. If the tank was friendly, its crew could not miss the wreathed sword-and-sun insignia on the *Victor*'s chest. If not, at least he wouldn't be a sitting target.

"Merde," he cursed aloud when he spotted the puff of white smoke from the Vedette's main gun muzzle.

He cut right, snapping ruby pulses from the paired Sorenstein 4.8cm lasers on the *Victor*'s left arm as he charged. The tank's shot furrowed the ground between his 'Mech's feet. Sortek leaned into the accelerator, jolting with the rough ride over the broken ground. He continued his harassment fire as he closed with the tank. Only two bursts from the Kuritan's autocannon scored, and they did no more than flake off some of the *Victor*'s armor plating in the 'Mech's lower left leg and upper chest.

At seventy meters, Sortek triggered the Pontiac, but the *Victor*'s violent motion threw off his aim. The hillside cratered around the tank. Belatedly, it began to move again.

Sortek tapped a correction into his targeting system and fired again. The high-velocity shells ripped into the tank as it churned at the already-torn ground, seeking purchase for a turn. The armor-piercers cut through the Vedette's ProTecTech plating as though it were merely lacquered wood. Chunks scattered on impact, and a second later, the whole vehicle burst in an eye-searing explosion.

The Marshal had no time to congratulate himself. Two more Vedettes crested the hill. *No more point in keeping it quiet,* he told himself.

"Sortek to Pangolin Base. Hostiles in sector Tango-Romeo seven-three-six. Need support."

Sortek opened fire on the tanks. Without waiting to see the results, he backed away. A gap in the hill afforded him a glimpse of an entire armored column moving up the reverse slope toward his position. He repeated his call, and this time got a response.

"Pull back, Marshal," the cool voice of the base comm officer advised.

"Too hot, Pangolin. They'll swarm me. I've got a whole company here."

There was a brief delay. "Understood, Marshal. We had a lance on its way up to the front. They're vectoring in on your position. Your luck is holding, Marshal. They should be there in ten."

"You'd better be right, Pangolin. If these Snakes get through me, they'll be in your laps in thirty."

"Understood, Marshal. Good luck."

Sortek's battle against the Kurita company was a seesaw affair—him trying to stay out of the line of fire; them trying to get as many vehicles as possible into position to fire on him. The Snakes lost no time adopting tactics that kept them out of range of his Pontiac cannon as much as possible. Meanwhile, the heat in the *Victor*'s cockpit rose steadily.

Just as he was giving up hope of a timely rescue, the shrill passage of long-range missiles announced the arrival of the Davion lance. The Vedette that Sortek had just crippled shuddered under the impact of the rockets. Black smoke boiled up through the gaps the warheads tore into its armor. As soon as he saw the survivors of the crew bail out, Sortek turned his attention to the next opponent.

The Davion lance, two *Enforcer*s, a *Dervish,* and a *Stinger,* stormed across the rolling hills. Their sudden, reckless attack stunned the Kuritans. A Vedette burst into a fireball under their concentrated fire.

The Pontiac's last cassette round clicked empty as Sortek bracketed the nearest Vedette with a burst of fire. The turret burst into flames as the main gun rocked free of its shattered mount to rattle down the Vedette's sloped armor. Its drive wheels mangled and treads shredded, the tank ground to a halt.

The odds had swiftly changed.

Outclassed by the newly arrived 'Mechs, the Kuritans withdrew. Sortek forbade pursuit. Feeling nervous about the Dracs' unheralded arrival, he wanted the lance nearby. "Take five," he called to his rescuers. "We're heading back to Pangolin Base as soon as I get this old warhorse's heat down."

"Tough fight, Marshal?" asked one of the Jocks. Sortek's comm board identified the signaller as Sergeant Sally Cantrell, the *Dervish* pilot.

"I wouldn't want to make this sort of thing a habit," Sortek allowed. "I'm bushed."

"Welcome to the club, Marshal." Leftenant Link's intonation was jovial, but Sortek sensed a bitter undertone. "If they're working us this hard with their groundpounders, what'll they do when they cut loose their 'Mechs?"

"We're about to find out." Cantrell's *Dervish* poked a rectangular forearm toward the north.

Ardan followed the line. Four Kurita 'Mechs were striding over the low ridge, spreading out into formation.

"*Chargers*," Link called out. "Gotta be with those shoulder baffles. They're too big to be *Griffins*, and they ain't got hand-helds. They'll be easy marks."

"Oughta be. They only pack small lasers. Won't be able to burn us at this range."

Two of the Kurita 'Mechs disappeared from Sortek's vislight scan in a cloud of smoke. Years of battle had taught him to recognize the signature exhaust of long-range missiles. "Break wide!" he ordered. "Evasive!"

The Davion BattleMechs scattered, but the surprise barrage had its effect. All of them took hits. The *Stinger* went down with a crippled leg.

"I don't think these things are *Chargers*," Cantrell said slowly.

"I think you're right," Sortek agreed. "The head's different."

"This is going to be a fight," Cantrell returned.

"Well, Marshal," Ling quipped, "your schedule just took another hit."

Sortek found the Jocks' easy banter reminiscent of his old command, but he hoped that they were not minimizing the problem. These 'Mechs, which he had tagged into his computer as *Charger-II*, were a rude surprise. And the appearance of enemy 'Mechs this far behind their lines was bad news. The Kuritans were on the move. He wondered how many more surprises the Dragon had in store.

64

West Cerant County, An Ting
Galedon Military District, Draconis Combine
11 August 3039

From the command lance's position in the hills west of the city, Dechan Fraser could look down on the city of Cerant. Eleven years ago, he had fought for his life and the continued existence of Wolf's Dragoons in that city. It didn't look that much different today. A shiver ran down his spine that had nothing to do with the cool breeze slipping down intermittently from the mountains.

Jenette reached over to place a gentle hand against his cheek. She tucked an errant strand of his blond hair behind his ear and away from the sleek pink skin at the side of his head, freshly shaven for better contact with the sensors in his neurohelmet. "You all right?"

"Yeah."

"It's the city, isn't it?"

"Yeah."

"Quite a conversationalist today."

He quirked the side of his mouth up in irritation.

"I feel it, too," she said, oblivious to his expression. One look at her face made him instantly contrite. "The ghosts are down there. All those lost Dragoons, asking why we're doing this."

"It does seem strange. The last time we were here, we were fighting the Ryuken. Akuma's Ryuken-*ichi*, to be exact."

"I'm glad Theodore ordered the name struck from the rolls," she said with sudden venom.

"Michi's idea," Dechan pointed out.

Jenette frowned. "Always Michi. He got us into this. He seems to be running our lives."

"We're not just paying back a debt," he reminded her. "You know there's more to it than that. We can't leave till the job's done. That's our mercenary honor. Even the Dragoon ghosts understand that."

She seemed unconvinced. "So why doesn't Michi answer our letters? Friends shouldn't abandon each other."

"He's still our friend, I think, and I know that he needs our help. We promised we wouldn't abandon him. That's why *we* don't leave." He reached for her hand, but she pulled it away and wrapped her arms around herself as though she were cold. "Isn't it?"

"I'm tired, Dechan. I want to go home."

Dechan understood her frustration and loneliness. *Home. As if they had one. Their home had been the Dragoons, until they'd left to follow Michi Noketsuna on his quest for vengeance.* The travails the three had shared made them friends, then led him and Jenette to agree to do all they could to help Michi see his goal through to the end. That promise had trapped them here among the Kuritans, fighting to save the realm of Takashi Kurita, the man against whom Colonel Jaime Wolf had sworn a blood feud. He wondered how the old Iron Man Tetsuhara would have resolved such a conflict of duties. Would Minobu have a better solution to Dechan's quandary than he'd had for his own?

The receiver in Dechan's ear buzzed, calling him to duty. He tapped it to life, and *Tai-shu* Kester Hsiun Chi's voice whispered to him.

"All is in readiness, Fraser-*san*."

Snapping into his new role as a commander, Dechan asked, "The Davion air?"

"Quite busy. They were not ready for our reserves. They seem especially surprised by the numbers of our *Sparrowhawk*s. After all, it is their design. Response to our ComStar-supplied *Hellcat* flights is encouraging as well. I think the professors at the New Avalon Institute of Science will be making some adjustments to Davion tactical doctrine."

"Then we will have a clear field for maneuver?"

"As much as I have been able to arrange. The Federated Suns troops do seem a little uncooperative, though. They have not yet surrendered," Chi said with a chuckle. His voice vacated Dechan's ear, leaving a sibilant, rushing sound that indicated the line was still active. In a moment, the gravelly tones resumed. "Please man your machines. I will need you to lead your Ryuken detachment into the attack soon."

"We'll be ready, Chi-*sama*."

"I am sure you will. Good hunting, Fraser-*san*."

The channel went dead with a click.

He stepped up to Jenette and put his arms around her from behind. "Time to saddle up."

She nodded as she turned in his embrace. "After this, we leave?"

"When we've finished our job."

Jenette hugged him tightly, face buried in the padded shoulders of his cooling vest. She pushed back and ran her soft gray eyes over his features. "Be safe." She kissed him lightly and slipped from his arms.

"Unity enfold you," he called softly as she trotted off to her *Hatamoto-kaze* BattleMech.

"Marshal Sortek! The Kuritans have breached the perimeter!"

The wail of the warning siren rose over the headquarters, as Sortek ordered the security lance scrambled. Directed chaos engulfed the room as men and women hurried to perform the tasks they had dreaded. The headquarters was to be abandoned. The door clattered open as an orderly carried the first armload of datadisks into the night.

Sortek turned to his adjutant. "Where and with how much, Jeanne?"

"North quadrant. Looks like two or three BattleMech regiments. We've got reports of their new heavies up and down the line. At least thirty of them."

"So many?" Sortek and Link's lance had barely escaped from a single lance of those machines two days ago. He shook his head. "Where'd they get all that stuff?"

"I don't know, sir."

"Well, intel doesn't seem to, either. If we make it out of this, it'll be their heads that roll, not yours." He massaged his red-rimmed eyes with both hands. "You oversee the evac. I'm going out to make sure our rear guard holds. See you at the DropShips."

She saluted his back as he ran for his 'Mech.

Dechan Fraser was tired, but his fatigue seemed to vanish when the battered and battle-scarred *Hatamoto-kaze* limped into the Ryuken camp. The eighty-ton 'Mech looked like it had been through a war. Which, of course, it had. Unlike his own *Hatamoto-ku,* the *H-kaze* showed heavy damage. The only area lightly affected was the chest plate, whose surface was blackened from missile exhaust and pitted by shrapnel marks. The 'Mech's radiator fin and one of the shoulder baffles were gone. The broad, flat sheaths that protected the antennae, and gave the 'Mech's head assembly the look of an ancient samurai helmet, dangled across its faceplate. The heavy armor on its left leg had been shredded and melted away. Tendrils of myomer pseudo-muscle floated through the gaps that revealed the cracked and pitted alloy structural members. No wonder the machine limped. Could the pilot have endured such destruction intact?

His fears were allayed when he saw Jenette climb whole and unharmed from the cockpit. He was waiting for her when she finished her descent. They held each other wordlessly for a minute before he broke the embrace to check out her condition. She was uninjured, but looked as beat as he felt. Even her smile was exhausted. He hustled her to the camp kitchen, thrusting a cup of hot tea into her hands until he could gather some food. They ate in silence, each finding the other's presence enough for the moment.

She placed her empty bowl on the ground. "The fight here is over?"

"I think so," he mumbled. "Davion DropShips have been lifting since midnight. They're burning straight for the jump point. An Ting has held, and without this system, the Davion thrust into Galedon will founder."

"Good." Her smile flashed in the darkness. "We'll be done soon."

Buoyed by what he took as her relief, he allowed the joy of a job well-done to fill his voice. "We taught Theodore's people well. The Ryuken fought a hell of a battle, more disciplined than I thought they'd be. The Iron Men would have been proud. These Jocks are almost as good as his old unit. They sure outshone the Eighth Sword of Light."

"You want another Misery?"

The bitterness in her voice, and the thought of the awful weeks on that barren planet where the Ryuken had fought the Dragoons, crushed his growing sense of accomplishment. His delight in the success of his charges turned to ashes as he remembered those bitter days on that bitter, cold world. The Dragoons had fought for their lives against all House Kurita could throw at them, including the old Ryuken regiments. The Dragoons had won, barely. Dechan's own lance had brought down the Iron Man . . . barely. He had no wish ever to experience anything like that again.

Had he rebuilt the unit that had almost destroyed the Dragoons, only to allow Takashi Kurita another chance? He forced away that fear and put assurance into his voice. "That can't happen again."

"Are you sure?" she asked softly.

In the night around them, Dragoon ghosts seem to echo her question.

65

Henschel Basin, Exeter
Kentares PDZ, Draconis March, Federated Suns
2 October 3039

"**F**uhito-*kun,* orbital reconnaissance confirms that the DropShips coming in are the Fourth Davion Guards," Theodore announced to the man seated in the forward couch of the BLR-1C *BattleMaster.*

His only response was a grunt.

Theodore took the rebuff in stride. He had no desire to interrupt his pilot's concentration. They were, after all, in the midst of a battle. One that he had best pay some attention to, instead of spending all of his time on system-wide operations. With deft finger motions, he reconfigured the main screen to display the area around the Samuelson Military Reservation, and slaved the secondary screens to the data feeds for the continental situation and the transatmospheric dispositions. He studied the displays, issuing orders to redirect Combine efforts to put more pressure against a poorly sited fire zone that he detected in the Davion defense. With a little more effort, Ryuken-*go*'s second battalion could crack the hedgehog of the Davion Militia's Thirty-fifth Combined Services Brigade and sweep through to raid the proving ground's laboratories.

The *BattleMaster* shuddered.

Rather than querying Fuhito, Theodore called up a window on the main screen. The 'Mech's systems were all nominal, though the schematic display of the *BattleMaster* showed reduced armor in the left-torso area. From the pattern, Theodore recognized a PPC hit. Local resistance must be stiffening. He was wise to leave Fuhito undisturbed.

He went back to his screens.

Fuhito pivoted the *BattleMaster,* but too slowly. The Davion *Warhammer*'s PPC blast caught his 'Mech in the left chest. The Fedrat Militia 'Mechs were old and time-worn, but their pilots fought hard. It was to be expected. They were defending their homes.

This pilot was a brave one. He had come on through the fire of the rest of the command lance to challenge the *BattleMaster.* The lesser machines of his companions had, with the aid of their armored support, engaged the attention of the other four Kurita 'Mechs. It was a valiant but hopeless effort. The *Warhammer* was battered, sparks and smoke trailing from its right-arm PPC. The *BattleMaster* was barely scratched until the Davion MechJock had scored with that last shot from the *Hammer*'s other PPC.

Fuhito elected to meet charged particles with like. He ripped off a blast from his 'Mech's hand-held Donal PPC. The blast struck the *Warhammer* high on the right shoulder, eating through armor to gouge a trough in the Davion machine's superstructure. Fire reached out through the opening as the alloy launcher-feed mechanism for the 'Mech's Holly SRM system burned, ignited by the heat transfer. Slowly at first, then with a sudden, shuddering crash, the Holly SRM launcher fell free of its mounting. The boxy launcher struck the protruding rear of the *'Hammer*'s autocannon and spoiled the pilot's aim before hitting the ground. There, it exploded in impotent fury as the loaded rack of missiles detonated from the heat of the flames engulfing the mechanism.

The *Warhammer* advanced, heedless of its loss.

"Meiyo to naru sensei, buso-senshi-san," Fuhito saluted aloud.

Conscious of his passenger, Fuhito dodged the big *BattleMaster* in among the trees dotting the slope where the machine stood. He was sure that the Davion Jock would follow. As soon as he had put enough of the tall trees between them to screen him from the enemy sensors, Fuhito brought the 'Mech to a halt, damping its heat output. He did not have to wait long.

The *Warhammer* came hunting, its functional PPC swaying back and forth as the pilot covered possible hiding places for his quarry. Unknowing, he bypassed Fuhito's position by thirty meters.

Regretting that he could not afford to meet this noble warrior in a fair battle, Fuhito opened the heat sinks and stepped the *BattleMaster* forward. The *Warhammer*'s pilot must have caught the rise in heat on his IR sensors. The Davion 'Mech started to turn as Fuhito unleashed the full complement of the *BattleMaster*'s formidable array of forward-mounted energy weapons. The Kurita 'Mech's own Holly launcher added its six missiles to the attack. Had the machine carried the usual pair of Sperry-Browning machine guns, Fuhito would have fired them as well. The *Warhammer* was a threat to the Kanrei and had to be eliminated as soon as possible.

The *Warhammer* staggered under Fuhito's flawless gunnery. The previously untouched armor over its lower rear torso vanished under the hellish energy that laved it. Out of control, it started to topple. The white brilliance of the fusion flame escaping its ruptured magnetic containment ate the upper half of the *Warhammer* before it had canted more than thirty degrees. The blackened stumps of its legs struck the ravaged earth. The torso had dissolved, and the Mech Warrior was gone, either blown out of sight or vaporized.

Fuhito turned the *BattleMaster* back the way it had come, moving to rejoin the rest of the lance.

Theodore felt the flicker of heat pass through the cockpit. Fuhito must have fired all of the 'Mech's weapons to tax its cooling system so. Under normal operating circumstances, the machine stayed cool, thanks to the Star League-vintage heat sinks that some ComStar clerk's mistake had left in it.

Those sinks were valuable, but not as precious as the command and control systems that took the place of the anti-personnel armament in this eighty-five-ton behemoth. They and the second seat, the commander's seat, were what really made this BattleMech live up to its name. They made it a true master of the battle. With this machine, the commander had a mobile, well-armored vehicle, able to survive on the battlefield. With the expanded cockpit, the machine could carry two men: the pilot, whose responsibility was the control of the *BattleMaster*'s power and the safety of the passenger, and the passenger, a battlefield commander who was free to worry about his real job, the command of his formations in battle. The commander could function without the distractions of keeping his 'Mech running, and without loss of command control when he came under fire and was forced to concentrate on simple survival.

Transmitting his current orders to the onplanet forces, Theodore wiped the main screen and brought up a display of overall strategic situation. He reviewed the planets involved in his counterthrust against the Davion invasion. Those on the Kurita side of the border, such as Fellanin II, Sadalbari, and Matar, had fallen easily at the start, their Davion occupiers confused and shocked by the sudden onslaught. Theodore had caught them as they prepared for their own attack; many had been hit while in transports.

More shocking to the Davion defenders, and to their High Command as well, was the sudden appearance of Kurita forces deep within their own space. Planets such as Cartago, Doneval II, and Clovis had not been expecting to be attacked while Davion was making its own push into the Combine. The DCMS intercept division, the ISF, the O5P, and the wary but still helpful ComStar people were for once in complete agreement. Hanse Davion—the Fox—had been caught off-guard.

So far, everything had gone like a finely choreographed program. Even the mercenary strikes at Le Blanc, New Ivaarsen, and Dobson had yielded suitable repayment for the investment. The Kurita counterattack, Operation Orochi, had proceeded with pleasing efficiency and success. On every world the Combine forces attacked, they had come down hard, formation after formation. Or so it had appeared. Every *buso-senshi* was doing the work of a 'Mech lance. Each unit was doing its best to look like more than they were, battalions acting like regiments. Theodore knew that Hanse Davion must suspect, at least, that the Combine had been re-arming far faster than could have been predicted. He hoped to fool the Fox by appearing to have more units than actually existed.

The apparent scale of Theodore's counterattack was designed to give the appearance that the Combine had enough resources and enough confidence in its defenses to launch a major offensive in the middle of an enemy invasion. His goal was to make Hanse Davion worry. To make him suspect that his intelligence apparatus had completely failed him. To make him fear for his own state's survival. It was that fear that would save the Dragon.

Theodore was gambling with the life of the Dragon, but he had no choice. The Combine's resources had been stretched dangerously thin. If Operation Orochi failed, the Combine would fall. But if he had been content just to defend the worlds of the Combine, the Draconis military would eventually have crumbled under the pressure of the mighty Davion-Steiner war machine. He was staking everything on this audacious operation.

The arrival of the Fourth Guards was the sign Theodore had been waiting for—the Fox had fallen for the bait. Theodore had been right in his assessment of Hanse Davion as a man who took few chances when playing for such high stakes. The Fox had chosen to protect his own instead of going for the Dragon's throat. Davion was no coward, but he was not foolishly blind, either.

Theodore checked the deep-space feed. The Davion Guards' DropShips were still on course for Exeter. The Guard would want Kurita blood. They would want to stop the Dragon before he took Robinson or thrust any deeper into their state. Theodore had succeeded in arousing Davion's fear.

Smiling with satisfaction, he fed course instructions through to Fuhito's screen.

Fuhito ran the *BattleMaster* up the hill, seeking a clear field for his sensors. At the crest, he halted and oriented the massive torso toward the distant Samuelson Military Reservation. The Kuritans had cracked the Davion defense. 'Mechs stalked through the outer reaches of the reservation, headed for the laboratory and testing compounds.

A pair of missiles smashed into the hillside at his right. Only one explosion geysered dirt, rocks, and vegetation against the *BattleMaster*'s leg. He gauged the origin point and snapped off a shot from the 'Mech's paired rear-defense lasers. The ruby pulses caught a deadfall, exploding it to flinders in a cloud of flash-heated steam. As the debris fell and the smoke cleared, he watched an infantryman stagger away, the flesh of his hands welded to the plastic of the launcher he had used. The man had survived firing on the Kurita 'Mech. Without thought, Fuhito triggered a single pulse that vaporized the stumbling figure.

Downslope, the *Dragon, Sentinel,* and *Crab* that made up the rest of the lance were prowling through the remains of the First NAIS Cadet Cadre. There would be no counterattack against the Samuelson Military Reservation.

The *BattleMaster*'s internal comm screen lit with a map, a projected course highlighted in red. Fuhito tapped an acknowledgement, satisfied that Theodore would read it on his screen when he could spare attention from his strategic concerns. He radioed the movement order to the lance. The expeditionary force had performed this smash-and-run routine across Exeter's northern continent, just as they had done on each planet they had hit between here and the Combine's border. Now it was time to withdraw. The Kanrei must have decided that they had done enough damage here.

Perhaps not quite enough, he thought, as the *BattleMaster* came on a staging area for Davion infantry. Fuhito charged his 'Mech forward, lasers flaring from its chest. At his right, the hunched, alien shape of Barnaby's *Crab* strutted, blasting with its heavy laser forearms. The Fedrat troops, surprised and demoralized by the sudden appearance of the Kurita 'Mechs, panicked to scatter in all directions. The Kuritans continued on, unscathed by the encounter.

Theodore's face appeared on the internal comm screen. "Everything in order, Fuhito-*kun*?"

"All clear, *Tono.*"

"Good."

"What's next, *Tono*?"

"Next we leave Exeter, Fuhito-*kun*. The Fox has taken the bait."

66

Breed System
Raman PDZ, Draconis March, Federated Suns
31 October 3039

Marshal James Sandoval took the crumpled fax out of his pocket. Straightening it, he stared again at the bitter order.
Recall.

All the forces under his command that had been tagged for the second wave were assigned new targets. His own First Robinson Rangers were to lead the attack to recover Breed. The second wave was indefinitely postponed, with all assigned resources being diverted to meet the threat from the Kurita counterattack. Postponed? More likely canceled. The chance had slipped by.

Only six months ago, they had struck the Combine, catching the Snakes unaware. Initial progress had been good. The lack of BattleMech support and counterattacks had only confirmed his belief that the Kuritans had not had time to rebuild those very expensive forces. What they did have was tied up in Dieron resisting the combined attacks that threatened to cut the Combine off from Terra.

It had all looked so good.

Then the Combine's resistance had stiffened. Even though the Davion forces were facing armies light on 'Mechs, the Kuritans held. Planets didn't fall when they were supposed to. The timetable of the invasion had begun to slip. Even then, Sandoval had not been especially worried. The Snakes might have been unprepared, but no one in his right mind would expect them to give up as easily as the Capellans had in the last war.

Then had come the assassinations against the officers of the Steiner front. It had thrown the Lyran thrust into turmoil. The Steiner advances had stopped almost instantly. The no-guts cowards had even gotten themselves kicked off Vega. He had heard a rumor that Katrina Steiner had panicked when she found an origami cat in the Royal Throne Room on Tharkad. James shook his head. An army had to be bigger than its leadership, stronger than its machines. While the Steiner troops had lots of heavy equipment, they seemed lightly equipped with determination. James felt betrayed. He knew that his father would be feeling even more so after all he had done to foster the alliance with those faint-hearted Lyran fancy-dressers.

He had never expected the Davion High Command to crumble, too. Sortek must have overrated the opposition on An Ting. It was the only explanation for the abandonment of the Galedon thrust. James knew better. From all he had seen, the Snakes had to be on the ropes. They were certainly ready to collapse all along his own front. Another push, and they would have.

Then the word had come that the thrice-damned Theodore Kurita had engineered a massive counterattack. Combine units had thrust deep into Federated Suns space, endangering Robinson. James stared sullenly at the faxes littering the small desk of his cubicle. He knew them too well. Supply bases gone. Militia units crushed. Combine planets retaken by the Dragon. AFFS units in danger of being cut off. New Kurita BattleMech units identified. Unexpected forces assaulting Davion worlds.

Everything was coming apart.

The door buzzed, and he tapped the switch to open it. Sir Michael Hallbrock stepped through. He flashed James a brief, apologetic smile. "Time for the approach briefing, Jimmy boy."

"I'll be there in a minute."

Hallbrock started to leave, but stopped halfway through the doorway.

"You done good, Jimmy. The Old Duke will be proud."

James didn't bother to look at him. "We're turning our backs on our last chance to crush the Combine. They've got to be weak, too spread out. If we could just keep pushing."

"Ain't a war ever been fought without a soldier carrying a politician on his back, Jimmy."

James sighed. "Sir Michael, you and my father fed me history when I was growing up. You told me tales of how warriors saved the day, rescued the maiden . . . slew the dragon. The MechWarrior always pulled it out when everybody else had lost hope."

"And you're wondering what's wrong with you that you're not the hero?"

James bit his lip. The old Colonel knew him too well.

"A good soldier follows orders," Hallbrock said softly.

"Even when he knows they're wrong?"

"Are you so sure that they are? Are you willing to bet the lives of millions that you are right about how weak the Kuritans are?"

After a moment of silence, James shook his head.

"I figure Hanse Davion feels the same way." Hallbrock straightened up. "Weak or not, them Snakes are holding Breed and we've got orders to take it back. The men are waiting, Marshal."

James forced a shallow smile. "Go on. I'll be along in a minute."

Hallbrock nodded. The door hissed softly as it cut off James's view of the lanky old Colonel. James sat, glumly staring at the clutter on his table. He felt the frustration building until it burst forth, and his arm swept out to knock all the fax sheets and data disks to the floor.

Drained of emotion, he stood slowly and walked through the mess to the door. He had an assault briefing to run.

67

Kirkwood Manor, Conqueror's Pride, Proserpina
Benjamin Military District, Draconis Combine
12 December 3039

The night was scented with the heavy, sweet odor of
yoruhana blossoms. Occasionally, insects blundered through
the light pools thrown by the stone lanterns, whirring gems
of iridescent chitin. The garden was an island of serenity.

Yasir Nezumi was at ease here, despite the kimono that
clung to the sweat brought out by the warmth and humidity.
The manor belonged to a yakuza leader, a minor official of
the *Boshi-gumi* clan. It was a near-perfect replica of a
Muromachi shoen complex and a sign of the progressive
changes made under the enlightened rule of the Dragon.
Each day, more of the war-ravaged world was returned to
productivity. One day, the Amerigo continent would be re-
claimed as well. When that day came, the *Boshi-gumi* clan
would be strong; they owned much of its land. The future
was bright for those of the clans.

A kagetaka called from the bushes.

Nezumi started, and a nervous anticipation filled him. The
kagetaka was not native to Proserpina, and though common
on worlds across the Inner Sphere, it was a species not yet
reintroduced to this planet. He cleared his throat. He wished
his voice to be heard clearly. It was important to make a
good impression. He was not dealing with the ordinary here.

"The war against the Davion and Steiner *teki* is going

well. Our enemies retreat, cowed and chastened for their temerity. Lord Theodore is triumphant in arms.

"Now that the danger to the Combine is past, it is time to
consider the proper ordering of things. The long years of
waiting for an appropriate moment are over, and we must
turn our eyes to the future. With the invader returned to his
own space, we can now attend to internal matters.

"For years, Takashi Kurita has hindered our lord. Un-
justly. Unwisely. The mantle of the Dragon has passed from
Takashi-*sama*. Men of vision have seen this for some time,
but they thought it prudent to refrain from action. Now the
truth must be recognized. All loyal citizens must do what
they can to see that an orderly transition proceeds, that the
old and faltering give way to the strong and vital."

He paused, letting the garden's silence engulf him.

"It is Kanrei Theodore's desire," he added.

Having stated his case, he relaxed. A beetle buzzed by his
ear and down past his shoulder to bump into a lantern at his
side. Its gossamer wings folded under its carapace as it
landed. Concerned with matters knowable only to an insect,
it crawled off into the darkness. "Is there anything else to be
said?" Nezumi asked the night. The silent serenity of the
garden went undisturbed. He waited a minute, but there was
no answer from the bushes or the trees. He repeated his
question. Nezumi sat quietly for another two minutes.

Had he been wrong?

He would not know any time soon. Resigned, he stood up,
groaning as he straightened. The price of advancing age, he
lamented. His knees and back were painfully stiff as he
walked the path of carefully chosen and placed stones. As
he neared the bushes at the edge of the garden, his concern
over his aches vanished. A speck of white arrested his passage, a folded rice-paper figure standing on one of the path's
stones. It was an origami cat.

He smiled with pleasure. He had served the Kanrei, and
he knew the Kanrei rewarded those who served him well.

68

Temujin Starport, Conqueror's Pride, Proserpina
Benjamin Military District, Draconis Combine
14 December 3039

Yasir Nezumi was waiting just inside the roped-off area of
the Temujin Starport receiving area, standing prim and
straight in his dark businessman's jacket. Behind the yakuza
oyabun, the crowd milled in sudden excitement as Theodore
walked down the ramp from the DropShip *Tetsuwashi.* A
chant of *"Banzai!"* arose, and Fuhito held back Theodore's
aides. Alone, the Kanrei walked into the acclamation, acknowledging it graciously. As he reached the *oyabun,* the
man made a formal bow.

"Welcome back, Kanrei."

"*Domo,* Nezumi-*san.*" Theodore smiled as he rose from
his bow. He thrust out his hand, and the stocky *oyabun* took
it firmly and pumped it vigorously. "I'm pleased that you
could take time from your business to be here to meet me.
Tomoe has spoken highly of your patriotic organization's
outstanding aid. I'm honored."

"*Iie, Tono.* It is my honor to take part in welcoming home
the victorious Dragon."

"Hardly victorious, *Oyabun.* We're still at war with the
Federated Suns and the Lyran Commonwealth."

Nezumi shrugged away the significance of that remark.
"They have almost completely withdrawn from our planets.
The *teki*'s assault is finished."

"As is ours," Theodore confided. "You know as well as

anyone how thinly spread we were within our wedge into Davion space. We couldn't have continued much longer, but they did not know that. It doesn't matter. We achieved our aim and impressed our determination on Hanse Davion."

Theodore stepped away from the *oyabun,* intent on clearing the receiving area. Over his shoulder, he added, "There's still the hornet's nest in Dieron that needs my attention. I will be heading there tomorrow."

"Your generals are well-trained and efficient, *Tono*. They can handle the minor operations in that district," Nezumi called aloud. Then he lowered his voice so that it carried no further than Theodore's ears. The *oyabun*'s manner shifted to that of friendly conspirator. "Wouldn't Luthien be a better choice for your next destination? It is your due."

Theodore was puzzled by Nezumi's obsequious behavior, but he had no time to ponder it. As they broke through the cordon, well-wishers, anxious officers, and toadying courtiers surrounded him, cheering and calling. Smiling, Theodore turned to the task of greeting his subjects.

Working his way through the crowd with an ease he wouldn't have been capable of two years ago, he spotted two familiar faces, Dechan Fraser and Jenette Rand. They stood aloof from the others, private and separate, despite rubbing shoulders with Kuritans. He greeted them, surprised but pleased that they were here. They were concerned about something and desirous of a private meeting. Assuring them of his attention as soon as possible, he arranged a meeting for that evening. Theodore turned, looking for an aide. None was in sight, but he saw Nezumi still standing at the fringes of the crowd. "Nezumi-*san*," he called. "Can you arrange an escort for my friends?"

"*Hai*, Coordinator," Nezumi responded with a sharp bow.

Theodore froze.

"I'm not the Coordinator."

Nezumi smiled broadly. "Is it not time for the cat to strike?"

Theodore's eyes went wide, his composure gone as dread flooded him. "What have you done?" he said softly.

Fearing that he already knew the answer only too well, Theodore pushed his way through the crowd. He did not head for Nezumi or for the limousine that awaited him. He ran back toward the DropShip, calling out orders for lift-off.

69

His footsteps echoed from the walls as Theodore pounded down the corridor. Otomo guards moved to defensive positions as he approached, readying their heavy-barreled stun rifles. They relaxed as soon as they recognized him, slapping their weapons against the hard plasteel of their cuirasses and bowing their helmeted heads. Theodore paid them no heed.

The last door loomed before him, its brass fittings gleaming in the soft radiance of the glow panels. Theodore hit it hard, jarring to a stop when the door remained firmly in place. His palm had slipped from the handle before he could turn it far enough to disengage the latch. With a curse, he twisted it savagely. Flinging the door wide, he entered the Peony Room, coming to an abrupt halt as he found the man he sought.

Takashi Kurita stood with his back to the door, apparently halted in mid-motion. The Coordinator wore his tan DCMS uniform. Its spotless surface glistened in the soft glow from the paper-shielded glow bulbs scattered throughout the chamber on black lacquered stands. The uniform's creases and folds were barely disturbed by Takashi's motions as he lifted an exquisite, cut-glass decanter in his left hand and poured dark amber fluid into the ice-filled tumbler in his right hand. Takashi returned the decanter to its place among the trays of food and rack of bottles on the table. He stoppered it before turning slowly to face his visitor.

"A very dramatic entrance," he observed wryly. He lifted his glass in mock salute, but did not drink. "Come to boast of your successes?"

Theodore sensed the waves of hostility rolling toward him from the Coordinator. *Just like old times,* he thought. "They are not mine alone. The Combine has drawn together to do this."

"Without me."

"Without you."

Takashi stepped away from the table of refreshments, walking slowly across the room. The soft light threw diffuse and enormous shadows against the gleaming, gold-framed paintings on the walls and the low beams of the elaborately raftered ceiling, as though some hunched giant were walking past. Takashi stopped when he reached the small elevated platform that held the carved chair of state. The Coordinator turned to face his son. "Am I such a useless old man that I must be confined here, surrounded by your lackeys?"

"I did what seemed best. You charged me with the military affairs of the realm. This invasion was one such affair. I didn't wish to disturb your serenity."

"I am not a blind dodderer," Takashi snapped. "Save your courtly excuses for the masses and the fawning toadies of the court. *I* am the Dragon, you insolent pup! This is *my* realm still. Not yours!"

Theodore burned with anger. If the Coordinator had been allowed to control the DCMS during this war, the Combine would have been devastated. Takashi did not understand the new army Theodore had built. If Theodore's agents had not prevented Takashi's orders from going beyond the palace on Luthien, the Combine would have been crippled, if not destroyed. All save the order to hold fast in Dieron had been inappropriate to the vital strategy Theodore was pursuing—and even the Dieron order had been given for the wrong reasons.

Theodore had acted to save the Combine, and his face flushed with anger that his father could question that dedication. Feeling the warmth on his cheeks, Theodore was ashamed that he had let the emotion show. He was angrier still when he saw satisfaction flash into his father's eyes.

"At least you have the grace to be embarrassed by your

conduct," Takashi said harshly. "It is of little comfort. By ignoring me, you threw away a chance to rip out Hanse Davion's throat. Your retreat from Exeter was far too premature. Some have called it cowardly."

The Coordinator continued to berate a silent Theodore. Takashi expressed his contempt for the Kanrei's strategic sense as demonstrated by his conduct of the war, detailing each and every military decision with accuracy that could only mean that the Coordinator had eyes and ears in Theodore's command staff. Takashi was too well-informed to have pieced the material together from individual officers, even if the Warlords had been his spies. Theodore was sure that Constance and her O5P would not have leaked such sensitive material. It could only mean that, in spite of the Director's assurances to the contrary, Subhash Indrahar continued to play his double game, balancing father and son to his own advantage and charting his own course for the survival of the Dragon.

Takashi ranted on. The Coordinator's topic shifted from the poor military decisions to the failure of his son as a warrior. Takashi found Theodore's abandonment of the thrust into the Federated Suns particularly cowardly.

After all these years, the man still did not understand. Theodore tried to push the emotion from his mind, to sink into the calm that would sustain him through what was to come. He was distracted by a sparkle of light from the crystal decanter. His eyes fastened on the convoluted patterns, following their angles. He studied their intricate precision, seeking regularity and pattern to slow his racing mind and to soothe his spirit. Perversely, his discomfort grew. Theodore started again to trace the flow of incisions in the surface of the bottle. A shape emerged amid the abstract angles of the pattern. He drew in his breath, his mind blazingly clarified. Takashi's words continued to hammer on Theodore's ears, but their pounding rhythm lost coherency. Takashi's surface sheen of contempt and disappointment slid away under Theodore's enhanced perception, laying bare the Coordinator's underlying, long-nurtured hatred and jealousy.

Theodore's hand slid down to the holster at his side. The hard, cool ivory of the handgrip snugged firmly into his palm as he slipped the flap open and gripped the Nambu.

Takashi stopped speaking. Their eyes locked. Theodore read pure contempt in his father's ice blue eyes.

"So ka," Takashi said quietly. He straightened his shoulders, the years and faint signs of infirmity left by his stroke vanishing. He lifted his glass to his lips.

Theodore drew his pistol, firing as the gun rose.

Takashi fell over backwards, rolling toward the tall chair of state. He lay still. Glass shards stood like icebergs in a spreading sea of amber fluid. Time ceased to flow for Theodore, the instant frozen and he with it.

From the gloomy upper rafters, a black shadow dropped to the floor, entering Theodore's consciousness before it reached his field of vision. The form crouched to absorb the force of its drop, then straightened smoothly, resolving into a human figure. The soft light of the room was absorbed by the dark clothing, obscuring all details save the hard, narrow shape of the sword hilt thrusting out over the shoulder. The apparition's face was masked, only the eyes visible: dark, lustrous, and utterly calm. Between them was a small black tattoo of a cat, its pose exactly like that of the one Theodore had seen hidden in the abstract design of the decanter's decoration. This person was a nekogami, a superb and implacable assassin, skilled at innumerable forms of death and at one with the darkness.

"Iie, Tono," the shadow said in a soft, feminine voice. "You have given this into our hands. Your presence and participation are unnecessary and unwise."

Theodore swallowed. His calm was cracking, leaving him too aware of the danger he faced. He turned his gun on the nekogami.

"This is not my wish."

The shadow stood silent, unmoving. By the dais, Takashi groaned.

As if prompted by the sound, the nekogami said, "I do not understand, *Tono*."

"There's been a misunderstanding. A well-meaning man took an initiative that was not welcome. He misread my intentions."

"I have been contracted," the voice stated flatly. "The nekogami honor is bound to the completion of the contract. My death is bound to that of the man Takashi Kurita."

"I will not be a party to his murder."

The black-suited figure stiffened. Theodore tensed, then relaxed, sensing no impending attack. She bowed.

"I believe I understand now," she affirmed in a voice so

soft that Theodore almost missed the words. "It is most regrettable."

The woman bowed again, deep and long. As she straightened, she tugged on something within her hood. She made no further movement.

Theodore watched her eyes. They were pools of the night in which she had been nurtured. Her utter, unattached calm was gone, replaced by a strange sort of peace. Then the life was gone from those dark eyes, and her body started to crumple to the floor. Before the corpse hit the polished parquet, there was a flare from within the hood. The mask that had concealed her face dissolved, taking her features with it. None would ever know what face she had worn when she was not creeping among the shadows.

The stench of burnt flesh filled Theodore's nostrils, nauseating and vastly out of place in the elegant Peony Room.

Unity Palace, Imperial City, Luthien
Pesht Military District, Draconis Combine
9 January 3040

Fuhito Tetsuhara and his dozen *buso-senshi* guards, the *Ryu-no-tomo,* or Dragon's Friends, bulled their way through the gathering of gawkers in the corridor leading to the Peony Room. Their 'Mechs and almost two dozen more waited outside the palace grounds, the piloted machines walking protective sentry. Fuhito fretted at the slow progress of his group, but was reluctant to force passage through the courtiers and functionaries. They all outranked him socially, and he had no idea what had happened in the room. He only knew that Theodore had headed there after ordering Fuhito to gather the warriors from the DropShip *Tetsuwashi* and follow.

He had acted as quickly as possible, but it had taken precious time to unlimber the BattleMechs and march them from the port. The Kanrei had long outdistanced them. They had only reached the outer halls of the palace when the distance-muffled shot had reached his ears. The dismounted *senshi* had increased their pace, only to be slowed by the crowded corridors.

The Otomo guards moved to refuse entrance to him and his group, but Theodore's raised hand stayed them. Relieved to see his lord safe within the room, Fuhito ordered the MechWarriors to aid the Otomo in guarding the door. He slipped between two brawny Otomo and entered the room.

Fuhito scanned the room as he passed the guardsmen. He was shocked to see the state of the Coordinator. Takashi sat in his carved chair, bloodied and pale. A man wearing the master's insignia of the Brotherhood of Physicians and two red-robed Pillarine Adepts attended him, cleaning his cuts and dressing them with plastiflesh. Fuhito had seen enough injuries to know that at least one of those wounds was beyond the magic of the spray binding and would leave a scar.

The obvious culprit lay sprawled near the center of the room. Two men were examining the body of the nekogami. A court functionary, his back to Fuhito, stood at the feet of the corpse, and Ninyu Kerai knelt near the body, examining the gray ash near the disfigured face of the assassin. The redheaded ISF man said something to his companion that Fuhito could not hear.

Theodore stood in conversation with his wife and his cousin Constance. As Fuhito approached, the Kanrei put down the decanter he was holding and turned to face him. He acknowledged Fuhito's bow with a nod.

"*Sho-sa* Tetsuhara, I've a different task for you than I expected. I want you to take temporary command of the Otomo. *Chu-sa* Ii has found the attack on the Coordinator beyond his honor."

"*Hai!*" Fuhito was surprised by the order. He was not surprised that the Otomo commander had committed seppuku for his failure to protect the Coordinator. That was expected. But to do so before the investigation was completed and all were certain that the Coordinator was safe? *Chu-sa* Ii had shown a shocking lack of sense for his duty, an unbalanced sense of honor.

"Have the corridors cleared," Theodore continued. "Assure everyone that the Coordinator is safe. I will have a public announcement at . . ." He looked at Constance with a raised eyebrow.

"We should be finished here in an hour, *Tono*," she replied to his unspoken question, turning from the Pillarine *jukurensha* to whom she had handed the decanter.

Theodore consulted his ringwatch before finishing the sentence he had left hanging. "Six."

A new presence intruded on the small group, the functionary Fuhito had seen near the body. Fuhito realized with a shock that the man was Subhash Indrahar, the dreaded Director of the ISF. Behind the Director and to one side stood

Ninyu, showing no sign of his usual sarcastic half-smile. "Do you think that wise, Kanrei?" Subhash queried. "The Coordinator's injuries from the shattered glass and his subsequent fall are light, but he is dazed and disoriented. He will not be ready to speak so soon."

Fuhito watched their eyes lock, felt the play of *ki* energy between them. Absorbed with trying to interpret the energies, he started when Theodore spoke.

"I'm doing what I deem necessary."

"Very well," Subhash said quietly. He adjusted his gold-rimmed spectacles, seating them more firmly. "You seem to be well-supplied with advisors whose words you heed. I will attend to the Coordinator."

Theodore paused a moment, seeming to weigh the Director's words. "I understand," he said finally.

Subhash bowed, brief and shallow, then turned his back on them. The Director strode directly across to the group around the Coordinator, dismissing the Pillarines. Ninyu watched, shifting his attention between the Kanrei and the Director. His face was stiff, as though he fought to control his thoughts. Reaching a decision, he cleared his throat.

"Kanrei," he began, holding out a packet wrapped in plain white silk. "Here is something for Michi Noketsuna."

Theodore accepted the offering and looked questioningly at Ninyu.

"It's some information that might be of interest to him. Recordings made by one Jerry Akuma. It seems that Akuma felt it necessary to secretly record his meetings with certain persons. The recordings are quite revealing. There is, of course, a copy for you. It may tell you something about your father as well."

"*Domo,* Ninyu-*kun.* I hadn't thought you interested in helping Michi-*kun.*"

"I'm not, but these recordings may encourage him to slither back under the rocks he crawled from. The Dragon will be better off without him and the bad company he keeps."

"These are not fabricated, are they?" Constance asked. Her voice contained only curiosity, but Fuhito suspected her words held more. Once again, he was out of his depth among the subsurface meanings that seemed to fill the court and ensnare the lords of the Dragon.

"The truth is damning enough," Ninyu snapped. He

stepped back, and without bowing first, walked halfway across the room before stopping. He seemed unwilling to join those around the Coordinator, but in his covert glance back to Theodore, Fuhito saw his reluctance to return to the Kanrei's group. He stood in the middle of the room for a moment, indecisive. Then he settled his shoulders and strolled slowly out past the Otomo.

"There is trouble brewing," Constance warned. "He is both more and less than one of your companions. Trust him with little."

"I trust him as I must," Theodore stated. "He's completely loyal to the Dragon. As long as the Combine's survival is threatened, he will never betray it."

"He is a small spider, learning the ways of the master weaver at the heart of the web," Constance observed. "He and his teacher may not see your interests and those of the Dragon as one and the same."

Theodore shook his head. "I can't afford to worry about that now. Besides, he won't be a danger for some time to come."

"Any time is too soon," Tomoe asserted.

"That is true, To-*chan*. But we must deal with the present right now. The future must wait for tomorrow." Without looking at Fuhito, Theodore added, "Isn't that right, Fuhito-*kun*?"

"*Hai, Tono!*"

Unity Palace, Imperial City, Luthien
Pesht Military District, Draconis Combine
18 June 3040

Piotr Hitsu, the man Theodore knew as a *kuromaku* of the yakuza, entered the audience chamber only after the guards had withdrawn from the room. Hitsu looked worn, aged more than the years since their last meeting could rightly claim. The *kuromaku* walked slowly across the floor, his limp more pronounced than when the two had met on Corsica Nueva.

A young boy followed him into the chamber. The boy, impeccably attired in a brilliant white *kataginu*, was dark-complexioned and thin, clearly no relation of the stocky, pale Hitsu. Something about the boy's face reminded Theodore of one of the *oyabun* that Hitsu had gathered into an alliance to serve the Combine. The lad, nervous and ill-at-ease in the formal garb, carried a half-meter cube whose shiny, lacquered surface reflected the surroundings as perfectly as a silvered mirror.

The *kuromaku* approached the platform where Theodore knelt. From three meters away, he bowed. He came forward another two steps and bowed again before kneeling.

"I'm pleased to see you again, Hitsu-*san*," Theodore began affably. "It's been too long since we have talked face to face as friends should."

"You friendship honors an undeserving old man, Kanrei."

"Nonsense. Have you brought word from the *oyabun*? They have been silent and invisible these last few months."

"Things will soon be as they were, Kanrei." Hitsu smiled weakly. "Assuming the satisfactory conclusion of today's business."

"If not word from the *oyabun*, what then is today's business, Hitsu-*san*? Your request for this meeting was not specific."

"The business is honor," Hitsu informed him. The *kuromaku* settled himself firmly, resting his palms on his legs just above his knees. He drew a deep breath, and letting some of it loose in a sigh, stared directly at Theodore. The old man's dark mahogany eyes glinted harshly. "Honor and apology."

Hitsu waved the boy forward. With awkward movements the boy rose, padded forward softly, and placed the box on the dais, just to Theodore's right. He bowed raggedly before returning to his place behind the *kuromaku*'s left shoulder.

"Nezumi-*san* has atoned," Hitsu stated.

Theodore didn't need to look into the softly humming box to know that it held the refrigerated head of Yasir Nezumi. The *oyabun* had paid for his ambitious mistake with his life. He also suddenly realized that the boy must be Nezumi's son.

"Nezumi-*san* was rash," Hitsu continued. "But he was mine as *oyabun* of the *oyabun*." The old man ignored Theodore's start at his announcement.

"Nezumi-*san*'s shame is canceled by his act. My shame remains. As his *oyabun*, his actions are my actions, and his honor is mine.

"He used your name in unknowing contravention of your will. His ignorance was, of course, no excuse. He acted without my permission or consent, which he would not have received even had I knowledge of his plans. But neither is my ignorance an excuse."

As he spoke, Hitsu removed a pair of white handkerchiefs from an inner pocket, one silk and one cotton. He laid them on the floor in front of himself, silk to the left, cotton to the right.

"This is unnecessary," Theodore protested, suddenly aware of the old man's intent. *Yubitsume*. The ritual finger-cutting atonement of the yakuza. Though he wished to forbid the action, he knew that it was bad form to refuse. And this man was necessary to Theodore, to the Combine. If Theodore refused his offering, the old man's sense of honor would be outraged. Hitsu would slit his belly in shame. Theodore could not allow that. Even before he had known that Hitsu was *oyabun* of the *oyabun*, he had felt that the man's resources, advice, and knowledge were immensely valuable to the Combine. "Your intent is sufficient for me, Hitsu-*san*."

The old man closed his eyes briefly, but said nothing. Instead, he removed a plain, scabbarded knife from within his jacket. With deliberate slowness, he freed the shining steel from the lacquered wood. Placing the scabbard at his left side, he laid the knife down at his right knee, edge toward himself. Hitsu placed his palms flat against the *tatami* mats and bowed deeply. He straightened and extended his left hand, palm down and fisted except for an extended little finger, to rest on the mat. He took the knife in his right hand, reaching across to rest the edge against the first joint.

Theodore dropped his eyes and nodded, unwilling to let the old man mutilate himself more than the minimum. He heard the crackle of cartilage as the blade bit home. When Theodore looked up again, Hitsu had wrapped the cotton cloth around his shortened finger, holding its loose ends in his fist. The old man pushed forward his offering, wrapped in the silk handkerchief.

"Please accept my apologies."

Theodore reached out and took the offering. He placed it by his right side, next to the lacquer box. Unsure of the proper ritual response, he bowed.

"*Domo, Tono.*" Hitsu bowed. "Honor is satisfied, and I have business that requires my attention. With your permission?"

Theodore nodded. The *oyabun* of the *oyabun* stood stiffly and walked from the room clothed in his dignity, his shame washed away in blood. The boy, green-faced, followed.

The Kanrei remained kneeling, contemplating the box and the small white package with its incarnadine stain at one end.

"You handled that well."

Startled from his musing, Theodore spun. He had risen halfway to his feet and started to pull his gun from its holster before he realized that he knew the voice. Too well. He returned the Nambu to its resting place and fastened the flap. He finished standing and bowed.

Praise was something he was not used to hearing from his father.

Takashi smiled tightly as he slid the painted panel closed behind himself, obviously relishing the surprise Theodore had not quite suppressed. "You still need better control if you are to be Coordinator."

"I don't want to be Coordinator."

Takashi barked a short laugh. "Do you think I did?"

Of course you did, Theodore replied silently. *It's your life.* Aloud, he said, "You've embraced the office wholeheartedly."

"*Hai.* I have." Takashi stepped down from the dais and walked to the outer wall. He opened the *shoji* panels, letting in sunlight as he spoke. "I was very unhappy when my father Hohiro recalled me to Luthien. All I looked for was a life serving the Dragon. I was a warrior, the strong arm of the Dragon who savaged our enemies. But my father knew that the Combine needed a strong heir. One who was more than a simple samurai.

"It is curious, is it not, that our greatest enemy has a similar history? Hanse Davion also wished to be a simple soldier. It is said that the Fox was raised to expect other things from his life than the burden of rulership. But he had an elder brother to insulate him from the concerns of state while I had only my blind devotion to the Dragon. When Yorinaga Kurita killed Davion's older brother Ian on Mallory's World and Hanse became Prince, he did not have the benefit of training at the court before taking his office. But he has prospered nonetheless.

"He did not wish the burden. Nor did I."

Nor I, Theodore echoed in his thoughts.

"Personal desire is a weakness," Takashi asserted. "I learned that as I learned what the Dragon required of me. Courage. Audacity. Tenacity. In time I learned the wisdom of a ruler. The foremost tenet of that cruel wisdom is that one must, and will, do whatever is necessary for the health of the realm. It was an education."

I have been educated, too, Theodore thought. *How strange that I should hear you speak my own thoughts. Frightening, too. I had never thought of you that way.*

"I won't take the office from you. Being Kanrei is enough for me."

"The *office,*" Takashi hissed. "You cannot still be so naive to believe that I would be satisfied with an empty title. You have done all you can to usurp my power, and you pretend that you spare me by leaving me a title. *Power* matters, boy! Not titles. Why you have balked at taking my life as well eludes me. Unless the reason lies in your weakness."

Theodore wanted to ignore the barb, but found himself trying to defend his position, knowing all the while that his defense was just the sort of weakness his father meant. "Being Kanrei is sufficient for me."

"A transparent subterfuge," Takashi accused.

"*lie.* It is a matter of honor."

"What honor is there in a weakling?"

"Honor lies not in strength but in integrity. The teachers you yourself set before me drilled that very deep. The ancient code of *bushido* is a warrior's ethic, but it draws deeply from the well of Confucian wisdom. The ancient sage laid down laws, laws I have sought to follow. One of those dicta, repeated in our own family's book of honor, states that a man may not live under the same heavens as the slayer of his father. To me that dictum means more than a simple justification for seeking revenge for a death.

"I won't be ... I can't be ... a patricide."

"You are weak."

Theodore said nothing.

"But perhaps not so weak as I have previously thought," Takashi conceded. "Though you have had some success in penning me until now, you still do not have the strength to be the Dragon."

"You're blind to my strength, then. It's there. You've molded your successor better than you think."

Takashi looked at him thoughtfully. "I will admit that you have had successes. Some have even impressed me. But those are soldier's victories. They give you no experience in the higher strategies of ruling a realm. The days for a ruler's wisdom are come again. Already the fighting fades, and we return to the old ways of raiding and harassment. The time of your eminence is past. I shall find the cracks in the walls you have built around me and escape your snares. I will again take up the power that is rightfully mine."

The Coordinator's face lit with fervor as he spoke. Theodore considered what he saw. Once he would have feared the threat, the hint of madness it contained. Now he only feared the results. His father cared deeply for the realm, but Takashi had let his own concerns blind him to its needs. Takashi had forfeited his right to rule. This was no time for weakness.

"You will do what is required of you as Coordinator," Theodore said. His voice was mild, but iron conviction underlay his words. "You will serve the realm as its figurehead while I attend to its health and well being. *Mine* is the vision that will see us through the future. *Mine* is the hand that will guide the realm. We mustn't fight and destroy the Combine between us. If you oppose me, I will have you sequestered."

Takashi's eyes narrowed.

"Then I shall not oppose you," he whispered rancorously. "In the open. We shall have our fights, boy. Do not doubt it. But you are right in one thing. We must attend to appearances. We must show the people, and our enemies—most especially our enemies—that we stand together, the head and the arm of the Dragon."

Even as the Coordinator held out his hands in a gesture of reconciliation, Theodore recognized that Takashi was taking the first step in his avowed plan to regain power. Takashi offered the illusion of accommodation, the appearance of conciliation. There would be no visible signs of dissent or weakness that their enemies might take as an invitation to try again. They would give the impression of strength and harmony to the outside, while remaining opposed.

Theodore embraced his father.

"The Draconis Combine is more important than either of us."

"*Hai*, my son. We agree on that. You have taken your first step in understanding what is required of you. Your first step in understanding me."

Not my first step, Theodore thought ruefully. *I understand you better than you know, Takashi, my father. I have, to my sorrow, become too much like you. In deed. In outlook. I wish it were not so, but it is. All that I thought made me different from you, better than you, has blown away on the breath of the Dragon.*

Are you so sure? a soft voice whispered in Theodore's head.

Tetsuhara-sensei!?

Your feelings are strong. That is good. Ninjo *and* giri *must be balanced. They are a circle, the yin and the yang. If one is too strong, the balance is broken. You must strive to maintain the balance.*

I have striven, sensei. I've failed.

A man cannot be said to have failed until after he is dead. As long as there is life, there is hope. Are you such a coward that you have abandoned hope?

I'm no coward, sensei.

Exactly. You are not your father. If you remember this, you will prosper.

I will remember.

When you go forth into the world, you must be your own man. You cannot live another man's dreams, nor be that which you are not. All that you do will be you, and you will be all that you do. You are your own karma.

Theodore started. Those were the exact words Tetsuhara-*sensei* had used when they had parted on the occasion of Theodore's departure for Sun Zhang Academy. On reflection, he realized that all of the *sensei*'s words were things that he had said to Theodore at different times and in different places. The conversation was a construct of Theodore's mind. But artificial or not, he recognized the timely wisdom of the *sensei*'s counsel.

The Dragon possesses five virtues, he reminded himself. *Bravery, audacity, and tenacity are but three. Even my father grants me those. The fourth is integrity, the one I had come close to abandoning. I must not allow myself to be so weak.*

Perhaps, this is the beginning of the fifth virtue, wisdom. If so, then I am the true heir to the Dragon.

Glossary

Throughout this book, Kurita officers and other officials are referred to by their ancient Japanese rank names or titles. The equivalents in English are:

Tai-shu	Warlord or General of the Army
Tai-sho	General
Sho-sho	Brigadier
Tai-sa	Colonel
Chu-sa	Lieutenant Colonel
Sho-sa	Major
Tai-i	Captain
Chu-i	Lieutenant
Buso-senshi	MechWarrior or AeroSpace Pilot
Kanrei	Deputy
Jokan	Noble Lady
Shudocho	Abbot, Master of an order
Jukurensha	Adept
Shoshinsha	Novice
Sensei	Master Teacher

Some other Japanese phrases that appear in this book and their translations:

Baka	Fool
Dekashita	Nice going!
Do	Kendo term: body armor covering abdominal area
Do itashi moshite	You're welcome
Domo arigato	Thank you very much

Gempuku	Rite of passage upon reaching manhood
Giri	Duty, obligation, justice
Hai	Yes
Hakama	Skirt-like male garment worn by samurai over kimono on ceremonial occasions
Hara	Belly
Iie	No
Kabuto	Helmet
Kamishimo	Samurai ceremonial dress—kataginu and hakama color-coordinated
Kataginu	The triangle of cloth covering the shoulders and breast in ceremonial dress
Katakana	Japanese lettering
Katana	Sword
Kendo	Fencing—literally, "The Way of the Sword"
Ki	Heart, mind, spirit, feeling
Kobun	Soldiers of the yakuza
Konnichi wa	Hello
Kuromaku	"Fixer," gang go-between
Meiyo	Reputation, honor
Meiyo to naru sensei	"Respected teacher"
Men	Kendo facemask
Ninjo	Humanity, sympathy
Ninjutsu	Literally, "Art of Invisibility," the skill of the ninja
O-medeto	Congratulations!
Obi	Sash that goes with kimono
Ohayo	Good morning
Otomo	Palace guards
Otosan	Father
Oyabun	Yakuza ringleader
Ryu no tomo	"Dragon's Friends"
Seimeiyoshi-rengo	Federation of gangs
Senshi	Warrior
Seppuku	Samurai ritual suicide

Shikata ga nai	Approximately, "It can't be helped"
Shimatta	Exclamation of dismay
Shinai	Bamboo sword in kendo
Shitenno	In context, inner circle of advisors; literally, "Four devas"
Shizen	Nature
Shogi	Chess
Shoji	Paper door or panel
Shuriken	Throwing star or small dagger
So ka	1. Oh? How interesting! 2. Is that right?
Sugu	At once, immediately
Tachi	Nature, disposition,—second nature
Tatami	Straw floor-matting
Teki	Enemy, opponent, rival
Tengu	Long-nosed goblin
Tono	Lord
Wakarimasu-ka?	Do you understand?
Wakizashi	Shortsword
Yubitsume	Yakuza finger-cutting atonement

List of Abbreviations:

AFFS	Armed Forces of the Federated Suns
DCMS	Draconis Combine Mustered Soldiery
DEST	Draconis Elite Strike Team
HPG	Hyperpulse Generator. An interstellar communications device used by ComStar
IFF	Identification: Friend or Foe
ISF	Internal Security Force. The Kurita secret service
LCAF	Lyran Commonwealth Armed Forces
LRM	Long-range missiles, indirect fire missiles with high explosive warheads
NAIS	New Avalon Institute of Science
O5P	Order of the Five Pillars
PPC	Particle projector cannon, a magnetic accelerator firing high-

	energy proton or ion bolts. It is the most effective weapon available to a BattleMech
ROM	ComStar's secret service
SRM	Short-range missiles, direct trajectory missiles with high explosive or armor-piercing explosive warheads
VTOL	Vertical Takeoff/Landing, including helicopters and directed thrust aircraft

MORE HARD-HITTING ACTION
FROM BATTLETECH®

DARING ADVENTURES FROM
SHADOWRUN®

☐ **NEVER TRUST AN ELF by Robert N. Charrette.** Drawn into a dangerous game of political and magical confrontation, Khan—an ork of the Seattle ghetto—not only learns never to deal with a dragon, he also discovers that trusting an elf may leave you dead. (451783—$4.50)

☐ **STREETS OF BLOOD by Carl Sargent.** London, 2054. Shadows hide a sadistic murderer, somehow summoned from Victoria's reign to kill once more, as the razor readies his kiss. (451996—$4.99)

☐ **SHADOWPLAY by Nigel Findley.** Sly is a veteran who has run more shadows than she cares to remember. Falcon is a kid who thinks he hears the call of magic and the voice of the Great Spirits. Together, they must face deadly confrontation between the world's most powerful corporations. (452283—$4.99)

☐ **NIGHT'S PAWN by Tom Dowd.** Jason Chase's past has come back to haunt him. He must rely on his experience and everything he's got, as he comes face to face with an old enemy left for dead. (452380—$4.99)

☐ **STRIPER ASSASSIN by Nyx Smith.** Death reigns under the full moon on the streets of Philadelphia when the deadly Asian assassin and kick-artist known as Striper descends on the City of Brotherly Love. (452542—$4.99)

☐ **LONE WOLF by Nigel Findley.** Rick Larson thinks he knows the score when it comes to Seattle's newest conquerors—the gangs. But when the balance begins to shift unexpectedly, Larson finds himself not only on the wrong side of the fight but on the wrong side of the law as well. (452720—$4.99)

Prices slightly higher in Canada.

Finally, the answer to the age-old question...
"What are we going to do tonight?"

VIRTUAL WORLD®

**FEATURING BATTLETECH®
AND RED PLANET™**

YOUR OPINION CAN MAKE A DIFFERENCE!

LET US KNOW WHAT *YOU* THINK.

Send this completed survey to us and enter a weekly drawing to win a special prize!

1.) Do you play any of the following role-playing games?
   Shadowrun ——— Earthdawn ——— BattleTech ———

2.) Did you play any of the games before you read the novels?
   Yes ——————— No ———————

3.) How many novels have you read in each of the following series?
   Shadowrun ——— Earthdawn ——— BattleTech ———

4.) What other game novel lines do you read?
   TSR ——— White Wolf ——— Other (Specify) ———

5.) Who is your favorite FASA author?
_____

6.) Which book did you take this survey from?
_____

7.) Where did you buy this book?
   Bookstore ——— Game Store ——— Comic Store ———
      FASA Mail Order ——————— Other (Specify) ———

8.) Your opinion of the book (please print)
_____
_____
_____

Name ———————————— Age ——— Gender ———
Address _____
City ——————— State ——— Country ——— Zip ———

Send this page or a photocopy of it to:
FASA Corporation
Editorial/Novels
1100 W. Cermak Suite B-305
Chicago, IL 60608